The Effects of Implementing Theme Cycles on Adult EFL Writers

主題探索式課程
對成人英文寫作學習者的影響

李利德　著

封面設計：實踐大學教務處出版組

DEDICATION

This book is heartily dedicated to my parents

for their unconditional love.

出 版 心 語

　　近年來，全球數位出版蓄勢待發，美國從事數位出版的業者超過百家，亞洲數位出版的新勢力也正在起飛，諸如日本、中國大陸都方興未艾，而臺灣卻被視為數位出版的處女地，有極大的開發拓展空間。植基於此，本組自民國 93 年 9 月起，即醞釀規劃以數位出版模式，協助本校專任教師致力於學術出版，以激勵本校研究風氣，提昇教學品質及學術水準。

　　在規劃初期，調查得知秀威資訊科技股份有限公司是採行數位印刷模式並做數位少量隨需出版〔POD＝Print on Demand〕（含編印銷售發行）的科技公司，亦為中華民國政府出版品正式授權的 POD 數位處理中心，尤其該公司可提供「免費學術出版」形式，相當符合本組推展數位出版的立意。隨即與秀威公司密集接洽，出版部李協理坤城數度親至本組開會討論，雙方就數位出版服務要點、數位出版申請作業流程、出版發行合約書以及出版合作備忘錄等相關事宜逐一審慎研擬，歷時 9 個月，至民國 94 年 6 月始告順利簽核公布。

這段期間，承蒙本校謝前校長孟雄、謝副校長宗興、王教務長又鵬、藍教授秀璋以及秀威公司宋總經理政坤等多位長官給予本組全力的支持與指導，本校多位教師亦不時從旁鼓勵與祝福，在此一併致上最誠摯的謝意。本校新任校長張博士光正甫上任（民國 94 年 8 月），獲知本組推出全國大專院校首創的數位出版服務，深表肯定與期許。諸般溫馨滿溢，將是挹注本組持續推展數位出版的最大動力。

　　本出版團隊由葉立誠組長、王雯珊老師、賴怡勳老師三人為組合，以極其有限的人力，充分發揮高效能的團隊精神，合作無間，各司統籌策劃、協商研擬、視覺設計等職掌，在精益求精的前提下，至望弘揚本校實踐大學的校譽，具體落實出版機能。

實踐大學教務處出版組　謹識

中華民國 95 年 9 月

PREFACE

There are those in my life that have influenced the journey and the process of this study. I would like to take this opportunity to gratefully acknowledge their influence.

To my advisor, Dr. Yueh-kuey Huang, I am particularly appreciative of her unfailing faith in me as I chose my topic, prepared the proposal, conducted the research, and wrote the dissertation. Her role as a facilitator promoted my learning autonomy. Her questions and suggestions caused me to deepen my own understanding of EFL literacy theory. Her warmth and encouragement helped me to complete this study.

Appreciation also goes to my committee members: Dr. Chun-chung Lin, Drs. Chung-kuen Yao and Chi-yee Lin, and especially Dr. Kristopher Kowal. Dr. Kowal took my vague ideas seriously at the very beginning of this study, read the early drafts and inspired me with constant encouragement. His untiring support makes me believe in my own potentials. I would also like to thank Drs. Hsiu-chieh Chen, Hwei-mei Chen, Rueih-lirng Fahn, Hsin-yih Shyu, Chen-hua Wang and Shih-chung Lee from Tamkang University for their instructions, which I incorporated in present research.

My mentors from Western Michigan University where I received my Master's degree should also be acknowledged. Dr. Constance Weaver first introduced the whole language philosophy to me and set the role model of a humanistic education. Dr. Allen Carey-webb led me into Paulo Freire's liberatory education. Dr. Robert Dlouhy participated all my paper presentations in TESOL annual convention and gave me generous comments. Dr. Loewe helped me in my research when I visited Michigan again in 1999.

I also owe my gratitude to Dr. Ching-hsi Perng from National Taiwan University. It is he who gave me, his previous student, the opportunity to start teaching reading and writing to adult EFL learners in the language center when I just came back from the States with my Master's degree in 1993. His confidence in me encouraged me to prepare the class with all my best and so paved the way for my research. My sincere thanks must also go to the students who participated in this study in the year of 2000-2001. Their perseverance in study and willingness in sharing helped me to reconfirm the philosophy of humanistic learning. Without their participation and interaction, this study cannot be completed.

Friends from TESOL Ph.D. program play an important role in my study. The endless hours of discussion, sharing of frustration and expectation, comfort and encouragement make this study possible. Brenda Chou volunteered to be a rater in my study and sacrificed her time and energy for reading my students' essays, journals, and portfolios. Because of her help, this study could stride a big step forward. Others like Peggy Huang, Bi-chu Chen, Jill Chi, Tony Hsu and Robert Chen (who passed away in May, 2001) colored my life in such difficult times and pushed me forward to reach the goal.

Friends from Feng-sheng Christian Fellowship accompany me through the study–like my brothers and sisters. When I was weak physically, they provided me with nutritional food and health guidance. When I was depressed and frustrated, they listened to me, comforted me, and prayed for me. When I was busy writing my dissertation, they took care of my parents: bringing food to them, chatting with them, and even providing medical supports. I am thankful for their unselfish love and support.

I am grateful to my elder sister, Dr. Jen-der Lee, who is always interested in my thinking and always the first reader of my many papers. She has constantly encouraged me in my educational endeavors and has given endless and caring love in my life. Her insistence and interest in intellectual quest enlightened my understanding of being a dynamic scholar. I also want to give thanks to my younger brother, Yuan-te Lee, whose love toward arts and cultures showed me the enjoyment of integrating learning and living.

My parents, Ta-Chung Li and Kuei-Shiang Tseng, have stood firmly with me and beside me during this process. They have always supported the journey, and constantly encouraged me to continue toward the goal at times when I thought I simply could go no further. It was their life-long inspiration that caused me to set such high aspirations in life, for they always made me believe in myself. I also want to thank my parents-in-law for their patience, understanding, and prayers.

A special thank you note must also go to my husband, Wei-ping Hsieh. For years, he listened to my dreams, dealt with my frustration, and shared my achievements. His faith, patience and tenderness help me to remember that love overcomes all the difficulties.

CONTENTS

CHAPTER 1

INTRODUCTION TO THE STUDY

1.1 Problem Statement

People in Taiwan are extremely interested in learning English. In addition to the existence of language schools for children, numerous courses are available for adults who have been out of school for many years. One of the courses offered is English writing, which is usually considered to have great value in building proficiency in the English language. Students, however, show a preference for listening and speaking in class and often show a reluctance to attend writing classes. They prefer listening and speaking courses because these offer practical skills to improve oral communication. They can immediately use these skills at work or while traveling. On the other hand, writing seems difficult, time-consuming, and irrelevant.

This state of mind results from the way English is taught. For a long time, EFL writing instruction in Taiwan has focused on grammar, spelling, and sentence structure. Writing courses, therefore, emphasize sentence pattern practice. Students are required to fill in the blanks to complete a sentence or re-arrange a sentence according to transformational rules. For those students who practice writing skills other than sentence making, a model-based paragraph writing practice is the most common approach. Usually students are asked to write a draft similar to a model paragraph. Teachers then correct and grade it based on grammatical accuracy. Having mastered the correct form, students move on to the next writing practice. The concern for grammar overrides that of idea generation. Focusing on sentence writing without idea development can make writing fragmental and irrelevant, which in turn, causes difficulty and frustration for learners.

Inspired by the concept of process writing and whole language education, teachers have recently implemented process-oriented or learner-centered approaches to writing instruction. However, most efforts are made on behalf of college level students. Adult learners seldom have the opportunity to experience this new approach when taking a continuing education writing class.

In addition to the method of instruction, materials selection is another factor contributing to irrelevance. Most textbooks on writing target college students, minorities in English speaking countries or illiterate adult learners. Adult learners in continuing education, however, don't fit this stereotype and usually have different interests. In the EFL context in Taiwan, for example, adult learners are usually highly educated professionals. They have a broad knowledge base resulting from their work and life experience. They are not only literate but can also be highly proficient in their native language. They may be false beginners[1] in terms of learning English, as they have already studied basic English in school. Choosing course material with no relevance to the lives of these students tends to distance them from the goals of the course.

With an increase in the population of adult learners who have a variety of backgrounds, experiences and motivations, bridging the gap between learners and the learning presents a great challenge for EFL writing educators in Taiwan. In order to make writing instruction and material relevant to adult learners and to fully develop their writing skills, it is obvious that the course must correspond to their linguistic and intellectual schemata. The concern for such needs is the reason for this study.

---

[1] See 1.4 Operational Definition of Terms

1.2 Purpose of the Study

The purpose of this study is to focus on the importance of relevant course material and to determine the influence that alternative ways of teaching may have on adult students of EFL writing. By so doing, the study hopes to provide a new direction for EFL writing instruction.

In order to highlight the importance of relevant material, authentic material theories and philosophies, learner-centered learning and liberatory education are reviewed. In particular, the concepts of whole language philosophy, the major concerns of Rogerian learning and the central beliefs of Freirean education are pursued. Research studies on EFL literacy in Taiwan seldom refer to or include the theories of Carl Rogers and Paulo Freire and little research has attempted to integrate Rogerian and Freirean learning into whole language philosophy. This study attempts to do just that. It is felt that such integration will bring new insight to EFL educators and raise awareness for the importance of the use of relevant materials in the writing instruction process.

The alternative way of instruction is the use of theme cycles. According to the literature, theme cycles integrate various learning skills and value the learning process. This seems to be one way of bridging the gap between learners and learning. Theme cycles have been widely applied in the native language environment and with ESL students, especially in elementary schools. Whether this can also benefit EFL adult students remains to be seen. This study is therefore aimed at investigating the use of theme cycles in the EFL adult learning context to gauge their influence on EFL adult student writers. As in all research studies, we hope to offer new insight into the philosophies and theories of EFL teaching methodology.

1.3 Significance of the Study

This study has theoretical and practical implications in describing the way students change as writers and how they perceive writing and the teaching methods used in a continuing education setting. The case studies and the data analysis from this research document the growth of adult EFL learners as they gain increasing confidence, while developing English literacy skills. The data also describe how students internalize and apply what they learn to daily life. In addition, the study highlights and portrays the increase in motivation when reading/writing is real and relevant.

A description of the writers and the classroom will inform two major audiences. The first audience targeted is the local post-graduate language center. This audience consists of reading/writing teachers and administrators. Many teachers and administrators might feel more comfortable trying or encouraging the use of new and different teaching methods if they could see their students changing and developing as writers in the classroom.

University-based researchers are the second audience. This study will augment the existing information available on EFL writing. It describes how the integration of Whole Language and the theories of Carl Rogers and Paulo Freire can function in a post-graduate level classroom and how the students can grow and develop into competent users of English. The study differs from previous research in Whole Language or Freirean Pedagogy since it focuses on highly-educated adult learners. The study also differs from previous research on Rogerian learning as its context is foreign language learning. Another way the study differs from previous research is in its inclusion of Voice[2] in the assessment of writing performance, its examination of the two attitudes – apprehension and self-efficacy and its emphasis on personal growth[3].

---

[2] See 1.4 Operational Definition of Terms
[3] See 1.4 Operational Definition of Terms

1.4 Operational Definition of Terms

Adult EFL writers—EFL student writers in this study generally refer to students in post-bachelor programs, including government employees who attended one-year (two-semester) English reading and writing classes with the researcher.

False beginners—These are people who studied basic English in school but still have difficulty in all aspects of its use (listening, speaking, reading, and writing) (Richards, Platt, and Platt, 1992).

Personal growth (Personal empowerment)—This refers to changes in the students, not including the building of skills and competencies (Heaney, 1995). It relates to gaining power as a confident and responsible learner (Rogers, 1983).

Theme cycles—the term "theme cycles" refers firstly to the recursive and spiraling process of knowledge construction and secondly to the cyclic learning process (Altwerger & Flores, 1994). As the word "cycle" implies, each step of the theme cycle in turn generates new steps, and theme cycle studies can often develop into subsequent studies when new and related questions are posed. In theme cycles, the students are involved in the entire process of theme development, from deciding on the topic, research materials, and information gathering. They share what they have learned (See Appendix A), and in the process, they learn how to learn.

Voice—"Voice is the use of language to paint a picture of one's reality, one's experiences, one's world" (Wink, 2000, p. 70). Also, according to Peter Elbow (1998b), "Writing *without voice* is wooden or dead because it lacks sound, rhythm, energy, and individuality. … Writing *with voice* is writing into which someone has breathed. It has that fluency, rhythm, and liveliness that exist naturally in the speech of most people when they are enjoying a conversation. … Writing *with real voice* has the power to make you pay attention and understand—the words go deep. … it is a matter of hearing resonance …" (p. 299).

NES—It stands for native English speakers.

ESL—It stands for English as a second language.

EFL—It stands for English as a foreign language.

1.5 Research Questions

This paper focuses on the following questions:

A. What changes are apparent in writing performance of adult EFL writers after they engage in theme cycles learning? Specifically, do their writing skills improve in terms of content, organization and use of language? Do they communicate their personal views and effectively voice their opinions in their writing?

B. What changes do adult EFL writers reveal in their attitudes toward English writing after they engage in theme cycles learning? Do they show less anxiety and exhibit more confidence while writing English?

C. How has the use of theme cycles affected their personal growth and personal empowerment? Do they present self-directed learning and show reflection on learning and living?

1.6 Chapter Content

This paper contains six chapters. The first chapter is an introduction. The second chapter reviews the literature. It begins by reviewing ESL writing, including its definition and teaching methods. It then focuses on the popular but controversial approach—whole language philosophy—to consider how whole language defines writing and how this philosophy can promote literacy development. Next, the researcher narrows the discussion to current research on whole language in Taiwan, followed by a discussion on Carl Rogers' whole-person learning and Paulo Freire's education of liberation. Special attention is paid to the unity (common beliefs) of these three theories. Finally, there is a discussion of theme cycles.

The third chapter concerns methodology and contains the rationale for the research methods used. Three major research methodologies are used in this study: the ethnographic method, the case study and the teacher as researcher. The pilot study describes preliminary research conducted by the researcher in prior years (1993-2000). From these observations and research findings, the researcher carried out this formal study in the 2000-2001 school year. The formal study depicts the class and its setting, the participants, the teacher-researcher and her teaching philosophy, typical classroom activities and the informed consent procedure. The purpose is to provide a clear portrait of the class, the participants, and the learning process. The researcher then introduces the materials and instruments used in the study and the procedures used in implementing theme cycles and data collection. Finally, the method of data analysis is described.

The fourth chapter is on data presentation. The data include the students' personal profiles, essay scores, results of questionnaires and portfolio evaluation. The personal profile is a description of the student, introducing educational background, English writing experience and the project theme in this study. Essay scores are the average scores gained from two raters and represent the students' pre- and post-prompt writing and the first and last drafts of each student's essays. The results from the pre- and post-class questionnaires on writing self-efficacy and writing apprehension were also presented. The portfolio evaluation consists of numerical scores and written comments of the two raters. All of the data were presented case by case. After all the data were presented, the researcher gave a profile of the class as a whole. This collection of data is analyzed in chapter five.

The fifth chapter is a discussion and analysis of the data. The analysis was conducted according to the category. According to the students' prompt writing scores, the researcher categorized the students into three groups: improved from weak to good; improved from average to good and improved from weak to average. For writing self-efficacy, there are three categories: confidence increased from low to high, from low to middle and from middle to high. For writing apprehension, there were also three categories: anxiety reduced from high to middle, from middle to low, and from high middle to low middle. The numerical scores of the portfolio were calculated from the average scores given by the two raters. The evaluation is also presented in three categories according to scores: superior, between superior and good, and good. Eight students are discussed and analyzed in these case studies. Writing performance, writing attitude and other changes concerning the perception of writing and perception of life is discussed with regard to each student.

The sixth chapter presents conclusions and recommendations. With a summary of the study, including major findings, the implications and recommendations for future studies were presented. This paper ends with the final conclusions.

CHAPTER

REVIEW OF THE LITERATURE

2.1 Content and Rationale for Selection

This study concerns the effectiveness of implementing theme cycles learning, focusing especially on the changes in writing performance of adult EFL writers, their attitudes towards writing, and their personal growth and empowerment. Since it covers several broad research areas, this chapter will discuss important literature from these areas. First, the progress of ESL and EFL writing instruction in Taiwan will be briefly reviewed. Second, literature related to whole language philosophy and its application in both ESL and EFL writing in Taiwan will be discussed. Third, an overview of Carl Rogers' whole-person education and its similarities with whole language philosophy will be presented. Fourth, Paulo Freire's education of liberation and the tenets it shares with whole language philosophy and Carl Rogers' whole-person education will be addressed. Fifth, research studies that describe theme cycles in ESL learning are summarized.

The study of ESL writing began with the theory of behaviorism, through the theory of schema, constructivism, semiotics and communication, and continued with the theory of process writing and whole language (Y. M. Chen, 1998). Its progress is neither linear nor pendulum-like; instead, it is recursive. A review of the history of ESL/EFL writing helps explain the need to implement whole language philosophy in present day EFL writing classes and also provides a possible reason for the difficulties of adapting to fluency-first or learner-centered learning.

Whole language philosophy includes various disciplines and has been applied at various levels and in different settings. In this study, as adult EFL writers are the main focus, the literature review related to whole language application will concentrate on the use of whole language in university-level ESL/EFL writing classes or in adult literacy programs. Also, although the focus is on adult learners, studies related to non-literate adult learners or immigrants to an English speaking country will not be included as the emphasis in this research is on highly educated professionals. They are not similar to either the new immigrant or non-literate segments of the population. The discussion of the whole language approach will start with the whole language view of writing, with its views of language, language learning, and the roles of teacher and learner. This decision was made because many research studies have discussed the definition and theoretical background of whole language, but little research has discussed writing directly from a whole language perspective or explicitly connected writing with the core beliefs of whole language.

The inclusion of Carl Rogers' whole-person education and Paulo Freire's education of liberation results from the unity in diversity they share with whole language. Their emphasis on the democratic relationship between teacher and student and their respect for learners as whole beings with potential enhance the humanistic concerns in whole language. In response to teachers' hesitation to embrace new insights such as whole language and to respond to their frustration from only adapting whole language "activities," the inclusion of both Rogers' and Freire's views of the teacher's role and personal empowerment is necessary. It is hoped that EFL writing teachers will extend their concerns beyond methodology and seek changes within themselves.

Theme cycles learning is an alternative for the application of whole language and is the focus of this study. However, because the concern is adult EFL learners, the discussion will focus on using theme cycles in ESL/EFL settings at an adult level. Studies related to applying theme cycles in an NES environment or at the elementary school level will be addressed only as supporting references. The purpose is to ensure that the literature review relates closely to the study.

2.2 Historical View of ESL/EFL Writing

2.2.1 Definitions of ESL Writing and Methods of Teaching ESL Writings

The field of ESL writing has gone through many changes over the past decades. From the 1940s to the 1970s, the audio-lingual method (ALM) of language teaching, which emphasized oral skills, considered writing to be a tangential language skill. In fact, during the years that ALM was in ascendancy, writing was actually excluded from ESL teaching programs (Reid, 1993). Up to the early 1970s, writing was included in some ESL classrooms but limited to teaching sentence-level construction and grammatical sentence structures (Kroll, 1991). Students were instructed to copy a sentence or to fill in the blanks to complete a sentence. At that time, writing was considered nothing more than sentence making. Since this philosophy of controlled writing came from the ALM, its instruction emphasized the prevention of errors. In the late 1970s and early 1980s, ESL writing, under the influence of NES writing theory and practice, moved from strictly controlled writing to guided writing. Students were instructed to answer a question by structuring sentences into a short paragraph. The emphasis of this instruction was on vocabulary building, reading comprehension and grammar. In addition to guided writing, language-based writing was welcomed in the early 1980s. This method viewed writing as a way to "reinforce grammatical structures, idioms, and vocabulary" (Raimes, 1983, p. 3). Thus, the emphasis was placed on language components, such as a specific verb tense, the use of adjectives or a particular sentence structure. Students were usually instructed to practice sentence-combining techniques (Kameen, 1978; McKee, 1983; Pack & Hendrichsen, 1981; Shook, 1978). The common beliefs underlying controlled writing, guided writing, and language-based writing are closely related to the beliefs of behaviorist psychology; that is, it is hoped that "with constant practice of correct structures, students will learn the language and will, therefore, be able to transfer the repeated skills to original utterances" (Reid, 1993, p. 27). However, according to research into the acquisition of a second language, language learning, which includes writing, is a process that the learner controls and to which the learner contributes rather than being limited to "stimulus-response" behavior (Bialystok, 1990; Fromkin & Rodman, 1988; Hatch, 1992; Krashen, 1981, 1982; Rivers, 1964, 1968).

During the 1980s, a new model of teaching ESL writing emerged, which was the pattern/product approach. With the awareness that writing classes should not be grammar classes, ESL writing teachers started to view writing as an effective method for a learner to generate proper discourse for the purpose of communicating with others in a new language (Raimes, 1985). ESL writing classes, therefore, focused on the concepts of paragraph development, such as the thesis statement, the topic sentence and organizational strategies in different patterns—process, cause and effect, comparison-contrast, etc. Students were instructed to re-order scrambled paragraphs, identify proper topic sentences, and write topic sentences for paragraphs whose topic sentences had been removed (Barnes, 1981; Reid, 1982; Rice & Burns, 1986; Wohl, 1985). The advocates believed that by so doing, ESL students would be well prepared to meet the requirements in academic proficiency examinations.

Since the early 1980s, many ESL teachers, influenced by NES research done by Peter Elbow (1973, 1998a), Donald Murray (1982, 1985), and Nancy Sommers (1980), have begun to accept and implement process writing into their teaching (Blanton, 1987; Spack, 1984; Spack & Sadow, 1983; Zamel, 1980, 1982, 1983). Writing was viewed as a process of discovery and as a procedure "relies heavily on the power of revision to clarify and refine that discovery" (Taylor, 1981, p. 8). The emphasis was placed on topic exploration, drafts sharing, and revision. Students were encouraged to express personal feelings, experiences, and reactions. Thus, students were instructed to write in journals, in which they concentrated on recording interesting ideas, rather than grammar and organization (G. Jacobs, 1988). However, though process writing was intended to reduce the anxiety level of the student by allowing the expression of interesting ideas in journal writing and promoting the activities of discovery beyond language components, ESL process-writing textbooks were still often language-based. Practice in vocabulary development, word skills, and grammar features, like singular/plurals, verb tenses, pronouns, etc., was still the focus of ESL writing instruction (Reid, 1993; Smoke, 1987). Besides, in the 1990s, the strong emphasis on process writing worried some ESL teachers and researchers. The proponents of the process-product approach found that the movement towards expressive and personal writing sometimes caused difficulties for ESL student writers. They thought students who were not familiar or comfortable with the conventions and expectations of narration and expression would lose direction in their writing practice (Johns, 1991; Santos, 1992). As a result, ESL teachers started turning more towards the academic writing needs of their students.

At the end of the 1980s, ESL teachers, moving from the ALM objectives of correcting all the students' errors to the concept of viewing errors as necessary to developmental progress, began paying attention to the process of composing and revising. Students were expected to know the differences between English and their native language so as to strengthen their ability to monitor weaknesses in the process of revision and editing. Other methods, such as contrastive analysis (Kaplan, 1988; Nickel, 1989), error analysis (Janopoulos, 1992; Santos, 1988), and the application of the concepts of coherence and cohesion (Connor, 1984; Johns, 1986) were paid attention at the same time. The common belief underlying these methods was that writing done by ESL students had different error patterns and different conventions of coherence and cohesion from NES writers. Thus, students were usually instructed and investigated in a "contrastive" way. Meanwhile, under the influence of process writing, the communicative and collaborative approaches to ESL writing were developed. The communicative approach places emphasis on the authentic audience and purpose of writing (Leki, 1989; Purves & Purves, 1986; Reid, 1993; Schachter, 1990; Schenk, 1988; White, 1987). Students were asked to write authentic pieces, such as an advertisement or a petition letter, and to keep their audiences in mind. The advocates of collaborative teaching and learning viewed writing as a process of negotiation and so stressed "the negotiation of meaning between student writers and their audiences, sequential processes of drafting and revising composition, and the development of learners' abilities to diversify their capacities for written expression" (Cumming, 1989, pp. 82-83). The hope was to stimulate students' participation in order to improve their English writing. Students were instructed to generate ideas in small groups and to gather, organize, and share materials with their peers.

Also in the middle of the 1980s, another trend emerged, called "whole language." Enlightened by the whole language philosophy, ESL writing entered a new era. Writing, for the first time, was considered an integral part of learning a language and according to the whole language perspective, since language is whole, writing should be learned from whole to part (De Carlo, 1995; Edelsky, Altwerger, & Flores, 1991; Freeman & Freeman, 1988; Rigg, 1991). In a whole language class, there is no isolated skill training, no decontextualized word memorization, no irrelevant sentence making, and no machine-like paragraph practice. Instead, students are encouraged to read authentic materials, such as literature, storybooks, and magazines (Lim & Watson, 1993), to write reading responses or dialogue journals (Arthur, 1991; Hall, 1994; Lamb & Best, 1990; Peyton, 1990; Peyton & Reed, 1990; Peyton & Staton, 1992), to participate in peer sharing and editing, to make portfolios (Valencia, 1990; Hansen, 1992), and to conduct self-evaluation. Meaning-making, critical thinking, and problem-posing are the concerns. The concept of "fluency first and accuracy later" subvert the traditional thinking of ESL writing (MacGowan-Gilhooly, 1991; 1996a, 1996b).

The impact of these new ideas was so overwhelming that it persuaded some ESL writing teachers to embrace the philosophy but it also turned some others away. Those who held on to the assumptions that words must precede sentences and sentences must precede paragraphs seriously questioned the mode of learning from whole to part. Those who were used to the skill-oriented curriculum cynically doubted the validity of meaning-driven course design. The slogan of "back-to-the-basics" was representative of this recurring syndrome, which, in turn, fired the debate: process vs. product, meaning vs. form, and fluency vs. accuracy. With this debate still going strong, ESL writing theories and pedagogy along with NES research entered 2000, the year of millennium.

2.2.2 The Instruction of EFL Writing in Taiwan

Most theories that we have about EFL writing are largely based on research in NES and ESL writing and are usually applied to classroom learning a decade or more later.   Taiwan is no exception.

Before 1981, the year the Ministry of Education announced the inclusion of English composition in the Joint College Entrance Exam, high school English teachers had no idea how to teach English composition. What they usually emphasized in class were language components, like verb tenses, parts of speech, and sentence structure.   Influenced by the grammar translation method (GTM) and the ALM, teachers paid a great deal of attention to students' accurate memorization of isolated words, common idioms, and "beautifully-written" sentences from literary works. Students were instructed to memorize words and phrases and to practice transformational grammar.   Dixson's *Essential idioms in English*, McCallum's two volumes of *Idiom drills: For students of English as a second language* (1970), and Ko's *New English Grammar* were a must for almost every student.   In the years after the 1981 announcement, the resulting struggles and confusion were frequently heard in teachers' conversations.   With doubts about the proficiency of their students' English, teachers did not believe that EFL students could write a complete composition in English.   The underlying principle was that language should be studied from part to whole and in sequence.   The common question was "How can they compose an article, if they don't have enough vocabulary or aren't familiar with all the sentence patterns?"   This suspicion spread all over Taiwan and shadowed the possibilities for learning EFL writing.

EFL writing research in Taiwan also focused mainly on the effectiveness of grammar instruction, pattern practice, guided writing, and error analysis (Y. M. Chen, 1998).   The writing product and accuracy were the chief concerns; writing practice rather than writing per se was the emphasis.   Lin (1984) discussed the use of students' cognitive schemata on writing. Chang (1984) emphasized the importance of practicing sentence making and transformational grammar. Wang (1984) stressed guided writing and error analysis. Teng (1985) talked about punctuation, discourse structure, and organization. Liu (1986, 1987) argued for the efficiency of making outlines, re-writing, and recognizing different rhetorical modes. Guang (1986) also emphasized guided writing. Apparently, writing was limited to the sentential level and was treated as an isolated skill. Good writing was defined as an "error-free" piece. Good writers were the ones who made "no mistakes" in their writing.

Then in the late 1980s, influenced by the theory of semiotics (Saussure, 1966) and the notion of the communicative approach (Hymes, 1972), the research began to show different concerns (Y. M. Chen, 1998; Cheng, 1998, 1999, 2001; Yao, 1997). Katchen (1987) and Nash (1987) began discussing the integration of writing, speaking, and reading. H. C. Chen (1988) and Nash, Hsieh, & Chen (1989) investigated the use of computer-assisted instruction (CAI) in writing class. Chang (1988) reported the possibility of letter exchange between high school students and college students. For the first time, writing was not considered as an isolated skill and communication as a purpose of writing was emphasized.

From early in the 1990s, process writing began to draw the attention of EFL writing teachers. A single final draft was replaced by multiple drafts and error analysis was replaced by revision, re-writing, and editing. Uchniat (1990), Kao (1993), Tung (1995), and Y. M. Chen (1996, 1997) either reported the implementation of multiple-draft writing or investigated the efficiency of peer editing. Since then, though skill-based writing instruction remains dominant, the process of writing and the sharing and response between writers and readers have been acknowledged.

Along with process writing, whole language philosophy in an ESL setting has had a dramatic impact on EFL writing. In the late 1990s, almost a decade or more later than NES or ESL, whole language philosophy gained respect among EFL writing teachers in Taiwan. Some teachers began helping students explore ideas through the use of a literature log or journal writing (Huang, 1997, 1998). Others encouraged students to undertake research projects (Li, 1997, 2001). Authentic literature and theme exploration were naturally integrated into the so-called "four skills" (i.e. listening, speaking, reading and writing). The teacher-student conference and student-student interaction enhanced collaboration in the writing process. Continuing assessment based on observation, multiple drafts, interaction, and portfolios challenged the traditional single-draft assessment. The shift from product to process and from accuracy first to fluency first was initially slow, but significant, to both teachers and students. However, facing the reality of large classes and test-oriented education, teachers often taught from proc-ess-writing textbooks with a language-based approach and used whole language activities as skill-building practices. This backwardness re-flected the beliefs of EFL writing teachers. Teachers must be the "change agent." Unless teachers change their beliefs, it will be diffi-cult to completely change the pedagogy of EFL writing in Taiwan.

2.3 Writing in a Whole Language Perspective

Whole language has been recognized for decades. Since Ken Goodman published his book *What's Whole in Whole Language* in 1986, the term "whole language" has been ardently discussed (Bergeron, 1990; Bird, 1987; K. Goodman, 1992; Y. Goodman, 1989; Krashen, 1999; Newman & Church, 1990; Watson, 1989; Weaver, 1988, 1994). In addition, the concept of whole language has been widely applied in various contexts. What exactly the whole language philosophy is and to what degree it influences ESL/EFL writing deserve a closer look.

Writing as a Meaning-making Process

Influenced by Rosenblatt (1978), whole language asserts that learning is a transactional process, in which meaning is constructed. That is, meaning is not found within the reader/writer or in the text, but rather in the transactions that occur as one reads and writes (Freeman & Freeman, 1998). While reading, the cues provided by the print combined with our previous knowledge of language and the world allow us to create and construct a unique interpretation. Like reading, writing is a meaning-making process (Goodman, 1986). When we write, we continually revise our thoughts, meanings, and linguistic expressions to discover new meanings (Edelsky et al., 1991). Writing, therefore, as Samway (1992) said, "is not simply a mechanism for expressing preconceived, well-formed ideas; instead, it allows one to explore and articulate one's thoughts" (p. 3). F. Smith (1983, 1994b) also argued that writing involves integrating global and local conventions with one's global and local intentions. This concept was restated by Samway (1992) as "when we write we try out our theory of the world and in the process discover what we know and think" (p. 3). Through writing, our thinking is enhanced.

In addition, writing is viewed as a recursive process (Samway, 1992). Since writers need to continually revise what they have written in order to discover new meaning, writing cannot be merely a simple, static, or linear process of composing, like pre-writing, writing, and revision. Instead, in the process of writing, ideas are generated and altered, as are plans and goals, because writers are constantly re-reading and re-evaluating their writing and organization. This phenomenon was described by Harste, Pierce, and Cairney (1985),

> Reading and writing are events which involve insights into the making and shaping of ideas in time and space. Cognitively both reading and writing are driven by a search for a unified meaning, or "text." In this search for a unified meaning, readers and writers begin with what they know, but in this process learn, that is, go beyond what they know. Readers and writers do this by constantly shifting perspectives from reader to writer, from speaker to listener, from participant to spectator, from monitor to critic, during the process of reading and writing (p. 3).

Writing as an Integral Part of Language Learning

Hamayan (1989) in her report, *Teaching writing to potentially English proficient students using whole language approaches*, argued that,

> Writing activities must be part of the entire language experience in which the students are engaged. It is more meaningful, and therefore easier, for students to write about things that they have just listened to, spoken or read about, or experienced (p. 1).

This view of writing is matched with the core belief in whole language philosophy.

In the whole language perspective, language can be presented in different modes, such as oral, written, or sign language. Since each of these modes is a system of linguistic conventions for creating meaning, there is no hierarchical connotation implied. In addition, whole language proposes that language is a super-system composed of interdependent and inseparable sub-systems, like phonological, graphic, graphophonic, syntactic, semantic and pragmatic systems and gestures (Edelsky et al., 1991; Goodman, 1967). It is asserted that when language is being used, all these systems are present and interdependent. In other words, "if systems have been artificially removed or if systems don't work together, then even if it looks or sounds like language in use, it isn't" (Edelsky et al., 1991, p. 12). Goodman (1986) also claimed that language is inclusive and indivisible. He further explained that "words, sounds, letters, phrases, clauses, sentences, and paragraphs are like the molecules, atoms, and subatomic particles of things. ... If you reduce a wooden table to the elements which compose it, it's no longer a table" (p. 27). The core belief is stated as language is language only when it is whole. Along with this concept, language is "predictable." F. Smith (1994a) in *Understanding Reading* stressed that language is predictable because it comprises these interdependent systems working together simultaneously. Though the process of using the subsystems of language as cues to make predictions is usually not conscious or deliberate, both Goodman (1969) and F. Smith (1994a, 1997) believed that predictability is an intrinsic feature of language.

This belief has a direct influence on language learning from the perspective of whole language. Since language is language only when it is whole, language learning should take place from whole to part (De Carlo, 1995; Edelsky et al., 1991; Freeman & Freeman, 1989, 1998; Goodman, 1986; Weaver, 1988, 1990, 1994). In other words, language should not be divided into pieces for the sake of learning. Learning a language does not merely consist of learning its components or subsystems. Learning each language skill (reading, writing, speaking, listening) separately is not the same as learning the entire language. As Goodman (1986) said, "The whole is always more than the sum of the parts and the value of any part can only be learned within the whole utterance in a real speech event" (p. 19).

Therefore, writing, as with other language modes, should no longer be considered as an end unto itself, but as an integral part of the entire language learning process. As Harste et al. (1985) claimed,

> There is … no 'pure' act of reading or writing—writers talk, read, write, listen, draw, gesture, all in the name of writing; readers discuss ideas they find problematic, listen, sketch, underline and do a number of other things, all in the name of reading. The multimodal and social nature of reading and writing make these processes complex events, but the very complexity of these events supports learning by allowing language users to shift perspective from reader to writer, speaker to listener, experiencer to spectator, spectator to critic (pp. 3-4).

Writing as a Self-generated and Self-actualizing Activity

In a whole language perspective, language is personal because it is driven from within by the need to communicate. Though we also need to follow the norms to make communication successful, each person's language still retains his/her personal characteristics (Goodman, 1986). In terms of language learning, whole language advocates also accept the tenets of Piaget's (1955) developmental stages and believe in Dewey's (1963) learning by doing. They believe that learning occurs when "people act on and interact with the environment" (Freeman & Freeman, 1998, p. 24) and that "learning is best achieved through direct engagement and experience" (Edelsky et al., 1991, p. 24). Therefore, a learner-centered curriculum, which draws on the students' background, interests, and strengths, is considered optimal. In this learner-centered learning, students bring a rich and varied background of experiences and talent to the classroom, and take ownership of their learning. Learning, as a result, not only becomes relevant, real, and meaningful, but also enhances students' self-esteem (Gust, 1994).

Writing also shares these features. Students like to write about themselves (Freeman & Freeman, 1998). If students can write of their experiences, share their inner feelings, and present their unique thoughts, they will naturally be more motivated to write. As Ueland (1987) argued, writing can be a joyful, lively, and satisfying activity if it uses a person's creative power. Whole language teachers believe that when given the chance to do so, students begin to write more; and the more they write, the more likely they are to improve (Hamayan, 1989).

Writing as a Process of Social Invention and Interaction

In a whole language perspective, language is not only personal but also social. We must search for the norms and conventions shared with the community to make communication successful (Goodman, 1986). This belief, interwoven with Halliday's functional grammar and Vygotsky's Zone of Proximal Development (ZPD), results in the belief that language learning is a process of social invention.

Halliday's (1977) functional grammar investigates the relationship between the different aspects of language and the social functions that different language structures fulfill. The notion of ZPD, proposed by Vygotsky (1978, 1986), emphasizes the importance of collaboration and stresses that through such collaboration, students can transcend their individual limitations. In other words, in ZPD, with support, people can achieve more with collaboration than they can individually, and are thus able to incorporate this collaborative effort into their individual repertoires (Engstrom, 1986; Vygotsky, 1978). It seems that processes which first occur inter-subjectively (between people) and eventually take place intra-subjectively (within a person) (Vygotsky, 1978, cited in Edelsky et al., 1991).

In this sense, writing, an integral part of language learning, should be a process of social interaction. Instead of merely assigning topics and word or page requirements, as many teachers used to do, whole language teachers "often guide their students through the writing process, from initial efforts at determining what they will write about to eventual 'publication' and/or public celebration of their writing" (Weaver, 1994, p. 366-367). Whole language writing teachers serve as allies, helping students strengthen their pieces, instead of being perceived as an adversary, correcting and evaluating students' first and only drafts. Besides the interaction with teachers, students also "talked to classmates about their ideas and shared their writings, soliciting ideas for improvement and submitting finished works to be celebrated by their peers" (Weaver, 1994, p. 367).

These concepts revolutionize both NES and ESL writing. More and more writing teachers are implementing these holistic and naturalistic approaches in their classrooms and are receiving positive feedback from their students.

2.3.1 Pertinent Research on Whole Language Application in ESL Writing

Historically, whole language was associated with literacy instruction at the elementary school level, but when second-language acquisition theory (Flynn, 1986; Flynn & O'Neil, 1988; Gass & Madden, 1985) has developed over the past decade, particularly with regard to language learning processes and strategies (Faigle, Cherry, Jolliffe, & Skinner, 1993; Feeley, Strickland, & Wepner, 1991; Mitchell, 1982; Moll, 1990; G. Murray, 1980) and the role of interlanguage (Gaies, 1976; Gass & Selinker, 1992; Kaspar & Blum-Kulka, 1993; Nehls, 1988; Selinker, 1991), whole language advocates have become more aware of the similarities between children and adults as language learners.

Clearly, whole language proponents believe that learning proceeds from whole to part and that for optimal learning, texts must be authentic, activities must be meaningful, and learning must be student-centered. This is not only compatible with learning a language orally but also with learning the written language. It is not only true for children acquiring their native language but is also valid for both children and adults when learning a foreign language. It is no wonder that the whole language view of writing has been widely applied in various ESL contexts.

One of the most successful examples in an ESL classroom was conducted by Adele MacGowan-Gilhooly (1991, 1996b) at City College in the City University of New York. She encouraged students to focus on writing about things that were interesting and important to them and not to worry about mistakes, as mistakes would take care of themselves. In order to reach the fluency goals set, students wrote a 10,000 word "book," practiced daily freewriting, read 1,000 pages of fiction, responded in journals, and worked in small writing and reading groups in class. They used writing to express themselves, to tell stories, to discover ideas, to think, and to learn. Accordingly, they began experiencing writing with comfort, control and confidence. This fluency-first writing curriculum, reversing the traditional grammar-first sequence, brought "concrete evidence of its effectiveness in the form of higher scores on standardized reading and writing tests, as well as the qualitative evidence of improvement in the students' written work and reading abilities" (Loewe, 1998a, p. 269).

Another example was the one described in Nelson's book, *At the Point of Need* (1991). Nelson emphasized that grammar should be taught within the context of writing, and she described a five-year, fluency-first writing program at the post-secondary level. She suggests that changes in writing must follow changes in awareness and behavior. When the students are freed from formulaic structures, organization patterns arise more naturally. Also, when the anxiety over correctness felt by students is reduced, real fluency and accuracy emerge. Karin, a first-year international student, supported Nelson's belief. Karin's writing changed for the better, having a strong, personal voice and greater accomplishment in global features (like idioms, articles, prepositions, and the like), when she could choose her own topics and rewrite or discard any of her work (Nelson, 1991).

The chief discoveries found in Nelson's longitudinal teacher-research relate to the students' gradually taking responsibility for their own work, the phenomenon of breakthrough in the students' writing and the development of tutors/teachers.   The ESL students Nelson and her tutors worked with changed from dependent to interdependent and finally to independent; conversely, the tutors/teachers changed "from a highly directive stance to one of adviser, if required" (Nelson, 1991, p. viii).   This change is closely related to the phenomenon of breakthrough in the students' writing.   During this process, the tutors/teachers "found that the most acceptable and effective teaching was to give the help the students asked for when they asked for it—that is, as the students perceived the need" (p. ix) and with such teaching at the point of need, improvement in grammar, structure, and punctuation in the students' essays was apparent. Consequently, students successfully transferred their writing competence from self-initiated writing to academic essays on assigned topics.   All in all, Nelson's research is impressive and since it has been applied in different countries (The United Kingdom, Korea, The People's Republic of China, etc.) with different students (kids, adults, gifted, mentally challenged, etc.), the philosophy and framework she reveals confirms the applicability of the use of whole language components in ESL writing.

Mary Anne Loewe (1998a, 1998b) also shared her experiences using whole language with ESL students in public schools as well as in university-level Intensive English Programs (IEP).   For ESL students in public schools, she adapted Brian Cambourne's (1988) model of literacy acquisition and added a few accommodations.   What she emphasized was

(1)   The student should be immersed in language, which means making both oral and written language comprehensible
(2)   Learners need to receive demonstrations of how texts are constructed and used
(3)   Maintain high expectations of the student
(4)   Give the student responsibility for his or her learning
(5)   Students must be allowed to use the language
(6)   Allow students to approximate language features

(7) Give the student an appropriate and timely response (Loewe, 1998b, p. 246-256).

She also emphasized implementing theme cycles in a classroom by referring to Popp's (1996) procedure for establishing a theme cycle. To Loewe, such theme explorations "offer students the opportunity to collaborate meaningfully on a project while honing their language skills" (Loewe, 1998b, p. 252). She emphasized the use of dialogue journals with ESL students, and used Gunkel's (1991) Japanese student as a successful example. This fourth-grade Japanese student made dramatic progress in writing within four months (Loewe, 1998b). Similar results using dialogue journals to promote writing can be seen in J. Clark (1992), Hamayan & Pfleger (1987), and Manning & Manning (1989).

As for ESL students at the university-level, Mary Ann Loewe (1998a) also offered guidelines for "helping students achieve grammatical accuracy through awareness development and strategy training, contextualized instruction such as theme units, grammar instruction integrated into the other IEP program components of reading, writing, speaking, and listening, and the adoption of a student-centered syllabus" (p. 260). As Loewe observed, most university-level intensive English programs generally maintain an isolated four-skill approach. Thus, it is considered necessary to implement a more contextualized study in classrooms, such as offering content-based integrated skill classes, or combining grammar with other skills, i.e. speaking, listening, reading and writing, or making the syllabus more student-centered. In her case, she chose teaching through theme units in each class as a way of contextualizing language study. In order to contextualize the study, she tried to build upon the students' previous learning experiences, allowing a focus on use as well as usage. She exposed the students to meaningful language use, taking into account the interests and needs of the students, and incorporated the eventual use the learner would make of the language (Brinton, Snow, & Wesche, 1989). The conclusion is

second-language learners are immersed in communicative reading and writing events, developing strategies needed for becoming lifelong learners of languages. Skills such as grammar are acquired by the meaningful use of the language, through analysis and discussion of sentences in written text and in their own speaking and writing, and in 'teachable moments' of direct, individualized instruction (Loewe, 1998a, p. 272).

Other studies further documented the successful use of whole language techniques in working with ESL students. These include Freeman & Freeman (1991, 1992, 1998), Hsu (1994), Jama (1992), Manning & Manning (1989), Manning, Manning, & Long (1994), Mills & Clyde (1990), Nigohosian (1992), Ridley (1990), and Wilson (1993).

2.3.2 Current Research on Whole Language Application in Taiwan

The discussion, research, and application of whole language in an ESL context have attracted the attention of language teachers in Taiwan. Those who are frustrated with traditional skill-based instruction are interested in meaning-oriented and learner-centered whole language classes. Those who are curious about the effectiveness of whole language investigate its theory, philosophy, and applicability. Therefore, more and more university-based researchers have reviewed the literature on whole language philosophy (Chao, 1994, 1995; Y. M. Chen, 1994, 2001; Luo, 1998; Shen, 1991; Tseng, 1998; T. H. Yu, 2001), implemented whole language principles in their classrooms (Y. M. Chen, 2001; Huang, 1997, 1998; Li, 1996, 1997, 1998a, 1998b, 2000a, 2000b, 2001; Liou, 1991; Lu, 2002; Tseng, 1997), or conducted projects cooperatively with elementary school teachers (Shen, 2000, Shen & Huang, 1997).

Y. M. Chen (1994) reviewed the origin and philosophy of whole language and discussed the view of language learning and the roles of teachers and learners. She also conducted participant observation in an elementary school to investigate the effectiveness of whole language application. The results of her study support the conclusion that whole language implies whole person, whole learning, whole teaching, whole activity, whole language, and whole environment. ... Whole language theory seems to be universally true, and it can be practiced and applied to various levels of education, including secondary (in subject-structure), and higher and adult education. Not only can it be applied to first language learning, but also to second language learning. Its ultimate goal in education is to foster self-recognition, self-growth, and self-development of individuals to the fullest extent (pp. 390-391).

Y. M. Chen (2001) further discussed the characteristics and theoretical framework of teaching reading in a whole language way. She utilized the strategies suggested by Heald-Taylor (1989) to connect students' reading with the real world. These strategies are themes, listening to literature, dramatization, role playing, interpretative drama, and puppet plays. She also reviewed reading strategies proposed by various researchers (Chaptman & Anderson, 1996; Crawford, 1993; Froese, 1991; Krashen, 1985; Newman, 1985; Peetoom, 1986; F. Smith, 1994a, 1997), such as pre-reading, guided reading, and post-reading. What she did not provide was the procedure to implement whole language in a reading classroom or an investigation of the effectiveness of the application. In addition, Y. M. Chen did not focus on an EFL environment, so its applicability is still a myth.

Tseng (1998) introduced Goodman's psycholinguistic view of whole language and Harste and Burke's socio-psycholinguistic view of whole language. She not only clearly interpreted their philosophy but also discussed the possibility and difficulty of implementing whole language in Taiwan. Tseng (1997), based on her teaching experiences, indicated the possible difficulties: course design and materials preparation, different beliefs held by teacher and students, and the challenge of the non-traditional role of the teacher. She also emphasized that the only solutions to these difficulties in implementation are the teacher's on-going reflection, reflection on course design and every event that happens in class, and teacher's participation in a support group, sharing the frustrations and enjoyment of whole language application in class.

Tseng (2000) published a book for elementary teachers in Taiwan who would like to use whole language in class. In this book, she first reviewed the major English teaching methods and how whole language differs. She then introduced how to implement whole language in an EFL pre-school curriculum. Taking her own class as an example, Tseng provided a clear picture of implementation, putting theory into practice.

However, all the research mentioned above is not directly related to writing per se. The research studies which focus mainly on the use of whole language in a writing class are those conducted by Shen (2000), Shen and Huang (1997), Huang (1997, 1998), and Li (1997, 1998b, 2001). Shen (2000) and Shen and Huang (1997) used whole language principles in elementary Chinese writing classes. Since whole language was originally intended for NESs, the L1 learners, Shen investigated whether it was possible and acceptable to implement this philosophy in classes where students learn Chinese as their first language. He used one grade 3 and one grade 5 writing class as the subjects for his experiment. Designing the course around themes, he received mixed results, where the grade 3 experiment almost failed, except for publication promoting students' writing interests, and the grade 5 result was very successful. Shen concluded that the key to successful whole language application in writing activities was the teacher's beliefs on writing (Shen, 2000; Shen & Huang, 1997).

Further research mainly focusing on EFL writing instruction was that carried out at Tamkang University (Huang, 1997, 1998). Huang and other professors in the English department at Tamkang University, followed Adele MacGowan-Gilhooly's (1996b) "Fluency First" and designed a literature-based integrated writing curriculum for their sophomore English majors. They read authentic books, watched movies, had discussions in class, and wrote journals and final projects. This implementation reversed the traditional skill-based and skill-separated view of learning. It integrated reading into writing courses and also emphasized discussion and sharing during the writing process. The results, according to Huang (1997, 1998), were mostly positive, especially in terms of the students' writing performance and their self-perception of being a writer.

Within the last two decades, whole language has been rapidly implemented in language classrooms, from English speaking countries to ESL environments. Though doubts, hesitation and even resistance still exist, many studies have reported positive outcomes as a result of the application of whole language. These studies pave the way for a revolution in EFL writing education. For example, the awareness that writing should not be taught in isolation has been introduced to EFL writing instructors. The emphasis of the reading-writing connection has been reinforced by the studies on literature-based or theme-based instruction. In addition, research has supported the idea that learner-related (authentic and relevant) materials greatly increase motivation when compared to pre-scheduled lessons and promote better writing skills than sentence pattern or model-based paragraph practices. It is also impressive that research indicates significant changes in the learning attitudes and perception. To some extent, whole language philosophy has not only revealed problems but has helped overcome major hindrances in traditional EFL writing education.

However, being a teacher of adult EFL writers, the researcher recognizes that there is a gap between the studies that have been done and the investigation of the effectiveness and applicability of using whole language in adult EFL classes. Since some research has suggested that the teachers' writing belief is the key to success, the researcher has strived to enhance the diverse and alternative roles of teachers and students by incorporating Carl Rogers' whole-person education and Paulo Freire's liberatory education in a whole language classroom.

2.4 Carl Rogers' Whole-Person Education

Carl Rogers, a distinguished psychiatrist and educator, the founder of "client-centered" or "non-directive" theory, was born in 1902 and died in 1987. He devoted his entire professional life to enhancing human communication. He not only proposed and promoted a new approach, known as the "non-directive," "client-centered," and "person-centered" approach in psychotherapy, but also introduced these characteristics of person-to-person relationship to all the helping professions, such as psychology, social work, education, ministry, and the like (Kirschenbaum & Henderson, 1989; Jiang, 2001).

Rogers (1983; Rogers & Freiberg, 1994) believed that students are unique individuals with full potential. The purpose of education is to facilitate each individual's potential so that they can develop their competence and personality. Rogers (1983) also insisted that both the intellectual and emotional selves of students should be respected in the process of learning (Jiang, 2001; Rogers, 1983; Rogers & Freiberg, 1994). His whole-person concept has been adopted in various educational settings and has led to a humanistic way of learning (Rogers, 1983).

2.4.1 Characteristics of Rogerian Learning

The best-known contribution of Carl Rogers is the "core conditions" for facilitative (or non-directive, person-centered) counseling practice. The core conditions include congruence, acceptance, and empathy.

Congruence, also referred to as realness, means that the feelings a person experiences are available to him/her and to his/her awareness. In other words, the person is able to live these feelings and is able to communicate them if they are appropriate. Acceptance, also known as prizing and trust in Rogers's writing, is a non-possessive caring for another person. In such caring, a person shows his/her confidence in imperfect human beings. Empathy is not simply getting into others' shoes or following certain techniques, like repeating the last words the client has said (Rogers, 1961a, 1961b, 1980). Empathy involves attentive and non-judgmental listening and understanding.

However, Carl Rogers's contributions are not only in counseling psychology or psychotherapy but also in education. In his later years, Rogers found that his ideas about interpersonal relationships were useful and suitable for all human relationships. Thus, he expanded his research into education, and his facilitative counseling has been widely applied to various educational settings. His educational reform contains features like teacher as facilitator, learner-centered learning, and ways of building freedom.

Teacher as Facilitator

> Not long ago, a teacher asked me, "what changes would you like to see in education?" I answered the question as best I could at the time, but it stayed with me. Suppose I had a magic wand that could produce only one change in our educational systems. What would that change be?
> I finally decided that my imaginary wand, with one sweep, would cause every teacher at every level to forget that he or she is a teacher (Carl Rogers, 1983, p. 135).

Carl Rogers more than once mentioned that teaching "is a relatively unimportant and vastly overvalued activity" (Rogers, 1983, p. 119). He disagreed with the definition of teaching as instructing someone else. To him, the imparting of knowledge only makes sense in an unchanging environment. Since our world is continually changing, the goal of education should be viewed as the facilitation of learning. He also suggested that an educated person is the one who has learned how to learn instead of relying on static knowledge. The qualities of Rogers's facilitative learning, according to his theory of person-centered counseling, include realness, prizing-acceptance-trust, and empathic understanding.

Realness, the basic element of facilitative learning, suggests that the teacher is a real person with convictions and genuine feelings toward her/himself and toward the students. In other words, the teacher is a real person instead of a "faceless embodiment of a curricular requirement" or "a sterile tube through which knowledge is passed from one generation to the next" (Rogers, 1983, p. 122). Prizing-acceptance-trust is another important element in facilitative learning. What Rogers meant here is the prizing and acceptance of the learner as an imperfect human being with many feelings and many potentialities. Such trust and love make learning more effective. Moreover, empathic understanding is essential in facilitative learning. A facilitative teacher views the world through the eyes of the students. In other words, the students are simply understood and accepted, with no evaluation or judgment from the teacher's own preferences.

To Rogers, as long as a teacher has this attitude, he no longer is a teacher. Instead, he is a facilitator—giving students freedom, life, and the opportunity to learn. Rogers believed, "If only one teacher out of one hundred dared to risk, dared to be, dared to trust, dared to understand, we would have an infusion of a living spirit into education that would ... be priceless" (Rogers, 1983, p. 131).

Learner-centered Learning

A person-centered mode of learning emphasizes the teacher's sense of security within her/himself to have essential trust in the capacity of others to think for themselves and to learn for themselves. With this precondition, it is possible to implement other features of person-centered learning.

Rogers proposed that the whole class should be involved with curriculum planning or course design, so that the facilitator (teacher) and the learners would share the responsibility for learning. The teacher/facilitator provides the learning resources within herself and from her own experiences and encourages the whole class to add resources from their own knowledge and experience. As for the learners, they are responsible for their own choices and can develop, individually or cooperatively, their own learning program according to their interests, curiosities, and resources. With this atmosphere of realness, trust, and understanding listening, the facilitative learning climate is nurtured, first by the facilitator and gradually by the whole class. The learning process and interaction in the process are given equal emphasis. Both the teacher and the students then come to the understanding that learning from each other is as important as learning from books.

In addition, the evaluation of learning is made primarily by the learner, and results will usually show that the learner, in such a self-chosen and self-initiated learning atmosphere, tends to invest his whole person in the learning process and that such learning "tends to be deeper, proceeds at a more rapid rate, and is more pervasive in the life and behavior of the student" (Rogers, 1983, p. 189).

Building Freedom

Besides the strong statement, "teacher as facilitator," Rogers also suggested ways to build freedom in learning.

One of the suggestions is to create circumstances that will involve students with real experiences and problems; providing resources is another. Using contracts, involving community, peer teaching, grouping, utilizing encounter groups and self-evaluation are some of the other suggestions. Among these methods, the use of contracts is especially effective and interesting. Contracts are usually used for "activities, motivation, and reinforcement to help students achieve cognitive objectives" (Rogers, 1983, p. 150). Also, the use of contracts can be a way of evaluating students. With student contracts, students "become searchers after knowledge, not passive and temporary recipients of it. They can enter into the process of learning and discover what an adventure it is" (Rogers, 1983, p. 153).

2.4.2 The Shared Beliefs of Rogerian Learning and Whole Language

Though whole language advocates seldom mention Carl Rogers and his whole-person education, it is evident that there are similarities. The most obvious shared characteristic is the emphasis on humanistic education. In order to achieve the goal of a humanistic education, they both advocate changing the role of teacher from a dominant examiner to a facilitator or helper. Both also value a learner's potential and the possibility of their transformation. They respect learners as unique, capable and whole beings, and believe students have the ability to take responsibility for their own learning and self-evaluation. A student's intellect and his likes and dislikes are seriously considered in curriculum design, as is teacher-student and student-student interaction. In other words, they both promote learner-centered learning, in which teachers act as facilitators, providing enough support for learners and learning, and learners hold the ownership of making choice and decision. It is no wonder that when Weaver, Chaston, & Peterson (1993) mentioned the theoretical basis of the whole language perspective, they included the work of the humanistic psychologist, Carl Rogers.

2.5 Paulo Freire's Education of Liberation

Paulo Freire, a Brazilian educator, was born in 1921 and died of heart failure in 1997. He is considered the most influential thinker in education in the late 20th century (Bentley, 1999; Gadotti, 1994; Gadotti & Torres, n.d.; "People You Should Know," n.d.). Though he is not as well-known as John Dewey, Freire "certainly made a number of important theoretical innovations that have had a considerable impact on the development of educational practice—and on informal education and popular education in particular" (M. K. Smith, 2002, p. 1). The ideas in his most well-known and popular book, *Pedagogy of the Oppressed* (1970), discuss the confrontation between the oppressor and the oppressed, especially in the political context of Brazil. However, the application of his response to the pedagogy of the oppressed goes well beyond the context of the political or economic aspects of Brazil (Berthoff, 1985; Elias, 1994; Gadotti, 1994; Freire, 1985, 1994; Freire, Fraser, Macedo, Mekinnon, & Stokes, 1997; Shor, 1987; M. K. Smith, 2002). It is no surprise that the same ideas have been applied and discussed in the educational field, with regard to adult literacy, second language learning and critical pedagogy (Bartolome, 1994; Freire et al., 1997; Freire & Macedo, 1987; Graman, 1988; Rigg, 1985; Shor, 1987; Shor & Freire, 1987).

2.5.1 Characteristics of Freirean Pedagogy

Paulo Freire held that students have great potential. Learners, especially adults, are knowledgeable because of their life experiences.

They may not know the target language or the subject matter but they have the ability to trigger and utilize the system of association. Freire (1970) claimed that students should not be considered as empty vessels, passively waiting to be filled; instead, they are living creatures with ideas, experiences, knowledge, and dignity. Therefore, education should not be like depositing money in banks—depositing canned lessons into students' empty brains, but should be conducted in a dialogical way. Both teachers and students can be information providers and receivers. Consequently, the relationship between teachers and students is dynamic instead of fixed (Freire, 1970, 1993). The dialogical way of learning encourages student-generated materials, where students usually bring up issues that really concern them. Through deeply reflecting on life and society, Freirean pedagogy enhances humanistic concerns, personal growth/empowerment, and critical thinking. All these are essential to language education, writing included. Therefore by utilizing a dialogical way of learning, Freirean pedagogy is applied to learner-centeredness.

Liberatory Education Versus Banking Education

Though Freire's critique of education was not new (Heaney, 1995), he definitely drew our attention to the weaknesses in education, especially adult education. To Freire, "adult education, whether for remediation or for career advancement, generally replicates patterns of earlier schooling: a … model of instruction which fosters respect for authority, experts, discipline, and good work habits" (Heaney, 1995, p. 1). This type of education cannot empower learners; instead, it silences the learners and treats them as second-class citizens. Banking education forms a relationship between teacher and student, which is narrative in nature. The teacher is narrator and the students are the listeners. The teacher plays the role of output while the students play the role of input, not vice-versa. Whatever the teacher narrates, the students take for granted by note taking, reciting, and repetition. Students are thus objectified. They don't have the chance to reflect; their way of thinking is pre-determined. Students in this situation are trained to accept reality through recitation instead of experiencing it for themselves. They don't know why they must accept this knowledge, and they soon lose the desire to inquire about the essence of existence, because to do so is considered abnormal and against authority. Memorization cannot help them to build relationships with the world, the self or others. Thus, it is difficult for learners in these circumstances to engage in critical thinking or reflection. Reflection and critical thinking, fostered through observation and participation, results in thinking and making changes. Also, when memorization is emphasized, students have no exposure to analysis. They tend not to ask "why" or "how." It is not surprising that banking education considers men as "adaptable, manageable beings" (Freire, 1993, p. 54).

Freire challenged this type of education and the relationship between teacher and student. He proposed a "liberating education," which liberates both teacher and student by emphasizing the act of cognition rather than the transferring of information. Liberating education regards men as conscious beings, who act and reflect upon their world in order to transform it. The process of recognizing their existing reality and transforming that reality is the process of humanization. In order to reach the goals of liberating education, the teacher-student contradiction found in banking education must be resolved. Only when the role of teacher is not a dominant one and the role of the student is not an oppressed one, will real learning occur. As Gadotti (1994) rephrased Freire's saying in his book *Extension or Communication* (1971), "whoever is just 'filled' by others, with just content that contradicts his own way of being, does not learn" (p. 42). Paulo Freire's liberating education highlights the practice of freedom as the basis for education. Thus, how can the contradictory teacher-student relationship be resolved? It can only be through dialogue.

A Dialogical Versus an Anti-dialogical Way of Learning

One of the important concepts in Paulo Freire's writing is dialogical pedagogy versus anti-dialogical pedagogy. In Chapter 4 of *Pedagogy of the Oppressed*, Freire (1993) made a distinction between anti-dialogic and dialogic theory. The characteristics of anti-dialogic theory include the necessity to divide and conquer in order to achieve domination, manipulation, and cultural invasion, while the characteristics of dialogic theory are collaboration, union, organization, and cultural synthesis. Paulo Freire links education to the struggle of the oppressed class, so both dialogic and anti-dialogic theory can be more widely applied than from only political or social perspectives.

Dialogue, for Paulo Freire, is not only a way of making friends or a tool for controlling others, but a part of human nature. As Gadotti's *Reading Paulo Freire: His Life and Work* (1994) says, Paulo Freire believed, "Human beings are constructed through dialogue as they are essentially communicative" (p. 29). Through dialogue, human beings discover, construct, and process knowledge. It is a natural way of discovery. Since schools are places for human beings to discover knowledge, in the view of Freire, dialogue should be included as a teaching strategy in education.

However, most schools present the "dialogue" in a vertical way, in which the teachers speak and the students listen. The educators command and the students obey. Freire considered this way of teaching with these pseudo dialogues as "anti-dialogic pedagogy." To him, anti-dialogic pedagogy is manipulation. Without the freedom to voice their own views and opinions or to participate in reciprocal interaction, the learners are prevented from stating their points of view, which in turn fosters ignorance and dependence. In anti-dialogic pedagogy, the teacher and students are antagonists instead of interlocutors.

In contrast, the dialogue that Paulo Freire emphasized is a horizontal relationship. It values respect for those involved in dialogue. They may be different, with different views, but they are never antagonists. Tolerance, another virtue of dialogue is the key to accepting those who are different. Thus, for Freire, the dialogue that should be included in schools is such that "schools should always listen to what their pupils say about what is taught to them" and in which schools are "making continuous evaluations" (Gadotti, 1994, p. 29). Such dialogue is fed by love, humility, hope, faith, and confidence (Friere, 1970, 1993). From what Freire insisted in dialogic pedagogy, we can see that education, for him, is part of the process of humanization. As Freire argued,

> Through dialogue, the teacher-of-the-students and the stu-
> dent-of-the teacher cease to exist and a new term emerges:
> teacher-student with the students-teachers. The teacher is no
> longer merely the-one-who-teaches, but one who is himself taught
> in dialogue with the students, who in turn while being taught also
> teach. They become jointly responsible for a process in which all
> grow (Freire, 1993, p. 61).

While mentioning dialogue, Freire (1993) unashamedly stressed the importance and power of love. He believed that "love is the most crucial characteristic of dialogue and the constitutive force animating all pedagogies of liberation" (McLaren, 1999, p. 53). He claimed:

> Dialogue cannot exist, however, in the absence of a profound
> love for the world and for people. The naming of the world,
> which is an act of creation and re-creation, is not possible if it is
> not infused with love. Love is at the same time the foundation
> of dialogue and dialogue itself. It is thus necessarily the task of
> responsible Subjects and cannot exist in a relation of domination.
> Domination reveals the pathology of love: sadism in the domi-
> nator and masochism in the dominated. Because love is an act
> of courage, not of fear, love is commitment to others. No
> matter where the oppressed are found, the act of love is com-
> mitment to their cause—the cause of liberation. And this
> commitment, because it is loving, is dialogical. As an act of
> bravery, love cannot be sentimental; as an act of freedom, it
> must not serve as a pretext for manipulation. It must generate
> other acts of freedom; otherwise, it is not love. Only by abol-
> ishing the situation of oppression is it possible to restore the
> love which that situation made impossible. If I do not love the
> world—if I do not love life—if I do not love people—I cannot
> enter into dialogue (Freire, 1993, pp. 70-71).

In addition to love, Freire strongly declared that dialogue cannot exist without humility, intense faith in humankind, hope, and critical thinking

(Freire, 1970, 1993). These features are not only essential to dialogue but also vital to education. To Freire, without these features there is no dialogue; without dialogue there is no communication, and without communication there can be no true education. Authentic education—liberating both teachers and learners—must involve the dialogic way of pedagogy.

2.5.2 The Shared Beliefs of Freire, Rogers and Whole Language

Though McLaren (1999) argued that, "Freirean pedagogy is often erroneously perceived as synonymous with whole language instruction, adult literacy programs, and new 'constructivist' approaches to teaching and learning based on Vygotsky's work" (p. 51), whole language philosophy and Freirean Pedagogy indeed share certain similarities in their philosophy. The view that learning is best achieved through direct engagement and experience, the emphasis on empowering both teachers and learners, and the value of critical thinking and problem posing are the primary points of similarity.

In the discussion of learning, Edelsky et al. (1991) used Freire's language to further elaborate the active participation of students—"education must therefore encourage students to become knowing Subjects (with the power to act on their reality) rather than passive Objects (vessels to be filled by the teacher)" (pp. 24-25). The inquiry of what and how to study is centered around the learners in whole language philosophy. It encourages students to shape their own topics and to write and rewrite their own lives rather than meaninglessly and repeatedly check certain sequence charts in workbooks. Similarly, teachers are encouraged to observe and to negotiate with students to generate learning themes rather than simply follow the pre-packaged textbooks assigned by an outside force. This perspective is parallel to Freire's statement (1993):

> The teacher presents the materials to the students for their consideration, and re-considers her earlier considerations as the

> students express their own. The role of the problem-solving educator is to create, together with the students, the conditions ... (p. 62).

In so doing, both teacher and students are empowered so as to take back control of their teaching and learning.

In addition, whole language advocates believe in the importance and necessity of critical thinking and problem posing. To them, both features are necessary ingredients of all learning and in turn, ideally engage students in acting on and transforming sociopolitical reality (Edelsky et at., 1991). From this perspective, whole language has the potential to be a liberatory pedagogy (Edelsky et at., 1991). Edelsky et al. made this further explanation:

> Whole language eliminates the grouping for reading and the tracking that ensure unequal access to 'cultural capital' (i.e., certain texts, vocabulary, knowledge, analyses). It devalues the major language-based devices for stratifying people. It makes teachers the authors (not 'deliverers' or 'managers') of curriculum. In other words, it helps subvert the school's role in maintaining a stratified society. ... Between its actual subversion of particular means of oppressive ranking in school (leading to even more oppressive stratifying in life) and its (unfortunately often unused) potential for critique, whole language could well be as 'pedagogy of resistance and possibility'[1] (Edelsky et al., 1991, p. 54).

At this point, both whole language and Freirean pedagogy share features with liberating education.

Except for the fact that Freire did not defend the principle of non-directivity in education as Rogers did, they share many common points in pedagogy and in the defined roles for teacher and learners. First,

---

[1] Edelsky et al. (1991) borrowed the term "pedagogy of resistance and possibility" from Aronowitz & Giroux (1985) *Education under siege: The conservative, liberal, and radical debate over schooling.* South Hadley, MA: Bergin & Garvey.

they both believed that men can solve their problems on their own as long as they are motivated to do so. Second, they both considered that education should be centered on the students and learning rather than the teacher and teaching. Students should be the master of their own learning and should be responsible for their growth and self-evaluation. Third, both Freire and Rogers respected the student as a whole being, a complete person with intellect, feelings and emotions. Fourth, both of them tried to bridge the teacher-student gap generated by the traditional banking education (Gadotti, 1994). All these similarities match the core beliefs of whole language philosophy.

2.6 Theme Cycles: A Whole Language Application

The term "theme cycles," which concerns the integration of various learning areas, learners and the world, is popular in literacy development, and its proponents know full well that this term is closely related to the concept of whole language philosophy and the education of liberation.

2.6.1 Definition of Theme Cycles

As Bess Altwerger and Barbara Flores explained in their article "Theme Cycles: Creating Communities of Learners" (1994), "Theme cycles are our way of rethinking curricular integration" (p. 2). In a theme cycle, learners (both students and teachers) are the center of learning. They brainstorm and negotiate the topics together, based on their interests, life experiences, knowledge, and curiosity. There are no pre-set topics or pre-chosen reading materials. All the reading, discussion, writing, and sharing is initiated and generated by the learners.

Usually, the learning process using theme cycles contains the following steps. First, learners brainstorm and discuss their interests, inquiries, and concerns so that they can negotiate a theme selection. Second, after the theme has been selected, learners have to negotiate some more in order to decide whether or not the theme is worthy of further investigation and where they can find related reading materials. Third, while re-investigating, learners begin to conduct reading, sharing, and authoring. They share what they have read related to the theme they have chosen and also share what they have written on the theme. Fourth, after discussion of their reading and writing, learners begin to revise and edit their own writing pieces. Fifth, after editing and revision, learners present their writing to the class, after which it is published in an anthology and placed in a portfolio. Sixth, by continuing to share, learners gain new ideas for the next theme cycle learning. (Altwerger & Flores, 1994).

Connie Weaver also mentioned the differences between "theme units" and "theme cycles" according to Altwerger's distinction (Weaver et al., 1993).

> A theme unit, Altwerger said, was teacher-oriented, with the topic predetermined and the teacher responsible for planning and organizing, based on his or her learning goals. In contrast, Altwerger conceptualized theme cycles as student-oriented, with the topic negotiated and students and teacher sharing responsibility, based on the knowledge, interests and questions both could contribute (p. 12-13).

2.6.2 Application of Theme Cycles

The methods of application of theme cycles can be different. Castro (1994) shared her way of implementing theme cycles in a third-grade bilingual class. To her, "one of the goals of the theme cycle is to integrate the different content areas and disciplines within the theme but not to force this integration" (p. 10). Thus, she along with her students brainstormed and voted on the themes they would like to explore in the year. In order to begin the process, each one of them listed five things they already knew about the theme and another five things they wanted to know. Then, they began theme cycle learning with the whole class, half-class groups, small groups, individually, in workshops, or in a learning station setting. Each student was also required to conduct a learning project of their own choice. Castro (1994) emphasized,

> it is important to remember that all these learning experiences were based on the questions the learning community generated at the beginning of the cycle as well as on the questions that emerged from their newly acquired knowledge (p.11).

This was Castro's way of implementing theme cycles in her elementary class.

However, using theme cycles is not merely a way of integrating content areas. To Andrews-Sullivan and Negrete (1994), a theme cycle is a way of knowing. They view theme cycle processes as a way for teachers and students to reconstruct knowledge based on their need to know. Also, the theme cycle process restored and empowered the students' voices. Through various scenarios such as whole class (reading aloud, observing an event, story-telling), pairs of students (reading buddies, writing partners), small groups (authors' workshop, literature study), committees (research teams, issue/interest groups), and individuals (observation logs, learning logs, mini research), their voices were heard. They learned how to make choices and decisions and see that everything is connected to something else. "Students become more assertive, take more risks, and experience a rebirth in their curiosity" (Andrews-Sullivan & Negrete, 1994, p. 17).

Timothy Shanahan (1997) had a deep insight into the purposes and effective ways of implementing thematic units in language learning. To him, simply "adding writing to the reading curriculum does not necessarily mean that students will improve in reading" (p. 14). "Improved learning is only likely to be the result if reading and writing are combined in appropriate ways" (p. 14). Thematic unit learning is an alternative. Proponents of thematic units usually claim (1) that integration will lead to greater amounts of learning (Beane, 1995; Lehman, 1994), (2) students will have a firmer grasp of the ideas that are studied (Lipson, Valencia, Wixson, & Peters, 1993; Nissani, 1995), (3) students will be able to apply what they learned to real problems (Schmidt et al.,

1985), and (4) students will have greater motivation (Lehman, 1994). However, with careful scrutiny, Timothy Shanahan (1997) revealed that improved motivation is probably the only positive outcome with convincing evidence. Some other research (Friend, 1985; Mansfield, 1989; Olarewaju, 1988; Schell & Wicklein, 1993; Wasserstein, 1995) supported Shanahan's statement and also emphasized the improved attitudes of students towards learning.

Thus, Shanahan (1997) provided a few guidelines for successfully implementing thematic units into language learning. First, he suggested that "thematic units should add intellectual depth to the curriculum" (p. 16). When the preference of the majority is to design fun units, Shanahan argued for the necessity to design units which would create a greater depth of knowledge. Second, Shanahan emphasized that "successful integration requires a great deal of attention to the separate disciplines" (p. 16). Unless we focus equally on reading and writing, students cannot gain insight into both skills. Third, Timothy argued that "curricular boundaries are social and cultural, not just cognitive" (p. 17). Thus, "integrated instruction will serve literacy learning best if it focuses on genres as cultural ways of communicating, and on being able to translate information from one form to another" (p.17). Finally, Shanahan stated that "integration does not do away with the need for direct explanation or drill and practice" (p. 18). In other words, even though students can gain valuable learning while conducting their own personal inquiries, there is a need for mini lessons and guided practice.

Dirkx and Prenger (1997) proposed an integrated theme-based approach (ITB) for adult learners. Though the target group of this approach is not ESL/EFL adult learners, the spirit of the study may still be helpful for ESL/EFL educators. The ITB approach was grounded conceptually in a transdisciplinary, (as opposed to a multidisciplinary or interdisciplinary approach), or real-world view of the curriculum. Since adults always bring a wide array of experience to educational programs in order to help them make sense of what they are trying to learn, and since adult learning is most effective when it is viewed as contextual, the ITB approach focuses on the life context of students to make their

learning more meaningful and relevant.   In addition, the teachers in the
ITB approach begin

> to develop goals and objectives, curricular materials, teaching
> strategies, and assessment tools only after they understand the
> life context and life goals of their learners (Dirkx & Prenger,
> 1997, p. 5).

In Gutloff's (1996) way of putting it, the integrated theme approach not
only represents a way of thinking but also develops the instruction,
which integrates all the competencies (i.e. academic skills, process skills,
and life skills) into a general idea or theme that is meaningful to the
learners.   The purpose is to arouse motivation, improve retention, and
enhance personal transformation, which is closely related to "the unfin-
ished self" described by Freire (1970) and Shor (1992).

METHODOLOGY

This chapter covers the methodology used in this study.   First, the researcher provides the rationale for the research methods.   Second, the pilot study and the design of the formal study are addressed.   Third, materials and instruments used in the study are described.   Fourth, the procedures of both theme cycles implementation and data collection are illustrated.   Fifth, the researcher briefly mentions the methods used for data analysis.

3.1 Rationale for the Research Methods

Both qualitative and quantitative methods were used in this study. However, since a small set of quantitative data, such as essay scores, were used for categorization and as supporting evidence for further description, statistical results should be interpreted in this light.   Also, no comparison groups or control groups were used in this study; therefore, no conclusion should be drawn about the superiority of one type of teaching method over another.   As indicated previously, this study was designed to provide a portrait of a small class of students.   Such a portrait contains students' writing performances, their affective responses to writing—self-efficacy and apprehension, and their changes over time.

3.1.1 Ethnographic Methods[1]

In order to examine adult EFL writers and the changes in their writing performance over time after having engaged in theme cycles learning, ethnographic methods such as participant observation, inter- viewing, and gathering written sources were used (D. M. Johnson, 1992). As D. M. Johnson (1992) argued in his book *Approaches to Research in Second Language Learning*, these methods are used "to see reality from the participants' point of view," which necessitates a great deal of time on-site and cannot be attained through a few short visits which are never adequate (p. 143). Thus, the researcher conducted observations throughout the year while she participated in co-learning with the stu- dents. The researcher also conducted interviews, mostly informal and gathered a variety of written materials such as students' journals, essays, and e-mails. It is believed that these methods were most appropriate because they allowed the researcher to obtain direct and detailed infor- mation about the learners and their learning. These methods also en- abled the researcher to accurately depict the class and the students, and so they provide the fullest picture of changes in the students' writing performances, attitudes, and perceptions. These changes were evi- denced through examination of their writing pieces, pre- and post-class questionnaires, and final self-evaluation and portfolios.

3.1.2 Case Study

In addition to the use of ethnographic methods as tools to collect data and to frame research, case studies were used to present and ana- lyze the data. Since the case study is "the primary vehicle for emic inquiry" (Lincoln & Guba, 1985, p. 359), it is believed that this method is adequate in studying the nature of this small EFL reading/writing class.

---

[1] Though Watson-Gegeo (1988) questioned, "For some, ethnography has become a synonym for qualitative research, so that any qualitative approach may be called ethnographic in whole or part, as long as it involves observation in non-laboratory settings" (p. 575), the term used in this study still takes its broader definition in ESL research.

The case study allowed the researcher to effectively demonstrate the interplay between the teacher and the students. The case study also made "thick description" (Denzin, 1990; Lincoln & Guba, 1985; Patton, 1990; Wu & Lee, 1995) possible so that the researcher could provide a sufficient base for transferability of judgment. Thus, even though "the findings of a case study cannot necessarily be generalized to other learners" (D. M. Johnson, 1992, p. 77), these findings may be a "natural basis for generalization" (Lincoln & Guba, 1985, p. 120), as long as the findings are epistemologically in harmony with the reader's own experience.

Triangulation was applied in this study as well. Triangulation was believed to be necessary because the use of multiple sources of data could prevent the researcher from relying on initial impressions and could establish and enhance the development of valid constructs during this study (Goetz & LeCompte, 1984).

3.1.3 Teacher as Researcher

The teacher as researcher has an advantage in this study because it is thought to be consistent with the emic knowledge and whole language philosophy. Whole language philosophy encourages teachers to take an active role as researcher within the classroom (Hydrick, 1991; Vacca & Rasinski, 1992) and to co-construct learning with the students (Edelsky et al., 1991; Brown & Mathie, 1991; Newman, 1985). In addition, ideas from ethnographic studies of education also support the teacher-researcher as a way of describing and understanding the meaning created within classrooms between the teacher and students (Brophy, 1988; Merriam, 1988). Since the researcher in this study taught the class herself, she had the chance to actively participate in the construction of knowledge with her students and to engage in a form of action research as she continually reflected on her practice. The research questions raised in this study came from her eagerness to understand her students and her desire to improve the quality of the students' learning experiences.

The techniques of the teacher-researcher as well as ethnography in education allow teachers to make the strange familiar, while observing their own classrooms. This capacity of observation not only benefits individual teachers but improves their knowledge of teaching (Cochran-Smith & Lytle, 1993). Additionally, teacher-research allows teachers to solve problems actively and to investigate innovative programs and their results, which, in turn, enhances the curriculum. All in all, the major advantage of teacher-research is that teachers have unique insider knowledge about the classroom, which an outside researcher may not be able to access in its entirety. Therefore, the teacher-researcher design in this study was most appropriate.

3.2 The Pilot Study

The pilot study was not done in one semester or one school year with one specific class. Instead, the pilot study was the result of an on-going effort during a span of seven years (1993-2000) with many students of diverse backgrounds. The pilot study can be divided into three phases. In the first phase, the understanding of adult learners and their perceptions of English reading/writing were examined. The second phase looked at adult reading/writing instruction and materials examination. The third phase tested the application of learner-centered and thematic learning. While it is helpful to describe them in sequence, the three phases were interrelated and sometimes overlapped.

It all started in 1993, the year the researcher began teaching reading/writing courses in this language center[2]. In the first four years, the classes were for career men and women from the general population and during the last three years they were for government employees. The students were from various professions: some were in business, some were elementary school teachers, some were arts or computer program designers, and some were nurses, soldiers, or lawyers. They came to

---

[2] This is the language center of a national university in Taipei.

the language center for various reasons, but with the same goal—to improve their English. However, according to the interviews, students revealed that they were eager to learn speaking/listening rather than reading/writing. They ended up in a reading/writing class because the classes for speaking/listening were full up when they tried to register. In other words, they came to class with weak motivation—they wanted to learn spoken English, but not reading and writing. They did not consider reading and writing to be practical. In their work and while traveling, they needed to speak and listen more than they needed to read and write. The perception was that reading and writing were tedious. From their previous experiences of learning English at school, they interpreted reading as checking the dictionary and memorizing vocabulary and writing as sentence making, pattern practice, and memorization of model articles. The passive participation and the pressure of a great deal of memorization discouraged them and scared them away from reading and writing before they had experienced any enjoyment.

Greatly inspired by the whole language philosophy, the researcher aimed to explore whether the whole language method could be successfully incorporated into EFL learning in Taiwan. However, out of a concern for the learners who viewed learning as sitting in class and listening to a teacher lecturing, the researcher implemented the concepts of whole language into the class little by little with care. From 1993 to 1996, the researcher scheduled one-third of class time for grammar instruction, one-third for reading instruction, and the remaining one-third for group discussion. In order to encourage students to be active learners and to promote interaction in class, time was allocated for reading. This was usually conducted as group reading, collaborative retelling and brainstorming, peer sharing, editing and dialogue journal writing. Besides, in order to enhance the learners' awareness of both authorship and audience, publishing[3] of the students' essays was always included in the curriculum (Li, 1998b). Over the years, the students gave consistently positive feedback to this whole-language-oriented class.

---

[3] Publishing students' essays refers to compiling students' final drafts in an anthology.

However, there remained a concern over whether or not the one-third of time spent on grammar discussion might negatively reinforce the form-over-meaning mode of thinking. Taking the concepts from Nelson's *At the point of need* (1991) and Weaver's *Teaching grammar in context* (1996), the researcher, from 1997, changed the curriculum by giving grammar lessons when the students were in need of such help. As a result, most of the class time was spent on reading discussion, idea generation, and draft discussion. Grammar lessons were not pre-planned or taught separately and systematically; instead, the discussion of word choice, sentence structure and discourse usage was mainly initiated by students when involved in draft discussions. Using students' writings, the whole class brainstormed better ways of expression. In so doing, students reviewed grammar rules while revising their writing, which made grammar more lively and more relevant.

In addition to the instruction, selection of materials was also a concern. In the beginning, the researcher used textbooks designed for ESL/EFL students. Students studied the reading text in the textbook and wrote essays based on what they read. Various topics were suggested by the teacher/researcher, but students could still choose their own topic. Through observation and interaction with the students, however, the researcher found that most ESL/EFL textbooks were designed for school-age students, and almost none was suitable for highly educated adult learners. The researcher therefore decided to go beyond the use of textbooks and began searching for articles or stories that would be of interest to the students in the hope of evoking a stronger reaction with more relevant reading matter. As a result, stories/essays discussing human relations, values, family, society and the like were suggested. Students immediately showed more interest and generated more ideas for writing. However, regardless of the efforts the teacher/researcher made on materials selection, no one specific genre appealed to all students: some liked stories, some favored news articles, some were interested in life issues, and still others in politics. Therefore, in order to really meet students' interests and needs, the teacher/researcher attempted to form theme-based learning.

For the classes from 1998 to 2000, a magazine, which contained about 10 themes per volume, was selected as the reading material. The whole class studied all the themes together, but students could choose their favorite for the writing of responses and essays. In so doing, students had more choices and became more involved in their learning. Since the students showed more potential in their writing with greater choice, the researcher decided to take a risk and allow them complete freedom of choice to read and write what they liked. The results of this experiment constitute the theme of this research.

In addition, during the 1999-2000 school year, the researcher carried out extensive exploratory observations. The goal of these explorations was to check if the students' perception of reading/writing had changed while participating in a whole language class and to also test the research instruments. Data collected using the Writing Self-Efficacy Questionnaire (See Appendix E) and the Writing Apprehension Questionnaire (See Appendix F) suggested that the students' perception of writing did change and that, for many students, this was their first experience of a humanistic learner-centered English language class.

During informal interviews, some students expressed their discovery of reading for pleasure and writing to discover the inner self. They liked to read and write in this way, on their own. Other students began to verbalize their enjoyment in reading and to participate more in classroom discussion.

In addition to these anecdotal findings, the researcher defined four categories of writing components to be used in an analytic rating scale. The categories are voice, content, organization, and language (See Appendix C), and are rated based on students' essays and journals. She developed and tested the Portfolio Assessment Form (See Appendix D) and Final Self-Evaluation of Writing and Reading sheets (See Appendix G), based on the portfolios and their reflection on the learning process. She was also able to decide the Coding System used in qualitative analyses (See Appendix H), according to interaction with students. All the rating scales, assessment forms, self-evaluation sheets, and the coding system were based on other research studies done in similar content areas.

3.3 Design of the Formal Study

3.3.1 The Class and the Setting

An adult EFL reading and writing class was the site for the study. This class was a Level 1 class of the Government Employees English Program (GEEP), sponsored by the language center of a national university in Taipei city. The courses were offered on a yearly (two-semester) basis, in 7 levels covering all skills. Reading/writing was a required subject for all the students.

During the 2000-2001 school year, the students in Level 1 had their reading/writing class with the researcher, who has taught in this language center since 1993. The class met once a week for three hours in a language lab. At the front of the room there was a teacher's desk along with computer facilities. Seats were arranged in rows of movable chairs. Each student's table was equipped with facilities for language practice, such as tape recorders and earphones. On either side, at the front, there was a color-TV set for watching videotapes or DVDs. There was also a public announcement (PA) system in the classroom.

The class was mainly person-centered and whole language-based. From the first class beginning Sept. 25, 2000, the students were informed that they would be engaged in a theme project. For the first semester, each student had to choose to read and write about a topic of their own choice and interest. The reading responses could be written in journals or in essay form. At the end of the first semester, each one had to make an oral presentation to briefly summarize what had been read. For the second semester, a non-fiction English book, *Tuesdays with Morrie*, was chosen as the main reading material, based on its content and level of interest to the students. This book also served as the stimulus for continuing theme exploration. Students read the book at home and participated in group discussions in class. The reading responses could also be included in journals and essays. Also, at the end of the second semester, each student had to make an oral presentation on this book. Each one also had to prepare his/her individual portfolio, which contained a preface and all writing samples (See Appendix B).

3.3.2 The Participants

The participants in this study were reading/writing Level 1 students in the Government Employees English Program (GEEP). During the 2000-2001 school year, 119 out of 212 applicants passed the exam required to enroll in GEEP. There were 16 students on the list of names for Level 1; however, only 11 students participated in this reading/writing class. Among these 11 students, three did not complete the class for a number of reasons. Thus, this study only includes the 8 students who completed the class and turned in all their assignments.

This student group comprised 1 male and 7 female students. Their ages ranged from 25 to 45 years. Two of them held bachelor's degrees; the other 6 had received their master's degrees in the fields of transportation management, land economics, forest industry, social welfare, social work, and business management. Except for one studying abroad for half a year, none of them had studied abroad. Their years of learning English varied, but most of them had little experience in learning English writing.

3.3.3 The Teacher-Researcher and the Teaching Philosophy

As indicated, the researcher taught this class based on the framework of whole language philosophy, Carl Rogers' whole-person education, and Paulo Freire's education of liberation. To incorporate these concepts into the classroom, the researcher attempted to create a safe environment, in which both the intellectual self and the emotional self were accepted, critical thinking and risk taking were encouraged, and reciprocal dialogues and active participation were expected.

The reading-writing connection was also emphasized in this class. The researcher encouraged students to conduct theme reading based on their interests, concerns, and background knowledge, and to write their reading responses in journals or essays. Besides sharing the written word, the students also spent a great deal of time in group discussion, class discussion, and oral report.

In addition, the researcher stressed that writing is not an isolating but a social activity, which welcomes real audiences and the exchange of ideas, and that written pieces should, in the main, be appreciated and not corrected. Therefore, with the students' agreement, their journal writing was shared with the whole class via e-mails. In the second semester, the researcher even designed an on-line discussion board for students. The opportunities for writing in a real social context promoted each student's self-perception of being a writer.

The researcher conducted the class in a dialogical way. She usually started the class with an invitation of inquiries. These inquiries were related to the students' lives, concerns or social events, and were explored in the dialogue between her and the students. The researcher also made close links between these dialogues and the follow-up reading/writing activities. Most of the time, the themes emerging from the dialogues would be the focus of the students' journals, essays, or theme reading. In these dialogues, each student was respected as a unique individual. Their thoughts and reflections were greatly valued. Also, through the dialogues, the researcher learned how to design the curriculum, how to choose reading materials, and how to respond to the students' sharing.

The reading materials selected for this class were mainly based on the concerns and interests of the students. The genres covered consisted of essays, fables, short stories, news articles, jokes, song lyrics, movie scripts, and non-fiction books. Besides their self-selected theme reading, students would sometimes suggest news articles, stories, or books for class discussion. This self-generated theme reading in addition to class discussion made reading and writing more relevant and interactive.

Publishing was another emphasis of this class. It consisted of two types: one was the collection of students' essays, and the other was the students' individual portfolios. According to whole language philosophy, publishing students' writing gives them a sense of authorship, which in turn, motivates student writers to engage in more authentic writing and empowers them to keep their voice and identity. Each semester, the students contributed the final drafts of their essays and the researcher compiled them into an anthology, which was given to each student as a "souvenir." Moreover, in the second semester, students designed their own portfolios to show their achievements in the learning process. Multiple drafts of essays, journals, oral reports, e-mails, reading materials, and self-evaluation forms were included to fully illustrate the students' achievements. The last class of the school year was designed as a celebration party where students shared their portfolios and the accomplishment and enjoyment of becoming a reader and writer.

In brief, the researcher's teaching philosophy was consistent with whole language philosophy—viewing writing as an integral part of learning. Her teaching philosophy also matched Carl Rogers' whole-person learning in treating a student as a whole being with full potential and with both an intellectual and an emotional self. In addition, the researcher's teaching philosophy was in harmony with Paulo Freire's education of liberation in believing that true dialogue between teacher and students cannot exist without profound love, humility, intense faith in humankind, hope, and critical thinking.

3.3.4 Typical Classroom Activities

The class met from 6:25 to 9:05 p.m. on Mondays. The usual sequence of activities is as follows:

1st session (6:25–7:15): Greeting and warm up
Inviting inquiries
Linking the inquiries with reading or
writing activities
2nd session (7:20–8:10): In-class reading and writing
Discussion of reading or composition
3rd session (8:15–9:05): Discussion on theme reading
Posing new inquiries

The sequence was flexible, and it changed frequently when there were suggestions generated by students or when the students engaged whole-heartedly in discussion.

As mentioned above, the researcher started the class with a greeting and inquiry period. She not only invited inquiries from students but also shared her own views on various matters. Usually, she linked these questions to the reading and writing done in class so as to bridge the gap between school learning and real life. Then, the students would engage in individual silent reading, group reading, and group discussion. Sometimes, they would also do impromptu writing and immediately share their opinions in written form. At other times, students would review different rhetorical modes of essay writing, such as cause-effect, definition, comparison-contrast, for a better understanding of writing conventions. There was also time for them to share their theme reading, which could be opinion exchange, vocabulary building or meaning construction. The following two examples further illustrate the typical activities in class.

Date: March 5, 2001

1st session: Greeting and Inviting Inquiries

* Both students and teacher shared the difficulties of being modern people
    1. Dull life
    2. Busy schedule
    3. Hard to say *no* to culture (from theme reading—*Tuesday with Morrie*)
* Linking the inquiries with a discussion topic on the CNN Website—"Can you really do whatever you want?"
    1. Inviting students to share their opinions and experiences
    2. Encouraging students to go on the web and to voice their opinions, especially on issues related to Taiwan
* Linking the concept of speaking up for Taiwan with Peggy's journal writing on "Freedom of Speech"
    1. Peggy shared her journal writing with the class

2. Brief discussion on the issues of comfort women and freedom of speech

* Closing the inquiries session by introducing the discussion board designed by the researcher: http://home.kimo.com.tw/ll5245 and encouraging students to share their ideas on this on-line discussion board

* Linking the discussion with the study of *Cause-Effect*
    1. Review what the students knew about the rhetorical mode of cause-effect essay writing
    2. Study of "focus on effect" and "chain reaction" types of writing

2nd Session: In-class reading or writing, discussion of reading or composition

* Linking the discussion with the study of *Cause-Effect* (Continued)
    1. Practicing cause-effect writing using student-generated ideas
    2. Students' sharing their writing practice

* Discussion of theme reading—*Tuesdays with Morrie*
    1. Group sharing and discussion on pp. 26-47
    2. Using Role Sheets to facilitate students' participation

3rd Session: Discussion of theme reading and posing new inquiries

* Discussion of *Tuesdays with Morrie* in groups (continued)
* Linking the discussion with other reading
    1. exploring the theme—busy modern life
    2. sharing and distributing the article "Logging off in Nantucket" from the Times magazine
    3. making connections between Mitch's life (described in *Tuesdays with Morrie*), the life described in "Logging off in Nantucket" and the lives of the students.

* Encouraging students to write journals and to get on the discussion board to share their opinions

March 12, 2001

1st session: Greeting and Inviting Inquiries

* Students freely sharing their outside reading
    1. Joyce voluntarily sharing her reading of *The Education of Little Tree* and *The Little Prince*, by showing the great impression she had on human relationships and the relationship between humans and nature
    2. Ken talking about his preparation for the entrance exam for graduate school and also his reading of *Harry Potter*
* Teacher sharing her love of *The Little Prince* and exchanging ideas with Joyce and others
* Other students and teacher responding to Ken's anxiety and the busyness of entrance exam preparation, showing their understanding of this "stressful" time
* Linking the sharing and discussion with the articles posted on our discussion board
    1. forgetting and being forgotten
    2. Can we really say No to our culture?
    3. being the big cheese or a small potato
* Peggy and Judy sharing their postings on the discussion board
* Linking the inquiries with reading or writing activities
    1. Reading and discussing the article "Logging off in Nantucket"
    2. Brainstorming the meaning
    3. Joyce, Peggy, Judy, and Henry sharing their guesses and also the level of difficulty in reading this article
    4. Students helping to clarify the meaning of this article
        i.   Joyce helping a lot on vocabulary (ex. chalked)
        ii. Lin helping a lot on culture (ex. 1-800)
        iii. Ken helping a lot on internet/computer information

2ⁿᵈ Session: In-class reading or writing, discussion of reading or composition

*   Continually exploring the theme of "freedom of speech"
    1. Peggy providing an article "Cartoon of Wartime 'comfort women' irks Taiwan" from the New York Times (March 2, 2001)
    2. Silent reading or pair discussions
    3. Explaining key phrases, paragraphs, and ideas
    4. Discussing the issues and different attitudes towards Japan from the Korean, Taiwanese, and Chinese peoples' points of view.
        i.   Joyce showing anger about the weaknesses of the Taiwanese
        ii.   Peggy fighting for the freedom of speech
        iii. Jerry emphasizing the fact of national/cultural differences, e.g. Korea—a country full of hatred
        iv.   Henry questioning Jerry's opinions by asking about the stance and features of our own country
*   Reading and discussing another article on a similar topic
    1. Briefly reading and discussing the article "Free speech, even if it's distasteful" from the Taipei Times (March 3, 2001, editorial)
    2. Quickly sharing important passages and messages in this article
    3. Students noticing the different spelling systems: Tung Yun and Han Yu, and asking for further investigation on these two systems.
    4. Discussing the statement made by the writer in the last two paragraphs
        i.   In regard to backtracking on democratic rights caused by barring Kobayashi

3ʳᵈ Session: Discussion on theme reading and posing new inquiries

*   Discussion of theme reading—*Tuesdays with Morrie*
    1. Sharing and discussing the book in groups (pp. 48-68)
    2. Not using Role Sheets (students forgot)

* Linking the discussion with other reading
    1. Sharing and distributing a short story "Thank you, Ma'am" for home reading and encouraging students to make connections between Mitch/Morrie (from *Tuesdays with Morrie*) and Roger/Ms. Jones (from "Thank you, Ma'am")

As indicated, this class was not preceded by a pre-determined syllabus (though there was indeed a tentative syllabus for the office); it was neither linear nor sequential. All the reading, writing, and discussion emerged from students' concerns and social events. The reading materials were provided by either the teacher-researcher or the students. The teacher was not the only person that provided information; instead, both teacher and students were information givers and receivers. The learning content could even be changed according to the students' prompting. As in the second example (March 12, 2001), students noticed the different Pin-Yin systems—Tung-Yun and Han-Yu—used in different magazines and newspapers, like the New York Times and the Taipei Times. They suggested that they should spend some time on this issue in order to have a better understanding of both systems. Therefore, we had a thorough discussion on these systems the following week, from historical background to the current debate, and compared and contrasted the phonetic alphabets in the two systems. This discussion, completely initiated by students and supported by the teacher, successfully led them to the study of comparison and contrast, another rhetorical mode of essay writing. In addition, this discussion made them recognize the fact that literacy is indeed involved with cultural and political issues.

To conclude, there were no so-called typical classroom activities. What this class had was a never-ending dialogue between the teacher and the students. All the learning took place and developed from this intensive interaction.

3.3.5 Informed Consent

Students read and signed the statement of Informed Consent (See Appendix I & J). In order to eliminate the fear of frankly presenting their opinions in writing, students were asked to voluntarily sign the consent form after they had finished taking the course. None of the data were published in any research study before the consent form had been signed. In addition, according to the ethics of research, the names of all participants were deleted from all the material and replaced with a pseudonym. In other words, the students' identities remained confidential. Since all eight students, who completed the course, signed the consent form, there is no violation of the ethics of research.

3.4 Materials and Instruments

The materials used in the research study included prompt writing, reading selections, portfolios, analytic rating scales, portfolio assessment forms, questionnaires, self-evaluation forms, field notes, and reflective journals.

Prompt writing. Each student produced two pieces of prompt writing based on the same topic. The first one was written at the first class on Sep. 25, 2000, and the second one was written at the last class on June 8, 2001. The topic was about the new policy of teaching English in elementary schools. The comparison between these two served as an indicator of the improvement in their writing.

Reading selections. Reading selections were divided into three kinds. One was the students' theme reading, conducted by the students themselves at their leisure. The themes varied and could be travel tips, ecology, music or anything else. Another was in-class reading, mostly provided by the instructor but sometimes by the students. The themes and genres also varied. They could be essays, news articles, short stories, jokes or song lyrics. The last was a best seller, *Tuesdays with Morrie*, read by the students at home and studied in group discussion in class.

Portfolios. Students designed their own individual portfolios with limited help from the instructor. Besides the preface written by each student to evaluate their own learning, portfolios also contained the multiple drafts of their essays, journal writing, their messages posted on the discussion board, the manuscripts of their oral reports and their e-mail correspondence with the instructor during the school year. Some students also included the syllabi, reading materials and all the handouts distributed in class. The individual portfolios served as an example of the various aspects of learning.

Analytic rating scale. The analytic rating scale, based on the ESL Composition Profile (Jacobs, Zingraf, Wormuth, Hartfiel, & Hughey, 1981), originally contained five weighted categories, in which content is the first and most heavily weighted. The others are organization, vocabulary, language use, and mechanics. Each category has four levels, which are very poor, poor to fair, average to good and very good to excellent. This study revised the ESL Composition Profile into four categories (voice[4], content, organization, and language) with equal weight given to each one. Each category was equally divided into five levels—very good, good, average, weak, and very poor. The total score was 100 (See Appendix C). It was hoped that the equal weight given to each category would result in a holistic analysis.

Portfolio assessment form. The portfolio assessment form used in this study is a revised version of the Portfolio Review Form (Rolheiser, Bower, & Stevahn, 2000). It contains four categories: quality of work, creativity and originality, evidence of effort, and evidence of growth. Each category has 10 points, ranging from 10 & 9 (superior)

---

[4] According to Peter Elbow (1998b), "Writing *without voice* is wooden or dead because it lacks sound, rhythm, energy, and individuality. ... Writing *with voice* is writing into which someone has breathed. It has that fluency, rhythm, and liveliness that exist naturally in the speech of most people when they are enjoying a conversation. ... Writing *with real voice* has the power to make you pay attention and understand—the words go deep. ...it is a matter of hearing resonance ..." (p. 299). Voice seems important to writing. Thus, in this study, "voice" is included as a rating category and refers to authenticity, uniqueness, individuality, and resonance.

to 4, 3, 2, & 1 (limited). The total score is 40. There is space for raters to provide written comments (See Appendix D).

Writing self-efficacy questionnaire. The writing self-efficacy scale, developed by Shell, Murphy, & Bruning (1989), originally consisted of 28 items, with a score ranging from 0-100, that asks students to rate their confidence while communicating in writing (writing tasks) and performing certain writing skills (writing skills). Shell's study, assessed with Cronbach's alpha (α), reported reliability scores of .92 for the tasks scale and .95 for the skills scale. This study revises Shell's writing self-efficacy scale into a 7-point Likert scale, ranging from 7 (extremely sure) to 1 (extremely unsure), in order to better locate students' preferences. Furthermore, in this study, items 3, 15 and 20 are omitted as they contain a cultural bias. Thus, the total number of items is 25. Reliability, assessed with Cronbach's alpha, is .98, indicating a high internal consistency for the scale. The students were asked to fill out the questionnaire twice: in the first class and then in the last class. The comparison between these two serves as an indicator of their attitudinal changes (See Appendix E).

Writing apprehension questionnaire. The writing apprehension scale measures a person's tendency to approach or avoid writing. Daly & Miller (1975) developed a 26-item instrument, originally in the form of 5-point Likert scale. Cronbach's alpha coefficient was .83 for elementary students (Pajares & Valiante, 1997) and .93 for high school students (Pajares & Johnson, 1996). This study revises Daly & Miller's writing apprehension scale into an 8-point Likert scale according to social cognitive guidelines (Bandura, 1986, cited in Pajares & Valiante, 1994). Reliability, assessed with Cronbach's alpha, is .88. The students were asked to fill out the questionnaire twice: in the first class and in the last class. The comparison between these two serves as an indicator of their changes on attitude (See Appendix F).

Final self-evaluation form. The self-evaluation form contains two parts. The first part includes ten open-ended questions related to English writing, and the second part includes another ten open-ended questions related to English reading. The questions vary from the quantity of their reading and writing to their perception of being a reader

65

and writer of English. The self-evaluation form shows the students' self-perception of learning (See Appendix G).

Field notes. Classroom observations, participation records, and e-mail correspondence were kept and coded in Microsoft Word, referenced by session number. The notes served as the evidence for the building of trustworthiness[5].

Reflective journal. The instructor's reflective journal was kept and coded in a notebook. Entries were made in this notebook after each observation. These entries were not typed, but each page was numbered for reference in the audit trail. The records in this journal also served as the evidence for the building of trustworthiness and conformability.

3.5 Procedures

3.5.1 Procedures of Theme Cycles Implementation

Pre-Implementation

Before deciding on a theme for exploration, students in the first class were encouraged to jot down their personal interests, concerns, and inquiries, which could relate to their professional training, life experiences, or simply to their curiosity. With analysis and synthesis, the teacher-researcher suggested a tentative core theme—life. Then, with the trials of sharing certain reading materials and with the observations of students' reactions, the core theme—life—was confirmed. According to research, the theme for adult learners should be as broad as possible so that they can freely integrate their life experiences in a theme study.

---

[5] According to Lincoln and Guba (1985), the qualitative definition of trustworthiness is related to "credibility," "transferability," "dependability," and "confirmability." They are the naturalist's equivalents for the conventional terms "internal validity," "external validity," "reliability," and "objectivity" (pp. 300-328).

The core theme was a broader theme for the whole class to make a connection to. Under the umbrella of the core theme, students were encouraged to individually develop their own project theme. Based on their own interests and concerns and on the inspiration gained from the core theme reading, the project themes gradually emerged. The process of such decision making was not linear, but recursive and spiral. Usually, students would begin with a theme related to their professional background, which they later changed as they looked for more challenging topics. Some students would return to the theme they abandoned earlier because of its close relationship to their lives. Thus, the theme selection was not done as "one command with one action." The selection went back and forth in the first few weeks, sometimes even during the whole school year.

Thus, in the stage of pre-implementation, no one knew what themes would be discussed and explored. Students had the freedom to choose whatever they wanted to explore, and the teacher played the role of facilitator only. In the second semester, the core theme continued, and the individual project themes were more closely related to humanism. This direction was not planned, but formed automatically with the concerns of the students. During the first semester, students shared their concerns about their busy lives, culture, health, and social issues in their journals. Also, in the final oral presentation of their theme project, a student mentioned a best seller, *Tuesdays with Morrie*. Because of his brief introduction, the whole class agreed to use this book as the main reading for the second semester. In so doing, the core theme—life—was re-emphasized and further explored. By then, the two phases of pre-implementation were complete.

Implementation

Let's take lessons the class studied in *Tuesdays with Morrie* as examples.

The story of *Tuesdays with Morrie* is told by a young man, Mitch, about the life and death of an old professor, Morrie. Though they were teacher and student, they shared a bond similar to that of father and son. In order to explore the theme of father and son or of an old man and a young man, a folk song sung by Dan Folgbert was chosen as an introduction. The song titled "Leader of the Band," describes how a son appreciated and was influenced by his father. The guitar-played melody and the poetic lyrics brought a powerful feeling of nostalgia to these adult learners. The class listened to the song several times and then formed into groups to read and discuss the lyrics. They first shared the meaning of the lyrics and the impression they had of the song, and then reflected on their own experiences with their parents or mentors. The theme was thus explored in meaningful ways.

The theme *"Love"* provides another example of implementing theme cycles in class. In the beginning, the class watched an episode of the movie *Fiddler on the Roof.* In the chosen episode, the second daughter and her boyfriend tell the father they are getting married. Undaunted by the father's rejection, the young couple say to the father, "We are not asking for permission, but your blessing." This strong statement surprised the father and caused tension in the relationship. An episode from another movie, *Father of the Bride,* with a similar conflict raised in a culture that values tradition, was played in class. In this film, the daughter tells her parents at dinner time that she is going to marry a guy she met in Rome. The father is surprised and disapproves of his daughter's decision. He questions the boy's profession and uncertain future, and tries to dissuade her from her decision. However, the daughter says to her father, "George, I love him." By addressing her own father by his first name, the daughter tries to put herself on an equal footing with her father, and by professing her love for the boy, the daughter infers that "love will conquer all." These two episodes, though describing different people in different cultures and time periods, reveal universal issues—love and the generation gap. The younger generation fought to make their own decisions, while the older generation questioned their traditions and value systems.

With the theme of love and the generation gap established, the class went on to watch the remainder of *Fiddler on the Roof.* This time the father asked the mother whether she loved him. This old couple, surprised by their daughter's frank expression of love, began to look introspectively at their 25-year marriage. The father kept asking the mother "Do you love me?" but the mother, like all the women in her culture, avoided saying the word "love." She answered her husband by saying, "For 25 years, I've washed your clothes, cooked your meals, cleaned your house, given you children, milked the cow, ..." Comparing this shyness shown on the traditional woman's face with the direct statement made by the young daughter, the meaning of love implied by the different generations became interesting. Next, the class listened to the song "Do you love me?" while reading the lyrics. Afterwards, the class read a poem taken from a famous book, *The Prophet,* by Kahlil Gibran. The poem, "Your Children are not Your Children," emphasizes that parents are like a bow and the children are like the arrows. The bow should follow the intention of the archer, Heaven, and shoot the arrow at the proper time in the proper direction. With the concepts gathered from the movies, the song, and the poem, students were encouraged to orally share their experiences and opinions in class and then in written form in their journals, essays and e-mails.

Post-implementation

The post-implementation stage contained three parts: presentation, publishing, and gaining new ideas.

Presentation referred to on-going journal sharing and the final oral report, like Author's Chair discussed in Graves and Hansen (1983). The final oral report was each student's summary and reflection on their theme reading projects. Students briefly introduced their theme project by explaining the reason for their choice, how they found the related reading materials, and a brief description of the contents. Rather than simply presenting a monologue, there was a Question & Answer session right after each student's oral report to encourage interaction. The on-going journal was shared via e-mail or on the message board. Before the on-line message board was set up by the teacher-researcher, the journals sent to the teacher's e-mail box were forwarded to the whole class with the permission of the writers. After the on-line message board was set up, some of the journals were directly posted on the board by the students themselves. By so doing, students created reader awareness by writing to communicate instead of merely completing an assignment.

Publishing referred to the anthology that was compiled and to individual portfolios. The compiled anthology was a collection of all the students' essays. When they knew that the essays would be included in the collection, students paid more attention to revisions. Most of the time, they submitted the fourth draft for publishing. The individual portfolios were a collection of each student's work—journals, essays with multiple drafts, and e-mail correspondence, messages on the board, manuscripts of oral reports, reading materials and so on. In the preface, students shared their reflections on the learning process. The individual portfolios represented the learning process and achievements of each student.

Gaining new ideas refers to the alpha and omega of the cyclic learning process. Through the on-going exchange of ideas, students gradually formed new interests and inquiries. This renewed curiosity usually led them to further investigate specific themes or to start a new journey of theme exploration. Thus, the cycle of theme learning would go on and on.

The purpose of doing all these post-implementation activities was to show that though reading/writing may be a solitary act, it can also be social, interactive, and lively.

3.5.2 Procedures of Data Collection

Timetable of Data Collection

(Fall 2000 - Spring 2001)

Timetable	Methodology
1st Class (Sept. 25)	- Pre-prompt writing on new policy of teaching English in elementary schools - Background information and interest
2nd Class (Oct. 2)	- Pre-class questionnaires on writing self-efficacy and writing apprehension
3rd Class (Oct. 9)	
4th Class (Oct. 16)	- Collection of essay 1-1 and journal (1)
5th Class (Oct. 23)	- Collection of essay 1-2
6th Class (Oct. 30)	

Timetable	Methodology
7th Class (Nov. 6)	- Collection of essay 1-3
8th Class (Nov. 13)	- Collection of journal (2)
9th Class (Nov. 20)	- Collection of essay 2-1
10th Class (Nov. 27)	- Collection of essay 2-2
11th Class (Dec. 4)	
12th Class (Dec. 11)	- Collection of essay 2-3 and journal (3)
13th and 14th Class (Dec. 18 and Jan. 8)	- Collection of project report - Observation of project report - Compiled the 1st anthology of students' essays
15th Class (Feb. 19)	
16th Class (Feb. 26)	
17th Class (March 5)	- Collection of journal (4)
18th Class (March 12)	
19th Class (March 19)	- Collection of essay 3-1
20th Class (March 26)	- Collection of essay 3-2
21st Class (April 2)	- Collection of journal (5)
22nd Class (April 9)	- Collection of essay 3-3
23rd Class (April 16)	
24th Class (April 23)	- Collection of essay 4-1
25th Class (April 30)	- Collection of essay 4-2 and journal (6)
26th Class (May 7)	
27th Class (May 14)	- Collection of essay 4-3
28th to 29th Class (May 21 to May 28)	- Collection of project report - Observation of project report - Collection of individual portfolios
30th Class (June 4)	- Compiled the 2nd anthology of students' essays - Post-prompt writing on new policy of teaching English in elementary schools - Post-class questionnaires on writing self-efficacy and writing apprehension - Collection of Final self-evaluation of reading and writing - Collection of reading and writing records

Data Collection

The data were collected at the language center, from a reading/writing class of the Government Employees English Program (GEEP) in Taipei, Taiwan, over the school year, 2000-2001. This particular class was selected because the researcher has been an instructor at this language center since 1993 and the structure of the thirty-week course allowed the researcher to compile data and observations over an extended period of time. The reading/writing course met for three hours a week for the duration of a typical 30-week school year—14 classes during the first semester and 16 during the second.

Since the pilot study suggested that changes would occur in the students' work and in their perception and enjoyment of reading over time, various types of data were collected. The types of data collected are listed below:

1. Pre-prompt and post-prompt writing on the new policy of teaching English in elementary schools
2. The first and final draft of each essay
3. Pre-class and post-class questionnaires on writing self-efficacy
4. Pre-class and post-class questionnaires on writing apprehension
5. Final self-evaluation forms, including the records of reading and writing
6. Individual portfolios, including preface, essay drafts, journal entries, manuscripts of oral reports (also messages posted on discussion board, e-mail correspondence, reading selections, final self-evaluation form, and handouts)
7. Teacher's field notes and reflective journals, including on-going observations and informal interviews

In examining the participants' writing performance, their pre- and post-prompt writing and the first and final draft of each essay were collected for rating analytically. Eight pre-prompt writings and eight post-prompt writings were collected, along with 64 essay drafts (2 drafts

* 4 essays * 8 students).   Besides the researcher, another experienced university writing teacher, who had taught English writing for more than 10 years, rated the 16 prompt writings and 64 essay drafts.   Scores from the two raters were averaged to create the final writing scores used in this study.   The correlation between the total scores of the two raters for all subjects was .62 (p $<$ .01, 2-tailed).

In order to examine the participants' attitudes toward English writing, participants were asked to fill out the 25-item *writing self-efficacy* and the 26-item *writing apprehension* questionnaires at the beginning and end of the school year.

In order to examine whether or not participants had become self-directed learners, the participants' portfolios and final self-evaluations were collected.   Preface, essay drafts, journal entries, and manuscripts of oral reports were required, while messages on the discussion board, e-mail correspondence, reading selections, final self-evaluation forms, and handouts were optional.

For the purpose of performing triangulation analysis, teacher's field notes and reflective journals were also kept and coded throughout the whole school year in order to examine the participants' learning from diverse sources.

3.6 Data Analysis

Both quantitative and qualitative analyses were used in this study. The purpose of the quantitative analysis was to investigate the writing performance and attitudes of the participants as a whole, while the purpose of the qualitative analysis was to detail the individual changes made during the research study.

To analyze the essays, a comparison of the means was applied for prompt writing drafts.   The results would serve as an indicator to show the differences in the initial formative stage of an essay, the differences in editing the final stages, and the differences in overall writing performance.

The paired-sample t-test[6] was used to analyze the data of participants' writing attitudes obtained from pre-class and post-class questionnaires on writing self-efficacy and writing apprehension.

Besides quantitative analysis, the triangulation approach was used in this study to investigate the transcribed and coded qualitative data (See Appendix H). It was hoped that the combination of quantitative and qualitative analysis would provide a thorough explanation of the study results.

---

[6] According to James Dean Brown's award-winning book (1988) *Understanding research in second language learning: A teacher's guide to statistics and research design*, "The *t* test applies regardless of the size of the two samples and is, therefore, much more commonly used in language studies" (p. 165). Thus, the t-test was used in this study to analyze the data obtained from questionnaires.

CHAPTER

DATA PRESENTATION

This chapter presents the data. First, basic information of the class and each student's personal profile are introduced. Second, students' prompt-writing and essay scores are presented. Third, students' responses to questionnaires on writing self-efficacy and writing apprehension are displayed. The chapter concludes with an evaluation of the students' portfolios, followed by a general profile of the class.

4.1 Basic Information of the Class

As shown in Table 4.1, 2 students were under 30 years of age, 4 students were in their 30s, and the other 2 were over 40 years of age. Two out of the 8 had their bachelors' degrees, while the other 6 had earned their masters' degrees in various disciplines.

Six of the students had had general English instruction for about 10 years, while 2 had studied English for more than 10 years. As for English writing, when they came to this class, 4 students had learned English writing for several years and the other 4 students had had no expo-

Table 4.1: Personal Information of the Class

Basic Information	Age			Education (Degree)		English (yrs.)		English Writing (yrs.)			Studying Abroad (yrs.)	
	<30	30-39	>40	Bachelor	Master	≤ 10	>10	None	1-5	>5	No	Yes
Number	2	4	2	2	6	6	2	4	3	1	7	1

Note: N = 8

sure to English writing. With the exception of one student who had studied abroad for half a year, none of them had studied abroad.

4.2 The Case Studies

A description of students' personal profiles includes such basic information as their major, profession, years of learning English and English writing, and reasons for attending this course. All the information was obtained from written interviews, informal interviews, and observation. Furthermore, the theme cycles that the students were engaged in will be touched on briefly. The information was gathered from their essays, journals, theme reading, and oral reports. The case studies are presented in alphabetical order.

Students' writing performance was classified into 4 categories (Voice, Content, Organization, and Language) with 5 levels in each category (Very Poor, Weak, Average, Good, and Very Good) according to the analytic rating scale (See Appendix C). The categories were scored as follows: Very Poor (VP) from 1 to 5, Weak (W) from 6 to 10, Average (A) from 11-15, Good (G) from 16-20, and Very Good (VG) from 21 to 25. The total scores for each writing piece would thus range from 4 to 20 (VP), from 24 to 40 (W), from 44 to 60 (A), from 64 to 80 (G), or from 84 to 100 (VG).

Writing attitudes in this study are broken down into two parts: writing self-efficacy and writing apprehension. The data include the distribution of the frequency checks on each item of the questionnaires, the pre- and post-Mean gained from the questionnaires, and the bar charts giving a visual representation of their progress.

In this section, evaluation of the students' portfolios is presented. Four categories (Quality of Work, Creativity/Originality, Evidence of Effort, and Evidence of Growth) and four criteria (Superior, Good, Average, and Limited) are used in the evaluation. Quality of Work refers to the students' knowledge of content and their skill in communicating

Table 4.2: Anne's Basic Information

Info. Name	Age	Education	Profession	Years of Learning English	Years of Learning English Writing	Years of Studying Abroad
Anne	32	Master's degree in Transportation Management	Civil Aeronautics Administration	10 years	None	None

ideas. Creativity and Originality refer to the students' voices in writing and the depth of reflection shown in that writing. Evidence of Effort refers to students' perseverance in learning and the amount of reading and writing they completed. Evidence of Growth refers to the depth of reflection on their lives and their concern for learning. It also measures their progress as a reader and writer and their perception of such.

Regarding the criteria, scores of 9 and 10 are rated as Superior, 7 and 8 are Good, 5 and 6 are Average, and scores 1, 2, 3 and 4 are judged as Limited. The total scores for each portfolio range from 40 to 36 (Superior), from 32 to 28 (Good), from 24 to 20 (Average), and from 16 to 4 (Limited). Besides showing their scores, a summary of written comments made by the two raters will also be presented.

4.2.1 Anne

4.2.1.1 Anne's Personal Profile[1]

Anne, a woman in her early 30s, graduated from a national university with a master's degree in transportation management. She was working in CAA (Civil Aeronautics Administration) as a secretary of the Director General at the time she attended the class (Em-A-1). She had not studied abroad and had no experience of learning the writing of English even though she had studied English for 10 years while attending school (Em-A-2). Her reason for attending the class was, as she put it,

---

[1] All students' names in this study are pseudonyms.

> Sometimes, I got a phone call from a foreigner. When I received the call, I answered 'please wait for a moment' immediately, [and] then I transfer[r]ed the phone to my colloques [colleagues]. That's why I am here,[.] I want to speak English well, listen English well (Em-A-1).

With the hope of improving ability in English, Anne started studying English with the researcher and other classmates in the 2000-2001 school year.

4.2.1.2 Anne's Writing Performance: Essay Scores

Anne wrote 4 essays in multiple drafts. Essay 1 was "The Effect of Bad Weather Condition on Air Traffic," the original title of which was "Taking Airplane in Bad Weather Days" when she wrote the first draft. While revising, Anne changed part of the content and also the title. Essay 2 was "What Means Success in My Opinion?" The first essay was based on her theme reading which she carried out during the first semester. She read the articles "Pleasing the Passenger (for Airports)," "An Urgent Need for New Noise Standards," "'Codeshare' Benefits Far Outweigh Downside," "Electronic Ticketing" and "Concorde - Will it

Table 4.3: Anne's Essay Scores

Categories / Essays	Voice	Content	Organization	Language	Total
Essay 1-1	15.5 (A-G)	18.5 (G)	17.5 (G)	14.0 (A)	65.5 (G)
Essay 1-3	18.5 (G)	21.0 (VG)	21.0 (VG)	21.5 (VG)	82.0 (G-VG)
Essay 2-1	19.5 (G)	17.5 (G)	16.0 (G)	16.5 (G)	69.5 (G)
Essay 2-3	22.0 (VG)	22.0 (VG)	21.5 (VG)	19.5 (G)	85.0 (VG)
Essay 3-1	21.5 (VG)	21.0 (VG)	20.5 (G-VG)	18.5 (G)	81.5 (G-VG)
Essay 3-3	23.0 (VG)	22.5 (VG)	22.0 (VG)	21.0 (VG)	88.5 (VG)
Essay 4-1	20.5 (G-VG)	19.5 (G)	19.0 (G)	15.0 (A)	74.0 (G)
Essay 4-3	22.0 (VG)	21.0 (VG)	21.5 (VG)	21.0 (VG)	85.5 (VG)
Pre-prompt	18.5 (G)	9.0 (W)	10.0 (W)	13.5 (A)	51.0 (A)
Post-prompt	19.0 (G)	16.5 (G)	18.5 (G)	16.5 (G)	70.5 (G)

Ever Fly Again?" The second essay she wrote was a discussion on her life in the rhetorical mode of definition writing. Essay 3 was "What happened to the Young People?" the ideas being generated by her concern for and observation of society and also from her reading of *Tuesdays with Morrie*. Essay 4 was "The difference of life before and after the marriage," the ideas coming from her own observations and experiences as well as her reading of *Tuesdays with Morrie*.

As Table 4.3 shows, Anne's voice improved during the learning process. Her essay 1-1 was rated at the A-G Level and essay 1-3 at the Good Level; essay 2-1 was rated Good and essay 2-3, Very Good. Her voice in essay 4-1 was G-VG and essay 4-3 was Very Good. Although the essays 3-1 and 3-3 were rated at the same level—Very Good, essay 3-3 had the higher score. Voice in her pre-prompt and post-prompt writing tested at the same level—Good—but the post-prompt writing had the higher score.

Regarding content in Anne's writing, Table 4.3 shows that Anne moved from a Good level to a Very Good level for her essays 1, 2 and 4. Both essays 3-1 and 3-3 stayed at the same level—Very Good—with scores increasing in 3-3. The content in her pre-prompt and post-prompt writing showed reasonable progress, from Average to Good.

For the organization of Anne's writing, Table 4.3 reveals the same pattern of progression, which was from Good to Very Good, with the exception of essay 3 and prompt writing. The organization in Essay 3 was improved from G-VG to VG, and the organization in Anne's prompt writing went from Weak to Good.

As for language use in Anne's writing, her language performance in essay 1-1 was at an Average level, but essay 1-3 was in the Very Good range, as was her essay 4. She scored the same for essay 2—Good, and she moved from Good to a level of Very Good for her essay 3. The prompt writing, as Table 4.3 shows, went from an Average level to Good.

All in all, Anne's essay performance went from Good to a Very Good level, and her general writing performance indicated by her prompt writing went from Average to Good.

4.2.1.3 Anne's Writing Attitudes: Results of Questionnaires

As Table 4.6 shows, before taking this course, Anne had absolutely no confidence in her English writing. The mean of the 25-item writing self-efficacy questionnaire was 1.9 on the 7-point Liker scale. However, after taking this course, the mean of the same questionnaire was 4.7, which showed Anne's progress in writing self-efficacy. As for writing apprehension, the mean of the 26-item writing apprehension questionnaire was 6, which intimates that Anne was very anxious about her writing in English before taking the course. However, after taking the course, the mean was reduced from 6 to 4.1, on the 8-point Liker scale.

Table 4.4: Frequency Check of Anne's Writing Self-Efficacy

Frequency	Scale	7	6	5	4	3	2	1
Tally Marks	Pre				//	###	### /	### ### //
	Post		### ///	### ////	///	///	//	
Frequency	Pre	0	0	0	2	5	6	12
	Post	0	8	9	3	3	2	0

Note: Total Number of Items (N) = 25

Table 4.5: Frequency Check of Anne's Writing Apprehension

Frequency	Scale	8	7	6	5	4	3	2	1
Tally Marks	Pre		### ### //	### //	////	/	/	/	
	Post		/	///	### ///	###	###	///	/
Frequency	Pre	0	12	7	4	1	1	1	0
	Post	0	1	3	8	5	5	3	1

Note: Total Number of Items (N) = 26
Note: Item 2, 3, 6, 9, 10, 11, 12, 14, 15, 17, 19, 20 and 23 are coded in a reverse way.

Table 4.6: Means of Anne's Responses to Questionnaires

Questionnaires	Means	Pre-Q (Mean)	Post-Q (Mean)
Writing Self-Efficacy		1.9	4.7
Writing Apprehension		6	4.1

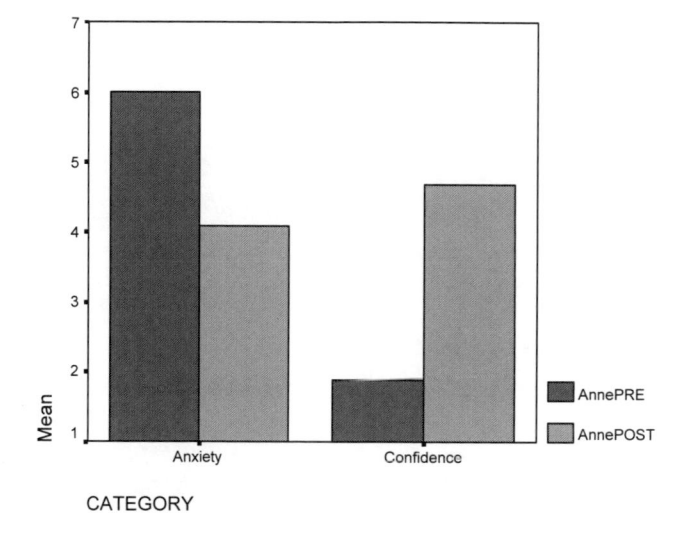

Figure 4.1: Results of Anne's Questionnaires

4.2.1.4 Anne's Personal Growth/Empowerment: Portfolio Evaluation

The evaluation of Anne's portfolio shows her overall achievements for the year 2000-2001. As Table 4.7 shows, the quality of her work was scored at 8, which falls into the Good category. Both Creativity/Originality in her work and Evidence of Effort shown in her learning process were scored 7.5, also in the Good scale. The highest score in her portfolio was 8.5 given for Evidence of Growth, which is between the scale of Good and Superior. Her total score was 31.5, in the Good category.

Table 4.7: Mean Scores of Anne's Portfolio

Category	Quality of Work	Creativity and Originality	Evidence of Efforts	Evidence of Growth	Total
Mean Scores	8 (G)	7.5 (G)	7.5 (G)	8.5 (G-S)	31.5 (G)

Summary of Written Comments on Anne's Portfolio

The written comments for Anne's portfolio were presented as follows:

1. Quality of Work

From her essays, revisions and summaries, we can see that she is quite proficient in conveying her ideas.

She showed her knowledge of flight and air transportation. Her ideas were developed through revision of her essays. Her journals conveyed ideas clearly.

2. Creativity and Originality

From the essays such as "What means success in my opinion?" we know that she is a mature person, capable of independent thinking.

Both the pieces on "success" and "young people" revealed her personal voice. She reflected on social issues and the safety of flight.

3. Evidence of Effort

Her improvement in the later drafts of her essays is the best evidence of her effort.

She tried hard and completed the study. She completed her theme reading. Her journal entries were done properly.

4. Evidence of Growth

As mentioned in her preface, the class enabled her to collect and reflect on meaningful experiences in her life. She considered reading as not only a language training activity but also as something from which she could learn about life—"life study," as she put it.

She started looking at life from different perspectives. She formed new concepts of the reading and writing of English. She was strongly motivated to continue reading and writing English.

5. Other comments

Her gracious attitude toward people around her was impressive. She thanked a lot of people in her preface.

4.2.2 Jenny

4.2.2.1 Jenny's Personal Profile

Jenny, a female, 34, graduated from a national university with a master's degree in transportation and was working in the Transportation Management Division of CAA (Civil Aeronautics Administration) (Em-Je-1). She had never studied abroad and had no experience of learning English writing. She was not sure how many years she had studied English, but knew that she had not practiced her English for a long time, probably not since she graduated from school (Em-Je-2). The reason she wanted to attend this class was mentioned in her written interview,

> Sometimes I would receive e[E]nglish complain letters, and I have to understand the content, then I find that my english is so poor. So, I decsided [decided] to come here, and I hope I can improve my english ability (Em-Je-1).

Jenny has a little daughter, who was staying in Hua-Lien with her parents, and she had to fly to Hua-Lien every weekend (O-4). That made it impossible for her to do any homework during the weekends. However, she still tried her best to attend classes and finished her assignments on time.

Table 4.8: Jenny's Basic Information

Info. Name	Age	Education	Profession	Years of Learning English	Years of Learning English Writing	Years of Studying Abroad
Jenny	34	Master's Degree in Transportation	Works in Civil Aeronautics Administration	Not sure	None	None

4.2.2.2 Jenny's Writing Performance: Essay Scores

Jenny's four essays were "The Urban Mass Transportation--Light Rail Transit," "What's a Good Composition?" "Try and Try Again," and "My Feeling Toward Rote Learning and Active Learning."

The first one was based on her theme reading about her profession and work. The second one was from her experiences of writing English composition. By writing this essay, she tried to clarify the definition of good composition. The last two essays were mainly based on her reading of *Tuesdays with Morrie* and her reflections on her life. The third one was about advice her former professor had given her and her gratitude towards him. The fourth one was about different types of learning. By taking her own learning as an example, she compared and contrasted rote and active learning styles.

According to Table 4.9, Jenny's voice was rated as Average in essay 1; however, she made progress in the following essays. Except for essay 2-1, which was at the G-VG level, the other essays all fell into the category of Very Good. In her prompt writing, she progressed from Average to Good.

The content of Jenny's essays improved with her continuing practice. In essay 1, her content was scored Good. However, in essays 2

Table 4.9: Jenny's Essay Scores

Categories Essays	Voice	Content	Organization	Language	Total
Essay 1-1	15.0 (A)	19.0 (G)	17.0 (G)	14.5 (A)	65.5 (G)
Essay 1-3	14.0 (A)	18.5 (G)	16.5 (G)	15.0 (A)	64.0 (G)
Essay 2-1	20.5 (G-VG)	21.5 (VG)	22.0 (VG)	20.5 (G-VG)	84.5 (VG)
Essay 2-3	21.0 (VG)	21.0 (VG)	22.5 (VG)	20.5 (G-VG)	85.0 (VG)
Essay 3-1	22.5 (VG)	21.0 (VG)	20.0 (G)	18.5 (G)	82.0 (G-VG)
Essay 3-3	21.5 (VG)	21.5 (VG)	21.0 (VG)	21.0 (VG)	85.0 (VG)
Essay 4-1	21.5 (VG)	20.5 (G-VG)	21.5 (VG)	20.5 (G-VG)	84.0 (VG)
Essay 4-3	22.5 (VG)	21.5 (VG)	22.0 (VG)	22.0 (VG)	88.0 (VG)
Pre-prompt	12.0 (A)	6.5 (W)	6.0 (W)	5.5 (VP-W)	30.0 (W)
Post-prompt	20.0 (G)	19.0 (G)	20.0 (G)	18.0 (G)	77.0 (G)

and 3, the content of both draft 1 and draft 3 were rated Very Good. Even though the content of essay 4-1 fell back to G-VG, she made progress in essay 4-3 after revision. In her prompt writing she showed an improvement in the content category from Weak to Good.

Similarly, Jenny showed improvement in the category of organization. In essays 1-1 and 1-3, her scores were Good. In essay 2 and essay 4, she scored Very Good. In essay 3, she made an improvement in organization from Good to Very Good. Although the organization of her pre-prompt writing was Weak, her post-prompt writing was Good.

The use of language in Jenny's essays also improved. In essay 1, her language was ranked at an Average level. However, in essay 2, she scored G-VG for language. In essay 3-1 and essay 4-1, her language score remained at the Good or G-VG level, but the language in her essay 3-3 and 4-3 improved to Very Good. The most obvious improvement made was in her prompt writing. In pre-prompt writing, her language was rated VP-W, but in post-prompt writing, she had a score of Good.

All in all, Jenny made progress in her essays, from Good to Very Good. In prompt writing, she improved from Weak to Good.

4.2.2.3 Jenny's Writing Attitudes: Results of Questionnaires

Table 4.12 shows the results of Jenny's questionnaires. Based on the 25-item questionnaire, her writing confidence level before class was 2.6 on a 7-point Liker scale, and after class, her writing confidence increased to 5.2. Also, her writing anxiety was decreased. Before class, the mean of the 26-item questionnaire was 5.1 and after class, the mean decreased to 2.2.

Table 4.10: Frequency Check of Jenny's Writing Self-Efficacy

	Scale	7	6	5	4	3	2	1
Frequency								
Tally Marks	Pre			/	⧼⧽ /	⧼⧽ /	⧼⧽ /	⧼⧽ /
	Post	/	⧼⧽ ⧼⧽ //	⧼⧽ ///	/	//	/	
Frequency	Pre	0	0	1	6	6	6	6
	Post	1	12	8	1	2	1	0

Note: Total Number of Items (N) = 25

Table 4.11: Frequency Check of Jenny's Writing Apprehension

	Scale	8	7	6	5	4	3	2	1
Frequency									
Tally Marks	Pre	//	### //	///	////	////	///	//	/
	Post				//	/	////	### ### /	### ///
Frequency	Pre	2	7	3	4	4	3	2	1
	Post	0	0	0	2	1	4	11	8

Note: Total Number of Items (N) = 26
Note: Items 2, 3, 6, 9, 10, 11, 12, 14, 15, 17, 19, 20 and 23 are coded in a reverse way.

Table 4.12: Means of Jenny's Responses to Questionnaires

Means	Pre-Q (Mean)	Post-Q (Mean)
Questionnaires		
Writing Self-Efficacy	2.6	5.2
Writing Apprehension	5.1	2.2

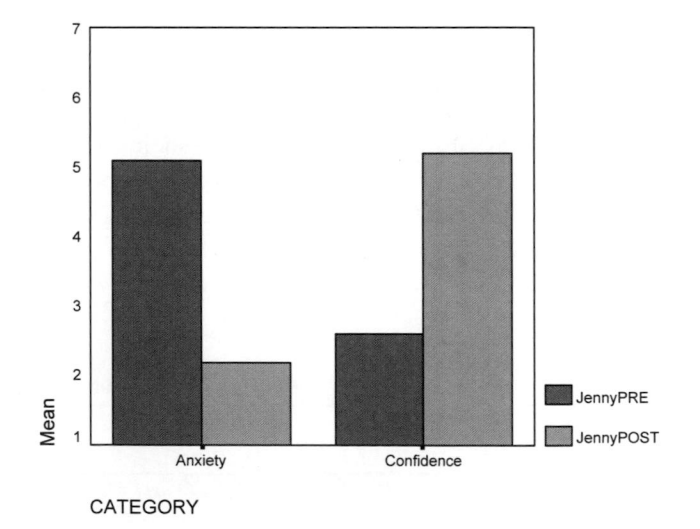

Figure 4.2: Results of Jenny's Questionnaires

4.2.2.4 Jenny's Personal Growth/Empowerment: Portfolio Evaluation

Jenny showed superior achievement in her portfolio. She was given a score of 8.5 for both Quality of Work and Creativity/Originality. Her Effort and Growth were obvious: for Effort she scored 10 (maximum score) and for Growth she scored 9.5. Her total score was 36.5, showing excellent performance in the process of learning.

Summary of Written Comments on Jenny's Portfolio

The written comments on Jenny's portfolio are summarized as follows:

1. Quality of Work

Her portfolio abounds with a great deal of interesting information, concerning both the class and the material she learned in class. She expressed herself well in formal and informal writing (e-mails).

She conveyed her ideas clearly, especially in the 3rd and 4th essays. She showed her knowledge of the issue, especially in the 1st essay about Taipei MRT.

2. Creativity and Originality

She showed creativity in compiling and editing her portfolio. The content of "Acknowledgements" and e-mails demonstrates her creativity and depth of reflection.

Her writing gradually improved and her voice grew stronger and stronger.

3. Evidence of Effort

She compiled her work thoroughly. Her drafts show improvement in her writing. Her e-mails show her growth in reading and demonstrate her active learning attitude.

Table 4.13: Mean Scores of Jenny's Portfolio

Category	Quality of Work	Creativity and Originality	Evidence of Efforts	Evidence of Growth	Total
Mean Scores	8.5 (G-S)	8.5 (G-S)	10 (S)	9.5 (S)	36.5 (S)

She spent almost all her free time on reading, writing, and discussion to formulate new ideas.

4. Evidence of Growth

Jenny became more confident as a reader and writer of English during the learning process. She was able to find the answer to her inquiry about the meaning of life.

She changed from being anxious about the English language to being confident. She viewed learning as an endless process. She reflected deeply on her life.

5. Other comments

Jenny is a very hard-working learner and the improvements shown were obvious. She experienced so many "first times" during this course, which is her great achievement.

4.2.3 Judy

4.2.3.1 Judy's Personal Profile

Judy was in her mid-30s. She graduated with a master's degree in Land Economics from a national university. She was working for the Council of Agriculture (Em-Ju-1). She studied abroad for half a year and had been learning English for almost 10 years. However, she had never studied the writing of English (Em-Ju-2). She came to this class because she needed to improve her English. She wrote,

Table 4.14: Judy's Basic Information

Info. Name	Age	Education	Profession	Years of Learning English	Years of Learning English Writing	Years of Studying Abroad
Judy	34	Master's Degree in Land Economics	Council of Agriculture	Almost 10 years	None	Half a year

English is very important for my job, not only promotion but also getting more che[a]nces to go abroad. I am still afraid of learning English when I was young. So, I hope that I can overcome this mind and improve my English ability (Em-Ju-1).

Her eagerness to learn and her insistence to "go for it" were shown in her written interview, where she wrote, "Although I am busy every day, I decide to come here. I will enjoy what I learn" (Em-Ju-1). She was busy in her career as well as at home with her family. She had a little boy at home to look after (O-8).

4.2.3.2 Judy's Writing Performance: Essay Scores

The four essays written by Judy were "The Impact of 'Let Go of Stress'," "What is 'Happiness'," "How to Avoid Being an Emotional Person" and "A Traveling with Tour vs. Self-help Trip." The first one was based on her outside reading, and the second one was for practicing the rhetorical mode of definition writing. The third was a reaction to *Tuesdays with Morrie,* and the fourth was her theme reading on travel. She chose all her topics according to what she read both in class and at home. In her writing, she shared her understanding of and reaction to certain issues.

Table 4.15: Judy's Essay Scores

Categories Essays	Voice	Content	Organization	Language	Total
Essay 1-1	17.5 (G)	15.5 (A-G)	14.5 (A)	13.5 (A)	61.0 (A-G)
Essay 1-3	21.0 (VG)	21.5 (VG)	21.5 (VG)	19.0 (G)	83.0 (G-VG)
Essay 2-1	16.0 (G)	15.0 (A)	14.0 (A)	14.0 (A)	59.0 (A)
Essay 2-3	17.5 (G)	18.5 (G)	17.5 (G)	18.0 (G)	71.5 (G)
Essay 3-1	20.0 (G)	19.0 (G)	15.0 (A)	13.0 (A)	67.0 (G)
Essay 3-3	22.0 (VG)	21.0 (VG)	21.0 (VG)	20.5 (G-VG)	84.5 (G)
Essay 4-1	17.5 (G)	19.5 (G)	19.0 (G)	18.0 (G)	74.0 (G)
Essay 4-3	21.5 (VG)	22.5 (VG)	22.0 (VG)	21.0 (VG)	87.0 (VG)
Pre-prompt	8.5 (W)	6.5 (W)	7.0 (W)	6.5 (W)	28.5 (W)
Post-prompt	19.0 (G)	18.0 (G)	20.5 (G-VG)	18.0 (G)	75.5 (G)

Is personal voice evident in her writing? Table 4.15 shows that she improved her writing voice from Good to Very Good in essays 1, 3 and 4. Though she stayed at the same level (Good) for essays 1 and 2, she improved in the drafts of her essays 2-1 to 2-3. In prompt writing, her voice improved from Weak to Good.

In terms of writing content, the scores fell in the A-G category for essay 1-1 and Very Good for essay 1-3. For essay 2-1, the content was Average, but after revision, the content of essay 2-3 was Good. In both essay 3 and essay 4, Judy improved her writing content from Good to Very Good. The content of her pre-prompt writing was Weak but that of her post-prompt writing was Good.

The improvement in the organization of her writing was more obvious. The organization of essay 1-1 was Average but increased to Very Good for essay 1-3. Essay 3 was also Very Good. In essay 2-1, the organization was Average while essay 2-3 was Good. Essay 4 showed an improvement from Good to Very Good. As for prompt writing, she made progress from Weak to G-VG.

Judy's use of language in her essays was weaker than other aspects of her writing, but the scores in Table 4.15 still indicate improvement. In essays 1 and 2, her language improved from Average to Good. In essay 3, it improved from Average to G-VG, and in essay 4, she made further improvement from Good to Very Good. Language in prompt writing, as in other aspects, went from Weak to Good.

All in all, Judy's essay was rated from Average to Very Good, and her prompt writing was rated from Weak to Good.

4.2.3.3 Judy's Writing Attitudes: Results of Questionnaires

The mean of the 25-item questionnaire on writing self-efficacy indicates the changes in Judy's learning after taking this course. Before the class, her writing confidence on the 7-point scale was 2.8 but moved to 3.5 after taking the course. The change in her writing apprehension is also shown in Table 4.18. The mean of the 26-item questionnaire on writing apprehension was 4.5 before the class and decreased to 3.6 after taking the course.

Table 4.16: Frequency Check of Judy's Writing Self-Efficacy

Frequency	Scale	7	6	5	4	3	2	1
Tally Marks	Pre		/	////	////	////	##	## //
	Post	/	////	////	///	////	///	## /
Frequency	Pre	0	1	4	4	4	5	7
	Post	1	4	4	3	4	3	6

Note: Total Number of Items (N) = 25

Table 4.17: Frequency Check of Judy's Writing Apprehension

Frequency	Scale	8	7	6	5	4	3	2	1
Tally Marks	Pre	## /	##	/		///	//	//	## //
	Post		##	////			##	## //	##
Total	Pre	6	5	1	0	3	2	2	7
	Post	0	5	4	0	0	5	7	5

Note: Total Number of Items (N) = 26
Note: Items 2, 3, 6, 9, 10, 11, 12, 14, 15, 17, 19, 20 and 23 are coded in a reverse way.

Table 4.18: Means of Judy's Responses to Questionnaires

Questionnaires	Means	Pre-Q (Mean)	Post-Q (Mean)
Writing Self-Efficacy		2.8	3.5
Writing Apprehension		4.5	3.6

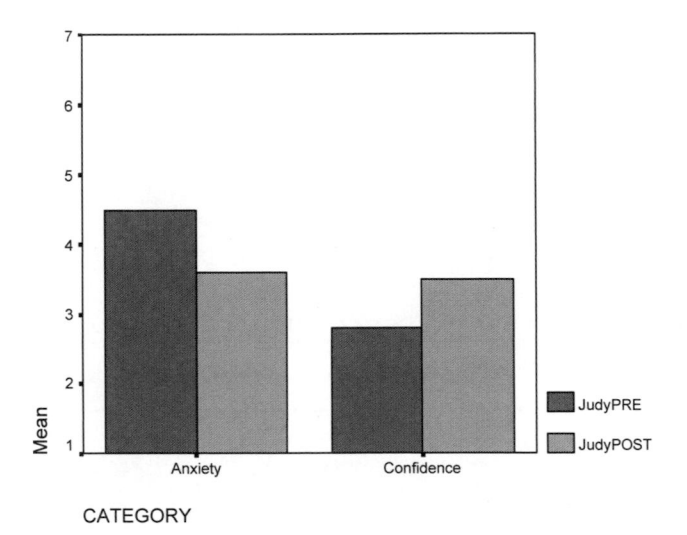

Figure 4.3: Results of Judy's Questionnaires

4.2.3.4 Judy's Personal Growth/Empowerment: Portfolio Evaluation

Judy's portfolio showed superior achievement. Except for Quality of Work, the other three categories (Creativity/Originality, Effort, and Growth) showed scores of 9 which is rated as Superior. The Quality of Work score was 8, which falls into the Good category.

Table 4.19: Mean Scores of Judy's Portfolio

Category	Quality of Work	Creativity and Originality	Evidence of Efforts	Evidence of Growth	Total
Mean Scores	8 (G)	9 (S)	9 (S)	9 (S)	35 (G-S)

Summary of Written Comments on Judy's Portfolio

The following written comments describe Judy's portfolio, which shows her achievements in the process of learning.

1. Quality of Work

Judy's work is rich with ideas and personal observations. She made a marked cumulative improvement in her language ability over time, which is clearly exhibited in her later works: the oral report on "Travel" and reflections on Tuesdays with Morrie.

Her theme reading on travel and New York City is informative. She conveys ideas clearly.

2. Creativity and Originality

Obviously, Judy is a person with original and creative thinking, e.g. her definitions about "happiness," her thoughts about the issue of racial discrimination in both the U.S. and Taiwan, etc.

All the essays and journals show her strong voice, especially in regard to youth issues and her reaction to Tuesdays with Morrie.

3. Evidence of Effort

The quantity and quality of her writings are the best evidence of the effort she made to fulfill both the class requirements and the need for self-actualization.

She tried very hard to continue the study, even though she had commitments to her family. She made time for reading and writing, and in fact did more than what was required. She actively posted and responded to messages on the on-line discussion board.

4. Evidence of Growth

Her works are abundant with thoughtful reflections on personal experiences. This shows in her meditations on "death" and "love" after reading Tuesdays with Morrie, and her opinions about parents' expectations for and influences on their children after listening to the song "Leader of the Band." Her writings demonstrate her personal growth after deep reflection on the issues involved.

She reflected on personal concerns and human relations.   She became more interested in English reading and writing and more confident in sharing her ideas in her writing.

5. Other comments

Judy is a reflective, conscientious, and industrious student.   The progress made in her writing ability is amazing, e.g. her Chin-glish expressions were markedly reduced in her later works.   Her preface is also a wonderful piece of work.

4.2.4 Joyce

4.2.4.1 Joyce's Personal Profile

Joyce, who had just turned 40 when the class began, graduated with a master's degree in Forest Science/Industry (Em-Jo-2).   She worked for the Bureau of Standards, Metrology and Inspection, with a specialty in the establishment and modification of national standards in the wood and paper industries (Em-Jo-1).

She had not studied abroad and had no experience of learning English writing, though she had studied English since junior high school (Em-Jo-2).   She was single, living with her parents and aged grandparents (O-10).   Life to her seemed to be a sack of responsibilities, if not a burden.   She came to class with a dream, "I ... hope in this class can guide me to increase more and more of my sight, and to understand more and more of what is yet unknown to me" (Em-Jo-1).

Table 4.20: Joyce's Basic Information

Info . Name	Age	Education	Profession	Years of Learning English	Years of Learning English Writing	Years of Studying Abroad
Joyce	40	Master's Degree in Forest Science and Industry	Bureau of Standards	Since Junior High	None	None

4.2.4.2 Joyce's Writing Performance: Essay Scores

Joyce's four essays were "Organic Food," "Ecological Environment," "Human Relationship in a Modern Society," which was originally titled "How to Maintain Well Relationships," and the fourth one "Gain and Loss." The first two essays were based on her theme reading, her profession and her job. The last two were based on reading *Tuesdays with Morrie* and reflections on her life.

According to Table 4.21, Joyce displayed a Good voice in most of her essays, except for essays 2-1, 3-3 and 4-3. In essay 2-1, her voice was rated as Average, but she made progress in revision. In essay 3-3, she showed G-VG for voice, which revealed a little improvement from essay 3-1. Also, in essay 4-3, she scored Very Good in voice, which was an improvement from essay 4-1. Her prompt writing also showed improvement in the category of voice. In pre-prompt writing, her voice was rated as Weak, while in post-prompt writing, she was rated Average.

In the category of content, Joyce was often rated as Good. In essay 1-1, she had Good content, and after revision, she attained the level of Very Good. In both essays 2 and 3, she provided Good content in the first drafts and had G-VG content with revision. In essay 4, she showed the most obvious progress: from Average to Very Good. As for her prompt writing, she made progress from Weak to Average.

Table 4.21: Joyce's Essay Scores

Categories Essays	Voice	Content	Organization	Language	Total
Essay 1-1	17.5 (G)	18.5 (G)	15.0 (A)	13.5 (A)	64.5 (G)
Essay 1-3	20.0 (G)	21.5 (VG)	20.5 (G-VG)	19.5 (G)	81.5 (G-VG)
Essay 2-1	15.0 (A)	18.0 (G)	15.5 (A-G)	12.5 (A)	61.0 (A-G)
Essay 2-3	19.0 (G)	20.5 (G-VG)	19.0 (G)	18.0 (G)	76.5 (G)
Essay 3-1	18.0 (G)	17.0 (G)	16.0 (G)	12.5 (A)	63.5 (A-G)
Essay 3-3	20.5 (G-VG)	20.5 (G-VG)	19.0 (G)	17.0 (G)	77.0 (G)
Essay 4-1	17.5 (G)	14.0 (A)	12.5 (A)	15.0 (A)	59.0 (A)
Essay 4-3	22.5 (VG)	22.0 (VG)	21.0 (VG)	20.0 (G)	85.5 (VG)
Pre-prompt	9.0 (W)	7.0 (W)	6.0 (W)	5.0 (VP)	27.0 (W)
Post-prompt	14.5 (A)	12.5 (A)	12.5 (A)	9.5 (W)	49.0 (A)

In terms of organization, Joyce's essay 1-1 was rated as Average and was changed into G-VG level with revision. The organization of essay 2-1 was at the level A-G, and she brought it up to Good in essay 2-3. Both of her essays 3-1 and 3-3 showed Good organization. In essay 4-1, the organization was Average, and essay 4-3 was rated as Very Good for organization. The organization of her prompt writing improved from Weak to Average.

Joyce showed the same pattern of improvement in the category of Language. All the essays she wrote showed progress from Average to Good after revision. As for her prompt writing, she improved from Very Poor to Weak.

All in all, Joyce made progress in her essays from Average to Very Good and from Weak to Average in her prompt writing.

4.2.4.3 Joyce's Writing Attitudes: Results of Questionnaires

Joyce showed changes in her attitude towards writing confidence and writing anxiety as indicated by the means of the 25-item questionnaire on writing self-efficacy and the 26-item questionnaire on writing apprehension. Before class, her writing confidence level was 4.5, on the 7-point Liker scale. After taking the course, her confidence level was raised to 5.5. Her writing anxiety level was 4.2 before class, which decreased to 3.0 on the 8-point Liker scale after taking the course.

Table 4.22: Frequency Check of Joyce's Writing Self-Efficacy

	Scale	7	6	5	4	3	2	1
Frequency								
Tally Marks	Pre	/	////	ЖЖ /	ЖЖ ЖЖ	////		
	Post		ЖЖ ЖЖ ////	ЖЖ ////	//			
Frequency	Pre	1	4	6	10	4	0	0
	Post	0	14	9	2	0	0	0

Note: Total Number of Items (N) = 25

Table 4.23: Frequency Check of Joyce's Writing Apprehension

	Scale	8	7	6	5	4	3	2	1
Frequency									
Tally Marks	Pre		ﷻ ///	//	/	//	////	ﷻ //	//
	Post		///	//	/		ﷻ	ﷻ ﷻ /	////
Frequency	Pre	0	8	2	1	2	4	7	2
	Post	0	3	2	1	0	5	11	4

Note: Total Number of Items (N) = 26
Note: Items 2, 3, 6, 9, 10, 11, 12, 14, 15, 17, 19, 20 and, 23 are coded in a reverse way

Table 4.24: Means of Joyce's Responses to Questionnaires

Means Questionnaires	Pre-Q (Mean)	Post-Q (Mean)
Writing Self-Efficacy	4.5	5.5
Writing Apprehension	4.2	3.0

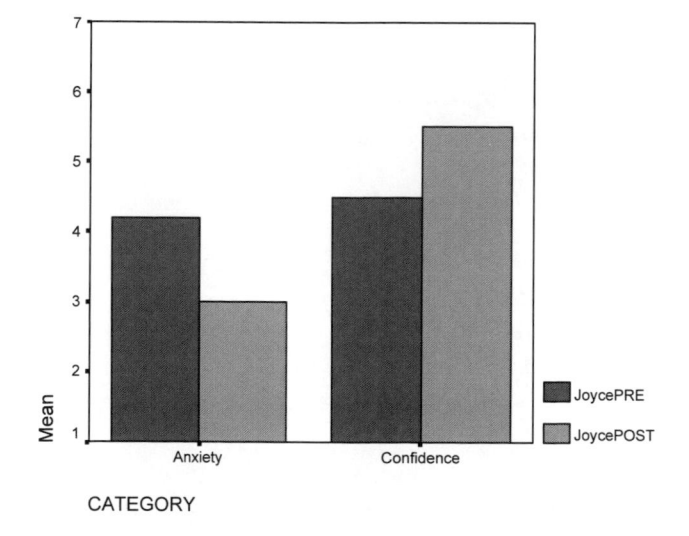

Figure 4.4: Results of Joyce's Questionnaires

4.2.4.4 Joyce's Personal Growth/Empowerment: Portfolio Evaluation

Joyce's portfolio showed her achievements. Both the Quality of her work and her Creativity and Originality were scored at 8. She was given a score of 9 for her Effort and 9.5 for her Growth. Her total score was 34.5, indicating her good-to-superior achievement.

Summary of Written Comments on Joyce's Portfolio

In addition to the mean scores, the written comments on Joyce's portfolio show all aspects of her accomplishment.

1. Quality of Work

Her essays are filled with brilliant ideas, good insight and great concern for our living environment. She demonstrated a high proficiency in conveying ideas in English, especially in her final drafts.

She was poor in English writing in the beginning but made progress during class.

2. Creativity and Originality

She demonstrated her originality in philosophical thinking and dialectic argument.

Her essays "Human Relation" and "Gain and Loss" showed her originality.

3. Evidence of Effort

The substantial improvement in her multi-draft essays, both in quality and quantity, was good evidence of her effort.

She tried hard to complete the reading and writing assignments, especially in the different genres.

Table 4.25: Mean Scores of Joyce's Portfolio

Category	Quality of Work	Creativity and Originality	Evidence of Efforts	Evidence of Growth	Total
Mean Scores	8 (G)	8 (G)	9 (S)	9.5 (S)	34.5 (G-S)

4. Evidence of Growth

She felt that, from the class, she had learned not only how to read and write English, but also how to live.   The topics she engaged in and the way she dealt with them demonstrate the depth of her reflection and personal growth.

Though her reading and writing still have room to grow, she has shown, in journals, essays and extra-curricular reading, steady growth as a reader and writer.

5. Other comments

Her ambition in undertaking serious issues for her topics should be admired.   She obviously was able to handle her subjects well, though she made grammatical mistakes once in a while.   This language use problem does not undermine the substance of her writings.

She obviously grew as a reader and writer and learned how to live more fully.

4.2.5 Ken

4.2.5.1 Ken's Personal Profile

Ken, a man in his mid-20s, graduated from a National University with a Bachelor's degree in Fire Protection and Prevention.   He was working in the Emergency Response and Rescue Center of the Fire Department of Taipei County (Em-K-1).

Table 4.26: Ken's Basic Information

Info. Name	Age	Education	Profession	Years of Learning English	Years of Learning English Writing	Years of Studying Abroad
Ken	27	Bachelor in Fire Protection and Prevention	Fire Department	Since Junior High	Since Junior High	None

He had studied English, including English writing, since junior high. He was one of the two in class who had studied English writing before attending this class. He had no experience of studying abroad but this was one of his goals (Em-K-2) and one of the reasons he attended the class. As he revealed in his written interview,

> I came here just want to improve my English ability, include listening and speaking. So that I want to get the opportunity to go to the abroad, like USA and Canada (Em-K-1).

Besides this, he had a higher goal, as he put it, "I will do my best to learn and hope that I can toward my English ability to a new space that I can't dare to think!" (Em-K-1). Ken is a promising young man, full of energy and dreams. His effort showed in his reading and writing and in his preparation for graduate school (O-18, 21, 23). At the end of the school year, he passed the Entrance Exam to graduate school and is now studying in a national university for a master's degree. He lived alone in Taipei and his parents and elder sister were in Kaoshiung. During the school year, his elder sister got married, so he kept thinking about moving back to Kaoshiung to be with his parents (O-24). The concern he showed for his parents and family was similar to the concern he had for society and human beings, which was clearly revealed in his writing.

4.2.5.2 Ken's Writing Performance: Essay Scores

The four essays written by Ken were "DVD and Home Theater," "The Doctor," "Feeling Sorry for Yourself," and "Sense and Sensibility." The first one was based on his theme reading—Movies and DVD players. The second one was based on his life experience and practice in the rhetorical mode of definition writing. The third and fourth essays were reactions to the best seller *Tuesdays with Morrie*.

According to Table 4.27, Ken's voice in his writing was Average in essay 1-1 but improved to Good in essay 1-3 after revision. In essay 2, Ken was rated for voice at the Good level, for both essays 2-1 and 2-3. In essay 3, Ken's voice was rated at the level of Very Good for both 3-1 and 3-3. In essay 4, his voice went from Good to Very Good. The obvious improvement in voice was observed in prompt writing. In pre-prompt writing, he was judged to be Average, while improving to a Very Good rating in post-prompt writing.

In the category of content, Ken was rated Good except for the essays 2-1 and 4-3. In essay 2, he made progress from Average to Good, and in essay 4, he made progress from Good to Very Good. Again, his prompt writing showed an improvement from W-A to G-VG.

The pattern of improvement in the category of organization was similar to that of content. Except in essays 2-1 and 4, Ken showed Good organization. In essay 2, Ken improved from Average to Good, and in essay 4, he made progress from G-VG to Very Good. The organization of prompt writing went from Weak to Very Good.

The language in Ken's essays was also mostly Good, except for essay 1-1 and essay 2-1. In both essays 1 and 2, Ken made progress from Average to Good. He also showed language improvement from Weak to Good in his prompt writing.

All in all, Ken made progress in his essay writing, mainly from Average to G-VG, and prompt writing indicated progress from Weak to G-VG.

Table 4.27: Ken's Essay Scores

Categories / Essays	Voice	Content	Organization	Language	Total
Essay 1-1	14.5 (A)	16.5 (G)	19.0 (G)	12.5 (A)	62.5 (A-G)
Essay 1-3	17.5 (G)	19.5 (G)	18.0 (G)	19.0 (G)	74.0 (G)
Essay 2-1	17.0 (G)	13.5 (A)	13.5 (A)	13.0 (A)	57.0 (A)
Essay 2-3	19.0 (G)	16.5 (G)	17.0 (G)	16.0 (G)	68.5 (G)
Essay 3-1	21.5 (VG)	18.5 (G)	18.5 (G)	18.5 (G)	77.0 (G)
Essay 3-3	22.0 (VG)	20.0 (G)	20.0 (G)	20.0 (G)	82.0 (G-VG)
Essay 4-1	20.0 (G)	19.5 (G)	20.5 (G-VG)	18.5 (G)	78.5 (G)
Essay 4-3	21.0 (VG)	21.0 (VG)	21.0 (VG)	20.0 (G)	83.0 (G-VG)
Pre-prompt	13.0 (A)	10.5 (W-A)	9.0 (W)	6.0 (W)	38.5 (W)
Post-prompt	21.5 (VG)	20.5 (G-VG)	22.0 (VG)	19.0 (G)	83.0 (G-VG)

4.2.5.3 Ken's Writing Attitudes: Results of Questionnaires

Ken showed improvement in both writing confidence and writing anxiety. The mean of the 25-item questionnaire on writing self-efficacy was 2.6 before classes and increased to 4.1 after classes.

The reduction of his writing apprehension was indicated by the reduction of the mean, obtained from the 26-item writing apprehension questionnaire. Before taking this course, Ken's anxiety level was 4.5, and it was reduced to 3.0 after taking the course.

Table 4.28: Frequency Check of Ken's Writing Self-Efficacy

Frequency	Scale	7	6	5	4	3	2	1
Tally Marks	Pre				/	### ### ###	### /	///
	Post		###	###	### /	### //	/	/
Frequency	Pre	0	0	0	1	15	6	3
	Post	0	5	5	6	7	1	1

Note: Total Number of Items (N) = 25

Table 4.29: Frequency Check of Ken's Writing Apprehension

Frequency	Scale	8	7	6	5	4	3	2	1
Tally Marks	Pre		/	###	### /	### ////	###		
	Post				//	////	### ### //	### ///	
Frequency	Pre	0	1	5	6	9	5	0	0
	Post	0	0	0	2	4	12	8	0

Note: Total Number of Items (N) = 26
Note: Items 2, 3, 6, 9, 10, 11, 12, 14, 15, 17, 19, 20 and 23 are coded in a reverse way.

Table 4.30: Means of Ken's Responses to Questionnaires

Questionnaires	Means Pre-Q (Mean)	Post-Q (Mean)
Writing Self-Efficacy	2.6	4.1
Writing Apprehension	4.5	3.0

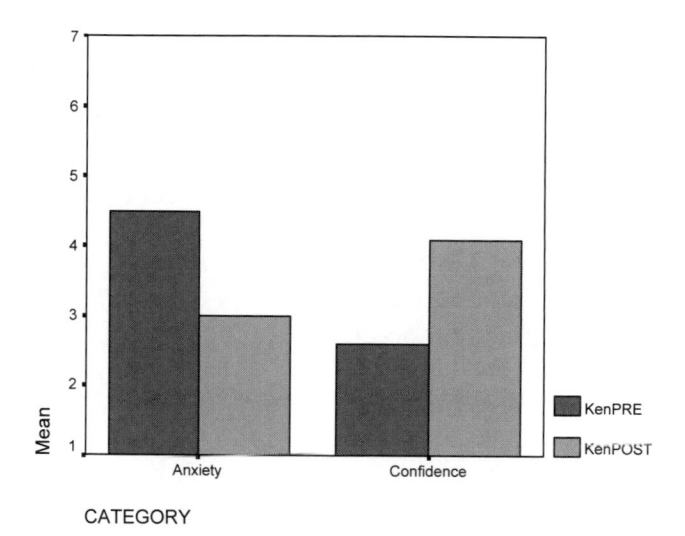

Figure 4.5: Results of Ken's Questionnaires

4.2.5.4 Ken's Personal Growth/Empowerment: Portfolio Evaluation

Ken's portfolio scores were all around 8. Quality of Work was scored 7.5 or Good on the scale. Both Creativity/Originality and Effort were an 8, also falling into the Good category. The highest score in his portfolio was given for his Growth, which scored a Superior 9. Ken's total score was 32.5, a little higher than Good.

Table 4.31: Mean Scores of Ken's Portfolio

Category	Quality of Work	Creativity and Originality	Evidence of Efforts	Evidence of Growth	Total
Mean Scores	7.5 (G)	8 (G)	8 (G)	9 (S)	32.5 (G-S)

Summary of Written Comments on Ken's Portfolio

Ken's portfolio demonstrated his achievements. Written comments are presented below.

1. Quality of Work

In his writing, he demonstrated knowledge in his field of interest. He wrote knowledgeably about MRTs, DVDs, and movies he enjoyed. Though his proficiency in English is not high, he could still functionally express himself. His revisions showed progress in his English.

He is knowledgeable about DVDs and movies. He successfully integrated English learning with movie watching. His ideas were generally clear but sometimes he got stuck.

2. Creativity and Originality

He has his own thoughts, e.g. he felt Gibson's heroic behavior in "Braveheart" was unnatural. Also, his opinions about taking naps during work or in class were rather unconventional.

He integrated English reading/writing, even listening/speaking, with movie watching. He had sensitive observations and reflections on daily life, such as in "Busy life," "Chinese School," "Feeling sorry for oneself," "Droupouts," "Japanese comic books," ...etc.

3. Evidence of Effort

His report on "movies" is a good demonstration of his efforts. It is a piece of work full of information and reflection. He also said in his "Preface" that he had read many good articles. His notes and remarks on the articles he wrote is also evidence of his effort.

He worked hard on reading and writing. While he had to prepare for the graduate school entrance exam during the semester, he still had time to write of his dilemma in his essays and journals.

4. Evidence of Growth

He gained much personal growth by attending the class. He said in the Preface that by reading the articles, he had the chance to explore the depth of his mind and to discover a part that was previously un-

known even to himself.   He also said that he found his strengths and weaknesses in writing during the process of learning to write.

He reflected greatly on life and on the different ways of learning English.   He formed the habit of reading and writing English.

5. Other comments

Though Ken made grammatical mistakes frequently, his writing was generally understandable.   Thus, perhaps grammatical accuracy isn't as important as content in determining the quality of a piece of writing.

4.2.6 Lin

4.2.6.1 Lin's Personal Profile

In her 40s, Lin graduated from a National University with a Master's degree in Business Management, and worked at the Taiwan Power Company (Em-L-1).

She had no experience of studying abroad.   She studied English writing for 1 year before attending this class (Em-L-2).   She is a mother with a teenage daughter about to enter senior high school at the time Lin joined the class (O-11).   She is a career woman and also a housewife.   Besides taking care of her husband and daughter, she also took care of her parents-in-law, who live with them (O-17).   However, no matter how busy and tiring her life would be, she always displayed a peace of mind when she came to class.   She seemed mature and usually provided profound insight to the class.

Table 4.32: Lin's Basic Information

Info.\n\nName	Age	Education	Profession	Years of Learning English	Years of Learning English Writing	Years of Studying Abroad
Lin	43	Master's Degree in Business Management	Taiwan Power Company	10 years	1 year	None

105

4.2.6.2 Lin's Writing Performance: Essay Scores

Lin's four essays were "Cancer Risks," "Difference in Urban and Rural Life," "Women," and "Family Problem." All the topics were based on her concerns and life experiences. She put theme reading responses in her journals and oral reports but not in her essays.

According to Table 4.33, her voice in essay writing was better than Good. For essays 1, 3, and 4, she made progress from Good to Very Good, and for essay 2, she showed her Very Good voice in both essays 2-1 and 2-3. She even started her pre-prompt writing with Good voice and showed an improvement in post-prompt writing with Very Good voice.

In the category of content, Lin made similar progress to that of voice. The content in essay 1-1 was rated as G-VG and improved to Very Good in essay 1-3. In essays 3 and 4, the content improved from Good to Very Good. She scored Very Good for content in essays 2-1 and 2-3. The content of her prompt writing improved from Weak to Very Good.

As shown in Table 4.33, the pattern of improvement in the category of organization was the same as that of content. Lin showed progress from G-VG to Very Good in essay 1, and from Good to Very Good in essays 3 and 4. Both of her essays 2-1 and 2-3 fell into the Very Good

Table 4.33: Lin's Essay Scores

Categories Essays	Voice	Content	Organization	Language	Total
Essay 1-1	19.0 (G)	20.5 (G-VG)	20.5 (G-VG)	17.0 (G)	77.0 (G)
Essay 1-3	21.0 (VG)	21.0 (VG)	21.5 (VG)	21.0 (VG)	84.5 (VG)
Essay 2-1	21.5 (VG)	21.5 (VG)	22.0 (VG)	21.0 (VG)	86.0 (VG)
Essay 2-3	21.5 (VG)	21.5 (VG)	23.5 (VG)	23.0 (VG)	89.5 (VG)
Essay 3-1	19.0 (G)	19.0 (G)	18.0 (G)	18.0 (G)	74.0 (G)
Essay 3-3	21.5 (VG)	21.5 (VG)	22.0 (VG)	22.0 (VG)	87.0 (VG)
Essay 4-1	20.0 (G)	20.0 (G)	19.5 (G)	18.0 (G)	77.5 (G)
Essay 4-3	22.5 (VG)	22.5 (VG)	22.0 (VG)	21.5 (VG)	88.5 (VG)
Pre-prompt	16.0 (G)	9.5 (W)	9.0 (W)	11.5 (A)	46.0 (A)
Post-prompt	22.0 (VG)	21.0 (VG)	20.0 (G)	20.5 (G-VG)	83.5 (G-VG)

category, with the 2-3 score being the higher. The organization of her prompt writing went from Weak to Good.

Lin showed similar patterns of improvement in the language category. She made progress from Good to Very Good in essays 1, 3, and 4, and scored Very Good for language in both essays 2-1 and 2-3. Her prompt writing showed language improvement from Average to G-VG.

All in all, Lin's essays were well written. Except for prompt writing, all the essays were scaled from Good to Very Good. General progress for prompt writing went from Average to Good.

4.2.6.3 Lin's Writing Attitudes: Results of Questionnaires

Lin's attitude towards writing changed after taking this course. Her writing confidence level, as gauged by the mean from the 25-item writing self-efficacy questionnaire, improved from 4.2 to 5.8, on the 7-point Liker scale. The mean score from the 26-item questionnaire on writing apprehension showed that the level of her writing anxiety dropped from 4.2 to 3.3, on the 8-point Liker scale.

Table 4.34: Frequency Check of Lin's Writing Self-Efficacy

	Scale	7	6	5	4	3	2	1
Frequency								
Tally Marks	Pre		//	## /	## ## ///	////		
	Post	///	## ## ///	## ////				
Frequency	Pre	0	2	6	13	4	0	0
	Post	3	13	9	0	0	0	0

Note: Total Number of Items (N) = 25

Table 4.35: Frequency Check of Lin's Writing Apprehension

	Scale	8	7	6	5	4	3	2	1
Frequency									
Tally Marks	Pre		##	///	///	///	## /	## /	
	Post			/	##	## /	## /	## /	//
Frequency	Pre	0	5	3	3	3	6	6	0
	Post	0	0	1	5	6	6	6	2

Note: Total Number of Items (N) = 26
Note: Items 2, 3, 6, 9, 10, 11, 12, 14, 15, 17, 19, 20 and 23 are coded in a reverse way.

Table 4.36: Means of Lin's Responses to Questionnaires

Means Questionnaires	Pre-Q (Mean)	Post-Q (Mean)
Writing Self-Efficacy	4.2	5.8
Writing Apprehension	4.2	3.3

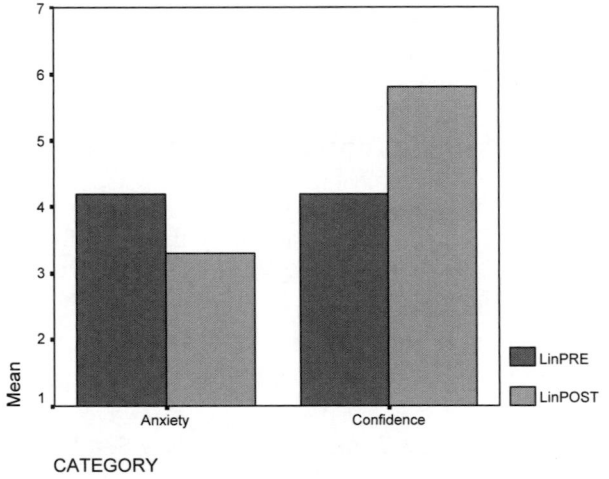

Figure 4.6: Lin's Questionnaires Outcomes

4.2.6.4 Lin's Personal Growth: Portfolio Evaluation

Lin showed superior achievements in all aspects of the course. She was given a score of 9.5 for both Quality of Work and Effort, 9 for Creativity and Originality, and 10 (maximum score) for Growth. Her total score was 38 out of 40, a near perfect performance and an indication of great progress as a reader and writer.

Table 4.37: Mean Scores of Lin's Portfolio

Category	Quality of Work	Creativity and Originality	Evidence of Efforts	Evidence of Growth	Total
Mean Scores	9.5 (S)	9 (S)	9.5 (S)	10 (S)	38 (S)

Summary of Written Comments on Lin's Portfolio

The written comments on Lin's portfolio illustrate all aspects of her achievements.

1. Quality of Work

In her work, Lin demonstrated her writing skill and her knowledge of the world. It was obvious that Lin has a rather good command of the English language.

She expressed herself well in English and conveyed her ideas clearly. She has much knowledge of life and social issues. Her theme reading was done well with meaningful responses.

2. Creativity and Originality

Her remarks after reading a story, such as "The Unicorn in the Garden," shows that she has an original mind. Also, her opinions on what encourages students to learn show that she is capable of critical thinking.

All her pieces reveal her personal voice and her personal viewpoint on life issues. She reflects tenderly but profoundly on reading and life.

3. Evidence of Efforts

The richness of her work is a good demonstration of her effort. She also made a great deal of effort revising her essays.

She always read, no matter how busy she was. She read and wrote more than was required. That she read whatever interested her proved her learning was self-directed.

4. Evidence of Growth

Lin is a keen observer of the people around her. She shows great understanding and compassion for those related to her. Her pieces, such as "Forgiveness" and "Marriage," demonstrate the depth of her reflection and her concern for the people she cares about.

She reflected not only on writing but also on her daily life, e.g. her interaction with her daughter. She has made a habit of reading and writing English and constantly looks for new books to read and share with others.

Table 4.38: Maria's Basic Information

Info. Name	Age	Education	Profession	Years of Learning English	Years of Learning English Writing	Years of Studying Abroad
Maria	31	Bachelor's Degree in Land Management	Taipei City Government	18 years	3 years	None

5. Other Comments

It was very enjoyable to read what Lin had written. Her English is quite good and her work is rich with insightful observations and empathetic understanding.

4.2.7 Maria

4.2.7.1 Maria's Personal Profile

Maria, in her thirties, graduated from a Private University with a Bachelor's degree in Land Management, and worked with the Taipei City Government (Em-M-2). She had no experience of studying abroad. She had studied English writing for 3 of her 18 years of English learning (Em-M-2). She liked traveling a lot, so she wanted to improve her English. Her dream was to study in Britain in the near future (O-18). She was full of ideas and imagination. She loved the beauty in everything (O-6, 13, 17). These characteristics were clearly revealed in her writing. She was single.

4.2.7.2 Maria's Writing Performance: Essay Scores

Maria's four essays were "Olympics Games and Sydney" (the original title was "Olympics Games in the World"), "Prague—European City of Culture 2000," "Love" and "Morrie Schwartz and the Buddhists." The first two were based on her theme reading and interest. The last two were mainly based on the reading of *Tuesdays with Morrie* and her own life experiences.

Table 4.39: Maria's Essay Scores

Categories Essays	Voice	Content	Organization	Language	Total
Essay 1-1	14.0 (A)	15.5 (A-G)	17.0 (G)	14.5 (A)	61.0 (A-G)
Essay 1-3	17.5 (G)	18.5 (G)	17.0 (G)	18.0 (G)	71.0 (G)
Essay 2-1	13.0 (A)	18.0 (G)	15.5 (A-G)	17.0 (G)	63.5 (A-G)
Essay 2-3	16.5 (G)	22.5 (VG)	21.5 (VG)	20.5 (G-VG)	81.0 (G-VG)
Essay 3-1	22.0 (VG)	20.0 (G)	19.0 (G)	18.5 (G)	79.5 (G)
Essay 3-3	23.0 (VG)	22.5 (VG)	21.0 (VG)	21.5 (VG)	88.0 (VG)
Essay 4-1	19.0 (G)	17.5 (G)	17.5 (G)	15.0 (A)	69.0 (G)
Essay 4-3	22.5 (VG)	22.0 (VG)	22.0 (VG)	21.0 (VG)	87.5 (VG)
Pre-prompt	12.0 (A)	12.5 (A)	12.0 (A)	13.5 (A)	50.0 (A)
Post-prompt	19.0 (G)	19.0 (G)	18.0 (G)	15.0 (A)	71.0 (G)

According to Table 4.39, Maria made progress in all aspects of essay writing. In the category of Voice, she made progress from Average to Good in both essay 1 and essay 2. In essay 3, she had Very Good voice. In essay 4, she improved from Good to Very Good. Her prompt writing also improved in Voice from Average to Good.

The content of Maria's essays showed an obvious improvement. In essay 1-1, the content was scored at A-G and rose to Good in essay 1-3. For essays 2, 3, and 4, Maria showed the same pattern of improvement—from Good to Very Good. The content of her prompt writing improved from Average to Good.

In the category of Organization, Maria scored Good for both essay 1-1 and essay 1-3. In essay 2-1, she had an A-G level of organization, but with revision, improved to Very Good in essay 2-3. For the remaining two essays—3 and 4, the same pattern of progress held, which was from Good to Very Good. The organization of her prompt writing went from Average to Good.

The progress in Maria's essays was obvious in her use of language. She scored Average for language in essay 1-1, moving to Good in essay 1-3. In essay 2-1, her language score was Good but after revision, was at the level of G-VG. In the same way, she had a Good score for language in essay 3-1, ending up with Very Good in essay 3-3. The most obvious progress was shown in essay 4. In essay 4-1, she was given an Average score, while in essay 4-3, she scored Very Good. As for her prompt writing, she had Average scores for language in both pre-prompt and post-prompt writing pieces.

All in all, Maria made progress in her essay writing from A-G to Very Good. Her prompt writing showed a general improvement, going from Average to Good.

4.2.7.3 Maria's Writing Attitudes: Results of Questionnaires

Table 4.42 shows the means resulting from the 25-item questionnaire on writing self-efficacy and the 26-item questionnaire on writing apprehension. As Table 4.42 reveals, Maria's writing confidence went from a 4.0 before the course to a 5.3 after the course, on the 7-point Liker scale. Her writing anxiety was at a 4.4 before and a 3.1 on the 8-point Liker scale, after taking the course.

Table 4.40: Frequency Check of Maria's Writing Self-Efficacy

	Scale	7	6	5	4	3	2	1
Frequency								
Tally Marks	Pre			*HH IIII*	*HH II*	*HH IIII*		
	Post		*HH HH III*	*HH I*	*HH I*			
Frequency	Pre	0	0	9	7	9	0	0
	Post	0	13	6	6	0	0	0

Note: Total Number of Items (N) = 25

Table 4.41: Frequency Check of Maria's Writing Apprehension

	Scale	8	7	6	5	4	3	2	1
Frequency									
Tally Marks	Pre		*I*	*III*	*HH II*	*HH IIII*	*HH I*		
	Post			*II*	*I*	*III*	*HH HH I*	*HH IIII*	
Frequency	Pre	0	1	3	7	9	6	0	0
	Post	0	0	2	1	3	11	9	0

Note: Total Number of Items (N) = 26
Note: Items 2, 3, 6, 9, 10, 11, 12, 14, 15, 17, 19, 20 and 23 are coded in a reverse way.

Table 4.42: Means of Maria's Responses to Questionnaires

Questionnaires	Pre-Q (Mean)	Post-Q (Mean)
Writing Self-Efficacy	4.0	5.3
Writing Apprehension	4.4	3.1

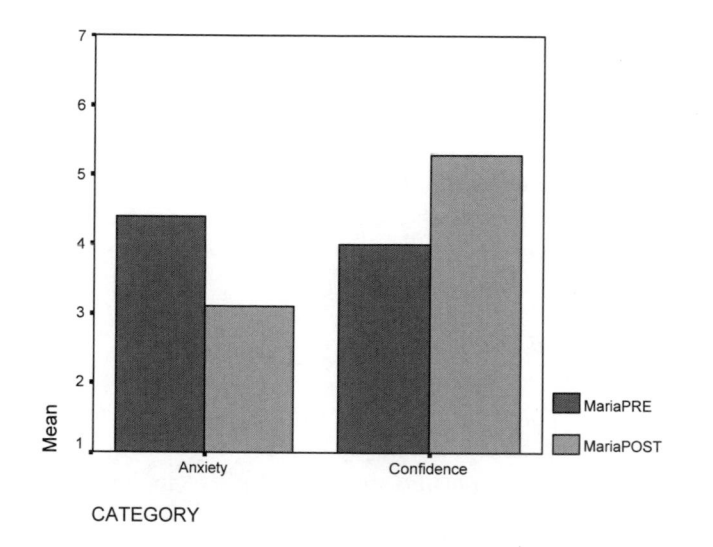

Figure 4.7: Results of Maria's Questionnaires

4.2.7.4 Maria's Personal Growth/Empowerment: Portfolio Evaluation

Maria's portfolio spoke for her achievements in the year of learning. She was given a score of 7.5 for the Quality of her work, and 8 for her Creativity and Originality. Both her Effort and Growth scored 9. Her total score was 33.5, falling between the categories of Superior and Good.

Table 4.43: Mean Scores of Maria's Portfolio

Category	Quality of Work	Creativity and Originality	Evidence of Efforts	Evidence of Growth	Total
Mean Scores	7.5 (G)	8 (G)	9 (S)	9 (S)	33.5 (G-S)

Summary of Written Comments on Maria's Portfolio

The written comments on Maria's portfolio follow and confirm the scores represented by her achievements in Table 4.43.

1. Quality of Work

Her work was rich with information and insight.

She took risks by tackling more difficult issues, which increased the difficulty of producing good quality. However, what she wrote illustrated that she gradually progressed.

2. Creativity and Originality

The cover page she designed and her reflections after reading Tuesdays with Morrie demonstrated her originality and creativity.

The first two essays did not show much originality, but the last two essays displayed her obvious creativity and originality, especially the piece on "Love."

3. Evidence of Effort

Her essay revisions showed the effort she made in her work.

Without doubt, she put effort into both theme reading and essay writing.

4. Evidence of Growth

The insightful and thoughtful ideas presented in the essays such as "Love" and "Morrie Schwartz and the Buddhists" showed evidence of Maria's personal growth. From her self-evaluation, we know that, with her practice, she has become a more confident reader and writer of English.

She showed progress in the 2nd semester in writing "Love" and in her responses to Morrie. She also developed as a reader by reading Tuesdays with Morrie.

5. Other comments

Her improvement, after revision of her essays, was impressive.

She did her best to read and write well. Although she still feels she has a long way to go in her reading and writing, she has shown progress in her writing and reading comprehension.

4.2.8 Peggy

4.2.8.1 Peggy's Personal Profile

Peggy, a woman in her late twenties, graduated from a national university with a Master's degree in Social Welfare and Social Work. She worked for the Council of Labor Affairs (Em-P-1). She had no experience of studying abroad. In her 11 years of English learning, she had studied English writing for 5 years (Em-P-2).

She came to this class to improve her English. In her written interview, she said,

> When I studied in the graduate school, I found my English become poorer and poorer. So, when I finished my thesis this semester, I think this is the best time to practice my English again (Em-P-1).

She was single, living in Taipei alone, while her family was in southern Taiwan (O-16). Her critical thinking skills and her concerns for society and human beings showed in her writing.

Table 4.44: Peggy's Basic Information

Info. Name	Age	Education	Profession	Years of Learning English	Years of Learning English Writing	Years of Studying Abroad
Peggy	27	Master's Degree in Social Work and Welfare	Council of Labor Affairs	11 years	5 years	None

4.2.8.2 Peggy's Writing Performance: Essay Scores

Peggy's four essays were "America Music," "The Titanic Riddle—Should A Good Feminist Accept Priority Seating on a Lifeboat?" "What do I See 'Girl lashes out at Dad in Court' event?" and "Web Bookstore vs. Traditional Bookstore." The first one was based on her theme reading—American Music. The second one was based on public discussion of the movie "Titanic" and her own observations. The third one was based on a real-life incident, her concerns and her profession. The fourth one was based on her own experiences.

As shown in Table 4.45, Peggy's voice was clearly heard in most of her essays. In essay 1, she scored Average for voice both the first and final drafts. In essay 2, she made progress from Good to Very Good in the Voice category. In essays 3 and 4, she scored Very Good for all of the drafts. In her prompt writing, she also presented her voice strongly. Her levels went from Good to G-VG.

In the category of content, Peggy also showed great skill. In essay 1, the content in both the first and final drafts was rated as Good. In essay 2, the content was Good for the first draft and Very Good for the final draft. As for essays 3 and 4, content was rated Very Good throughout. In pre-prompt writing, she showed Weak content but improved to a level of Good in her post-prompt writing.

Table 4.45: Peggy's Essay Scores

Categories Essays	Voice	Content	Organization	Language	Total
Essay 1-1	15.0 (A)	19.5 (G)	18.5 (G)	17.0 (G)	70.0 (G)
Essay 1-3	13.5 (A)	19.5 (G)	17.0 (G)	17.0 (G)	67.0 (G)
Essay 2-1	19.0 (G)	17.5 (G)	17.5 (G)	16.0 (G)	70.0 (G)
Essay 2-3	21.0 (VG)	21.0 (VG)	20.5 (G-VG)	20.5 (G-VG)	83.0 (G-VG)
Essay 3-1	22.0 (VG)	21.5 (VG)	21.5 (VG)	19.5 (G)	84.5 (VG)
Essay 3-3	22.5 (VG)	22.5 (VG)	22.5 (VG)	21.5 (VG)	89.0 (VG)
Essay 4-1	22.5 (VG)	22.5 (VG)	23.0 (VG)	20.5 (G-VG)	88.5 (VG)
Essay 4-3	23.0 (VG)	22.5 (VG)	23.0 (VG)	22.5 (VG)	91.0 (VG)
Pre-prompt	16.5 (G)	9.5 (W)	9.0 (W)	9.0 (W)	44.0 (A)
Post-prompt	20.5 (G-VG)	20.0 (G)	19.5 (G)	16.0 (G)	76.0 (G)

For organization, Peggy showed Good organization for both drafts of essay 1.   In essay 2-1, she also scored Good for organization, becoming G-VG in essay 2-3 after revision.   In essays 3 and 4, organization was rated Very Good for all drafts.   As for her prompt writing, organization was Weak in pre-prompt writing, improving to Good in post-prompt writing.

Language use in Peggy's essays also improved.   As Table 4.45 shows, in essay 1, her language was Good, the same as in essay 2-1, improving to a level of G-VG in essay 2-3.   In essay 3-1, her language score was at the Good level, becoming Very Good in essay 3-3.   In her last essay, her language score went from G-VG in 4-1, to Very Good in essay 4-3.   Also, in her prompt writing, language improved from Weak to Good.

All in all, Peggy's essay writing improved from Good to Very Good, and her prompt writing improved from a level of Average to Good.

4.2.8.3 Peggy's Writing Attitudes: Results of Questionnaires

Table 4.48 shows Peggy's writing confidence and anxiety level before and after completing the course.   The mean of the 25-item questionnaire on writing self-efficacy was 3.0 before the course and 3.9 after the course on the 7-point Liker scale.   As for writing apprehension, Peggy's writing anxiety level was measured at 3.8 before taking this course, dropping to 3.0 on the 8-point Liker scale after the course.

Table 4.46: Frequency Check of Peggy's Writing Self-Efficacy

	Scale	7	6	5	4	3	2	1
Frequency								
Tally Marks	Pre		//	///	///	//// //	////	////
	Post		/	////	//// //// /	//// //	/	
Total	Pre	0	2	3	3	7	5	5
	Post	0	1	5	11	7	1	0

Note: Total Number of Items (N) = 25

Table 4.47: Frequency Check of Peggy's Writing Apprehension

Frequency	Scale	8	7	6	5	4	3	2	1
Tally Marks	Pre		/	卌 /	///	////	///	卌 /	///
	Post	/	/	//	////	//	///	//	卌 卌 /
Frequency	Pre	0	1	6	3	4	3	6	3
	Post	1	1	2	4	2	3	2	11

Note: Total Number of Items (N) = 26
Note: Items 2, 3, 6, 9, 10, 11, 12, 14, 15, 17, 19, 20 and 23 are coded in a reverse way.

Table 4.48: Means of Peggy's Responses to Questionnaires

Questionnaires	Means	Pre-Q (Mean)	Post-Q (Mean)
Writing Self-Efficacy		3.0	3.9
Writing Apprehension		3.8	3.0

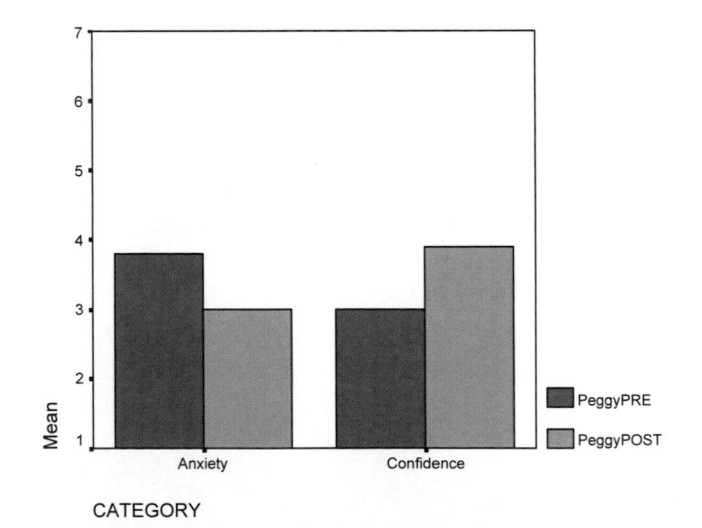

Figure 4.8: Results of Peggy's Questionnaires

4.2.8.4 Peggy's Personal Growth/Empowerment: Portfolio Evaluation

Peggy's portfolio showed all aspects of her achievements. She was given 8.5 for the Quality of her work, her Effort and her Growth. For Creativity and Originality, she scored a 9. Her total score was 34.5, falling in between Superior and Good.

Table 4.49: Mean Scores of Peggy's Portfolio Scores

Category	Quality of Work	Creativity and Originality	Evidence of Efforts	Evidence of Growth	Total
Means Scores	8.5 (G-S)	9 (S)	8.5 (G-S)	8.5 (G-S)	34.5 (G-S)

Summary of Written Comments on Peggy's Portfolio

Written comments on Peggy's portfolio, which reflect her learning and accomplishments, follow.

1. Quality of Work

Her portfolio is rich in information. Her essays demonstrated her ability to write well-organized essays.

Her ideas were conveyed clearly and she had good summaries and responses on what had been read. The last article "Web Bookstore vs. Traditional Bookstores" is full of vivid language.

2. Creativity and Originality

She raised many good questions in her writing, such as in "Freedom of Speech," and "What do I see 'Girl Lashes Out at Dad in Court' Event?" which shows that she has an inquiring mind.

Both her theme reading—Jazz—and journals on social events show her unique and critical way of thinking. She had some special concerns showing independent thought.

3. Evidence of Effort

She collected lots of information for her reports and did a great deal of reading for both her essays and her oral reports.

She put a lot of work into searching for information, especially for theme reading and on reading and writing.

4. Evidence of Growth

By answering the questions she raised in her writing, she grew not only as a reader and writer, but also as a person.

Her growth was not only evidenced in her writing but also in her determination to spend time with and take care of her family.

5. Other comments

Peggy frequently consulted references.   This could have a harmful effect on her writing as she had the tendency to use the expressions and words of others for convenience.

She is a deep thinker and a good writer of English.

4.3 General Profile of the Class

This section summarizes the improvements of the class as a whole. Writing performance, writing attitudes, and personal growth of the students are presented as an indication of the scope of this study.

4.3.1 Writing Performance of the Class

Table 4.50: Results of a Paired-sample T-test on the Prompt Writing of the Class

Source	Paired Differences			t-value	df	Sig.
	Mean	SD	SE of Mean			(2-tailed)
Pre−Post	-33.81	11.88	4.20	-8.052	7	.000

** p<.01, N = 8, 95% CI (-43.74, -23.88)   Note: α = .01, one-tailed (directional) decision

H_{01}: There is no significant improvement in students' writing performance after they had engaged in the learning of theme cycles.   (H_{01}: $\mu_{x1} \geq \mu_{x2}$)

H_{A1}: There is significant improvement in students' writing performance after they had engaged in the learning of theme cycles.   (H_{A1}: $\mu_{x1} < \mu_{x2}$)

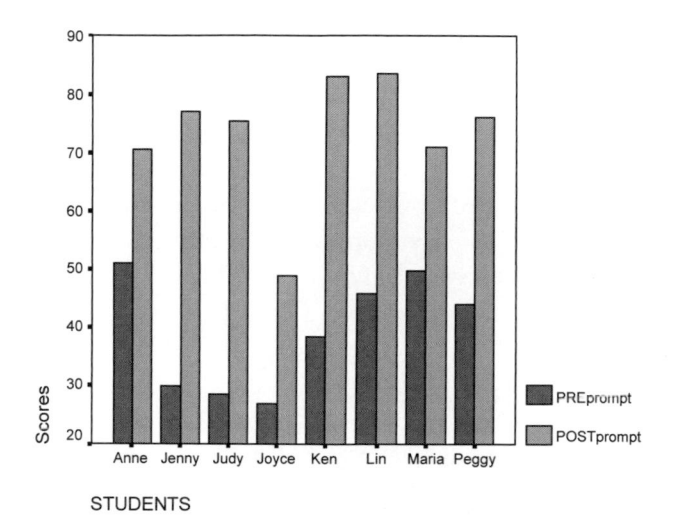

Figure 4.9: Writing Performance of the Class (1)

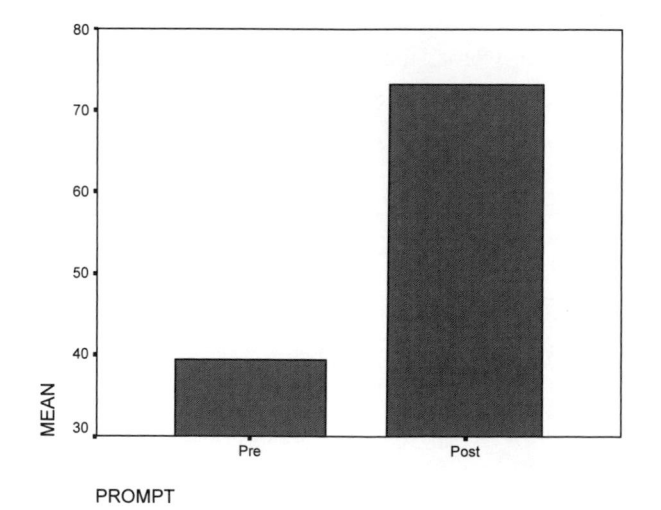

Figure 4.10: Writing Performance of the Class (2)

Table 4.50 shows the results of a paired-sample t-test on the prompt writing of the whole class. According to Table 4.50, $df = 7$ and $t = -8.052$. Compared with $t_{.01,(8-1)} = -2.998$ (critical value), it is obvious $-8.052 < -2.998$ ($t < CV$). Since this is a left single-tailed test, the null hypothesis (H_{01}: $\mu_{x1} \geq \mu_{x2}$) should be rejected. This means that students' post-prompt writing is significantly better than their pre-prompt writing ($p < .01$). In other words, the class as a whole increased its writing performance significantly.

4.3.2 Writing Attitudes of the Students

Table 4.51 shows the results of a paired-sample t-test on the writing self-efficacy of the whole class. According to Table 4.51, $df = 7$ and $t = -5.451$. Compared with $t_{.01,(8-1)} = -2.998$ (critical value), it is obvious $-5.451 < -2.998$ ($t < CV$). Since this is a left single-tailed test, the null hypothesis (H_{02}: $\mu_{x1} \geq \mu_{x2}$) should be rejected. This means that the mean of the students' post-class questionnaires is significantly better than the mean of their pre-class questionnaires ($p < .01$). In other words, the class as a whole increased its writing confidence significantly.

Table 4.51: Results of a Paired-sample T-test on Writing Self-efficacy

Source	Paired Differences			t-value	df	Sig. (2-tailed)
	Mean	SD	SE of Mean			
Pre−Post	-38.63	20.04	7.09	-5.451	7	.001

** $p < .01$, N = 8, 95% CI (-55.38, -21.87)   Note: $\alpha = .01$, one-tailed directional decision

H_{02}: There is no significant increase in students' writing confidence after they had engaged in the learning of theme cycles. (H_{02}: $\mu_{x1} \geq \mu_{x2}$)

H_{A2}: There is significant increase in students' writing confidence after they had engaged in the learning of theme cycles. (H_{A2}: $\mu_{x1} < \mu_{x2}$)

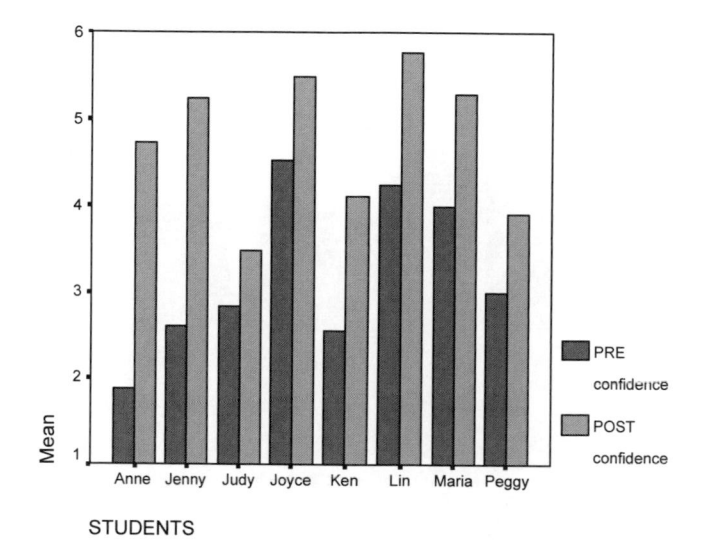

Figure 4.11: Results of Writing Self-efficacy of the Class (1)

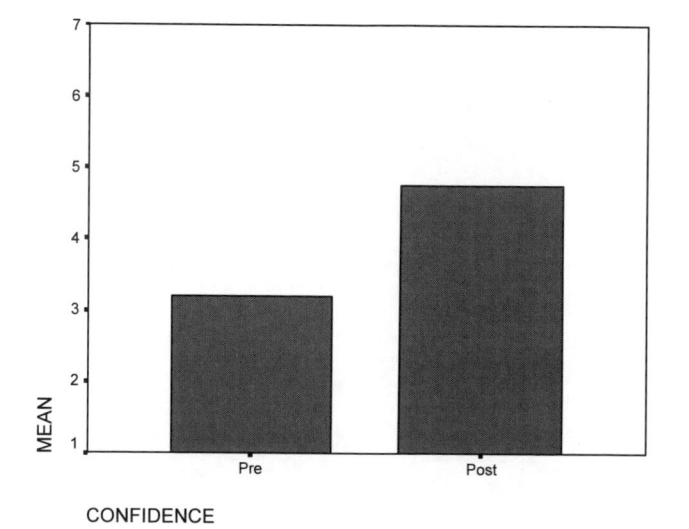

Figure 4.12: Results of Writing Self-efficacy of the Class (2)

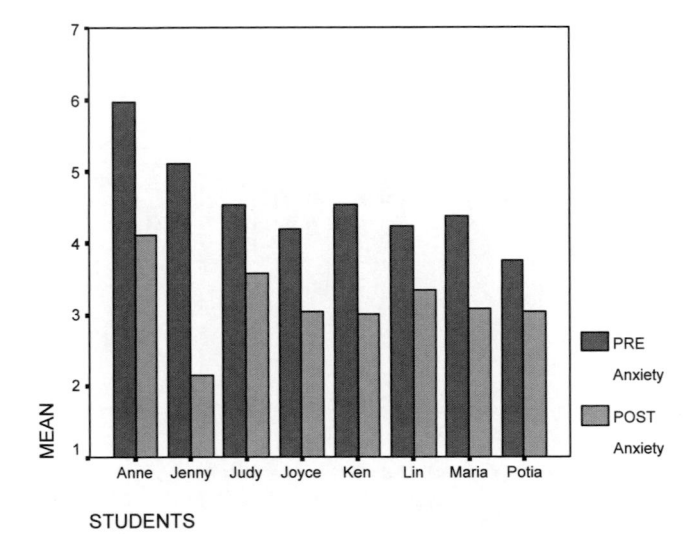

Figure 4.13: Writing Apprehension of the Class (1)

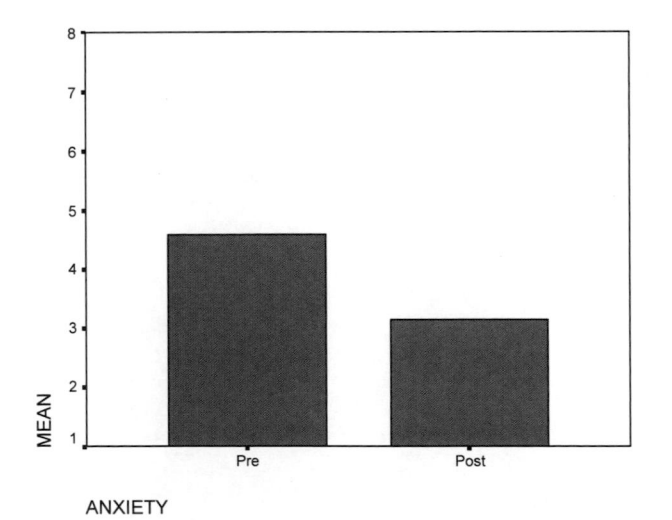

Figure 4.14: Writing Apprehension of the Class (2)

Table 4.52: Results of a Paired-sample T-test on Writing Apprehension

Source	Paired Differences			t-value	df	Sig. (2-tailed)
	Mean	SD	SE of Mean			
Pre — Post	37.00	18.72	6.62	5.592	7	.001

** p<.01, N = 8, 95% CI (21.35, 52.65)   Note: α = .01, one-tailed directional decision

H_{03}: There is no significant decrease in students' writing anxiety after they had engaged in the learning of theme cycles.   (H_{03}: $\mu_{x1} \leq \mu_{x2}$)
H_{A3}: There is significant decrease in students' writing anxiety after they had engaged in the learning of theme cycles.   (H_{A3}: $\mu_{x1} > \mu_{x2}$)

Table 4.52 shows the results of a paired-sample t-test on the writing apprehension of the whole class.   According to Table 4.52, $df = 7$ and t = 5.592.   Compared with $t_{.01,(8-1)} = 2.998$ (critical value), it is obvious $5.592 > 2.998$ (t>CV).   Since this is a right single-tailed test, the null hypothesis (H_{03}: $\mu_{x1} \leq \mu_{x2}$) should be rejected.   This means that the mean of the students' post-class questionnaires is significantly lower than the mean of their pre-class questionnaires (p<.01).   In other words, the class as a whole decreased its writing anxiety significantly.

4.3.3 Personal Growth and Empowerment

Table 4.53 shows all aspects of the results of the students' portfolios.   In terms of quality of work, one student had a Superior score, two were at the G-S level, and five were at the Good level.   Regarding their creativity and originality, three students were rated Superior, one fell into the G-S category, and 4 scored Good.   Five students were given a Superior score for effort in their learning, one was considered G-S, and two were rated as Good.   As far as growth was concerned, six students presented Superior growth and two showed a score of G-S.   Generally speaking, 2 out of 8 students showed Superior growth, 5 showed G-S growth, and one showed Good growth.

Table 4.53: Results of Portfolio Evaluation of the Class

Scale Category	Superior (10-9)	Superior – Good (9-8)	Good (8-7)
Quality of Work	Lin (9.5)	Jenny (8.5), Peggy (8.5)	Judy (8), Joyce (8), Maria (7.5), Ken (7.5), Anne (8)
Creativity/ Originality	Lin (9), Judy (9), Peggy (9)	Jenny (8.5)	Joyce (8), Maria (8), Ken (8), Anne (7.5)
Evidence of Efforts	Lin (9.5), Jenny (10), Judy (9), Joyce (9), Maria (9)	Peggy (8.5)	Ken (8), Anne (7.5)
Evidence of Growth	Lin (10), Jenny (9.5), Judy (9), Joyce (9.5), Maria (9), Ken (9)	Peggy (8.5), Anne (8.5)	
Total	Lin (38), Jenny (36.5)	Judy (35), Joyce (34.5), Peggy (34.5), Maria (33.5), Ken (32.5)	Anne (31.5)

DISCUSSION AND ANALYSIS
OF THE DATA

The discussion in this chapter will focus on individual students. The change in each student's writing performance, writing attitude and personal growth and empowerment will be discussed in the form of case studies. This will be analyzed using a variety of evidence to confirm the results and establish trustworthiness[1].

5.1 Analysis of Writing Performance

In discussing writing performance, the students' prompt writing was used as the main evidence, with other essays used as confirmation of the findings. Prompt writing was done in class during a limited time period and did not require any revision. The changes made in prompt writing, therefore, reveal improvement in idea generation and initial organization after the students had engaged in theme cycles learning. However, the students' potential in content development and organization/language revision is more clearly presented through essay writing. Accordingly, the students' multi-draft essays will also be used in dis-

---

[1] According to Lincoln and Guba (1985), the qualitative definition of trustworthiness is related to "credibility," "transferability," "dependability," and "confirmability." They are the naturalist's equivalents for the conventional terms "internal validity," "external validity," "reliability," and "objectivity" (pp. 300-328).

cussing the changes in their writing performance, in the hope of providing triangulation analysis.

These changes that came about in the students' writing are discussed and are based on the evaluation criteria of Voice, Content, Organization, and Language.

In this section, the discussion of the students' writing performance is based on the improvements shown in their total scores for prompt writing. The changes shown in prompt writing have been categorized into 3 groups: (1) Weak to Good, (2) Average to Good, and (3) Weak to Average. By so doing, the general progress of the students' writing performance is easily tracked.

5.1.1 Writing Performance from Weak to Good

According to the total scores of the students' prompt writing, 3 students improved in their writing from a Weak level to a Good level. These three students were Jenny, Judy, and Ken.

The following sections will discuss in detail the writing performances of Jenny and Judy. The discussion of Ken's writing performance is shown in Appendix K.

5.1.1.1 Jenny's Writing Performance

The scores of Jenny's prompt writing show that her performance improved from the level of W to G. The most obvious changes showed in her use of language.

Prompt Writing—All Aspects

Pre-prompt writing. In her pre-prompt writing (Ex. 1), it was obvious that Jenny was not mastering English vocabulary, sentence structure or writing conventions. Her articles had no title, no indention (s1, s3 and s4), wrong spacing between words, wrong punctuation (s3, s6) and incomplete sentences (s2, s5). Content was limited and her ideas were neither clearly presented nor fully developed.

Ex. 1 Jenny's Pre-prompt Writing

(1) I think to learn english is an very important things.   (2) So it it right to learn english as early as possible.

(3) I think it it good for children to learn english early , because they can learn it more quickly than adults.

(4) Now the age of children learning english is becoming low. (5) If government don't decide that children can learn english early.   (6) The parent would take children to learn english out of school .

Ex. 2 Jenny's Post-prompt Writing

(0) Teaching English in elementary school

(1) In mordern socity, education is becoming importantly. (2) And what we should teach our children in elementary school is discussed regularly and openly.   (3) Is it right to teaching English in elementary school?   (4) I think we should have our children to learn English in elementary school, because English is so prevalence in our socity.

(5) I have a 2-year-old daughter.   (6) Now she knows a few letters of English.   (7) I think she is very interesting in these letters, so she can find a lot of English letters in her life. (8) For example, she found lots of A. B. C in her pencils, clothes, shoes, cups, books etc.   (9) Everytime she found them, she would say "Mom, there is A. B. C", and I finally found there are so many A. B. C in our life.   (10) I think English is so prevalence in our life, so it it right to let our children to learn and to know them as early as possible.   (11) And they can fig-ure out what's the English words in their pencils, clothes and so on.   (12) There is no reason to prevent our children to know the words in their life earlier.

(13) The improvements of our society is becoming quickly, so I think it's right to let our children to contact the international languages.   (14) I think when they know what the international people said, they could improve themselve and follow up the steps of society easily.

Post-prompt writing. However, she did show progress in her post-prompt writing (Ex. 2). The post-prompt writing had a proper title (s0) and used indentation to indicate a new paragraph (s1, s5, s13). Though there were still spelling mistakes (*socity, themselves*) and incorrect parts of speech (*importantly, prevalence, interesting*), the number of incomplete sentences and misuse of punctuation was greatly reduced. Her thesis statement was correct (s4). Her ideas were adequately presented and developed with supporting examples and explanations (s8-11). Her conclusion reflected the introduction and restated her position on the subject (s13-14).

Essay Writing—Organization and Content

Jenny's essay writing gave more details of her progress. Her earlier drafts did not have a clear thesis statement or good development, but her later drafts usually provided clear explanations and examples to support the theme. In contrast to the rigid format shown in her early essays, her later essays conveyed her lively ideas by utilizing physical descriptions and narration.

Thesis statement, topic sentence, idea development. In her essay 1-1 "The Urban Mass Transportation—Light Rail Transit" (Es-Je-1), she wrote three paragraphs—the introduction, the body of the article, and the conclusion—to conform to the standard composition format. However, without the thesis statement, the introductory paragraph failed to adequately set up the whole article. The content in the middle paragraph showed that Jenny was knowledgeable about the topic, but her use of terminology without adequate explanation confused the reader, so the information she provided was not useful (Ex. 3). For example, there was no explanation for such terms as *exclusive R/W*, *separate R/W*, or *joint R/W* or for the relationship between LRT and these systems.

In essay 1-3, she did not make successful revisions to her thesis statement, but she developed her ideas with adequate explanations and clear examples in the body of the essay. She explained what *R/W* referred to (Ex. 4, s9-10) as well as expanding on the meaning and function of *exclusive R/W*, *separate R/W*, and *joint R/W* (Ex. 4, s11-18). Also, she provided examples, like *rapid transit system* and *conventional rail system*

(Ex. 4, s13, s16), to help the reader form a visual image of these systems and have a better understanding of the information. This revision not only confirmed her knowledge on this topic but also showed awareness of her audience. With the help of these detailed explanations, she conveyed the meaning of her writing successfully.

The difficulty in making a proper thesis statement was overcome when she composed the 2nd essay "What's a Good Composition?" (Es-Je-3/4). She wrote a clear thesis statement in essay 2-1 "… a good composition should include some characteristics such as paragraph unity, good structure, correct grammar and good words" (Ex. 5, s4). In essay 2-3, it was changed to "A good composition, …, should include some characteristics such as unity, good organization, correct grammar and good word choices" (Ex. 6, s6). This thesis statement successfully introduced the main ideas that would be discussed in the article. Besides the revision on the thesis statement, the introductory paragraph in essay 2-3 started with a discussion on the definition of good composition (Ex. 6, 3-4), in which Jenny's own opinions were offered (Ex. 6, s5-6). This way of mentioning other people's opinions first and then sharing her own thinking made the discussion natural and objective.

Ex. 3 The 2nd Paragraph of Jenny's Essay 1-1

> (4) There are many differences between LRT and conventional rail system or high-volume rapid transit system. (5) First, the coaches weight of LRT on the rail is relatively lower (so we called it "Light Rail"), and the impact of LRT to the environment is relatively smaller. (6) Second, the "right of way "(R/W) of them is difference. (7) Conventional rail system and rapid transit system are provided with exclusive R/W. (8) The LRT doesn't have exactly exclusive R/W, it is designed to suit varying situations with exclusive R/W, separate R/W and joint R/W, so its speed is more slowly than conventional rail system and rapid transit system. (9) Third , the construction time of LRT is more shorter, and the construction cost is relatively lower.

Ex. 4 The 2nd Paragraph of Jenny's Essay 1-3

(6) There are many differences between LRT and conventional rail system or rapid transit system. (7) First, the coaches weight of LRT on the rail is relatively lower (so we called it "Light Rail"), so the impact to the environment is relatively smaller. (8) Second, the "right of way "(R/W) is different. (9) R/W means the right (or priority) of using route. (10) R/W includes 3 categories: exclusive R/W (type A), separate R/W (type B) and joint R/W (type C). (11) Type A represents a monopolistic right of road. (12) It usually takes the form of overpass or underpass. (13) The rapid transit system is provided with exclusive R/W, for example. (14) Type B represents a semi-monopolistic right of road. (15) We usually use level crossing (railway crossing) to separate the other traffic. (16) For instance, conventional rail system is provided with separate R/W. (17) Type C represents non-monopolistic right of road. (18) We use traffic light to order the movement of different traffic. (19) LRT doesn't have exactly exclusive R/W. (20) It is designed to suit varying situations with exclusive R/W, separate R/W and joint R/W, so its speed is more slowly than conventional rail system and rapid transit system. (21) Third, the construction time of LRT is shorter, and the construction cost is relatively lower.

Ex. 5 The 1st paragraph of Jenny's Essay 2-1

(1) All of us have the experience of reading a composition. (2) However, what is a good composition? (3) I think a good composition is a piece of writing that is clear and vivid. (4) In other words, a good composition should include some characteristics such as paragraph unity, good structure, correct grammar and good words.

Ex. 6 The 1st paragraph of Jenny's Essay 2-3

(1) All of us have the experience of reading a composition. (2) However, what is a good composition? (3) Someone defines a good composition as an article that is creative, but someone takes it for granted that a formed article is a good one. (4) It is not easy to say which is more important in a good composition. (5) But I think a good composition is a piece of writing that is clear and vivid, and a formed article is usually clearer and more vivid. (6) A good composition, in other words, should include some characteristics such as unity, good organization, correct grammar and good word choices.

In addition, Jenny's use of topic sentences in each paragraph in the body of the article (Es-Je-4, s7, 11, 17, 20) was correct as they matched and explored the main ideas. The conclusion was short, only three sentences, but kept to the point (Es-Je-4, s25-27).

Descriptive and narrative expression. Jenny's progress was not limited to making a proper thesis statement, topic sentences, or idea development. She also demonstrated her ability to write physical description and narration.

In her 3rd essay "Try and Try Again" (Es-Je-5/6), she wrote about the influence that a professor had had on her. Instead of presenting this article in a moral teaching style, she made it more like story telling. She started the "story" with

I think I am an introvert, and I am not used to express my feeling in the public. Because of that, my teachers and classmates can't easily figure out the frame of mind. But Mr. Chang, one of my favorite professors, can understand what I feel, and would give me advice in the proper time (Es-Je-5-1).

Mr. Chang is a small man. He talks low and looks like a cold and detached guy. Due to his characteristic, I was strange to him initially. In fact, Mr. Chang is a friendly person, and his words usually encouraged people around him. I didn't realize it until the year I was going to graduate (Es-Je-6-2).

Like a story teller, Jenny built her story with a descriptive introduction. Besides giving us background information about Jenny's personality and telling us of the considerate Professor Chang and the help he offered Jenny, this introduction also revealed Jenny's deep gratitude towards Professor Chang. In order to pave the way for conflict and climax, she delayed the main plot of her story. Instead, she wrote more on Mr. Chang's appearance and personality. Her description of him as *a small man*, *talks low*, *cold and detached* (Es-Je-6, s5) seemed to contradict the depiction of him as *friendly* and *encouraged people* (Es-Je-6, s7). However, because of this contradiction, Jenny successfully created a climax, which carried us to the conclusion (Ex. 7).

Ex. 7 The 3rd paragraph of Jenny's Essay 3-3

> (9) At the end of my college year, I took a government examination. (10) After a far-reaching waiting, I was noticed that I was flunk. (11) I was disheartened and in low spirits due to that bad news. (12) One day when I went to the college department, I met Mr. Chang. (13) He talked to me on his initiative. (14) After the chatting of life, he told me a story about a successful man. (15) The successful man usually was asked how to achieve success, and he said the principal to achieve success is two words – right decisions. (16) Then, he was asked how to make right decisions, and he said the key point is just one word – experience. (17) Someone was curious and asked him how to get experience, and the man said "It's easy, just two words – wrong decisions." (18) Mr. Chang told me failure wasn't bad, because it was a good way to find the right way, so "Try and try again, and you can get what you want," he said. (19) I was encouraged and moved by his words, and "Try and Try again" has become my motto since that time. (20) Sometimes when I felt regret and wanted to give up something, I would remember Mr. Chang's words, and usually I would do my best to try once more. (21) I got a lot from these words.

Ex. 7 The Last Paragraph of Jenny's Essay 3-3

(22) Because of the excuse of busyness, I felt that motto is far away from me. (23) Recently when I read the story of Morrie and Mitch, I remembered Mr. Chang and his words. (24) I think I will keep those in mind again, and I would share it with others when I have opportunities.

This anecdote served as evidence of Mr. Chang's helpfulness and clarified the conflict caused by his inharmonious cold appearance on the one hand and his considerate disposition on the other. It also showed that Jenny understood and was capable of presenting plots according to a time sequence. By using time signal phrases *At the end of my college year* (Ex. 7, s9), *After a far-reaching waiting* (Ex. 7, s10), *One day ... I met Mr. Chang* (Ex. 7, s12), *After the chatting of life* (Ex. 7, s14), and a sentence with present perfect tense *has become ... since that time* (Ex. 7, s19), she developed the story event chronologically, which, in turn, promoted the readability of her story. Her mastery of narration was further illustrated when she told the story of a successful man within her own story. The complex construction of the story did not bother her; instead, she smoothly integrated a mini story into the main text (Ex. 7, s15-17). Without hardly any transition, she started the inserted story right after the statement "... he (Mr. Chang) told me a story about a successful man" (Ex. 7, s14). Also, followed directly by the saying "Mr. Chang told me failure wasn't bad, ..." (Ex. 7, s18), the story returned to the interaction between Jenny and Mr. Chang. It seemed that we, the readers, were actually listening along with Jenny to Mr. Chang's story telling. The ending of the story was brief and reconfirmed her determination to stick to her motto: try and try again (Es-Je-6, s22-24).

Essay Writing—Language

The most obvious improvement in Jenny's prompt writing was in language use, where her scores improved from the level of VP to the level of G. Similar progress was also noted in her essay writing, where her language scores improved from level A to level VG. Her awareness of language usage, such as word form, sentence structure, and spelling increased throughout the year. Her progress was beyond single word corrections and achieved clarification of meaning. She also demonstrated mastery in the use of direct and indirect statements.

Sentence structure. In Essay 1-1, she mistook *difference* for *different* (Ex. 3, s6) and misused *more shorter* for *shorter*. The sentence "... LRT *is become* famous ..." (Es-Je-1, s10) had wrong structure in the present perfect tense, and "... Government is *planing* to ..." (Es-Je-1, s11) contained wrong spelling. With revision, in essay 1-3, these errors were corrected. In the 2nd essay, she continued to show her ability in language revision. In Essay 2-1, s16 "The reader would misunderstand or confuse if the writer use incorrect tense or incorrect subject," there were errors in sentence structure (*would ... confuse*) and the problem of subject-verb agreement (*the writer use* ...). By utilizing the *verb be* and adjective *confused* and by changing *use* into *using*, she revised the sentence into "The reader would misunderstand or be confused when the writer using incorrect tense or subject" (Es-Je-4, s19). Also, in Essay 2-1, s19, she mistook the 3rd person singular *likes* for the preposition *like* in "We can use a different sentence structure likes participial phrase to develop the paragraph" and in Essay 2-3, she revised the sentence into "... we can use different sentence structures to develop the paragraph such as participial phrase" (s22) with another preposition phrase *such as*.

Word choice. Jenny's language progress was beyond the need for only single word correction. In the 2nd essay "What's a Good Composition," for example, when she mentioned the importance of unity, she first wrote "it makes the composition friendly and easier to be read" (Es-Je-3, s7) but then she changed it into "It makes the composition clearly and easily to be read" (Es-Je-6, s9). She not only revised *easier* into *easily* but also substituted *clearly* for *friendly* so as to precisely explain the influence of unity on composition. Also, in the same essay, she replaced *structure* (Es-Je-3, s9) with *organization* (Es-Je-6, s11) and rewrote the whole sentence from "...the structure of an article determines the quality of composition" (Es-Je-3, s9) to "... the organization of an article is an another factor that influences the quality of a composition" (Es-Je-4, s11). Rather than claim organization as a determinant, in the revised draft, she regarded it as one of the factors influencing the quality of a composition. By so doing, she both balanced the four components—unity, organization, grammar, and word choice—mentioned in her article and solved the contradiction caused by the two statements in Essay 2-1: "Paragraph unity is the most important component that a good composition should include" (s5) and "... the structure of an article determined the quality of composition" (s9). The term *the most important* and the word *determined* had common connotations but referred to different components, which caused ambiguity. Her effective word choice also appeared in the last paragraph of the 2nd essay. In Essay 2-1, when she concluded the definition of a good composition, she wrote "It can transmit the writer's main idea, opinions and feelings successfully" (s23). The word *transmit* was changed into *convey ... to ...* in Essay 2-3, "I can convey the writer's main ideas, opinions, and feelings to readers successful" (s26). The recognition of the nuance of the words was revealed in this change and her transactional view of writing was illustrated.

The importance of revision for meaning clarification was becoming obvious when she composed the 3rd and the 4th essays. In the 3rd essay, while describing Mr. Chang's personality, she first wrote "Due to his characteristic, he didn't famous in our campus. In fact, Mr. Chang is such a friendly person that everyone can make friends with him" (Es-Je-5, s5-6) but then changed it into "Due to his characteristic, I was strange to him initially. In fact, Mr. Chang is a friendly person, and his words usually encouraged people around him" (Es-Je-6, s6-7). *I was strange to him initially* rather than *he didn't famous in our campus* helped focus the description on the relationship between herself and Mr. Chang. *His words usually encouraged people around him* instead of *everyone can make friends with him* spoke more for Mr. Chang's inspiring character, which was supposed to be the main focus in this article. The efforts made to clarify meaning also appeared in the 4th essay "My Feeling Toward to Rote Learning and Active Learning" (Es-Je-7/8). In Essay 4-1, the 2nd paragraph, she discussed the first difference between these two learning styles.

She considered *the speed of getting answer* (Ex. 8, s4) as the first difference, and she argued that the teacher's instruction style was the reason (Ex. 8, s5-6). Because the instruction was based on the assumption that the process of learning is not important, students therefore learned by recitation and memorization (Ex. 8, s7-8). However, getting rid of *the speed of getting answer* as a criterion, she chose a more academic description *learning process* instead (Ex. 9, s4). Rather than consider the teacher's instruction style as the reason, she viewed these differences from the learners' viewpoint (Ex. 9, s5-9), which closely matched the title. This revision presented proper word choice, coherence, and the clarity of meaning.

Ex. 8 The 2nd Paragraph of Jenny's Essay 4-1

(4) The first difference between the two is the speed of getting answer. (5) In rote learning, teachers show answers to learners directly. (6) They teach class on the assumption that the processes of getting answers are not important. (7) So the learners know the answers very quickly, and the most important thing for them is to recite and memorize the answers. (8) Unlike rote learning, it gets answers so quick, active learning would take learners much time to find out the result. (9) For the active learners, the most important thing is to figure out the causes and effects and learn from it.

Ex. 9 The 2nd Paragraph of Jenny's Essay 4-3

(4) The first difference between the two is the learning process. (5) In rote learning, the learners get answers directly. (6) And the most important thing for them is to recite and memorize the answers. (7) They learned on the assumption that the processes of getting answers are not important. (8) Unlike rote learning, which gets answers so quick, active learning would take learners a lot of time to find out the result. (9) For active learners, the most important thing is to figure out the causes and effects of the problems and get answers from them. (10) Thus, the learning process of active learning is more complicated than rote learning.

Direct and indirect statement. In addition to the awareness of word choice, structure and meaning clarification, Jenny demonstrated her mastery in both direct and indirect statements. In Essay 3-3 "Try and Try Again," direct quotes and indirect quotes were successfully incorporated. In s17-18, for example,

> ... the man said "It's easy, just two words – wrong decisions." Mr. Chang told me failure wasn't bad, because it was a good way to find the right way, so "Try and try again, and you can get what you want," he said (Es-Je-6, s17-18).

She skillfully orchestrated three different ways of expressing essentially the same thing, for example, *the man said, "..."* (s17), *Mr. Chang told me ...* (s18), and *"...," he said* (s18). With proper punctuation—commas and quotation marks, she made the piece lively and vivid.

Essay Writing—Voice

Her writing voice benefited from this lively and vivid expression. Though voice is not always evident in language, Jenny's essays expressed the interweaving between language and voice and even with content and organization. Her voice was evident in almost all of her writing pieces.

In Essay 2-3, her voice was "heard" while arguing the definition of a good composition, "... I think a good composition is a piece of writing that is clear and vivid, and a formed article is usually clear and more vivid" (s5). In the 3rd essay "Try and Try Again," the whole article was full of her identity and personality. The story was presented with her authentic voice. The most noticeable example of her real voice was the 4th paragraph of her essay 4-3. While explaining the most important difference between rote learning and active learning, she composed the article as follows:

> The most important difference between rote learning and active learning is the lasting of memory. For me, it is easy to recite something, but it's easy to forget it too. For example, when I was in high school, I had to recite a lot of descriptions of history,

geography, the Three People's Principles and so on, but I can barely remember those descriptions now. In contrast, I can remember some phenomenons that I learned actively. For example, I still remember the phenomenon of specific gravity. I learned it from an experiment. When an equal weight of gold and silver are separately put into a full-water container, the overflows would not be equal. The reason is the specific gravity of gold is different from silver. It's very interesting. And I can't forget that I was eager to do some experiments like that. After school, I ran home immediately, went to the bathroom, filled the bathtub, and jumped into it. When I study the quantity of the overflow, I felt as if I were a scientist. I got a deep impression from active learning. (Es-Je-8-4)

Taking her experiences as an example, she not only delivered the explanation with vivid and lively language but also presented her real voice with uniqueness and resonance (Elbow, 1998b).

5.1.1.2 Judy's Writing Performance

According to her scores in prompt writing, Judy improved in all aspects from the level of W to the level of G.

Prompt Writing—All Aspects

Pre-prompt writing. Her pre-prompt writing (Ex. 10) had twelve sentences, full of wrong word choices (s2, s4), incorrect sentence structures (s1, s2), fragments (s2, s7), spelling errors (s9, s12), incorrect punctuation (s2, s3, s11), unclear messages (s5, s8, s10), and clichés (s12). The only correct sentence was "English is very popular in the world" (s6). The ideas were confusing and disconnected, and the development was neither logical nor adequate.

Post-prompt writing. Her post-prompt writing (Ex. 11) contained five paragraphs: one for the introduction, three paragraphs in the body of the work, and one for the conclusion. The introductory paragraph stated the advantages of mastering English and led the discussion to the reasons for starting English education in elementary school (s1-5).

In body paragraphs, she used enumeration to present her opinions. The three reasons supporting her agreement were children's memory (s6), habit formation (s10), and her wish for her child (s14). She gave some detail and explanation to help develop the content. The conclusion reconfirmed her support for this policy and suggested that the teachers, the reading materials and way of learning should be well designed in order to reach the goal (s16-17). Generally speaking, her post-prompt writing presented adequate content development and organization. Though there were still many language problems (s2, s3, s4, s6, s7, s9, s14, s16, s17), the meaning was not obscured and her voice (s12, s13, s17) was clearly heard.

Essay Writing—Organization and Content

Judy's writing progress in all aspects (content, organization, language, and voice) was not rapid or dramatic. Her understanding of content development, coherent organization, English conventions, and authentic voice was eventually revealed in a gradual improvement. Although, throughout the year of learning, she continued to use incorrect structure, improper words, incomplete ideas and illogical argument once in a while, her eagerness to present her ideas definitely increased the quantity of her writing.

Ex. 10 Judy's Pre-prompt Writing

(1) I agree this policy very much. (2) Because I ever heard the professionist said " The more learning English early the more depending English as mother-language easily".

(3) My English is very poor , so I don't hope my child is like me. (4) Maybe early learning is good ideal. (5) This is an international world. (6) English is very popular in the world. (7) If we want to promote ourselves and compete with other countries. (8) It's useless that English is too poor. (9) Basicly, you can't connect with othe people well. (10) How do you express your thinking and doing?

(11) For our country , learning English easily is absolutely a right policy. (12) Thrust me, we all can make it.

Ex. 11 Judy's Post-prompt Writing

(1) This is an international world. (2) You must communicate with other countries people, so it is very important to have the strong language ability. (3) English is thought a global language. (4) If we have good English ability, we will have superior competitive. (5) Thus I agree that learning English is necessary from elemantary school education.

(6) There are some reasons support my oppinion. (7) The first , children's memory are better than adults'. (8) They can remember the all accurate useages of English and have deep impression in their mind. (9) They also are easy to catch the right prounciation and speak naturally like their mother language.

(10) The second, even though children have mistakes in English usages, it is easy to correct them. (11) Their acceptance are higher than adult's. (12) I think it is easy to teach children than adult. (13) Perhaps from economic efficiency, it is more efficient to invest in children's than adult's

(14) The finally, because my English is very poor, I hope my child is better than mine. (15) If he can learn English from elementary school, I believe his English ability will be stronger than mine.

(16) To sum up, I support the policy that learning English should begin in elematory school. (17) However the teachers, the books and the learning ways and so on should be designed well, the effect of learning will appear out.

Idea development. In Essay 1-1 "The Impact of 'Let Go of Stress'" (Ex. 12), she discussed two kinds of stress—job stress and home stress—in two separate body paragraphs, but in Essay 1-3 (Ex. 13), she further developed each of these paragraphs into two paragraphs. That is, she stated the possible causes of job stress in one paragraph and then discussed a possible solution for reducing the stress in another paragraph. The same pattern was applied in the discussion on home stress. This change allowed her to add more detail to her statements and to focus on only one idea at a time. The details she added in the 2nd paragraph of Essay 1-3 were an example of this. After pointing out the two kinds of people who would probably have job stress, she further described the characteristics of these people by saying "They always keep nervous status, and fear that all things will be terrible. After a long time, they may get some disease, particularly in psychology" (Ex. 12, s9-10).

Ex. 12 The 2nd and 3rd paragraphs of Judy's Essay 1-1

(5) Job stress is so common, and is listed as a top health threat. (6) In my opinion, two kinds of people are easily to get job stress. (7) The first one who requests every step perfect for doing anything, something nit-picking. (8) The second one who is a wimp that can not reject anything from his boss. (9) For these people, the only way to release their stress is to change their thought. (10) Let them accept some unimportant defects or say "No" boldly, and don't depend the job on his life. (11) If people only work everyday and cannot find more interesting things around them, it would be sad. (12) After all, Life is short, we shouldn't waste our life in a single way.

(13) Home stress is another style, especially for working women. (14) They must deal with many things in the job and housekeeping. (15) So, they combine home and work stress due to their dual roles. (16) Their behavior is usually very terrible when they face the overloading stress. (17) Maybe they would hurt themselves or others. (18) The working women more need to learn how to release stress. (19) It's no way, just learn to "put down" that Buddha said. (20) Don't care anything that you feel unsatisfied and relax your nervousness. (21) You can search for some happy things to do and transfer stress to others, for example, enjoy a romantic tea time with your good friends, go shopping, do exercise and so on. (22) Remember it, don't put the big stressful women along. That's my opinion and my ways to release the stress of the working women.

Making expression concise. In addition to adding more details, Judy also shortened sentences to make expression concise. Like in the 1st paragraph of Essay 1-1, she wrote

> … Although everybody's stress is not the same extent, some people can tolerate the high level stress, some people just can tolerate the low level stress, anyway, for our health all the stress must be released through many kinds of methods (Essay 1-1, s4).

In Essay 1-3, she cut down the redundant expression *some people can tolerate the high level stress, some people just can tolerate the low level stress, anyway, for our health…* and revised the sentence into a more succinct one

> … Although everyone has different stress extent, all the stress must be released through the various methods (Es-Ju-2, s4).

Also, in Essay 1-1, while suggesting that working women should learn how to release stress, she stated "It's no way, just learn to 'put down' that Buddha said" (Ex. 12, s19), but in Essay 1-3, she completely deleted this sentence and made the suggestion directly in a better way as not to "care anything that you feel unsatisfied and relax your nervousness" (Ex. 13, s21). In the end of the same paragraph of Essay 1-1, she wrote "Remember it, don't put the big stressful women along" (Ex. 12, s22) but deleted it in Essay 1-3 because of its unclear meaning. The application of either additions or deletions to clarify what she meant showed Judy's skill in the presentation of her ideas.

Making use of examples. One of the features of Judy's writing was her preference for giving examples. In her prompt writing, she wrote "My English is very poor , so I don't hope my child is like me" (Ex. 10, s3). In her 1st essay, she stated "I am a working woman too. Those are my ways of releasing the stress" (Ex. 13, s23-24). In her 2nd essay "What is 'Happiness'" (Es-Ju-5/6), she again used an example. To support the thesis statement "No matter what you define this word (happiness); it may be up to your feeling" (Es-Ju-3, s3), she used a woman's reaction as an example:

Ex. 13 The 2nd, 3rd, 4th, and 5th paragraphs of Judy's Essay 1-3

Job stress is so common and listed as a top health threat, so it needs more time to overcome such a stress. In my opinion, two kinds of people are easily to get job stress. The first kind of people request that every step be perfect in doing anything, something nit-picking. The second ones are like wimps who cannot reject anything from their bosses. They always keep nervous status, and fear that all things will be terrible. After a long time, they may get some diseases, particularly in psychology.

For these people, the only way to release their stress is to change their thought. They need accept some unimportant defects or say "No" boldly and don't think that the job means their life. If people only work everyday and cannot find more interesting things around them, it would be sad. After all, life is short, we shouldn't waste our life in a single lifestyle.

Home stress is another style, especially for working women, but it seems easier to remove. Working women must deal with many things about the job and housekeeping. Thus, they combine home and work stress due to their dual roles. Their behavior is usually very terrible when they face the overloading stress. Maybe they would hurt themselves or others.

The working women need to learn how to release stress very much. It is better way to not care anything that you feel unsatisfied and relax your nervousness especially in home stress. You can search for some happy things to do and transfer stress to others for example, enjoy a romantic tea time with your good friends, go shopping, do exercise and so on. I am a working woman too. Those are my ways of releasing the stress.

… I know a woman who looks a little fat because of her overeating of fried chickens. I ever asked her, " Do you mind somebody's opinion for you ? " She firmly said "No" and told me that she didn't care about anyone's thinking. It is her greatest happiness to eat various delicious foods. I admire her courage, because she can ignore the general opinions of people. The more important, eating is easy to be satisfied; that means the happiness is not difficult to get (Es-Ju-4, s8-13).

In the following paragraph of the same essay, she re-emphasized this argument with another woman's story:

> ... there is a woman who makes friends with a married man. She told me that she just felt happy when she gets together with the man and she said their relationship belonged to the spiritual satisfaction. She didn't want to destroy his marriage or marry him in the future. She just pursued the happy feeling. What a special thinking is ! If we don't argue her behaviors, happiness seems not difficult to be defined (Es-Ju-4, s14-19).

In the 3rd essay "How to Avoid Being an Emotional Person" (Es-Ju-5/6), she continually used examples as supporting evidence. While talking about losing one's temper over a petty thing, she used herself as an example to give further illustration:

> ... I always fly into a rage for my son's toys not being cleaned up or his clothes being smudged and so on. In others' eyes, these are trivial things that are unworthy of caring. Perhaps, I should make a self-criticism and learn to control my temper (Es-Ju-6, s12-14).

The same strategy also appeared in the 4th essay "A Traveling with Tour vs. Self-help Trip" (Es-Ju-7/8). When she argued against the tight schedule planned by the travel agency, she backed up her opinion with examples:

> ... getting up early at 6:00 A.M., staying at a place for half an hour, having a meal for 20 minutes, going to a toilet for 10 minutes and so on. Like a military management, you cannot have more time to enjoy every scenic spot (Es-Ju-7, s9-10).

Also, when she investigated the travel contract in the last body paragraph, she took a well-known social event as an example to question the safety of traveling with a tour group:

> Did you remember the issue about Kang Ning travel agency ? The travel agency is generally acknowledged the biggest travel agency in Taiwan and is also a member of the Quality Assurance Association, but the manager still took all money of tourists away. From this issue, we must carefully choose the travel agency (Es-Ju-7, s23-25).

Essay Writing—Voice

Her preference for using examples benefited her writing in content, organization and voice. Because of the examples she used, she was able to develop her thesis fully and arrange the article in a logical order. Besides proving that she had knowledge of the issues, she revealed her strong personality by presenting unique opinions. Two examples of her strong voice can be seen in the above excerpts.

In Essay 2-3, after mentioning a woman's "spiritual satisfaction" in a love affair, Judy's voice comes through in her comments:

> However this situation has a question; that is, whether we can build our happiness on somebody's pain. If getting the happiness might hurt somebody else, we must doubt such happiness is not a real happiness (Es-Ju-4, s20-21).

In Essay 4-1, while describing a tour's tight schedule, she used "military management" as a vivid analogy and so this expression "Like a military management, you cannot have more time to enjoy every scenic spot" (Es-Ju-7, s10) aroused resonance.

Ex. 14 The Last Paragraph of Judy's Essay 1-3

... (28) Thus, you can choose your attitude to face the stress happily or unhappily. (29) If you keep the happy mind to face the stress, the stress would not be a stress. (30) To be modern people, we must accept the various stress bravely and use our wisdom to release it. (31) Stress is not really terrible. (32) The more important thing is the stress should become our energy.

Other evidence of Judy's authentic voice was obvious. In the last paragraph of Essay 1-3, she reconfirmed the importance of overcoming stress. She knew that, to many people, knowing was one thing but acting on it was another, so she emphasized an alternative view of stress with an encouraging tone. (Ex. 14).

In Essay 2-3, after discussing different definitions of happiness through various examples, she concluded the article with more short examples and strong statements (Ex. 15). The last examples, *To a vagrant, ...* (s25), *To a merchant, ...* (s26), *for me, ...* (s27) were presented with a repetitive technique and a parallel structure. This technique reinforced the thesis—that the definition of happiness is up to the individual and reflected the authenticity and intensity of her voice.

Ex. 15 The Last Paragraph of Judy's Essay 2-3

(22) To sum up, I think happiness means a harmless, personal feeling. (23) It can be defined as the fulfillment of a simple demand or more complicated satisfaction. (24) We cannot criticize anyone whose feeling is happy or not. (25) To a vagrant, it is happy for him to own a simple and crude place to sleep. (26) To a merchant, earning more money is happy. (27) However for me, when I am exhausted, going to bed is the greatest happiness. (28) It appears that your happy feeling depends on who you are or what situation you are at. (29) Anyway, the most important is that we should cherish our happy feeling and enjoy it.

Judy's real voice could also be heard in the 3rd essay when she explained the second reason for emotional behavior. She placed value on forgiveness and revealed her strong desire for a forgiving society (Ex. 16, s15-20). The question *"Why cannot we endure somebody's behaviors easily and forgive him or her?"* (s20) showed her candor and suggested a deep inquiry. Similarly, when she listed the third reason—complaints—that caused emotional behavior, she was again straightforward in revealing her thinking (Ex. 16, s21-27). The expression *...we are used to complaining* (s21) and *We seem to feel unsatisfied forever* (s22) prompted profound introspection. The statement *... when someone complains about something, his or her mood is impossible to be peaceful* (s25) reflected the truth and resonated with the audience.

Essay Writing—Language

In terms of language, Judy showed her progress in word choice, sentence structures, and punctuation. She also made progress by expressing herself more vividly.

Ex. 16 The 2nd paragraph of Judy's Essay 3-3

... (15) Second, we lack the heart of forgiveness. (16) If we could easily forgive the other people's unwitting mistakes, we won't put ourselves on emotional situation. (17) There are many cruel or harmful issues happened in our society, just because there is no forgiveness in people's mind. (18) Someone may be killed resulting from an incidental touch or look at another person. (19) How terrible it is ! (20) Why cannot we endure somebody's behaviors easily and forgive him or her ? (21) Third, we are used to complaining. (22) We seem to feel unsatisfied forever. (23) Complaining often happens every day for our work or life and so on. (24) We think complaining is nothing, but in fact, it really has affected our emotion. (25) You can observe the phenomenon when someone complains about something, his or her mood is impossible to be peaceful. (26) The voice or the look may express anger or depression. (27) It is enough to be identified that emotion is affected by complaining. ...

Sentence structure. In Essay 1-1, s4, she wrote independent sentences joined by commas, such as *some people can tolerate the high level stress, some people just can tolerate the low level stress* (s4), incorrect sentence structure like *Let them accept some unimportant defects or say "No" boldly, and don't depend the job on his life* (s10), misuse of comparatives in *The working women more need to learn how to release stress* (s18), and wrong parts of speech such as *... you can choose your attitude to face the stress, happy or unhappy* (s27). These errors were corrected in Essay 1-3. The comma-splice sentence was deleted to allow the meaning to flow more smoothly. The sentence with incorrect structure was changed to *They need accept some unimportant defects or say "No" boldly and don't think that the job means their life* (s12). By substituting *they* for *let them* and revising the phrasal verb *depend on* into a subordinate sentence *that* ..., she cleared up any confusion. She also changed the wrong-comparative sentence into *The working women need to learn how to release stress very much* (s20). Though the phrasal adverb *very much* was awkwardly put, she at least showed her recognition of the misuse of the word *more* in the first draft. She also rewrote the sentence with the wrong word-form so that it contained the correct word form: *...you can choose your attitude to face the stress happily or unhappily* (s28). This change showed that she was aware of different parts of speech.

Word choice and meaning clarification. Other evidence of Judy's awareness of language use was in the revision of the 2nd essay. She revised *...the most women* (Essay 2-1, s4) into *...most women* (s2-3, s4), and deleted the article *the* from the sentence *I think the happiness is ...* (Essay 2-1, s20) when she wrote Essay 2-3, s22. These changes showed her understanding of the use of the definite article *the*. Also, in the 2nd essay, she demonstrated her improvement in word choice. In Essay 2-1, she wrote *... I also care that somebody uses these words or other more severe phases to describe me* (s7). Though her intention was to use *phrases* instead of *phases*, she used none of them in Essay 2-3. Instead, she chose *idioms* for the revision (Essay 2-3, s7). In the same article, when she mentioned the love affair between a woman and a married man, she used the term *spiritual communication* (s15) in Es-

say 2-1 but chose *spiritual satisfaction* (s15) in Essay 2-3.   The connotation of *satisfaction* was closer to the meaning of happiness than that of
communication, which clearly depicted the woman's feelings.   Then,
when she commented on the love affair, she first wrote *If we don't debate her behavior,* ... (s19) in Essay 2-1 and revised it into *If we don't
argue her behaviors,* ... (s19).   Besides adding an inflectional mor-
pheme –s to the word *behavior* to form a plural, she changed the verb
debate into *argue.*   Since *debate* often suggests an indecisive answer,
while *argue* usually hints at a firm position, that she chose *argue* in the
statement paved the way for her following comments: *However* ... *If
getting the happiness might hurt somebody else, we must doubt such
happiness is not a real happiness* (Essay 2-3, s20-21).   At the end of
this article, while drawing conclusions for the definition of happiness,
she wrote in Essay 2-1 *So it depends on what your role or your timing is*
(s26) but she revised it into *It appears that your happy feeling depends
on who you are or what situation you are at* (Essay 2-3, s28).   To begin
the sentence with *It appears that* ... and to use indirect questions such as
depends on *who you are* ... and *what situation you are at*, she demonstrated her understanding and ability to utilize complex construction.   A
similar sentence pattern was also shown in the 4th essay when she discussed the time-saving advantage of planning a trip with a travel agency:
*it is no doubt that the former seems to save more of your time than the
latter* (Es-Ju-8, s7).   The use of a formal subject *it* plus a noun clause
that ... and the use of pronouns *the former* and *the latter* again proved
Judy's mastery of complex construction.

   Vivid expression.   Judy's language progress was more than error
correction, word choice, and sentence maturity.   The language she used
in the 3rd and 4th essay revealed evidence of vivid expression.   In Essay
3-3, when she described her anger toward her son, she wrote *I always fly
into a rage for my son's ... clothes being smudged ...* (s12).   The
phrasal verb *fly into a rage* seemed to carry the tremendous sound of her
shout, as the mother, and the word *smudged* formed a visual image of
her son's dirty clothes.   In Essay 4-3, when she mentioned the tour's
tight travel schedule, she wrote *Like a military management, you cannot
have more time to enjoy every scenic spot* (s10), and when she described

the situation of being deceived by travel agency, she emphasized help-lessness by saying *When you meet this situation, you are not able to express your discomfort, like a dumb person tasting bitter herbs* (s22). These two similes *like a military management* and *like a dumb person tasting bitter herbs* added colorful and lively expression to her work. The use of these vivid analogies revealed the long process of searching that Judy's writing had gone through and that she had reached new territory full of imagination and creativity.

5.1.2 Writing Performance from Average to Good

According to the total scores of students' prompt writing, 4 students improved their writing from Average to Good. They were Anne, Lin, Maria, and Peggy.

The writing improvement of Anne and Lin will be discussed in the following sections. The discussion of Maria's and Peggy's writing performance can be found in the Appendices L and M.

5.1.2.1 Anne's Writing Performance

According to Anne's prompt writing scores, her writing performance improved from level A to level G. The major changes were shown in content and organization.

Prompt Writing—All Aspects

Pre-prompt writing. In terms of organization, Anne's pre-prompt writing did not use titles (Ex. 17, s1) or paragraph indentation (Ex. 17, s7). She put all of her ideas into one paragraph and did not provide enough supporting sentences to fully develop the discussion. There was no obvious topic sentence or thesis statement to signal the main subjects in her writing. Lacking detail and a fully developed theme, Anne's essay failed to show her knowledge on the topic, which was, in this particular case, the new policy on English education in primary schools. The language she used in this piece contained several errors in sentence structure (Ex. 17, s1, 6), punctuation (Ex. 17, s1, 5, 6, and 7) and spelling (Ex. 17, s6, 7).   However, she used a strong voice in presenting her arguments, especially when she referred to her personal experience learning English (Ex. 17, s4, 5, and 6).

Post-prompt writing.   She did, however, make obvious progress in her post-prompt writing (Ex.18).   This time, Anne put an appropriate title on her article and added more detail to support her argument.   In this piece, there were five paragraphs, including introduction, 3-paragraphs in the body of the piece and a short concluding paragraph. Though the topic sentence and the thesis statement were far from perfect, by using enumeration, her points became clear and logical.   Also, because she had adequately organized and developed her ideas, her knowledge of the issues was evident.   Though there were still errors with sentence structure, punctuation and spelling, they were mostly minor and did not obscure the meaning.   Her strong voice could still be heard.   In general, Anne's post-prompt writing showed improved organization, language and content.   Her post-prompt writing is as follows:

Ex. 17 Anne's pre-prompt writing

(1) Talking about the new policy that teaching English in the elementary school . (2) It's a good idea.   (3) If children can learn English as young as possible, they may speak English more naturally and smoothly.   (4) The most important thing is how the teachers teach them.   (5) In the past , we learned English for passing the entrance examination, so we can read , but we can't listen and speak .   (6) If we do the same way, for elementary school , I cann't say that's good .

(7) Teaching English in elementary school is good , and I hope the children can learn English actively and full oriently , including listening , speaking , reading and writing.

Ex. 18 Anne's post-prompt writing

Starting Learning English from Elemantary School

It will be a good educational policy to start teaching English in elemantary school. There are more advantages than disadvantage for the students. The following will list some advantages.

Firstly, younger children have better ability to learn language. They aren't afraid of making mistakes when they are speaking English. Secondly, practicing is very important in learning language, so learning in elemantary school will provide students more time to practice. Children can learn English from daily life.

Then, if children have to learn English, the parents should have to learn English with their children. Because they concern and care their children so much, and children at that ages like to have conversation with parents, that will create more reactive learning chances.

finally, as English is more popular, why not to start learning it as early as we can. The children could have more time to learn it.

In conclusion, start to learn English earlier will make it easier and interesting.

Essay Writing—Organization and Content

Similar progress can be found in her essay writing. At the beginning of the class, Anne's essays were loosely organized and her ideas incoherent. The content lacked detail and was not properly developed. However, her later essays showed clear organization of ideas, a proper thesis statement and adequate explanation and development.

Logic and coherence. For organization, her essay 1-1 "Taking Airplane in Bad Weather Days" (Es-A-1) was loosely organized and some ideas seemed incoherent. For example, there was no thesis statement to set up the reasons for the whole article (Ex. 19) and the

Ex. 19 The 1st paragraph of Anne's essay 1-1

(1) In Taiwan, many people wouldn't like taking airplane in bad weather days, although, by statistics, airplane is the fastest and safest mode in the world. (2) Sometimes we feel uncomfortable and afraid that usually happen in raining days. (3) Especially the airplane is shaking or dropping down when it is flying through heavy clouds.

body paragraphs were weakly connected with the introduction (Ex. 20). If "Especially the airplane is shaking or dropping down when it is flying through heavy clouds" (Ex. 19, s3) was intended as the thesis statement, the theme of the article should have been a fear of flying in bad weather. The remainder of Anne's essay 1-1, however, was about flying in bad weather, how high-tech equipment is used to improve flight safety and how pilots' attitudes and skills influence the quality of the air travel (see Ex. 20).

This disconnection made her writing illogical and hard to understand. However, her essay 1-3 "The Effect of Bad Weather Condition on Air Traffic" (Es-A-2) showed better organization. In order to better

Ex. 20 The 4th and 5th Paragraphs of Anne's Essay 1-1

(13) We know the weather deeply impact the air traffic. (14) In order to prevent raining hurt the pavement of runway, the expert design special civil structure. (15) Using radar system, guiding lights system and communication system to guide and control the air traffic. (16) And also there are many kinds of high-tech equipment in the planes to keep connective. (17) People work very hard to ensure the flight safety.

The most important is the attitude and skill of pilots who control the craft. When the airplane takes off the pilots take the responsibility of the craft and passengers. If the pilots can handle the information of weather condition or the others, they can keep the plane away the unstable waves and make the passengers feel more comfortable.

> ### Ex. 21 The 1st paragraph of Anne's essay 1-3
>
> (1) In Taiwan, many people wouldn't like to take airplane in bad weather condition, although taking airplane is the fastest and safest way to travel in the world. (2) The weather apparently has a marked effect on the air traffic. (3) In addition to the passengers' feelings, the weather also has the impact on airlines' operation and flight safety.

connect the title, the introduction and the content, Anne not only re-wrote the content of her essay but also changed the title. By emphasizing the effect of bad weather conditions on air traffic, she could include the fear of flying as well as the use of high-tech equipment and the attitude and skill of pilots. As shown in Ex. 21, the revised introductory paragraph contained a clear thesis statement, which introduces the content of the essay.

From sentence (2) and (3), the reader expects the article to discuss the effect bad weather has on personal feelings, airline operation and flight safety. Such expectations were met in Anne's following paragraphs (Es-A-2). In the 2nd paragraph, Anne focused on personal feelings and gave examples from her own experiences and those of her friends. In the 3rd and 4th paragraphs, Anne mentioned systems, devices and rules that are in place for airports and airlines. In the 5th paragraph, she briefly mentions the importance of the attitudes and skills of the pilots.

Supporting statement. Besides organization, Anne showed progress in content development in her first essay. In essay 1-1, there was a lack of detail for supporting her statements (Ex. 20, p4), but in essay 1-3, she showed further development with more explanation and detail (Ex. 22).

Instead of saying "We know the weather deeply impact the air traffic" (Ex. 20, s13), she explains in essay 1-3 how weather influences air traffic (Ex. 22, s13, 14, 15). Also, in essay 1-3, she provides the figures for accidents caused by weather (Ex. 23, s16) and further describes the high-tech systems used to prevent accidents (Ex. 22, s17-21).

These revisions show that she has knowledge of the topic and is capable of fully developing an idea.

Her progress in both organization and content was more obvious in her second essay "What Success Means in my Opinions?" (Es-A-3/4) In essay 2-1, there were only two paragraphs with limited development (Es-A-3). Though she gave examples in both paragraphs in an effort to elaborate on her ideas, she actually switched back and forth using transitional phrases (Ex. 23, s2, 3, 4, and 8), without emphasizing the main ideas.

Ex. 22 The 3rd and 4th paragraphs of Anne's essay 1-3

(13) The airplane necds to have a flight plan for every flight, which should consider the weather condition, the flight route, the amount of fuel, and the available space for revenue. (14) If the weather of the destination airport is too bad to land, the airplane needs to transfer to another airport or turn back. (15) That is the reason why the airlines' operation cost and revenue are effected by the weather.

(16) According to CAA's announcement, the weather-related factor contributes to one third of airplane accidents. (17) In order to increase the flight safety, the governments and aviation industry invest a lot of money to develop high technique systems in expectation of reducing the effect of weather and avoiding turbulence encounters. (18) These advanced systems include the radar system, low altitudes wind-shear prediction system, guiding lights system and communication system, etc. (19) There are also many rules to decide whether the airplane could takeoff or land, such as the visibility, wind speed, wind-shear speed and the ceiling. (20) Every airline establishes the standard operation procedures to let the pilots follow up. (21) Before they get in the cabin, they are told the task hints including the weather information. (22) However, the natural power is so huge and unpredictable. (23) Something still happens just out of human beings' mind of before you can predict.

Ex. 23 Anne's essay 2-1

(1) When people think about personal success, almost, it equals to wealth or high position such as earning much more money than average, being famous or other particular perform-ance. (2) According to those criteria, I wonder how many people could be so-called success, and whether people without them are failures. (3) In my opinion, we cannot evaluate personal success only by wealth or social position, but also the achieving of de-sired results. (4) In other words, if you desired to be a house-wife, you could be success because of your contribution to your family. (5) Considering whether is success or not, that depends on what are your desired results, and it should be measured by yourself, not anyone else.

(6) During our lives, there are many role-playing in differ-ent situations, such like being children or parents in family, a boss or an employee in career, or a friend of others, etc. (7) Some people think a successful career is the most important thing, some others wish best to have a happy family, and some others emphasis the relationship. (8) However, we need to make a value judgement and decide the priority about what we face, otherwise, perhaps we will loss our direction.

However, in essay 2-3, she developed the article into five para-graphs, with details, examples, and explanation. She used "ascending enumeration" to present her opinions (Es-A-4). She re-arranged the introductory paragraph so that the introduction contained a clear thesis statement (Ex. 24, s4). In each of the body paragraphs, she also pro-vided clear topic sentences followed by supporting details. In the 2nd paragraph, the topic sentence was "First, considering being successful or not should be measured by yourself not anyone else, and that depends on what your desired results are" (Ex. 24, s5). In the 3rd paragraph, the topic sentence was "Second, the pleasure of success is not limited to the end of your efforts" (Ex. 24, s10). In the 4th paragraph, the topic sen-tence was "Then the most important thing is how to make you to be successful." These topic sentences reflect the main ideas stated in the thesis statement "... success should be more meaningful to our lives," and were followed by details supporting the topic sentence. The organization and development were adequate.

Idea generation. The differences shown in drafts 1 and 3 (usually the final draft) indicate the progress Anne made after revision. In addition, Anne's progress was also evident in the authoring stage (idea

---

Ex. 24 The 1st, 2nd, and 3rd paragraphs of Anne's essay 2-3

(1) When people think about personal success, almost, it equals to wealth or high position such as earning much more money than average, being famous or other particular performance. (2) According to those criteria, I wonder how many people could be so-called successful, and whether people without them are failures. (3) In dictionary, success refers to achieving of desired results. (4) In my opinion, success should be more meaningful to our lives.

(5) First, considering being successful or not should be measured by yourself not anyone else, and that depends on what your desired results are. (6) In our lives, there are many role-playing in different situations, such like being children or parents in family, a boss or an employee in career, or a friend of others, etc. (7) Some people think a successful career is the most important thing, however, some others wish best to have a happy family, and some others emphasize the relationship. (8) No matter what kind of person, I think he/she could be successful in his/her own life. (9) In other words, if you desired to be a housewife, you could be successful because of your contribution to your family.

(10) Second, the pleasure of success is not limited to the end of your efforts. (11) Although everyone desires success, I think life is also a process of learning. (12) In any effort, if you can enjoy each step in the process of improving, you will gain much. (13) On the other hand, if each step toward your goal is painful and tiresome, even if you reach your position, you may not be particularly pleased by your effort, which may seem to have too great for the reward.

generating and drafting). The 3rd and 4th essays show that she clearly presented her ideas and fully developed her arguments in the 1st draft. Though there were still errors with words and sentence structure, she certainly improved her strategies with respect to generation of ideas and conciseness, so that she could write a more complete 1st draft. For example, in essay 3-1 "What Happened to the Young People?" (Es-A-5), Anne had an introductory paragraph, three body paragraphs and a concluding paragraph. All were well-organized with a proper thesis statement (Ex. 25, s3), topic sentences (Ex. 25, s4) and adequate details and development (Ex. 25, s8-11). Her expression was fluent and cohesive.

Ex. 25 The 1st and 2nd paragraphs of Anne's essay 3-1

> (1) For some time now, sociologists have noted an alarming increase in rate of juvenile delinquency and suicide. (2) It could be easily found from news reports that young people taking illegal drugs, using violence, speeding illegally and committing suicide. (3) Why is it that young people in Taiwan choose that way to hurt themselves or some other people even those are their parents?
>
> (4) Did their parents work too much to have enough time caring them? (5) In the modern society, except male spent much time to make a living, more and more women contributed their ability in the job. (6) In dual-earner family, many children grew up with baby sitter instead of their parents. (7) Children didn't have much enough time to be together with their parents. (8) In a touching story which described a little boy and his very busy father. (9) The father gave little boy every thing except his time. (10) One day, the little boy borrowed some money from his father and asked how much his father's salary was. (11) He wanted to borrow money buying his father's time to be company with him. (12) I am happy for the father at last finding what his son wants. (13) And I also wonder that do we realize what we work hard for? (14) Perhaps while we are gobbling up something new, we have missed the more important things, such like watching out for their children.

Ex. 26 The 3rd paragraph of Anne's Essay 4-1

(10) Secondly, after she gets married, her life is more stable and less free. (11) She always has dinner with the same guy. (12) When she plans holiday activities, she has to consider her partner or family and spend a lot of time to deal with the relationship. (13) However, surrounded by those who love you and going outside in the same activity is a kind of happiness. (14) On the contrary, a single lady can control her time one hundred percent. (15) She can go to a movie at any time she wants and visit wherever she would like to. (16) But sometimes, when her friends all are busy, maybe she will feel lonely if she need a person to talk to or to join a party together.

This change in the authoring stage is also seen in her essay 4-1 "The Differences Between Before and After the Marriage" (Es-A-7). Essay 4-1 contained an introductory paragraph, three body paragraphs, and one concluding paragraph. She used enumeration again and led a comparison/contrast discussion about a woman's life before and after marriage. The central idea was the contradiction between a stable life and freedom (Ex. 26, s10). She contrasts the stability of married life with a lack of freedom (s13-14) and then remarks on the freedom experienced by single people who can at times be lonely (s14-16). She presents this parallel comparison/contrast, which enhances the logic in her expression.

Essay Writing—Language

In addition to organization and content, Anne improved her language use (e.g. in sentence structure, word choice, spelling, punctuation, etc.) in the process of learning.

Word choice and sentence structure. In essay 1-1, she wrote "In sunny days, airplanes take off and land more stable and smooth" (Ex. 27, s4), but in essay 1-3, she changed it to "In sunny days, airplanes can take off and land smoothly" (Ex. 28, s4). She conveyed her meaning more clearly by adding the auxiliary *can* and deleted the dangling modifier, *more*.   She also used the proper adverb *smoothly* to replace *smooth* or *stable*.   She continues in 1-1 "If we don't fear the height, taking airplane is exciting.   In raining days, the situations change, we can't see anything through the windows but feel upset" (Ex. 27, s6-7).   Though the only error in these two sentences was a comma splice, the way it is expressed in essay 1-3 shows an obvious improvement in sentence structure: "Not being afraid of the height, we can enjoy the flight trip. In contrast, we can't see anything through the windows but feel upset in raining days" (Ex. 28, s6-7).   By using the participial phrase *Not being afraid of the height* and transitional phrase *In contrast*, she solved the problem of the comma splice and varied her sentence structure.   In Essay 1-1, s8 started a new paragraph but in essay 1-3, s8-12 was in the same paragraph of s4-7.   Along with re-organization, Anne also worked on vocabulary and sentence structure.   She wrote, in essay 1-1, "A friend ever told me her first experience in a raining day.   She was ill over three weeks after landing at airport safely" (Ex. 27, s9-10).   She did not mention *what* experience on a rainy day and did not clearly show the connection between these two sentences.   However, in essay 1-3, she added *taking airplane* to clarify the experience her friend had referred to and used the causative verb *made* to connect these two sentences and to show a cause-and-effect relationship.   The revision in essay 1-3 was "My friend told me that her first experience of taking airplane in a raining day made her sick over three weeks" (Ex. 28, s9).   The last few sentences in this paragraph showed improvement in verb form and word choice.   In essay 1-1, s11 "There was one same experience I remembered," she used *one same* to describe an experience she had had, and in s12 "When the pilot broadcast we would flight through an unstable air waves, it suddenly became quiet in whole cabin while the airplane flied through it," she mistook the noun *flight* for the verb *fly*, used wrong past tense of the verb *fly* and used the improper subject *it* for the main clause.   She solved these problems in essay 1-3 by choosing different words and ways of expression.   In essay 1-3, s10, she wrote "As I remembered, I had the same experience, too."   She used signal phrase *As I remembered* to foretell that she was going to share her own experience and changed *one same* experience into *the same* experience.

In essay 1-3, s11 "When the pilot broadcast we would meet some turbulence, all passengers in whole cabin suddenly became quiet," she used *meet* to replace *fight through* and changed the improper subject *it* into the correct *all passengers*. She also substituted *turbulence* for *unstable air waves* and so presented her ideas precisely.

Ex. 27 The 2nd and 3rd paragraphs of Anne's Essay 1-1

(4) In sunny days, airplanes take off and land more stable and smooth. (5) And we can see cotton-like cloud in the sky and beautiful view of ground of getting smaller city. (6) If we don't fear the height, taking airplane is exciting. (7) In raining days, the situations change, we can't see anything through the windows but feel upset.

(8) There are some people don't take flight as possible as they can. (9) A friend ever told me her first experience in a raining day. (10) She was ill over three weeks after landing at airport safely. (11) There was one same experience I remembered. (12) When the pilot broadcast we would flight through an unstable air waves, it suddenly became quiet in whole cabin while the airplane flied through it.

Ex. 28 The 2nd paragraph of Anne's Essay 1-3

(4) In sunny days, airplanes can take off and land smoothly. (5) Then we can see cotton-like cloud in the sky and beautiful view of ground of getting smaller city. (6) Not being afraid of the height, we can enjoy the flight trip. (7) In contrast, we can't see anything through the windows but feel upset in raining days. (8) Moreover, the airplane's shaking and dropping down causes the passengers to feel uncomfortable and afraid while it flies through a heavy cloud. (9) My friend told me that her first experience of taking airplane in a raining day made her sick over three weeks. (10) As I remembered, I had the same experience, too. (11) When the pilot broadcast we would meet some turbulence, all passengers in whole cabin suddenly became quiet. (12) We couldn't feel safe later until the airplane landed.

Verb, preposition, and conjunction. More evidence of obvious language improvement is shown in the 3rd essay. The fragment "In a touching story which described a little boy and his very busy father" in essay 3-1 (Ex. 25, s8) was corrected with a complete sentence "There is a touching story describing a little boy and his very busy father" (Ex. 29, s8) by utilizing the phrasal verb *There is* and the proper form of *describe*. The wrongly structured sentence "He wanted to borrow money buying his father's time to be company with him" in essay 3-1 (Ex. 25, s11) was changed to "He wanted to buy his father's time with this borrowed money so that his father could be company with him" in essay 3-3 (Ex. 29, s11). She successfully rephrased the sentence with the use of the preposition *with* and the phrase conjunction *so that* and in so doing, illustrated her understanding of the complexity of the sentence structure. Her knowledge of sentence structure and her ability in error correction also show up in the following sentences. In essay 3-1, the confusing

---

Ex. 29 The 2nd paragraph of Anne's Essay 3-3

> (4) Did their parents work too much to have enough time caring them? (5) In the modern society, not only male spent much time to make a living, more and more women contributed their ability to the job. (6) In dual-earner family, many children grew up with babysitter instead of their parents. (7) Children didn't have much time to be together with their parents. (8) There is a touching story describing a little boy and his very busy father. (9) The father gave the little boy everything except his time. (10) One day, the little boy borrowed some money from his father and asked how much his father's salary was. (11) He wanted to buy his father's time with this borrowed money so that his father could be company with him. (12) I am happy for the father for his finding what his son wants at last. (13) And I also wonder whether we realize what we work hard for. (14) Perhaps while we are gobbling up something new, we have missed the more important things, such like watching out for our children.

word *for* in "I am happy for the father at last finding what his son wants" (Ex. 25, s12) was clarified in essay 3-3 "I am happy for the father for his finding what his son wants at last" (Ex. 29, s12). The misused direct question *do we realize* plus the question mark in "I also wonder that do we realize what we work hard for?" in essay 3-1 (Ex. 25, s13) was correctly changed to a proper indirect question with the subordinate conjunction *whether* in "I also wonder whether we realize what we work hard for" (Ex. 29, s13).

Subject-verb agreement. Anne's progress in language was not only observed in the revision and editing stages but was also revealed in the authoring and drafting processes. A large number of misspellings, wrong structures or word forms and incorrect tenses or connectors were markedly reduced in the fourth and last essay. Essay 4-1 (Es-A-7) contained few language mistakes, as did the revised essay 4-3 (Es-A-8). As seen in the 3rd paragraph of essay 4-1, the most obvious errors were the incorrect subject-verb agreement *she need* and the awkward word order *friends all are busy* in "… sometimes, when her friends all are busy, maybe she will feel lonely if she need a person to talk to or to join a party together" (Ex. 26, s16). She noticed the error of the incorrect s-v disagreement and revised it into *she needs* in essay 4-3 (Ex. 30, s16), but did not change the awkward word order. Incorrect s-v agreement is considered a less serious error as it does usually not impede understanding.

Ex. 30 The 3rd paragraph of Anne's Essay 4-3

(10) Secondly, after she gets married, her life is more stable and less free. (11) She always has dinner with the same guy. (12) When she plans holiday activities, she has to consider her partner or family and spend a lot of time to deal with the relationship. (13) However, surrounded by those who love you and going outside in the same activity is a kind of happiness. (14) On the contrary, a single lady can control her time one hundred percent. (15) She can go to a movie at any time she wants and visit wherever she would like to. (16) But sometimes, when her friends all are busy, maybe she will feel lonely if she needs a person to talk to or to join a party together.

Though incorrect word order is usually regarded as a more serious error, the awkward word order here did not seriously cause confusion in meaning. Therefore, it is felt that Anne made noticeable improvements in language during the learning process.

Essay Writing—Voice

Anne's strong personal voice was present in most of her writing pieces by presenting her thoughts with personality and identity.

In her first piece, pre-prompt writing (Ex. 17), she had already shown resonance by arguing

> In the past, we learned English for passing the entrance examination, so we can read, but we can't listen and speak. If we do the same way, for elementary school, I cann't say that's good (Ex. 17, s5-6).

Reflecting on her own experiences, she firmly stated her position on this subject. This strong statement distracted attention from mechanical mistakes and drew attention to her argument.

In essay 2-3, while discussing the definition of success, Anne's expression was unique. As she emphasized,

> ... considering being successful or not should be measured by yourself not anyone else, ... In other words, if you desired to be a housewife, you could be successful because of your contribution to your family (Ex. 24, s5, 9).

She further stated, in the same essay,

> ... Although everyone desires success, I think life is also a process of learning. In any effort, if you can enjoy each step in the process of improving, you will gain much (Ex. 24, s11-12).

In contrast, she continually said,

> ...if each step toward your goal is painful and tiresome, even if you reach your position, you may not be particularly pleased by your effort, ... (Ex. 24, s13).

With plain language, she powerfully delivered her words. She seemed genuine in the written presentation of her thoughts.

Anne's most inspiring expression appeared in the 3rd essay "What Happened to the Young People?" (Es-A-6). In essay 3-3, Anne discussed the possible reasons causing young people to go astray. She first questioned the time parents spent with their children, and then cast doubt on the present education system. Arguing against the emphasis on competition and scores, Anne firmly states,

> To release the pressure and balance the development of students' personalities, we should pay more attention to the education of students' good characteristics, potential talent or concepts of value. In fact, the grade in school doesn't mean the performance of life (Es-A-6, s21-22).

In addition, she strongly disagrees with the culture of silencing a failure. She asks,

> Didn't they ever hear any advice about how to deal with failure in their young life? In our culture, all parents hope their children will have a bright future, so they give children anything they want so as to push them to learn. However, people seemed not used to talking about love or their inner feelings. ... the culture seldom encouraged her people to experience life of all the good emotions and all the bad ones. Hence, some people hind their emotions inside instead of sharing with family or someone else. The young people have known what they were expected by their family, but they ought to know there is someone who will always stand by them too. No matter when they are in anguish or in fear, they always have someone to talk to. I think that should be better than holding back on the emotion and letting the problem getting worse (Es-A-6, s24-31).

To respond to the questions she raised in the title "What Happened to the Young People?" and in the thesis statement "Why is it that young people in Taiwan choose that way to hurt themselves …?" (Es-A-6, s3) and to suggest a possible solution to the problems discussed in the essay, Anne presented an introspective conclusion.

> Watching the news of young people on TV made me feel a little sad. I asked myself why they did this. Was there anything we could do for them? I hope this situation can be improved and can start from myself by keeping my eyes on them around me (Es-A-6, s32-35).

Anne, a novice in EFL writing, showed progress not only in organization, content, and language but also in presenting her voice. Through fully participating with the meaning she conveyed, she made her writing "a sound of a meaning resonating" (Elbow, 1998b, p. 311). Her writing is more than just words; it carries a depth of feeling and power.

5.1.2.2 Lin's Writing Performance

According to her prompt writing scores, Lin's writing was improved from an A level to the level of G-VG. The organization and content in her prompt writing showed the most obvious changes.

Prompt Writing—All Aspects

Pre-prompt writing. Her pre-prompt writing (Ex. 31) was about teaching English in elementary school. She started with the need to learn English from an international trade perspective (s1-4). Then, she used a further example to explain how poor English could hinder competition (s5-10). Finally, she used European countries as an example to argue against the belief that learning English can harm children's affinity for their mother tongue (s11-16). Generally speaking, Lin's pre-prompt writing contained a meaningful message. However, because she did not present her ideas in a logical way and did not fully develop the theme, the ideas in the article were disconnected, lacked fluidity and had little substance. Her language in pre-prompt writing was acceptable, showing clarity with few word choice or sentence structure errors. The misuse of punctuation (s4, 5, 6, 7, 10, 11, 14, 15) was her most serious problem and because of wrong punctuation, her ideas were disconnected. Her voice in the pre-prompt writing was quite strong, especially when she explained, with examples, the need to learn English (s10, 13).

Post-prompt writing. Lin could not attend the post-prompt writing class as she was on a business trip. Therefore, her last journal entry, composed near the end of the school year and written over a short period of time with no revision, was used as her post-prompt writing in this study. It can be argued that the only difference this made was in the choice of topic. Her post-prompt writing (the last journal entry) was her reading responses to *Tuesdays with Morrie* and had nothing to do with English education. Since the topic was chosen by herself, it is

---

Ex. 31 Lin's Pre-prompt Writing

(1) Taiwan is very small island. (2) So, trades between nations are very important. (3) We have excellent human resource and technology too.
(4) but, people in Taiwan need more foreign language ability..
(5) A campaign of techology idea. (6) Held in Hong-Kong last year. (7) The Hong-Kong , Singpore. (8) Taiwan and Korea teams all joined this game. (9) We didn't won. (10) Because our English expression was not good , even though, our idea was very good.
(11) In European. (12) The people learn many languages when they was child. (13) So don't worry Chinese will fade . (14) Because we learn English early. (15) So. (16) I agree this policy.

possible that the dramatic changes (see Table 4.32) in her writing scores came about simply because her interest in this topic inspired stronger motivation.   For this reason, the following discussion investigates her essay drafts in detail in order to demonstrate the validity of her general writing progress.

Essay Writing—Organization and Content

Lin improved her understanding and competence in the writing of English, especially in the aspects of content and organization.   All her essay drafts had clear themes but her later essays presented ideas with more examples and details.

Details and explanation.   Her essay 1-1 was "Cancer Risks" (Es-L-1).   She started by discussing her father's hospitalization and then the possibility of cancer prevention (Ex. 32).   She proposed three ways to help reduce the threat of cancers, like eating better, exercising regularly, and staying out of the sun (s10).   The main ideas in her introduction were properly conveyed.   The only problem resulting in confusion was the misuse and misplacement of punctuation, which will

---

Ex. 32 The 1st paragraph of Lin's Essay 1-1

> (1) My father went to hospital for routine examinations last year, the doctor told him "you must stay hospital for more detail check ". (2) After moved to patient room, from the nurse to the doctor, everyone asked him the same questions "Do you smoke cigarettes ? How long do you smoke cigarettes ? (3) Father always answered "I have smoked about sixty years " (4) After measured blood pressure 、 body weight and others examinations, the doctor said "We will arrange the operation for your lungs" (5) When hear this news, my mother and us were very worry. (6) Through four hours operation, my father was sent to "special take care room" (7) All his body put so many tubes, He looked pale and painful. (8) In my family and my company, so many people suffer the pain of cancer. (9) I always think about this that how can we reduce threaten of cancers. (10) By eating better, exercising regularly, and staying out of the sun, we can reduce their risks.

be discussed later. With details and explanations, she developed each point adequately in the subsequent paragraphs.

The ideas were also well organized. The introduction described her father's lung disease, caused by smoking, and revealed the motivation for her subject choice (Ex. 32). The body paragraphs discussed three ways to prevent cancer (Ex. 33). In the conclusion, she urged that we pay the same attention to diet, exercise, and sun-tanning, as we do to anti-smoking campaigns (Ex. 34). Generally speaking, she was knowledgeable on this topic and her ideas in this article were supported and properly stated.

Ex. 33 The 2nd, 3rd, and 4th paragraphs of Lin's Essay 1-1

(11) I am wonder something tasted wonderful but not good for our body, example people eat hamburger, cheese, French fries and pizza. (12) These common foods contain large amounts of saturated fat, which is the worst kind of fat. (13) Thought light and fat-free products are constantly being introduced to the consumer market, many people didn't choose this one, just because it doesn't taste better. (14) However, eating fatty foods can increase a person's chance for some kinds of cancer.

(15) In the past, people did more physical activity than people do today. (16) This is the generation that started the couch potato boom, and today's couch potatoes are bigger than ever. (17) Health experts said that the best way to attain a healthy weight again is to cut back on the amount of food and to exercise regularly

(18) In western societies value a tanned complexion, so on weekends people tend to flock to the beach or swimming pools and lie in the sun. (19) Many of these people don't use a safe sunscreen, and the result is that they often get sunburned. (20) Sunburn damages the skin, and repeated damage may lead to skin cancer later in life. (21) People have started to listen to doctors' warnings about this situation and more and more people are using proper sunscreens.

Ex. 34 The Last Paragraph of Lin's Essay 1-1

> (22) Cancer has been around since the earliest days of human existence. (23) Their risk of contracting this terrible disease decreases, if they either stop smoking or don't smoke at all. (24) Anti-smoking campaigns can be seen everywhere. (25) If the same amount of attention were given to proper diets, exercise, and sunscreens, perhaps the number of overall cancer cases would be reduced.

Topic sentence. However, in Essay 1-1, there was no precise topic sentence for each of the body paragraphs (Ex. 33, s11, 15, 18). After revision, there were proper topic sentences which depicted the focus of each paragraph. For example, she deleted *I am wonder* in "I am wonder something tasted wonderful but not good for our body" (Ex. 33, s11) to make the topic sentence clear. Also, she added a sentence to the 3rd paragraph so that the paragraph started with a complete topic sentence "Many people today are overweight, and being overweight has been connected to some kinds of cancer" (Es-L-2, s15). The revision to the 4th paragraph was also the addition of a topic sentence. Before jumping into the description of western people's predilection for sun-tanning, she mentioned the rising rate of skin cancer in general by adding the topic sentence "Finally, health officials are gravely concerned about the astounding rise in the cases of skin cancer" (Es-L-2, s19). With the changes to topic sentences, her body paragraphs were closely connected to the thesis statement in the introductory paragraph "By eating better, exercising regularly, and staying out of the sun, we can reduce the risks caused by cancers" (Es-L-2, s10).

Though the conclusion in essay 1-1 restated the main points properly and addressed her suggestions for fighting cancer, the revision in essay 1-3 exhibited more logical and coherent expression:

> Cancer has been around since the earliest days of human existence, but only recently has the public been aware of some risk factors involved. Anti-smoking campaigns can be seen every-

where. The risk for them to get the terrible disease would decrease, if people either stop smoking or don't smoke at all. If the same amount of attention were given to proper diets, exercise, and suntan oil, perhaps the number of overall cancer cases would be reduced (Es-L-2-5).

Idea development and coherence. Her 2nd essay was "Difference in Urban and Rural Life" (Es-L-3). Based on her own experiences—born in a small country town and now living in a big city, she compares and contrasts life in the city and in the countryside (Ex. 35).

In essay 2-1, she only mentioned that she was born in a small country town and had lived in Taipei for ten years (Ex. 35, s1-2), but, in essay 2-3, she added detail telling us when she moved to Taipei and that she had been happy in the countryside:

> I lived in a small country nearby Ping-Dong County when I was a child. The time I live in the country was my best time. I moved to Taipei in 1990. I have lived in Taipei for 10 years (Es-L-4, s1-4).

This added information paved the way for her conclusion "...differences exist, but none of these makes one place better than the other" (Es-L-4, s25).

In order to clearly convey her ideas, she discussed the differences point by point using enumeration. Friendliness, the pace of life, and a variety of activities were three points she wanted to explore (Ex. 36).

Ex. 35 The 1st paragraph of Lin's Essay 2-1

(1) I lived in small country nearby Ping-Dong County when I was child. (2) I have lived in Taipei 10 years since I married. (3) In fact, city dwellers all over the world tends to have similar life styles. (4) Perhaps some of the most notable differences in the lives of these two groups include degree of friendliness, pace of life, and variety of activities.

Ex. 36 The 2nd, 3rd, and 4th paragraphs of Lin's Essay 2-1

> (5) One major difference between growing up in the city and in the country is the degree of friendliness. (6) These urban apartment dwellers tend to be wary of unknown faces and rarely get to know their neighbors well. (7) The situation in a small town is often just the opposite. (8) Small-town people generally grow up together, attend the same schools and churches, and share the same friends. (9) As a result, rural people are much more likely to treat their neighbors like family and invite them into their homes.
>
> (10) Another difference is the pace of life. (11) In the city, Life moves very quickly. (12) The streets reflect this hectic pace and are rarely empty even late at night. (13) Life of them tends to be a series of deadlines. (14) In the country life is much slower. (15) Stores close in the early evening. (16) The people here seem more relaxed and move in a more leisurely way.
>
> (17) A third difference lies in the way people are able to spend their free time. (18) Although life in the city has it drawbacks, city dwellers have a much wider choice of activities that they can participate in, For example, they can go to museums, eat in exotic restaurant, attend concerts, and shop in hundreds of stores. (19) The activities available to people in rural areas, however, are much more limited. (20) Concert tours almost never include stops in country towns. (21) In addition, people who enjoy shopping might be disappointed in the small number of stores.

She concluded by saying that the differences did not make one superior to the other (Ex. 37).

All in all, the thesis sentence in her 2nd essay was clearly presented and fully developed and the ideas were well-organized and coherent.

Ex. 37 The Last Paragraph of Lin's Essay 2-1

(22) Life in urban areas and life in rural areas vary in terms of human interaction, pace of life and daily activities. (23) Other important difference exists, too, but none of these makes one place well than the other.

Originality and uniqueness. Her 3rd essay "Women" (Es-L-5) was her reaction to the movie "Crouching Tiger, Hidden Dragon." Instead of introducing the movie or summarizing the main plot, she discussed "the difference of women at age before and after 35" (Es-L-5, s3). Taking the two main female characters—Yu Shulien and Yuh Jiau-Long

Ex. 38 The 2nd and 3rd paragraphs of Lin's Essay 3-1

Women whose ages are over 35 are more like Yu Shulien, one of the main actresses in the movie. She always sacrifices herself for the family. She was to do many things that she should do without regret and complaint. For her lover she was so passive. For the others she always does as she would be done by. She obeyed the rules learning from the parents, the family and the society. In the appearance, she preferred to dignified clothes and she didn't like showing off herself very much.

A woman under 35 is like the other main actress, Zhang Zi-Yi. She's been looking for a vivid life. Unlike traditional women, who craved a well-ordered mode of life, the modern women are looking for excitement. She was active. She always does something whatever she really likes to do. She didn't care about the rules from society too much. She didn't need to accomplish so many responsibilities for her own life. She showed herself completely. For the man who she loved, she always takes initiative. In the appearance, she preferred to bright and sexy clothes. She also liked something new and she can change her ideas very quickly. She liked to contact friends very often and she even liked to use cell phone when she was walking.

as examples, she presented her observations and took the discussion further (Ex. 38). This creative comparison and contrast, with her mature language use, reinforced her uniqueness and authenticity.

In conclusion, she tried to maintain a balance between these two and suggested that a woman should "wisely choose one life style that she really wants" (Es-L-5, s31).

Ex. 39 The 2nd, 3rd, and 4th paragraphs of Lin's Essay 4-1

(5) When we were born, maybe we have lovely parents if we are fortunate. (6) They love us and give us a good education. (7) If we are fortunate maybe we have good brothers and sisters. (8) We can play together everyday. (9) However everything is not so perfect. (10) Though their personal characters cannot match with us, we must live together with them everyday. (11) Our lives are possibly miserable. (12) When we get married, we fall in love with our spouse. (13) But the relatives are the ones that we have no right to choice. (14) If we have right to choose the members of the family, the life will be easier and happier.

(15) In an eastern family, people share the space with family. (16) The privacy is not important traditionally. (17) Even though we cannot get along with our family, and we don't like to see them very much, they are always in our sight. (18) The conflicts are easy to happen. (19) If we own more space, and members in the family can respect each other, even though we don't like each other, the pressure of the relationship will be a little bit lower.

(20) Mothers always talk with children in imperative mood. (21) She didn't talked in the way the she talks with the father. (22) Many parents request children to obey their order. (23) Our parents always give us too much pressure. (24) Especially Chinese parents wish their children were outstanding in school. (25) And so many parents hope their children can help them do something that they didn't achieve.

The 4th essay "Family Problem" (Es-L-7) also contained well-supported ideas. Being concerned about the family problems prevalent in our society, she wrote this article, in which she discussed potential reasons for family problems. The reasons investigated were the close relationships of family members, lack of privacy and dominant parental attitudes (Ex. 39). The conclusion restated these points and a hope for the resolution of family problems.

In the body paragraphs, there were proper explanations for each potential problem she mentioned. However, in essay 4-1, some explanations lack coherence and logic. For example, in the 4th paragraph, she discusses the stress caused by parents but the sentence "Mothers always talk with children in imperative mood" (Ex. 39, 20) seemed to hint that only mothers would pressure their children and only mothers would cause family problems. Moreover, in the following sentence "she (mother) didn't talked in the way the she talks with the father" (Ex. 39, s21) ambiguity was raised. In what way does she suppose a mother talks to a father? How is that related to her main discussion of parents pressuring their children? With further consideration and revision, in essay 4-3, she changed *mother* to *parents* and deleted the entire statement referring to the way a mother talks to a father. She also re-organized her ideas so that they were expressed more powerfully. Similar problems shown in the concluding paragraph of essay 4-1 were resolved with revision in the conclusion of essay 4-3. In essay 4-1, she concluded the article by simply restating the points in a long sentence.

> If we can choose the member of family and live together, in the family we own more space and respect each other, and the parents know what we really are, then the problems of family will be decreased (Es-L-7, s28).

However, in essay 4-3, she summarized the points with the proper transitional words, which closely connected each point and presented the ending fluently:

Family is important to us. Especially when we were in the childhood, we got so much value that affected us deeply and widely from family. If parents don't pay more attention to or don't work out the space problems in the family, the children won't stop complaining. Consequently, the family won't be in harmony, either. The more space each one can own, the happier he or she is. If the parents know what children they have and respect children's choices, the problems of family will be decreased (Es-L-8-5).

Lin showed her understanding and competence in English writing, especially in the aspects of content and organization. All her essay drafts demonstrated a clear organization of introduction, body and conclusion. Most drafts contained proper thesis statements and topic sentences. She usually gave examples or provided details to further explain her ideas in order to fully develop the articles.

Essay Writing—Language

Lin also made progress in language, such as the use of punctuation and quotation marks, the awareness of pronoun agreement and sentence structures, and effective expression.

Punctuation. The most obvious progress was in the use of punctuation. As in her pre-prompt writing, her essay 1-1 included misused punctuation (Ex. 32, s2, 4, 6, 17) and poor spacing (Ex. 32, s1, 2, 4). While using direct quotes, she either misplaced the full stop and the quotation marks, such as *the doctor told him "you must stay hospital for more detail check"*. (Ex. 32, s1), or incorrectly omitted commas and periods before or after the quotation marks, like *Father always answered "I have smoked about sixty years"* (Ex. 32, s3), *the doctor said "We will arrange the operation for your lungs"* (Ex. 32, s4). With revision, the misplacement and misuse of punctuation were greatly reduced in essay 1-3 (Ex. 40).

Ex. 40 The 1st Paragraph of Lin's Essay 1-3

(1) My father went to hospital for routine examinations last year, and the doctor told him that he must stay hospital for further check. (2) After my father moving to ward, everyone asked him the same questions, "Do you smoke?" "How long have you smoked?" (3) Father always answered, "I have smoked for sixty years." (4) After my father being measured blood pressure, body weight and other examinations, the doctor said, "We will arrange the operation for your lungs." (5) When hearing this news, my mother and all of us worried very much. (6) After a four-hour operation, my father was sent to the intensive care unit. (7) Many tubes covered his body, and he looked pale and painful. (8) In my family and my company, so many people suffered the pain of cancer. (9) I always think about how we can reduce the threat of cancers. (10) By eating better, exercising regularly, and staying out of the sun, we can reduce the risks caused by cancers.

The same improvement was shown in her post-prompt writing, in the last journal entry "Money is not a Substitute for Tenderness" (Pr-L-2). Since this journal was her reaction to the reading of *Tuesdays with Morrie*, she quoted several of Morrie's statements and used the quotation marks properly, for example, *"Wherever I went in my life, I met people wanting to gobble up something new. ... Guess what I got?"* (Pr-L-2, s5-11), or *"There's a big confusion in this country over what we want versus what we need"* (Pr-L-2, s21).

Sentence structure. In her revisions, Lin also showed her awareness of pronoun agreement and basic sentence structure. In essay 1-1 "Cancer Risks," she had noun-pronoun inconsistency in "... light and fat-free products are constantly being introduced to the consumer market, many people didn't choose this one, just because it doesn't taste better" (Ex. 33, s13). The noun *products* is plural, while the pronouns *this one* or *it* are singular. The mismatched situation was revised into "... light and fat-free products are constantly introduced to the consumer market, many people don't choose those ones, just because they don't taste better" (Es-L-2, s13). She changed *this one* into *those ones* and *it* into *they*. Also, in essay 1-1, when she mentioned that tanned skin was valued in western society, she wrote "In western societies value a tanned complexion, so on weekends people tend to flock to the beach or swimming pools and lie in the sun" (Ex. 33, s18). Lin mistook the prepositional phrase *In western societies* for the subject of this sentence. By adding the proper subject *people*, she corrected the sentence into "In western societies, people value a tanned complexion, …" (Es-L-2, s20). Similarly, in the sentence "After moved to patient room, from the nurse to the doctor, everyone asked him the same questions …" (Ex. 32, s2), the subject was ambiguous. According to the sentence structure, it was *everyone* who should be moved to another place, but according to the context, she was referring to her father. Also, in the sentence "After measured blood pressure, body weight and others examinations, the doctor said …" (Ex. 32, s4), it was not clear whose blood pressure was taken and to whom the doctor was speaking. However, the revision in essay 1-3 showed that she now understood the structure of a participial phrase. By adding the subject *my father* to the phrase, the former sentence was revised to "After my father moving to ward, everyone asked him the questions, …" (Ex. 40, s2), in which it clarified which person moved to the ward, and the latter sentence was revised to "After my father being measured blood pressure, …, the doctor said …" (Ex. 40, s4), where it was clear which person had had his blood pressure measured. The problems with sentence structure were greatly reduced in her later essays. Each sentence had a subject and participial construction was done correctly.

Word choice and effective expression. In addition to the progress in sentence structure, she also made progress in word choice and effective expression. In essay 1-3 "Cancer Risks," she replaced *patient room* (Ex. 32, s2) with *ward* (Ex. 40, s2) and *special take care room* (Ex. 32, s6) by *intensive care unit* (Ex. 40, s6). She also revised *four hours operation* (Ex. 32, s6) into *four-hour operation* (Ex. 40, s6) and modified *my mother and us were very worry* (Ex. 32, s5) into *my mother and all of us worried very much* (Ex. 40, s5). In essay 2-3 "Difference in Urban and Rural Life," she changed *life in the city has it drawbacks* (Ex.

36, s18) to *life in the city has its drawbacks* (Es-L-4, s19).   In essay 4-3 "Family Problems," she shortened the sentence *the parents always use the dominant attitude toward the children* (Es-L-7, s4) into *the parents always dominate the children* (Es-L-8, s4) and changed the sentence *maybe we have lovely parents if we are fortunate* (Ex. 39, s5) into *we may have lovely parents if we are fortunate* (Es-L-8, s5).   These improved sentences were brief and concise.

Essay Writing—Voice

In terms of her writing voice, Lin was always straightforward in stating her opinion.   Her identity and personality were clearly seen in her writing.

In the 3rd paragraph of essay 1-3 "Cancer Risks," when she addresses modern people for their lack of physical activity, she humorously states, "This is the generation that started the couch potato boom, and today's couch potatoes are bigger than ever" (Es-L-2, s17).   In essay 2-3 "Difference in Urban and Rural Life," her description of city life arouses resonance:

> In the city, the pace of life moves very quickly.   The streets reflect this hectic pace and are rarely empty even late at night. Life of city dwellers tends to be a series of deadlines (Es-L-4-3).

In mentioning the many differences between urban and rural life, her last sentence reveals her unique views.

> Life in urban areas and life in rural areas vary in terms of human interaction, pace of life and daily activities.   Other important differences exist, too, but none of these makes one place better than the other (Es-L-4-5).

In Lin's essay 3-3 "Women," she described the differences between women before and after the age of 35.   In her opinion, women over 35 usually follow the rules of family or society and do not dress up, but women under the age of 35 usually search for excitement and prefer showing off by wearing attractive clothes.   In her conclusion, she did not favor either side. Instead, she honestly stated, "Which life style for women would be better? I don't know" (Es-L-6, s22-23). Because she didn't know which one is the better, she tried to be open-minded to the differences, and because of this, her concluding comments resonated:

> In my opinions, something may be old and unfashionable, but it is still precious. We need to keep it. On the contrary, something is fashionable and new, but it is good, too. Don't be afraid of changing. In the future, the world will be open and full of freedom. The woman has to wisely choose one life style that she really wants (Es-L-6-4).

Her voice was enhanced when she discussed family problems in her essay 4-3 "Family Problems." While discussing the problems caused by relatives, she attributed the difficulties in married life to not having the ability to choose one's own in-laws. Her straightforwardness seems to echo her life.

> When we get married, we fall in love with our spouse. However, the relatives are the ones that we have no right to choose. If we have right to choose the members of the family, the life will be easier and happier (Es-L-8, s12-14).

Then, when she described the lack of space for the eastern family, her voice directly conveyed her suggestion that privacy should be respected:

> In an oriental family, ... The privacy is not important .... If we own more space and if members in the family can respect one another, ... the pressure of the relationship will be a little bit lower (Es-L-8-3).

As for the problems caused by the tension between parents and children, she wrote without reservation:

The parents always give children too much pressure. Especially Chinese parents wish their children were outstanding in school. So many parents hope their children can accomplish whatever they didn't achieve. While developing their personality, children are not only led by school teacher but should also be encouraged to find out what they really want or like in their own life. They also need to know their abilities and try new things. In addition to reading the books that teachers want them to read, they also need to read books that they really want. In my opinions, many things are more important than the scores for students. Parents need to respect children as different individuals. Try to be open-minded to discuss the problems that they face and accept their opinions that they form from different perspectives (Es-L-8-4).

This argument offers proof of the progress she made in her writing voice and is evidence of the overall improvement in her writing.

5.1.3 Writing Performance from Weak to Average

In looking at the total scores of the students' prompt writing, only one student improved from Weak to Average. That student was Joyce.

5.1.3.1 Joyce's Writing Performance

Joyce's scores in prompt writing show that her writing improved from a level of W to an A. This overall change reflects progress in the categories of content, organization, and voice. Her scores in language increased from a VP level to W. Joyce's writing went from little substance with poor content, disconnected ideas, lack of organization, a weak authentic voice, and no mastery of English conventions to clear ideas, acceptable fluency, and originality. Her work still, however, included confusing words, idioms and grammar. The contrast between her pre-prompt writing and post-prompt writing illustrates the changes.

Prompt Writing—All Aspects

Pre-promt writing. In this pre-prompt writing (Ex. 41), she stated her opinions about the new garbage policy in Taipei City[2]. Besides giving the article no title, most ideas were presented unclearly (s3, s13) and were disconnected (s2-4, s8, s12). Her weak voice (s9-11) was further blocked by her poor language. The errors in word choice (s1, s2, s7, s12), sentence structure (s2, s3, s4, s6, s7, s8, s9, s10, s11), spelling (s10, s13), punctuation (s9, s10), and subject-verb agreement (s5) can be seen throughout the article.

Ex. 41 Joyce's Pre-prompt Writing

(1) The government has a new policy for garbage to politic in Taipei on August. (2) The new policy is that you must separt the garbage in home and must use the special bag.

(3) When you clean the garbage from recycle or non-recycle.

(4) In addition, the garbage must be used special bag.

(5) The city government hope the new policy can control the garbage growth. (6) and longer the burner age.

(7) Maybe when the new policy was publiced, people didn't like, they thought it is too difficult to do. (8) And the special garbage bag is too expensive, they can't accept. (9) But I believe the policy will succeed

(10) Because citizes can understand that it's important for garbage's separt. (11) and for our generation.

(12) Another, the city government must think again how to slow down the price of the garbage's bag and the size of the garbage bag.

(13) A good circulate have a good feature.

---

[2] Joyce was on a business trip when pre-prompt writing was done in the first class. Since she did not have the pre-prompt writing on English education at elementary school, the prompt writing (about new garbage policy) she had done for this program's entrance exam was used.

Post-prompt writing.   Her post-prompt writing, while not perfect (Ex. 42), clearly indicates her progress.   In terms of content, she used enumeration to present the reasons she supported elementary school English education (s7, s10, s14) and included explanations to further develop the thesis.   In organization, a thesis statement was given (s5-6)

Ex. 42 Joyce's Post-prompt Writing

(0) Learning English since elemantal school

(1) Now English language is more and more popular.   (2) It has been one of international main languages.   (3) And when should we begin to learn English?   (4) Elemantal school or Journal school?

(5) In my oppinion, I think learning language has to be early.   (6) I have some reasons to expain.

(7) First, children are like sponge.   (8) The more you give them, the more they absorb.   (9) So once the learning eduction begins early, children gain less and more knowledge.

(10) Second, we relate everythings with English around us, for example, television, computor, newspaper and commercial level.   (11) It is very easy to get.   (12) Let children learn from life.   (13) And we need not to force them learning.

(14) Third, if the children learn English since elemary school, they are interested in English evens as they grow up.   (15) Because English is a part of their life.   (16) They don't think speaking or seeing English are difficult.   (17) English might like their native-language.   (18) After all, I think no matter what learning language must begin early.   (19) Children are plastiability.   (20) Let them learn earlier, they will gain more.

(21) Beside, economical development are also speed information translation.   (22) Every parents don't hope their childre lose at the point of beginning.   (23) When Everyone learns, no one doesn't want to learn.   (24) Parents could push their children learning.

and expressed with acceptable fluency (s7-8, s12, s19-20), although ideas were still loosely organized with limited support. Her authentic voice in this article occasionally came through with descriptive language, such as ... *children are like sponge. The more you give them, the more they absorb* (s7-8) and with her straightforwardness, like *Let children learn from life. And we need not to force them learning* (s12-13). Though the meaning in this article was still sometimes obscure (s23), her language errors were greatly reduced.

Essay Writing—Organization and Content

The improvement in the detail of Joyce's four essays spoke for her writing progress. Improvement in organization and content was evidenced by supporting detail, proper explanations and logical development.

Ex. 43 The 1st and 2nd paragraphs of Joyce's Essay 1-3

> When you go to the supermarket to buy the vegetables or the fruits, which one do you choose? The beautiful and cheaper ones or the clumsy, wormy and more expensive ones? Those that don't be eaten by insects and look very beautiful seem to be more delicious. Maybe most people will choose the beautiful and cheap ones. Whereas when we choose them, if we should consider why they are so beautiful and why the insects don't eat them.
>
> Since World War II, agricultural productions have become industrialization and intension. The farmers usually use pesticides, fertilizers or other chemicals to increase the quality and quantity of agricultural products. Agricultural outputs have greatly increased; however, the ecology has also been polluted and damaged. It is the most terrible that the residues of pesticides, fertilizers or some chemicals are in corps and the contaminated foods endanger our health. As environmental pollution is accompanied by economic development, people begin to concentrate on the pollution problems. Organic agriculture is a new trend of developing agricultural products.

Knowledgeable about the topic. The 1st essay "Organic Foods" (Es-Jo-1/2) shows that she has professional knowledge on this subject. She used a wide range of vocabulary and developed the discussion into a seven-paragraph, three-page double-spaced article. From the length of the article, it is obvious that Joyce had the intention and motivation to communicate and she indeed communicated her ideas in a logical order. The introduction contained two paragraphs (Ex. 43). Joyce began the first paragraph with a series of questions. The question, on whether beautiful-looking fruits are safe, brought up the issue of over-using chemicals in agriculture, which in turn introduced discussion of the thesis—organic foods.

Ex. 44 The 4th and 5th paragraph of Joyce's Essay 1-3

> Because of the requirements for enhancing the quality and quantity of corps, the farmers usually use pesticides to control harm of pests and use fertilizers to accelerate the growth of corps and to look more beautifully for the vegetables' surface. In other hand, the farmers also use some chemicals to kill insects or remove wild-flower during planting days. Sometimes the farmers unconsciously use over pesticides, fertilizers and chemicals. The same the soil also absorbs over these substances. Once the soil can't dissolute these substances. These will cumulate in soil. The soil is polluted. Finally the soil can't be planted again. It will go to pot with time.
>
> The products of organic agriculture must be farmed and be processed by serious control. The ideal organic food must not contain any chemicals during planting, portage, storage and processing treatment. That is to say that organic foods are minimally processed to maintain the nature of the foods without artificial ingredients, preservatives, or other chemicals. The farmers use composes planting them. Organic foods come from healthy and non-pollution soil. We can eat them reassuringly after cleaning treatment.

The body of the work contained four paragraphs. The first of these briefly explained the meaning of organic agriculture emphasizing its advantages for food safety and environmental protection. The following two paragraphs (Ex. 44) contrasted the planting processes of non-organic and organic foods in order to emphasize the healthier and safer methods used by the organic agricultural industry. The fourth body paragraph explained why organic food is usually more expensive than non-organic food. The last paragraph concluded the article. It stressed the better nutrition value of organic food and why one should choose it. The main ideas in each paragraph were fully developed with adequate detail and supporting explanations. Her expression was considered fluent and acceptable. The 4th and 5th paragraphs were examples of this (Ex. 44).

The confusion in meaning was mainly caused by her language problems, which will be discussed later.

Ex. 45 The 1st and 2nd paragraphs of Joyce's Essay 2-1

From agricultural age to industrial age, commercial development leaded to a growth and activity of economy. However at the same time human population growth and increasing resource demands are also seriously destroy Earth's ecosystems. These is a result of civilization

Ecosystems supply us production of food, provision of pure and sufficient water, maintenance of bio-diversity and provision of recreation and tourism opportunities. For too long we have focused on how much we can take from our ecological environment and little attend how much we feedback to our ecological environment. Therefore we unconsciously have consumed the nature resources and have eroded the quality of the environment, for examples, illegal dumping of waste, degraded of agricultural lands, destruction of forests, and even too much tourism.

Logic and coherence. The 2nd essay "Ecological Environment" (Es-Jo-3/4) proved that she has professional knowledge of the content and indicates obvious progress in her organization. The 2nd essay contained seven paragraphs in the first draft and eight paragraphs in the second draft. In the beginning, she mentioned the imbalance between industrial/economic development and protection of the environment. Then, she discussed how land, water and forests benefit human beings. The last part of this article suggested possible solutions to protect the environment. The thesis was adequately presented and developed with proper explanations and illustrations. As for organization, the two drafts were different. In Essay 2-1, the ideas in the introductory paragraphs were loosely connected and expression was incoherent (Ex. 45).

A revised draft was presented in Essay 2-3 and was logically arranged with coherent expression, though there was still no concrete thesis statement.

The use of ... *the boom of population and increasing resource demands lead to a growing economic activity* (s1) successfully connected ideas—the growth of the economy, population and the need for resources. The sentence *However, Earth's ecological environments are also deteriorated at the same time* (s2) not only clearly stated her point but also made a connection to the previous sentence. Also, the re-arrangement of the 2nd paragraph (Ex. 46, s3-5) showed that she was aware of the need for coherence. She deleted the redundant expression in Essay 2-1 *Therefore we unconsciously have consumed the nature resources and have eroded the quality of the environment, for examples, illegal dumping of waste, degraded of agricultural lands, destruction of forests, and even too much tourism* (s6) and rewrote the ending of this paragraph as *We aren't aware of the natural resources' consumption and the erosion of the quality of the environments* (s5) to focus on the topic and to keep back something for the remainder of the discussion. In Essay 2-1, the description of river pollution needed to be more fluent (Ex. 47), but in Essay 2-3, because of proper arrangement, the same ideas were presented in a logical way, promoting fluency (Ex. 48).

Ex. 46 The 1st and 2nd paragraphs of Joyce's Essay 2-3

(1) From agricultural age to industrial age, the boom of population and increasing resource demands lead to a growing economic activity. (2) However, Earth's ecological environments are also deteriorated at the same time.

(3) Earth's ecological environments supply us food, pure and clean water, bio-diversity and recreation. (4) For too long time, we have focused on how much we can take from our ecological environment and have little cared how much we give again to them. (5) We aren't aware of the natural resources' consumption and the erosion of the quality of the environments.

Ex. 47 The 3rd paragraph of Joyce's Essay 2-1

Rivers are the important sources of our revival, but someone is for his own self-interest to destroy the rivers. Recently in south Taiwan a depraved company illegally dumped the chemical toxic waste into upstream of river that contributed water resources to the inhabitants on the spot. When our riverhead suffered the contamination, it must be leaded to public hygiene problem. Once it rains, the contaminating water will permeate to the ground, involuntarily the plant suffered to contaminate too.

Ex. 48 The 4th paragraph of Joyce's Essay 2-3

Water is the important source of our life, but certain factories discharge untreated water to rivers. When the rivers suffered from contamination, public hygiene problems ensued. On the other hand, when rivers flow into ocean, the polluted ocean will poison fishes. ...

Ex. 49 The 5th paragraph of Joyce's Essay 2-1

Forests over about a quarter of the world's land surface. Many developing countries today rely on timber for export earnings. At the same time, millions of people in tropical countries still depend on forests to meet their need everyday. Excess cutting has also leaded to loss of ecological functions.

Ex. 50 The 5th paragraph of Joyce's Essay 2-3

> Forests cover about a quarter of the world's land surface. Many developing countries' economies rely on timber export. At the same time, millions of people in tropical countries still depend on forests to meet their daily need. Excess cutting also led to loss of ecological functions. In developed counties, people have improved their living standards and lifestyle. Naturally, leisure and recreational activities have become a regular part of their lives. More and more outdoor recreation sites are needed and developed, which destroyed the original condition of ecological environments. People scared the animals away and also destroyed the bio-diversity.

Ideas supported. In the same article, Joyce demonstrated her ability to use supporting ideas. In Essay 2-1, when she discussed the environmental problems relating to forests, she only mentioned the economic reasons for cutting wood in developing countries (Ex. 49), but in Essay 2-3, she also explained how forests were being destroyed in developed countries (Ex. 50).

The revision on her conclusion illustrated her ability to use supporting expressions. In Essay 2-1, the conclusion was loosely organized (Ex. 51). Though the main ideas stood out, her expression was somewhat unclear due to a limited explanation. In Essay 2-3, the revised draft, the same conclusion was expanded into two paragraphs: one asked what we could do for the environment and the other suggested possible answers and re-emphasized the importance of ecological protection (Ex41). The statements in Essay 2-3 *Perhaps we can begin changing ourselves* (Ex. 52, s29) and *Even though we can't change everything, we can make a big difference by doing the little things* (Ex. 52, s31) answered the question of what can be done and closely linked the suggested solutions such as *recycling of wastes, less use of the plastic bags, saving electricity* (Ex. 52, s34). The last sentence in Essay 2-3 *We should love our earth and leave our future generation a beautiful environment* (Ex. 52, s38) further explains and supports the powerful statement at the end of Essay 2-1 *We don't have right to destroy the eco-logical environment of Earth* (Ex. 51, s27).

Fluent expression. The substantive development of the thesis and greatly improved organization were two major features in Joyce's essay writing journey. Similar to the 1st and 2nd essays, the 3rd essay "Human Relationship in Modern Society" (Es-Jo-5/6) was also a

---

Ex. 51 The Last Paragraph of Joyce's Essay 2-1

> We have to consider what we should leave to our genera-tion. During industries development we can't prohibit their de-velopment, but we should be from control pollution forward to resources' effective used. We can seek more efficient and less environmentally- harmful patterns of material use in modern societies. Today we should not only stress environmental protect but also consider important of ecology development forever. We only have a Earth. We don't have right to destroy the ecological environment of Earth.

Ex. 52 The Last Two Paragraphs of Joyce's Essay 2-3

> What can we do? We can't prohibit industrial development and can't stop the companies to pollute air and water. Perhaps we can begin changing ourselves. Sometimes life's biggest les-sons come from the smallest things. Even though we can't change everything, we can make a big difference by doing the little things.
>
> Now, besides controlling pollution, we should make good use resources. We can seek more efficient and less environ-mental-harmed materials. For example, recycling of wastes, less use of the plastic bags, saving electricity and so on. Today we should not only stress environmental protection but also con-sider the importance of ecology development forever. In fact we have only one Earth. We don't have the right to destroy the eco-logical environment of Earth. We should love our earth and leave our future generation a beautiful environment.

three-page long article with plenty of ideas and illustrations. Comparing the organization in Essays 3-1 and 3-3, we could see a huge difference. Improved coherence in Essay 3-3 showed that Joyce is able to present ideas logically. The title of Essay 3-1 was originally "How to Maintain Well Relationship," but since the majority of the content related to the reality of present day relationships with others, it was changed, in Essay 3-3, from a "how to" into "Human Relationship in Modern Society." She started Essay 3-1 with a sloppy introduction, in which the ideas were jumping all over the place and not well connected (Ex. 53), but the introduction in Essay 3-3 was well-organized, coherent and had adequate fluency (Ex. 54).

In Essay 3-1, the second sentence *The one of main reasons is economic development* (Ex. 53, s2) was a dangling expression. It was dangling because it used *one of* when there was no other reason mentioned in this paragraph and because it neither supported the previous sentence nor was linked to the following sentences. In Essay 3-3, therefore, Joyce deleted this sentence from the introductory paragraph (Ex. 54) and wrote an entirely new paragraph to further discuss the standoff relationship caused by socio-economic development (Ex. 55). This newly added paragraph supports the thesis and leads the discussion to various aspects affecting human relationships, such as evasion, lack of courage, being self-centered and mistrust. The way she rearranged her ideas and the way she developed supporting detail confirmed Joyce's progress in organization.

Ex. 53 The 1st paragraph of Joyce's Essay 3-1

> We can find that it seems more and more stand off between man and man. The one of main reasons is economic development. Most of the people wouldn't know their neighbor who lives at the next door. Walking the street, we can find that everyone have a poker-faced and seems to catch the time. Maybe we say that there are busy things full of our life day by day or there is a target that I must do. I don't have much time. When we are busy with business, we can find friends leave us alone.

Ex. 54 The 1st paragraph of Joyce's Essay 3-3

> In modern society, maintaining good human relationship is not an easy thing. Most of the people even don't know their next-door neighbor. On the street, we can find that most of the people have a poker face and seem to catch the time. We might have an excuse to say that there are too many things in our life or there are full schedules that we must achieve. If we keep saying we don't have much time, perhaps we may find we are so lonely when we need help. Friends leave us alone.

Ex. 55 The 2nd paragraph of Joyce's Essay 3-3

> What is reason causing the result? Perhaps we could explain the one of reasons that causing people relationship standoff is economical development. We could find the more developed our economy is, the more alienated human relationship is. In modern society, our pursuing aim is different from before. We have higher required standards. As we made requirements, we are always incognizant of freezing up somebody, maybe our families, our friends, our colleagues and so on. At the same time, we also isolated ourselves.

Essay Writing—Language

As was the case in her prompt writing, language was the biggest problem in her essay writing. From the 1st essay to the last one, she made errors in word choice, sentence structure and mechanics. Her organization was also impeded by her language problems. However, after revision, she showed progress in word form, word choice and sentence structure and so on. In addition to the correction of isolated words, she became aware of the context of precise expression and gradually used a wide range of vocabulary.

Word form, word choice, and sentence structure. In Essay 1-1, she made errors in word form (will *choice,* during *plant* … and *process*), word choice (to *insure* the food security, *non-destroy* to the ecology, organic food must not *use* any chemicals, the prices … are *more expen-*

sive ...), and sentence structure (*in other hand, use some chemicals to kill insects* ...; *the soil can't plant again*; *Perhaps we will think why organic foods are so expensive, they look like not at all*). In Essay 1-3, she corrected all these errors with proper word form (*choose*, during *planting* ... and *processing*), word choice (to *certify* food security, *harmless* to the ecology, organic food must not *contain* any chemicals, the prices ... are *higher* ...), and sentence structure (*In other hand, the farmers also use some chemicals to kill insects* ...; *Finally the soil can't be planted again*; *Perhaps we will think why organic foods are so expensive. They don't deserve it.*).

Also, in Essay 2-1, she had errors in verb form (it must be *leaded* to public hygiene problem, These *is* a result of civilization) and article (*a* growth, *a* Earth), but in Essay 2-3, she did not merely correct the errors (*an* Earth) but rewrote the whole sentence or revised the entire expression. For example, the sentence *It must be leaded to public hygiene problem* (Es-Jo-3, s9) was changed into *When the rivers suffered from contamination, public hygiene problems ensued* (Es-Jo-4, s12), and the statement ... *commercial development leaded to a growth and activity economy* (Es-Jo-3, s1) was revised to ... *the boom of population and increasing resource demands lead to a growing economic activity* (Es-Jo-4, s1). In so doing, she showed her understanding and awareness of language use in context.

Meaning clearly conveyed. Without isolating the incorrect word or phrase, her revisions in language usually helped convey precise ideas. Making revisions to context also appeared in the 3rd essay. In Essay 3-1, when she searched the reasons that caused people to be distant from one another, she wrote *We are able to find many reasons to explain why we don't have many friends. We can also find human is only one that finds evasion* (Es-Jo-5, s8-9) but it was changed to *Subjective mind also causes standoff. Sometimes we would find an evasion to explain why we can't maintain good relationship with other people* (Es-Jo-6, s14-15). These rewritten sentences presented her ideas in a more logical way and formed a proper topic sentence for the paragraph.

Besides improving correction and revision, Joyce also demonstrated the wide range of vocabulary she had developed throughout the year.   Some examples were as follows: *pesticides, fertilizers, contaminated, residua* in the 1st essay, *boom, deteriorated, bio-diversity, consumption, hygiene, ensue, spontaneously, ecosystems, accelerating* in the 2nd essay, *standoff, evasion, alienation, exculpate, affluent, misapprehension, substantial, dissension* in the 3rd essay, and *seesaw, inessential, detachment, sane, blessedness* in the 4th essay.

Essay Writing—Voice

Joyce's writing voice was not affected by her language problems. In fact, her authentic voice, which represented her personality, was clearly present in her work.

In Essay 1-3, when she explained the reason organic foods were usually expensive, she wrote *Organic foods are frail like a baby. They don't have any protection to resist the natural enemies* (s33).   With vivid language, she revealed her unique thoughts.   In Essay 2-3, her voice was obvious when she argued for environmental protection.   She said ... *For too long time, we have focused on how much we can take from our ecological environment and have little cared how much we give again to them* (s4) and

> ... Perhaps we can begin changing ourselves. Sometimes life's biggest lessons come from the smallest things. Even though we can't change everything, we can make a big difference by doing the little things (s29-31).

The 3rd essay was presented with Joyce's strong voice, in which she revealed her authentic opinions on human relationships.   Her voice was clearly present in the following passage:

> Subjective mind also causes standoff. Sometimes we would find an evasion to explain why we can't maintain good relationship with other people.   ... Evasion might be a subconscious behavior of protecting ourselves. We don't want to lose face. We don't have the courage in charge of our behaviors.   ...   In addition, we have too much choice at the affluent economic

scheme. As having choice, we concern which is better, and we don't always know how to treasure matters around us (Es-Jo-6, s14-25).

She went on to explain how we often do not treasure what we have and her voice became stronger in the description:

> ... We always split hairs for trifle. We anger and transfer our anger to another, especially the closest ones. We often unconsciously hurt them. Under the conditions, the feeling is also weak. We have to wait to be lonely to recognize the value of friends and families (Es-Jo-6, s 26-30).

Then, when she explained other factors contributing to the distancing of people, she wrote ...*more and more we care about our own benefits and ignore the viewpoints of other people* ... (s31) and *We usually guess the mind of others. We dare not speak our thoughts* (s33-34). These words seemed to come from the heart and seemed so real. At the end of this article, when she suggested ways for maintaining good relationships, she again presented her authentic thinking by saying *it is important to ... express our enthusiasm. The human relations have to be managed heartily* (s36-37), and

> ... We should open our mind and keep smile. Let our love transfer to everyone. ... love is the best medicine for unhappiness and offense. ... love can also resolve dissension (Es-Jo-6, s45-49).

As in the 3rd essay, the 4th essay "Gain and Loss" (Es-Jo-7/8) was full of Joyce's unique thinking and authentic voice. In the beginning, Joyce expressed her voice with figurative language: *Gain and loss are like two sides of seesaw* (Es-Jo-8, s1). Then, as she continued with this illustration, she wrote

> In our life, we might face many choices. Some are important, and some are inessential. And our emotion is also completely affected by our choice. Usually making a decision ..., we are hesitant. The main reason is that we know we would lose another chance. ... No matter what we choose, we think that is not the best. ... Actually, having choice is not only happy but also painful, because we have to take the responsibly to our choice (Es-Jo-8-2).

Since making decisions was stressful and painful, she suggested *Before we made a choice, we might learn how to detach. Only through detachment we could get calmness ... and we might feel happier* (Es-Jo-8, s18-21). For those who might think that detachment renders loss, she argues

> Loss does not represent what we really lose, and gain does not represent what we real gain. ... we should change the way of thinking and re-consider whether we gain what we don't expect is good or not (Es-Jo-8, s23-24).

To respond to her argument—gain may be loss and loss may be gain, she looked at the rush of modern life as an example:

> ... In modern society, we work hard. The final purpose is we want to pursue the good quality of life. However we might lose something during the pursuit, might not have our own time to get together with our families, or might lose our friends for commercial benefits. Sometimes we should give up some things. ... (Es-Jo-8-4).

When she restated the thesis at the end of the article, her unique thinking was again evident:

> Gain is loss and loss is gain. Gain might be not gain and loss might be not loss. Although gain and loss dominate our emotion,

we have right to decide if we are happy. Actually the real gain must have a little give up, some loss could take some real blessedness (Es-Jo-8, the last paragraph).

As shown in these excerpts, Joyce's voice was revealed in all her pieces and her unique thoughts aroused resonance in readers' minds.

5.2 Analysis of Writing Confidence

Writing attitudes in this study refer to writing self-efficacy and writing apprehension. Thus, for a discussion of the changes of writing attitudes, both the increase of students' writing confidence and the decrease of their writing anxiety shown in the pre- and post-Mean gained from the questionnaires will be investigated. Also, the distribution of frequency checks and any substantial changes in the response to certain items will be further scrutinized.

The *Writing Self-Efficacy Questionnaire* uses a 7-point Liker Scale, where low (L) is below 3.5; the middle range (M) is from 3.5 to 4.5; and high (H) is above 4.5. Thus, the increase in the writing confidence of the students is categorized into (1) from L to H, (2) from L to M, (3) from M to H.

5.2.1 Writing Confidence from Low to High

Only one student in the group, Jenny, increased the level of her writing confidence from Low to High.

5.2.1.1 Jenny's Attitudinal Changes on Writing Self-efficacy

Jenny's writing confidence changed dramatically. The results from the *Writing Self-efficacy Questionnaire* showed her confidence level increased from 2.6 to 5.2, going from a Low level to a High level.

The *Writing Self-efficacy Questionnaire* contains two subscales: writing tasks and writing component skills, and both indicated her improvement. In the first subscale focusing on writing tasks (Item 1-17), Jenny's writing confidence increased from 2.3 to 5.1, and in the second subscale, focusing on writing component skills (Item 8-25), her writing confidence went from 3.3 to 5.5. These numbers indicate that Jenny had experienced a tremendous breakthrough in the learning process and had begun to believe in her ability to communicate ideas through her writing.

Further evidence could be seen in the distribution of frequency checks. Before taking this course, Jenny had 18 out of 25 checks in the category of "no confidence" (point 1, 2, 3) but only 1 in the category of "confidence" (point 5, 6, 7). The other 6 checks fell in the category of "undecided" (point 4). However, after taking this course, she had only 3 out of 25 checks in the category of "no confidence" but 21 checks in the category of "confidence," including one check for extremely confident (point 7), 12 checks for strongly confident (point 6) and 8 checks for fairly confident (point 5). This pointed to a considerable increase in Jenny's writing confidence.

Regarding confidence in different writing tasks, Jenny's most amazing change came in her answers to Item-12 "Author a short fiction story." Before taking the course, she chose "extremely unsure" (point 1) as her answer, but after a year of learning, she felt "strongly confident" (point 6). The change from one end of the scale to the other showed her marvelous progress.

Her strong confidence in authoring a short fiction story was not just shown in the questionnaire but was also evident in her essay writing. The 3rd essay she wrote "Try and Try Again" was like a short story, in which she used description, built to a climax and presented her ideas with feeling. According to her final self-evaluation (SE-Je-1), this was her favorite piece and she felt wonderful about it. In addition, because she mentioned that she liked to read stories (SE-Je-2), her confidence in writing a short story may have come from her reading experiences.

Another remarkable change showed in her answers to Item-17 "Write a brief autobiography." Before learning, she showed a fair lack of confidence (point 3), but after learning, her response was "extremely confident" (point 7).

In addition to writing an autobiography or a short story, she gained confidence in other types of writing. For example, her confidence level in "compose an article for a popular magazine such as Newsweek" (Item-11) went from an extreme lack of confidence (point 1) to being fairly confident (point 5). Her belief in herself in "write a letter to the editor of the daily newspaper" (Item-10) went from a strong lack of confidence (point 2) to being fairly confident (point 5), and in "prepare lesson plans for an elementary class studying the process of writing" (Item-16) went from extremely lacking confidence (point 1) to having fair confidence (point 5). She also revealed her confidence in preparing lesson plans for an elementary writing class in her essay writing. Her 2nd essay "What's a Good Composition" discussed the components of a good composition. In this article, she not only gave a clear definition of what a good composition should be, but also provided a model—her own writing.

In addition, Jenny gained confidence in writing for functional purposes. Her response to the statement "Write an instruction manual for operating an office machine" (Item-4) showed her confidence increasing from a strong lack of confidence (point 2) to having strong confidence (point 6). The answers related to Item-3 "Fill out an insurance application" indicated her confidence growing from a fair lack of confidence (point 3) to having strong confidence (point 6). As far as learning to write was concerned, from the statements in Item-14 and Item-7, her increase in confidence had also improved. Item-14 asked whether she had confidence to "Write useful class notes" and Item-7 asked whether she believed she could "Compose a one or two page essay in answer to a test question." In the first question her confidence went from extremely lacking confidence (point 1) to being fairly confident (point 5). In the second situation she improved from fairly lacking in confidence (point 3) to having strong confidence (point 6). The change related to answering test questions also showed up in the comparison of her pre-prompt and post-prompt writing. If prompt writing was considered as an answer to a test question, her poor pre-prompt writing containing only a few sentences clearly reflected her lack of confidence, while her adequately developed and well-organized post-prompt writing echoed her growing confidence.

Jenny continued to exhibit this growing confidence when performing different writing skills. Most obvious were the answers to Item-25 "Write a paper with good overall organization (e.g., ideas in order, effective transitions, etc.)": which went from a strong lack of confidence (point 2) to having strong confidence (point 6). Others, such as the answers to Item-18 "Correctly spell all words in a one-page passage" and the responses to Item-24 "Organize sentences into a paragraph so as to clearly express a theme" increased from either strongly lacking in confidence (point 2) to being fairly confident (point 5) or from fairly lacking in confidence (point 3) to having strong confidence (point 6). In comparing all of Jenny's essays, it is not difficult to see how her writing confidence closely interacted with her writing performance.

5.2.2 Writing Confidence from Low to Middle

Four students improved writing confidence from a Low to a Middle level. They are Anne, Judy, Ken, and Peggy.

The changes in Anne's and Judy's writing confidence will be discussed in the following sections. The increase in the writing confidence of Ken and Peggy is discussed in Appendix N and Appendix O.

5.2.2.1 Anne's Attitudinal Changes on Writing Self-efficacy

Based on the results from the *Writing Self-efficacy Questionnaire*, Anne increased her writing confidence from 1.9 to 4.7 on the 7-point Liker scale, which means she increased from the Low to the Middle level.

When the two subscales are separately investigated, the results still clearly show that Anne's confidence increased. In the first subscale focusing on writing tasks, Anne's writing confidence increased from 1.7 to 4.6, and in the second subscale focusing on writing component skills, her writing confidence increased from 2.3 to 4.9. This is evidence that Anne built up belief in herself when writing in English, such as successfully communicating ideas in different writing tasks and confidently performing various writing skills.

For example, before learning, Anne's answer to Item-1 "Write a letter to a friend or family member" was 2, strongly lacking in confidence; however, after learning, her answer to the same question was 6, showing strong confidence. Her confidence in letter writing was not only shown in the results of the questionnaire but was also present in her interaction with the teacher-researcher. Once in a while, she wrote a few extra lines at the same time she sent her essays or journals by email; she also asked questions by e-mail. In the final self-evaluation of reading and writing, Anne mentioned, "I like to write e-mail ..." (SE-A-1). It seemed that her confidence level rose through her sending of e-mails to the teacher.

Besides writing e-mails, Anne also liked to write essays with enumeration (SE-A-1). Her confidence shown in this type of writing was revealed in the answers to Item-2 "List instructions for how to play a card game" and to Item-4 "Write an instruction manual for operating an office machine." For the former, Anne recorded an extreme lack of confidence (point 1) in the beginning but showed strong confidence (point 6) after learning. For the latter, Anne increased her confidence from strongly lacking in confidence (point 2) to strong confidence (point 6).

Anne also showed an obvious increase in confidence in her responses to Item-12 "Author a short fiction story." She was extremely lacking in confidence (point 1) in the beginning but showed fair confidence (point 5) at the end of the school year. In this regard, her confidence is also reflected in her final self-evaluation, in which she mentioned, "The majority [of her reading] is ..., ..., or story," and "Story [is her favorite genre to read]" (SE-A-2). Thus, it is possible that her confidence in authoring a short fiction story was influenced by her reading experiences and preferences.

As for confidence in writing skills, Anne showed a noticeable improvement. For example, the results from Item-22 "Correctly use plurals, verb tenses, prefixes, and suffixes" went from a strong lack of confidence (point 2) to strong confidence (point 6), while the answers to Item-23 "Write compound and complex sentences with proper punctuation and grammatical structure" went from extreme lack of confidence (point 1) to fair confidence (point 5). Even though in the results of the questionnaire, Anne showed only a moderate increase in organization (Q24 and Q25), she used strong statements in Question-9 in her final self-evaluation. To the question "What rules and conventions have you mastered?" Anne's answer was "The first one is outline your ideas that will help you structure your essay. ..." (SE-A-1). This answer indicates her confidence in expressing her ideas.

The message she posted on the notice board two weeks after the class ended shows her confidence in writing. She wrote,

> Dear all, [have] you ever read this article in "reflection"? After I read it I wondered when people behave like the ants? When we are used to or love someone or something, we difficultly leave away or give it up. Right? Although the ending is sad, it is still beautiful. Much people would like to [die] for the beauty. The following is this article. Share with you. ... (J-A-8-1)

Anne still read stories on her own and continually shared her reading responses. This self-directed learning showed that Anne's writing self-efficacy had increased.

Also, what Anne wrote in her essays and journals showed her beliefs in her writing. The topic selection ranged from very job-related professional issues, such as air transportation, to a variety of life issues, such as society and young people. The variety of topic selections reveals her confidence in communicating her ideas in different ways, which supports the increasing confidence shown in the questionnaire.

There is more evidence showing Anne's increasing confidence level in her final self-evaluation. She said, "I think my strength as a writer is ...that I have my own thinking [and] my own words to say about life and society et al.," and "I think I need to read more, practice more, [and] then I will get the potential to write well" (SE-A-1). That Anne believes in her writing potential is the best evidence of her writing self-efficacy.

5.2.2.2 Judy's Attitudinal Changes on Writing Self-efficacy

According to the results from the *Writing Self-efficacy Questionnaire*, Judy's writing confidence increased from 2.8 to 3.5 on the 7-point Liker scale, which means she went from a score of Low to the Middle level. By looking at the two subscales, we find that the improvement in her writing confidence shows up in the mean of the first subscale (from 2.8 to 3.7) but not in the second subscale (same score: from 3.0 to 3.0). In other words, while considering communication through different writing tasks, Judy had more confidence than before, but her confidence did not change her self-belief in her performance of various writing skills.

However, the distribution of frequency checks revealed details of the nuance. The first difference that is worthy of mentioning is the check numbers for point 7 (extremely confident). Before taking the course, no check fell on the scale at point 7, but after a year of learning, there was one check mark showing extreme confidence. This single point-7 response was an answer to the statement of Item-22 in the second subscale. Moreover, her responses to Item-22 "Correctly use plurals, verb tenses, prefixes, and suffixes" went from point 4 (undecided) to point 7 (extremely confident). This change indicates that Judy did make some progress in her confidence in mastering writing skills.

The second difference shown in the distribution of frequency checks was in the check numbers for point 6 (strongly confident). At the beginning of the class, there was only 1 response for point 6, but after a year, Judy had 4 responses for point 6. These four responses were the answers to four statements (Item-1, 3, 5, 6) in the first subscale. While Item-5 "Prepare a resume describing your employment history and skills" had the same response (point 6) before and after learning, others showed an obvious increase in confidence. The answers to Item-6 "Write a one or two sentence answer to a specific test question" showed the greatest progress: from point 2 (strongly lack of confidence) to point 6 (strongly confident). Item-1 "Write a letter to a friend or family member" first had Judy's response at point 3 (fairly lack of confidence), later increasing to point 6 (strongly confident). The answers to Item-3 "Fill out an insurance application" went from point 4 (undecided) to point 6 (strongly confident).

These changes indicated that Judy gained writing confidence in the areas of letter writing, test writing, and functional writing. A similar improvement in these areas was also shown in Item-10 and Item-7. Item-10 "Write a letter to the editor of the daily newspaper" was related to letter writing and Item-7 "Compose a one or two page essay in answer to a test question" was related to test writing. In both of them, Judy's responses went from point 1 (extremely lack of confidence) to point 5 (fairly confident).

In addition to the questionnaire results, Judy's confidence in letter writing was also revealed in her final self-evaluation. When asked "What kinds of writing do you like to write?" e-mail writing was her first choice (SE-Ju-1). As well, the great number of letters (almost 25 letters) (Em-Ju-1/25) she wrote to the teacher-researcher proved her fondness for letter writing.

5.2.3 Writing Confidence from Middle to High

Three students increased their writing confidence from the level of Middle to the level of High. They are Joyce, Lin, and Maria.

The increase of Joyce's and Lin's writing confidence will be discussed in the following sections. The discussion of Maria's attitudinal changes on writing confidence can be seen in Appendix P.

5.2.3.1 Joyce's Attitudinal Changes on Writing Self-efficacy

According to the results gained from the *Writing Self-efficacy Questionnaire*, Joyce's writing confidence increased from 4.5 to 5.5, equal to an improvement from the Middle level to High. The means of each subscale also showed the same progress: from 4.6 to 5.5 for the first subscale and 4.3 to 5.4 for the second one.

The distribution of her frequency checks gave details of the changes. The distribution shown in the pre-class questionnaire showed 11 out of 25 checks fell in the category of "confidence" (point 7, 6, 5), 10 for "undecided" (point 4), and 4 for the category of "non-confidence" (point 3, 2, 1). However, in the post-class questionnaire, there were 23 out of 25 for the category "confidence," 2 for "undecided," and none for the category of "no confidence." In other words, if the checks falling below 5 were considered as "no confidence," Joyce had 14 no-confidence checks before learning but only 2 after learning.

Her increase in writing confidence could be seen in various writing tasks. In terms of writing for functional purposes, the answers to Item-2 "List instructions for how to play a card game" indicated her progress, going from point 2 (strongly lack of confidence) to point 6 (strongly confident). Item-8 and Item-11 represented progress in composing a formal article. Her responses to Item-8 "Write a term paper of 15 to 20 pages" and to Item-11 "Compose an article for a popular magazine such as Newsweek" went from point 3 (fairly lack of confidence) to point 5 (fairly confident). In addition to the confidence shown in writing formal articles, the answers to Item-16 "Prepare lesson plans for an elementary class studying the process of writing" showed her confidence level on discussing the process of writing: increasing from point 4 (undecided) to point 6 (strongly confident). The increase of confidence on letter writing was shown in her answers to Item-1 "Write a letter to a friend or family member" and Item-10 "Write a letter to the editor of the daily newspaper." The former showed her confidence increased from point 3 (fairly lack of confidence) to point 6 (strongly confident). The latter indicated progress in confidence from point 4 (undecided) to point 6 (strongly confident).

As for the second subscale—focusing on writing skills, she also demonstrated improvement. The most obvious were the responses to Item-20 and Item-21. Item-20 "Correctly use parts of speech (i.e., norms, verbs, adjectives, etc.)" first had point 4 (undecided) as her response and then point 6 (strongly confident). Item-21 "Write a simple sentence with proper punctuation and grammatical structure" also showed her increase in confidence in writing skills going from point 4 (undecided) to point 6 (strongly confident).

All in all, Joyce's confidence in both writing tasks and writing skills increased.

5.2.3.2 Lin's Attitudinal Changes on Writing Self-efficacy

According to the results gained from the *Writing Self-efficacy Questionnaire*, Lin's writing confidence improved from 4.2 to 5.8, or from the Middle level to High. Both means of the two subscales also indicated the improvement. The mean of the first subscale increased from 4.4 to 5.7 and the mean of the second subscale went from 3.9 to 5.9. If the distribution of frequency checks is investigated, the increase in her writing confidence can be seen in the details. Before learning, only 8 out of 25 checks were for the category of "confidence" (point 5, 6, 7), 13 for "undecided" (point 4), and 4 for "no confidence" (point 1, 2, 3). Among these 8 "confidence" checks, there were only 2 for strong confidence (point 6) and 6 for fair confidence (point 5). There was no response for point 7 (extremely confident). However, after learning, all 25 of the checks fell in the category of "confidence" with none for "undecided" or "no confidence." These 25 confidence checks were distributed at 3 for extreme confidence (point 7), 13 for strong confidence (point 6), and 9 for fair confidence (point 5).

In the first subscale, regarding confidence in various writing tasks, the biggest change was in the answers to Item-14 "Write useful class notes," going from point 4 (undecided) to point 7 (extremely confident). Her confidence in writing for school was also shown in the responses to Item-6 "Write a one or two sentence answer to a specific test question": from point 5 (fairly confident) to point 7 (extremely confident). In addition, she also gained confidence in composing various types of articles. For example, the responses to Item-9 "Author a scholarly article for publication in a professional journal in your field," Item-12 "Author a short fiction story," Item-15 "Author a children's book" and Item-16 "Prepare lesson plans for an elementary class to study the process of writing" were changed from point 4 (undecided) to point 6 (strongly confident). As for "Author a 400 page novel" (Item-13), her answers went from point 3 (fairly lack of confidence) to point 5 (fairly confident). The statement of Item-17 "Write a brief autobiography" scored point 3 (fairly lack of confidence) before learning and point 6 (strongly confident) after learning. In the second subscale, regarding confidence on performing different writing skills, her responses to Item-23 "Write compound and complex sentences with proper punctuation and grammatical structure" and Item-25 "Write a paper with good overall organization" showed the most obvious changes: both went from point 3 (fairly lack of confidence) to point 6 (strongly confident). The answers to Item-19 "Correctly punctuate a one-page passage," Item-20 "Correctly use parts of speech," Item-22 "Correctly use plurals, verb tenses, prefixes, and suffixes" and Item-24 "Organize sentences into a paragraph so as to clearly express a theme" all went from point 4 (undecided) to point 6 (strongly confident) and clearly indicated the increase in her writing self-efficacy.

5.3 Analysis of Writing Anxiety

The attitudinal changes in writing apprehension were also investigated in this study. The *Writing Apprehension Questionnaire* uses an 8-point Liker Scale, where the middle level (M) is between 3.5 and 5.5; the high level (H) is above 5.5, and the low level is below 3.5. Thus, the decrease of their writing anxiety is categorized into (1) from H to M, (2) from M to L, (3) from higher M to lower M.

5.3.1 Writing Anxiety from High to Middle

One student in the group, Anne, decreased her writing anxiety level from High to Middle.

5.3.1.1 Anne's Attitudinal Changes on Writing Apprehension

According to the results from the *Writing Apprehension Questionnaire*, Anne reduced her writing apprehension from 6 to 4.1 on the 8-point Liker scale, which is the same as reducing her anxiety level from High to Middle.

In frequency check investigations, the distribution also indicated a lowering of her writing apprehension.   Before learning, 23 out of 26 checks fell in the level of "agree" (point 8, 7, 6, 5)—referring to anxiety, and 12 out of these 23 fell under "strongly agree" (point 7).   There were only 3 checks under "disagree" (point 4, 3, 2, 1)—referring to non-anxiety, and none for point 1 (extremely unafraid).   However, after a year of learning, 12 out of 26 checks indicated her anxiety with 1 out of these 12 showing as strongly anxious (point 7).   The checks for not being anxious increased from 3 to 14 where 3 were strongly un-afraid(point 2) and 1 was extremely unafraid(point 1).   Though some checks still fell in the middle of the scale, such as 8 for point 5 and 5 for point 4, the decrease in Anne's writing apprehension was obvious.

The biggest change in her attitude was her perception of writing. For example, before learning, her answer to Item-19 "I like seeing my thoughts on paper" was 3 (quite disagree), while after learning, her an-swer was 7 (strongly agree)[3].   Similar results were shown in Item-10 "I like to write my ideas down."   Her responses to the former statement went from 3 (quite disagree) to 5 (somewhat agree).   A decrease in anxiety and an increase in the enjoyment of writing English were also shown in her final self-evaluation.   To respond to Question-6 "What were your major accomplishments this year as a writer?" she considered "… trying to write my ideas on the paper in English" as one of her major accomplishments in the year (SE-A-1).

Besides showing her enjoyment of writing, she also revealed her increased fondness for sharing her writing with others.   The answer to Item-20 "Discussing my writing with others is an enjoyable experience" was 3 (quite disagree) before learning but was 7 (strongly agree) after learning.   Also, the answer to Item-12 "I like to have my friends read what I have written" was 2 (strongly disagree) before learning but a 5 (somewhat agree) after learning.   The acceptance of sharing writing with others not only reduced her writing anxiety but also helped her writing performance.   While answering Question-4 "What kinds of

---

[3]   For the positive statements (Items 2, 3, 6, 9, 10, 11, 12, 14, 15, 17, 19, 20 and 23) in this questionnaire, the answers are coded in a reverse way.   However, the original checks will be used in analysis in order to make simplify the discussion.

response help you most as a writer?" in her final self-evaluation, she said, "… discussion with classmates and teacher, … help me making my ideas clearer and re-structure my essay to be easier to read" (SE-A-1).

Her interest in sharing her writing was further illustrated by her responses to Item-6 "Handing in a composition makes me feel good" and Item-9 "I would enjoy submitting my writing to magazines for evaluation and publication." The answers to the former question went from 4 (somewhat disagree) to 7 (strongly agree), and the answers to the latter question went from 2 (strongly disagree) to 5 (somewhat agree). Finally, when she was asked whether "writing is a lot of fun" (Item-17), her first answer was 3 (quite disagree) but then became 6 (quite agree) after learning. All in all, part of the reason for the reduction in Anne's writing anxiety came from her increased interest in writing. The change from showing strong disagreement (point 2) to showing fair agreement (point 5) shown in the answers to Item-15 "I enjoy writing" is the proof.

5.3.2 Writing Anxiety from Middle to Low

Six students reduced writing anxiety from the Middle level to the Low level. They were Jenny, Joyce, Lin, Ken, Maria, and Peggy.

The decrease in writing anxiety for Jenny, Joyce and Lin will be discussed in the following section. The discussion on changes in writing apprehension for Ken, Maria and Peggy can be referred to in Appendices Q, R, and S.

5.3.2.1 Jenny's Attitudinal Changes on Writing Apprehension

The results from the *Writing Apprehension Questionnaire*, showed that Jenny's writing anxiety decreased from 5.1 to 2.2, or from Middle to Low. The details can be seen in the frequency checks of her responses. The responses of the pre-class questionnaire showed 16 out of 26 checks fell under the category of "anxiety" (point 5, 6, 7, 8) while 10 checks belonged to the "non-anxiety" category (point 1, 2, 3, 4). Among the 16 anxiety checks, 2 were for extreme anxiety (point 8) and 7 were for strong anxiety (point 7). Among the 10 non-anxiety checks, only 1 fell into the category of completely having no anxiety (point 1) while 2 fell in the area of strongly having no anxiety (point 2). However, the answers to the post-class questionnaire showed only 2 out of 26 checks fell into the category of "anxiety" and 24 out of 26 checks belonged to the category of "non-anxiety." Most importantly, the only 2 anxiety checks were for fair anxiety (point 5). That is, there were no checks for extreme anxiety (point 8), strong anxiety (point 7), or being very anxious (point 6). Moreover, in the 24 non-anxiety checks, 8 were for extremely having no anxiety (point 1) and 11 for strongly having no anxiety (point 2). These remarkable changes undoubtedly speak for the decrease in her writing apprehension.

The most obvious change in Jenny's writing apprehension was in her answers to Item-22 and Item-18. Item-22 stated "When I hand in a composition I know I'm going to do poorly" and Item-18 stated "I expect to do poorly in composition classes even before I enter them." Jenny responded to both of these statements with point 7 (strongly agree) before taking the course but with point 1 (extremely disagree) as her answer after she engaged in the learning of theme cycles. This big change was also reflected in Item-5. Before learning, Jenny fairly agreed (point 5) that "Taking a composition course is a very frightening experience" (Item-5) but after taking the course, she strongly disagreed (point 2) with this statement. Even her answer to the positive statement in Item-6 "Handing in a composition makes me feel good" showed a similar improvement: from point 4 (fairly disagree) to point 8 (extremely agree). Her positive attitude towards writing class or handing in a composition was also revealed in her final reflection—the preface of her portfolio. She said, "During the period of learning, … I am not afraid of writing as usual" (PP-Je-3) and "I usually get huge happiness when I finished writing. … It usually took me lots of time. But I know it worth" (PP-Je-5).

In addition, Jenny's perception of her writing ability changed when she reduced her anxiety level. Before learning, she responded to "I never seem to be able to clearly write down my ideas" (Item-16) with point 7 (strongly agree) and, after learning, her choice became point 2 (strongly disagree). Similarly, in answer to the positive statement "I feel confident in my ability to clearly express my ideas in writing" (Item-11), she showed a change from point 3 (quite disagree) to point 7 (strongly agree). Even while responding to statements like Item-23 "It's easy for me to write good composition," she still showed improvement from strong disagreement (point 2) to fair agreement (point 5).

With the obvious decrease in her writing anxiety, she became interested in sharing her writing with others. Her responses to Item-14 "People seem to enjoy what I write" were the evidence. She extremely disagreed (point 1) with this statement in the beginning, but then, after a year of learning, she quite agreed (point 6) that people would enjoy her writing. Also, regarding the statement "I am afraid of writing essays when I know they will be evaluated" (Item-4), she lowered her anxiety level from point 6 (quite agree) to point 2 (strongly disagree). Because she was getting fond of sharing writing with others and was not afraid of being evaluated, she changed her answers to Item-24 "I don't think I write as well as most other people" from point 7 (strongly agree) to point 2 (strongly disagree). All in all, Jenny's responses after a year of theme cycles learning, have changed dramatically. Consider the following: "I'm no good at writing" (Item-26) going from point 8 (extremely agree) to point 3 (quite disagree), "I'm nervous about writing" (Item-13) going from point 7 (strongly agree) to point 2 (strongly disagree), and "I avoid writing" (Item-1) going from point 6 (quite agree) to point 2 (strongly disagree).

5.3.2.2 Joyce's Attitudinal Changes on Writing Apprehension

According to Joyce's results from the *Writing Apprehension Questionnaire,* her writing anxiety decreased from 4.2 to 3.0, or from the Middle level to Low. Looking at the distribution of frequency checks, the details of this change can be seen. Before learning, 11 out of 26 checks fell in the category of "anxiety" and 15 in the category of "no anxiety." Among the 11 checks for anxiety, 8 responses were for point 7 (strongly anxious). Among the 15 checks for "no anxiety," there were 7 for point 2 (strongly unafraid) and 2 for point 1 (completely unafraid). However, after learning, Joyce had only 6 out 26 checks in the category of "anxiety" and 20 in the category of "no anxiety." Among the 6 checks for "anxiety," only 3 belonged to point 7 (strongly the 6 checks for "anxiety," only 3 belonged to point 7 (strongly anxious). Among the 20 checks for "no anxiety," there were 11 for point 2 (strongly unafraid) and 4 for point 1 (completely unafraid).

Joyce's changes in writing anxiety seemed to be a chain-reaction. While being asked whether "I like seeing my thoughts on paper" (Item-19), Joyce answered with point 5 (fairly agree) before learning, and had point 7 (strongly agree) as her answer after learning. Because she became more positive toward seeing her thoughts on paper, she showed less worry on Item-7 "My mind seems to go blank when I start to work on a composition": going from point 7 (strongly agree) to point 3 (quite disagree), and lowered her anxiety on Item-16 "I never seem to be able to clearly write down my ideas": from point 7 (strongly agree) to point 2 (strongly disagree). Similarly, in the beginning of the school year, she strongly disagreed (point 2) with "I feel confident in my ability to clearly express my ideas in writing" (Item-11), but quite agreed the statement (point 6) after a year of learning.

Since she felt she could express her ideas clearly in writing, she would not be afraid of handing in a composition. This change was shown in her responses to Item-22 "When I hand in a composition I know I'm going to do poorly": from point 6 (quite agree) to point 2 (strongly disagree). Consequently, her general feelings toward writing changed. For example, her responses for Item-13 "I'm nervous about writing" changed from point 7 (strongly agree) to point 2 (strongly disagree), and her answers for Item-17 "Writing is a lot of fun" altered from point 2 (strongly disagree) to point 7 (strongly agree). The most dramatic change was related to her self-perception as a writer. Her answers to Item-26 "I'm no good at writing" greatly changed from point 7 (strongly agree) to point 1 (extremely disagree). This change along with the above-mentioned attitudinal shift shows strong evidence of the decrease in Joyce's writing apprehension.

5.3.2.3 Lin's Attitudinal Changes on Writing Apprehension

According to the results gained from the *Writing Apprehension Questionnaire*, Lin's writing anxiety was reduced from 4.2 to 3.3, which means her anxiety level was lowered from Middle to Low. Investigating the distribution frequency of check marks gave more details.   Before the course, 11 out of 26 checks fell in the category of "anxiety" (point 5, 6, 7, 8), among which 5 were for point 7, referring to strongly anxious, 3 for point 6 (very anxious), and 3 for point 5 (fairly anxious). After learning, there were only 6 out of 26 checks belonging to the category of "anxiety," including 1 for point 6 (very anxious) and 5 for point 5 (fairly anxious).   There were none for either point 7 (strongly anxious) or point 8 (extremely anxious).   Moreover, before learning, there were 15 out of 26 checks falling into the category of "no anxiety" (point 1, 2, 3, 4) and after learning, 20 out of 26 checks belonged to the category of "no anxiety," among which there were even 2 checks for point 1 (completely unafraid).

The two checks falling on the scale at point 1 were the responses to Item-8 and Item-18.   While being asked whether "Expressing ideas through writing seems to be a waste of time" (Item-8), Lin quite disagreed (point 3) with this statement at the beginning of learning, and after a year of learning, she extremely disagreed (point 1). In answer to Item-18 "I expect to do poorly in composition classes even before I enter them," she chose point 3 (quite disagree) before learning and changed to point 1 (extremely disagree) after learning.   Besides revealing the decrease of Lin's anxiety in writing, these changes reflected how Lin viewed a composition class and how she viewed her own writing—process and product.

In terms of her views on composition classes, the responses to Item-5 "Taking a composition course is a very frightening experience" indicated the changes she made.   Before learning, she chose point 6 (quite agree) and after learning, she had point 3 (quite disagree) as her answer.   Similarly, in answer to Item-4 "I am afraid of writing essays when I know they will be evaluated," she first chose point 7 (strongly agree) and then changed it into point 4 (somewhat disagree).

In terms of her view of the writing process, she showed a decrease in anxiety in the answers to Item-7 and Item-16.   For the statement in Item-7 "My mind seems to go blank when I start to work on a composition," she responded with point 6 (quite agree) before learning, and answered with point 4 (somewhat disagree) after learning.   As for the statement "I never seem to be able to clearly write down my ideas" (Item-16), she answered with point 7 (strongly agree) in the beginning and chose point 5 (fairly agree) at the end of school year.

In terms of her self-concept about writing products, she showed a decrease in writing anxiety in her responses to Item-22, Item-23, Item-24, and Item-26.   While responding to Item-22 "When I hand in a composition I know I'm going to do poorly," she first chose point 4 (somewhat disagree) and then changed it to point 2 (strongly disagree). While being asked whether "It's easy for me to write good composi-tions" (Item-23), she answered with point 3 (quite disagree) before learning and responded with point 5 (fairly agree) after learning.   Also, to respond to the statement "I don't think I write as good as most other people" (Item-24), point 7 (strongly agree) was her answer at the begin-ning of learning and point 5 (fairy agree) was her response at the end of school year.   As for the statement "I'm no good at writing" (Item-26), she strongly agreed (point 7) with this statement before learning and then fairly agreed (point 5) with this saying after a year of learning.

Generally speaking, Lin reduced her writing anxiety from the Mid-dle level to Low, and this change helped her to perceive the writing of English differently.   The evidence was shown in her responses to Item-17.   Before learning, she somewhat disagreed (point 4) with the statement "Writing is a lot of fun" (Item-17), but after learning, she quite agreed (point 6).

5.3.3 Writing Anxiety from Higher Middle to Lower Middle

Judy was the only student in this study who lowered her writing anxiety from Higher Middle to Lower Middle.

5.3.3.1 Judy's Attitudinal Changes on Writing Apprehension

According to the results from the *Writing Apprehension Question-naire*, Judy's writing anxiety fell from 4.5 to 3.6 on an 8-point Liker scale.   This change represented a decrease from a higher Middle level to a lower Middle level.   The distribution of frequency checks showed similar outcomes.   Before taking the course, 12 out of 26 checks fell in the category of "anxiety" (points 8, 7, 6, 5) and 11 checks fitted in the category of "non-anxiety." Slight differences, 9 out of 26 for "anxiety" and 17 for "non-anxiety" were recorded after a year of learning. The most noticeable change was in the check numbers for point 8, which refers to extreme anxiety. In the pre-class questionnaire, Judy had 8 checks for point 8 (extremely anxious), but none in the post-class questionnaire. This change proved that there was indeed a lowering of writing anxiety, though it was not remarkable.

The investigation of the responses to each statement revealed that the biggest change came in Judy's perception of her writing. In answer to Item-4 "I am afraid of writing essays when I know they will be evaluated," she had point 7 (strongly agree) for the pre-class questionnaire but responded with point 1 (extremely disagree) for the post-class questionnaire. A similar decrease of anxiety was shown in the answers to positive statements, like Item-2 and Item-9. The responses to Item-2 "I have no fear of my writing being evaluated" were from point 1 (extremely disagree) to point 7 (strongly agree), and the answers to Item-9 "I would enjoy submitting my writing to magazines for evaluation and publication" were from point 1 (extremely disagree) to point 6 (quite agree). Without the fear of being evaluated, her attitude changed so that she was able to share her writing with others. The statement of Item-20 asked whether "Discussing my writing with others is an enjoyable experience" and her responses changed from point 6 (quite agree) to point 8 (extremely agree).

In addition, she showed her fondness of writing her ideas down in her answers to Item-10. Before learning, she responded to Item-10 "I like to write my ideas down" with point 5 (fairly agree) and, after a year of learning, she answered with point 7 (strongly agree). Item-3 was a similar statement "I look forward to writing down my ideas" to Item-10, and Judy chose point 8 (extremely agree) for both pre- and post-class questionnaires. These answers showed her expectation and eagerness of sharing ideas in the written form. Such assurance in writing was also reflected in the answers to Item-15 and Item-17. The direct statement in Item-15 "I enjoy writing" first scored point 6 (quite agree) as her answer and then got point 8 (extremely agree) at the end of school year. Similarly, she changed the responses to Item-17 "Writing is a lot of fun" from point 5 (fairly agree) to point 7 (strongly agree). Judy's view on composition changed as well. While being asked whether "Taking a composition course is a very frightening experience" (Item-5), she strongly agreed with it at first (point 7) and then quite disagreed with the statement (point 3).

5.4 Personal Growth and Empowerment

Based on Freire's arguments (Freire, 1970, 1993; Freire & Macedo, 1987) and Rogers' opinions (Rogers, 1961a, 1980, 1983; Rogers & Stevens, 1967), personal empowerment in this study refers to the efforts students made in their studies and personal growth is that which is developed through engaging in the learning of theme cycles. The main evidence used in this discussion will be portfolio evaluations. In addition, the students' final self-evaluation, the preface of their individual portfolio, their reading/writing log, and in-class sharing will also be discussed as support for the triangulation analysis.

In this section, based on their total portfolio scores, the students were divided into 3 groups: (1) Superior (40-36), (2) Good to Superior (36-32), and (3) Good (32-28).

5.4.1 Superior (40-36)

Two students received a rating of Superior. They were Lin and Jenny.

5.4.1.1 Lin's Personal Growth/Empowerment

Lin, in her 40s and married with kids, had to shoulder a lot of responsibility with her work and family commitments. However, she came across as an active learner and thinker. Throughout the year of learning, she not only increased her ability and confidence in reading and writing English, but also demonstrated her powers of observation and reflections on people and life (RJ-29).

Her theme project (Em-L-3) for the first semester revealed her interest in people. As she mentioned in her oral report, "I love to meet interesting people and hear about their stories. Therefore I chose some articles about people and [shared] five of the articles" (OR-L-1-1). Reading biographies brings her great enjoyment (SE-L-2) and sharing what she reads with others helps to make her a better writer (SE-L-1).

Lin's reading and writing is not limited to biography. She reads other materials with diverse genres and contents. According to her final self-evaluation, she read almost 50 articles and 2 books in the year of learning (SE-L-2) and wrote 22 pieces to communicate her ideas with others (SE-L-1). This great amount of reading and writing was a good demonstration of her effort, her self-directed learning, and the interest she developed in reading and writing (RJ-30). Her statement in the preface of her portfolio was a proof:

> How time flies. These two semesters passed so quickly. I enjoyed the reading process. I had a good time when I was reading. Every time I finish reading an article, it let me get into a deep thought (PP-L-1).

Perhaps she was referring to the deep thoughts she had after reading *Tuesdays with Morrie*. To respond to Morrie's views on forgiveness, she reviewed her parent's relationship and wished her aged parents would forgive each other, no matter how serious the hatred was that they concealed for years (J-L-11). Her frankness, sincerity, and maturity were revealed in her writing:

> When you forgive someone who is around you everyday, you clean a bright area in your heart and you also stop carving a dark corner in your heart.
> …Nobody is perfect. 'We can forgive ourselves before we die. Then forgive others' (J-L-12-2/3).

Her reaction to the discussion on marriage showed her understanding of the difficulty of managing married life and her reflections on keeping commitments and human relationships:

> Some of my friends got marriage problems. Some had problems getting into marriage. Some had problems getting out of marriage. Some had problems managing it. It's true, Morrie said, 'My generation seemed to struggle with the commitment. ... ... (J-L-11-1)
> ... ...
> In our culture, it's so important to keep a loving relationship with someone because our society does not give us it. In general, we are too selfish to take part in a loving relationship. We don't know ourselves. Of course we don't know what we want in the partnership. We get so many tests in our marriage. We must learn how to accommodate with partner. We also must learn how to respect, compromise and talk openly with the partner. The most important thing is the couple need to have a similar set of value in their marriage life. If not, they get a big problem (J-L-11-5).

Lin had an intense interaction with the texts she read, and this led her to re-consider the meaning of her life. The inquiries, like whether she spent time wisely and whether she pursued things that had value, pushed her to carefully investigate her present life:

> I worry that I put my valuable time in the wrong things. I spend so much time on asking myself frequently. In this world what is the most important thing I need to pursue for all my life? Is money? Is power? Or fame? (J-L-13-1)
> ... Every day I spend 8 hours on my work, but I think 8 hours are too much. I spend 25 years making money, but I also think 25 years are too much ... (J-L-13-2)

She is not tired of her work but is aware that her life could be more meaningful. Freire (1993) once mentioned,

> In problem-posing education, people develop their power to perceive critically *the way they exist* in the world *with which* and *in which* they find themselves; they come to see the world not as a static reality, but as a reality in process, in transformation (p.64).

Lin's careful investigation into her life showed that she is empowered to critically perceive the world and that she has experienced the two dimensions of the words: reflection and action (Freire, 1993). With profound introspection, she began to look at what she really wanted: to make changes in her life:

> ... I hope I could create new value when I am at work. While at work I am not just concentrated in the work itself and I care about people in the meantime. If I can help my colleagues, I will put down my work at hand. In the office I hope I can face people with smile instead of impatience (J-L-13-2).

Her determination to lead a meaningful life was not limited to her life at work but also included her family life:

> ... Every day I finish my work I am exhausted. The children want to talk with me, but I am impatient. Although the parents stay at home all day long after I go to office, I have no time ... communicate with them even when I finish work just because I am too busy. So I hope I can reduce the necessity for new goods and lead to a simple life (J-L-13-3).

Although leading a new life was not easy, throughout the year of learning, her resolution was enhanced. Her illustration in her theme report proved her willpower in pursuing a life with meaning and purpose:

> ... If we can really understand what we really want, maybe we can spend less time making money. We get more time ... do something we really want to do. ...
> ... we need to devote ourselves to loving others, and devote ourselves to our community around us. Giving to other people is what makes us feel alive. Devote yourself to creating something that gives you purpose and meaning. ... (OR-J-2)

After reading *Tuesdays with Morrie*, she started reading another English book *Who Moved My Cheese?* in her free time. She was greatly impressed by these books and quickly became a book lover. The statement she made in the preface of her portfolio was good evidence of this:

> ... This is also the first time I read a book thoroughly. I hope this would be a good start that furthermore leads me in the same way to read other English books (PP-L-1).

All in all, we can say that Lin demonstrated much growth in her reading, writing, sharing, and thinking.

5.4.1.2 Jenny's Personal Growth/Empowerment

Jenny, a mother of a two-year-old girl, was expecting her second child when the second semester started (O-27). Though her work was heavy and she was pregnant, she still completed the course with a great sense of achievement. Besides her improvement in writing performance, an increase in writing confidence, and a decrease in writing anxiety, she also experienced many "first times" in her life during the course:

> *Tuesday with Morrie* is the first English book that I have read completely.
> The first time I got e-mail from my teacher
> The first time I present in English.

> The first time to have a chatting place—*Learning Garden*[4]—to
> communicate with others
> The first time I made an individual portfolio in English
>
> (OR-Je-2-1)

These "first time" experiences revealed how challenging this course was for her and showed how proud she felt when she overcame all the difficulties. Most importantly, she did not stop trying after these "first times." While reading *Tuesdays with Morrie*, she started reading another book, an anthology of short stories, *Reflections*, and had almost finished reading it by the end of the school year (SE-Je-2-6). Nearly a week after the class was over, she wrote an e-mail to her teacher and gladly shared, "I bought some English books last night. One is *Daddy Long Leg*, and the other is *The Little Prince*. I hope I can read them completely, just like *Tuesday with Morrie*" (Em-Je-21). Her fondness for and motivation to read had been formed and she enthusiastically embraced it.

Her reaction to the first-time receipt of the teacher-researcher's letter was also positive. She immediately replied and said,

> It is very great to receive your e-mail. This is the first time I received e-mail from my teacher. I want to write a lot of sentences to you, but I don't have enough time, because I have to attend a meeting at 12:30. ...(Em-Je-4)

Her sincere explanation of not being able to reply was already a good reply and though she did not have time to write at that moment, she did continue writing e-mails to the teacher to negotiate the topic for her theme project, to ask for a leave, to discuss her writing pieces, or to share the difficulty and happiness of taking care of her daughter. The correspondence she shared with the teacher proved that she took the challenge seriously and made efforts to become competent. As Rogers

---

[4] *Learning Garden* is the name of the teacher-researcher's homepage, which links to the on-line discussion board, mainly designed for this class.

(1983) claimed, students are always full of the potential to break through as long as teachers react genuinely with attentive and non-judgmental listening and understanding.

The oral report Jenny presented in the first semester was her first time at presenting a project in English. She shared her theme project—the comparison of Taipei MRT and Washington D. C. Metro—with well-designed transparency. She introduced six differences between these two systems, such as single journey fares, stored-value tickets, group discounts, etc. (OR-Je-1). Though she felt nervous about her first-time oral presentation in English, she made a very good and informative speech, which not only provided the audience with valuable information but also illustrated the efforts she had made in searching for materials, reading, and summarizing (O-14).

Her excitement over her first-time exposure to an on-line discussion board was evident in her e-mail,

> … I have received your e-mail about 'New Message on the board' … I am very sorry that I haven't shown my opinions on the board. But it's no doubt that I often go to the web station. I added "Learning Garden" to my favorite stations when I saw it the first time. … (Em-Je-14)

That she also included the front page of *Learning Garden* in her individual portfolio proved how much she enjoyed having access to the chat room (O-29).

Besides *Learning Garden*, her portfolio is packed with lots of interesting information, which demonstrates her growth as a reader and writer and her personal development in the learning process. In the preface of her portfolio, she revealed how anxious she was in the first class:

> I remember the first time I attended this class. When Li-Te show us the syllabus and explained what we should do during the whole semester, I felt a shiver. Can I do it? Can I keep up with others? Can I write an essay? Can I understand

> what the teacher said?   There are a lot of questions in my mind,
> and I began to wonder if I could get my money back? (PP-Je-1)

Fortunately, she did not give up on learning or, more precisely, she did not give up on herself.   She faced the challenge with effort and perseverance.   Though she suffered a great deal when she got stuck with her writing, she was usually extremely happy when she was finished (PP-Je-5).   Though her search for writing themes and how to present them usually took her a lot of time, she firmly believed that it was all worth the effort (PP-Je-5).

Similar to a reflection on Freire's (1993) dialogical way of learning, she recognized that reading, along with thinking and discussion was most helpful in generating ideas in the learning process.   She considered herself a writer because of her positive feelings (SE-Je-1), and perceived herself as a reader because of her patience when reading (SE-Je-2-7).   Though she knew that her performance was not perfect, she believed that she had developed a deep interest in reading and writing (Em-Je-22).   It is no wonder that she continued reflecting in the preface of her portfolio as follows:

> ... Now I am going to graduate, ... it's very exciting.   Besides it, the most important thing is that I learned a lot during this year, it's the biggest treasure that I will cherish forever (PP-Je-2).   ... ...
> ... I totally agree that learning is a lifelong process, and I believe that the ending of this class would be my beginning of learning English (PP-Je-6).

In addition, during the learning process, Jenny was able to find the answer to her inquiry about the meaning of life:

> What's a meaningful life?   Is it called working hard?   Does it mean rich?   After reading the words of Morrie, I began to consider this question strictly.   After a long thinking, I got a definition about 'a meaningful life to me.'   I think the term a meaningful life signifies more loving, more giving and more

> sharing in my life. After recognizing it, I began to adjust some schedule and some attitude of mine. Now I pay more attention to my family, I spend more time with my daughter, and I am glad to share what I know with my friends. The Morrie's words have changed my life (OR-Je-2).

Spending more time with her daughter, she discovered the little girl's great potential for learning and was amazed at some of the words her two-year-old daughter came out with (Em-Je-15). Jenny's warmth was revealed naturally through her interaction with others. Besides volunteering to set up a mailing list for the class (Em-Je-18 & 19), she actively shared an article related to the in-class discussion: Should we care the important things or the emergent things (Em-Je-16)? Reflecting on her busy life and its negative consequences, she made up her mind to live differently:

> Most of us are busy in modern society. Lots of works are stacked for us to do everyday, and so we often forget to detach our feeling of annoyance. Sometimes we automatically vent our anger on somebody who's not to blame. It's not only hurt others but also ourselves. After reading the Morrie's words, I began to learn detach. And I feel I am happier than I was (OR-Je-2).

Jenny's reflections illustrated her experiences of "reading the word and the world" (Freire & Macedo, 1987). She not only decoded/encoded the words she read but also decoded/encoded the people and the community around her. She not only immersed herself in the pages but also found meaning in the visible and invisible messages of the world (Wink, 2000). With deep reflection, she was empowered in the process of decoding and encoding.

Furthermore, other than having complaints all the time, Jenny gave thanks to the people around her:

> I would like to acknowledge the enormous help given to me in taking this course. I wish to thank my husband; he inspired me to attend this training class, …. Then, I want to say 'thank you' to Mr. …, my colleague, who drove … me to [the class] all the time. Also, special thanks to all of my classmates, because of their accompanying; I found a lot of interests from learning. Mostly, I want to thank [the teacher]. For her patience, diligence and great concern. I think I developed a deep interest in reading and writing (Em-Je-22).

Her sincere thankfulness showed her tenderness and proved her determination to pursue a meaningful and harmonious life.

5.4.2 Between Superior and Good (36-32)

Five students' portfolios were scored between Superior and Good. They are Judy, Joyce, Peggy, Maria, and Ken.

Judy's and Joyce's personal growth will be discussed in the following sections. The discussion of Peggy's, Maria's, and Ken's personal growth is shown in Appendix T, Appendix U, and Appendix V.

5.4.2.1 Judy's Personal Growth/Empowerment

Judy's personal growth was evident throughout the school year and usually after deeply reflecting on the issues.

While responding to reading "Dropouts," she exclaimed "It is unbelievable to pay the dropout-students for claiming them to stay in class" (J-Ju-7-1), and emphasized "Learning is voluntary and cannot be compelled" (J-Ju-7-2). It was obvious that she insisted on keeping a balance between how to keep at-risk students in school and not wasting educational resources. Her responses to the modern fable "The Unicorn in the Garden" were also straightforward. Besides analyzing the main characters—husband and wife—in detail, she commented on the unhappy couple:

> ... It is so sad when the married relation develops such a result. In my opinion, this couple should learn how to respect and take care each other, so the marriage would be longer (J-Ju-8-2).

It seemed that this reading triggered her inner feelings and allowed her to hold a certain position, where such strong feelings helped her write from her heart. The close interaction she described in her reading-reflection-writing-empowerment was parallel with Freire's argument of reading the word and the world (Freire & Macedo, 1987) and was reinforced when she integrated reading with personal anecdotes and social events.

Impressed by the melody and the lyrics of "Leader of the Band,"[5] she reflected   on parents' worries and expectations:

> ... the process of being a famous artist or a musician is very hard. Many parents worry their children to suffer hardships and have economic problem in the future, so they generally master their children's thinking.   Some geniuses of art or music maybe disappear.   To hope one's children will have a bright future is the wish of all parents, but I told myself I should respect my son's aspiration even though he chose a work which I was really difficult to accept it (J-Ju-10-3).

Although her son was only in kindergarten and she already had a thorough understanding of what it took to be a good parent.   If there had been no deep reflection, it would have been impossible for her to include her son in this discussion.   From her description, we can see her reading/writing was closely connected with her life, and so she not only learned the target language but also sought the proper way to live.

The same connection was also offered in her discussion on committing crimes, racial discrimination, and provincial-identity complex. She believed "the social culture is full with love and care, people will

---

[5]   A song, sung by Dan Fogelberg, describes a son's gratitude to his father for giving him the freedom to choose what he loved—music—and gave him a gift—his talent in music—that he could not repay.

harm no one at all" (J-Ju-11-2), "… if we have love … in our mind, we will learn forgiveness and easily forgive others doing harm for us" (J-Ju-13), and "… if there are love and esteem exist in people's mind, what are the racial discrimination and the complex of province? They won't happen" (J-Ju-14-3). Judy was not a Utopian. Her emphasis on love and forgiveness was brought into play when she had to face a disagreement with her boss:

> I sometimes have a dispute with my chief for work. My chief is really firm in his view for something, even though the others agree my opinion. I also feel frustrated and even want to leave there. However, I check my communicational method again, I find me doing a wrong thing that is to express strong egocentric. I tried to consider the question from my chief's position. I got a little bit different situation. Thus I attained a conclusion that is to judge everything by more side consideration. Now I feel better to manage my work and also reduce the dispute with my chief (J-Ju-12-2).

Judy acquired the concept of love and the power of showing love from her reading, especially from the words of Morrie. She insisted that love should be expressed and spread because she was aware that "… Most people often cover up their feelings and finally regret that they don't express love for their main persons face to face" (OR-Ju-2-1). Judy thought love should be the foundation of everything, as Morrie said, "Without love, we are birds with broken wings" (Mitch, 1991, cited in OR-Ju-2-3). To her, love was shown in all aspects of life, such as family, marriage, society, and culture. The love of one's family cannot be replaced by money or fame. This love comforted her and always made her strong (OR-Ju-2). Love in marriage would make marriage permanent and terminate the assumption that marriage is the grave of love. The love of society and culture reminded her to give time and attention to the people around her. She had changed. The process of reading-reflection-writing-empowerment changed her, as she stated, "… these pages let me consider some things that I should change myself. I have also some decisions to plan my future. …" (J-Ju-9-4).

The immediate decision she made was to contact her previous teachers. Moved by the intimate relationship between Morrie and Mitch, she was thinking of her teachers during her school days:

> ... I envy Mitch had a good teacher. In my school time I had good teachers too. They helped me and gave me much edification. I cannot forget them, but I also have the defect that I am too lazy to contact with them. In fact, a greeting card or a phone call takes us only little time. Maybe I should contact with my teachers right now (J-Ju-9-3).

Besides trying to make contact with her former teachers, not wanting to lose contact with the teacher-researcher and her classmates in this study, she maintained and frequently used her e-mail to share her struggles with theme selection (Em-Ju-3, 4, 5), her happiness in completing a writing task (Em-Ju-7), her anxiety about oral reports (Em-Ju-6, 7), her expectations for the new semester (Em-Ju-8), her gladness over her younger sister's engagement (Em-Ju-6), the excitement of her son entering elementary school (Em-Ju-19), her sorrow over the loss of Mr. Chen[6] (Em-Ju-16), her disappointment over the ending of the school year (Em-Ju-14, 17-19), her future plans for life and learning (Em-Ju-20, 21, 23, 24), and her eagerness for the yearly class reunion (Em-Ju-22, 23, 25). Many of her e-mails showed her determination in investing in people and keeping in contact with significant people in her life.

In addition, she reconfirmed the decision she made on turning thirty:

> ... Mitch changed his life because of his uncle's death. He felt as if time were suddenly precious, water going down an open drain, and he could not move quickly enough. I have this feeling since I was thirty years old. Hence I told myself to cherish time and together with my family. Mitch knew time is

---

6   Chen Hsi-Sheng, an English teacher and also a graduate student in TESOL Ph.D. program at Tamkang University, died of liver disease on May 23, 2001. He was a classmate of the teacher-researcher.

> precious, so he was devoted to working and chasing his fame or
> money. ... Mitch ... depend the materials gain on an
> achievement and ignore the spiritual gain till he met Morrie. I
> felt lucky, for I always think the spiritual gain is forever. Thus
> I pursuit the spiritual satisfaction, I just worry I have no time to
> learn many things (J-Ju-9-2).

Her emphasis on the value of non-material satisfaction was evidenced
when she enjoyed a trip with her family to Bali (Em-Ju-10), when she
spent time on her son's schoolwork (Em-Ju-23), and when she once
again stated, "... life is changeable. I more cherish my everyday and
the reunion time with my family and friends" (Em-Ju-21). In pursuing
spiritual satisfaction rather than money and fame, she would like to
grow through constant learning:

> ... I depend on the work on my little part of life, so I still ar-
> range some courses to keep learning. It is including listening
> three speeches at weekend, attending the course of Knowledge
> Economy ... and going to the Ministry of Foreign Affairs to
> learn English at night. I feel dynamic and happy (Em-Ju-21).

It was obvious that Judy's perseverance with learning was permanent
and the quantity and quality of her writing were the best evidence of the
effort she was making to fulfill both the class requirements and the need
for self-actualization (RJ-29, 30).

In the year of learning, she changed her self-perception as a reader
and writer. Besides mastering the basic structures of English writing,
she placed value on the process of generating ideas. She wrote "Discussion is helpful to me" in becoming a writer (SE-Ju-1-4) and she
viewed her strengths as having many ideas and the ability to easily express them (SE-Ju-1-7), as she noted in her final self-evaluation. Similarly, she placed value on reading for meaning transaction and she
perceived that reading could only be improved by more reading
(SE-Ju-2). This change helped her build her self-confidence in learning English, which in turn brought her a great sense of achievement.
Though in her memory, "When I went to the [school] and began the first

class, I felt it was so long and difficult to finish this training course"
(Em-Ju-18), she indeed challenged her limitations and completed the
course. The preface of her portfolio gave evidence of her effort, her
thankfulness and her triumph:

> I don't know how to describe my present mood. Because I fi-
> nally finished my English studying course, I feel excited and
> proud. Looking back this one year, there are a stirring of emo-
> tion in my mind. I really want to thank my family for helping
> me to reach the dream of pursuing further education. Every
> time my sisters always took my son to go to my mom's home
> before I attending the class and my husband drove me to my
> mom's home after I finishing the class. When I went back my
> mom's home, my son had been full and taken a bath. I didn't
> need to spend any time caring him. Their support let me ac-
> complish the hard task. I am very lucky.
> I also want to thank [the teacher]'s teaching. Her professional
> guidance let me build up my confidence for English. I can hug
> English again and produce great learning enthusiasm. Her en-
> couragement is an important reason. I am never serious to learn
> English like this time. Even though I went to a cram school be-
> fore, I just a quiet person. I didn't dare to say any word. Poor
> English was always my nightmare. Through this course training,
> I don't boast of my progress, at least I can speak out bravely in
> public. In addition, the training of writing changed my English
> composition ability. I never thought English writing could be
> done so easy. Although the process of writing I met some prob-
> lems like structure, organization, no ideals and grammar mis-
> takes, I followed the teacher's leading and overcame these ob-
> stacles little by little. In fact, don't worry about your writing
> good or bad and don't care others opinions. More readings and
> writings are the best ways. That is the reason why I announced
> some writings on the board. I like each piece of writing in my
> portfolio. Because all writings stand for my painstaking effort, I
> regard them my achievement. I like the way of writing essays

too. Through the two drafts and the final article reinforce my impressions. I believe I won't do the same mistakes next writing. To sum up, I don't know how to express my appreciation for [the teacher]. I can say only "Thank you very much."
This semester we read the book of "Tuesdays with Morrie." Everybody had deep feeling and got many hints from this book. So did I. Because we used the type of discussing everyone's opinion, not only increased the feeling each other but also achieved many different thinking. I really have great achievement. Although the course was over, we mutually made an appointment to continue reading some English books. In the future, perhaps we can form a study group and go on keeping contact. Every time I went to the class, it was my happy time. I cherish the memory about learning with my classmates. Their friendship will imprint on my mind forever. I wish everybody a perfect life.

(PP-Ju)

5.4.2.2 Joyce's Personal Growth/Empowerment

Joyce, a professional in the field of engineering, read technical articles but seldom read anything that was moving or sensitive (OR-Jo-2-1). However, in this year of learning, she expanded her reading as well as her concerns.

In the first semester, her theme report was about the living environment, such as green industries, water pollution, the greenhouse effect, organic foods, and space trash. The reason why she paid attention to these issues was because she wanted to integrate all the knowledge she had studied in her school days:

> ... I concern this subject because I majored in chemical engineering in university and in graduate school I majored in forest engineering about modify of wood products industry. The scopes are big difference between chemical engineering and forest engineering. That how to get balance between both is my interested at all times (OR-Jo-1-1).

Her eagerness to find a balance between her two majors revealed that she was serious towards learning and in the application of what she had learned. Also, she considered theme exploration as an opportunity for her to investigate issues further. The way she integrated her professional knowledge, her concern for the environment, and her English course demonstrated her perseverance and how deeply she reflected on things (RJ-14).

In the second semester, her theme report was about life, which included death and the fear of aging. Besides discussing the things Morrie said, she also used Oscar Wilde's *The Happy Prince* for supporting references. This work was totally different from what she had reported in the first semester and she began to view these differences as a chance to take risks:

> Perhaps my major is about engineering, so most of my readings are more rational and less sensitive articles. This semester I read some sensitive articles. In my feeling, life is an endlessly learning course. Everyday we have different class to learn (OR-Jo-2-1).

She faced the challenges courageously, though there were difficulties: she either felt her thoughts were stuck or she did not know precisely how to convey her abundant ideas (Em-Jo-13). With patience and extraordinary effort (O-22, 23, 27, 28), she eventually composed wonderful essays, usually revised more than four times, and completed inspiring theme reports. The wide range of theme selection broadened her concerns and deepened her insight. As Rogers (1983) emphasized, when students have freedom to learn, they become searchers after knowledge and discover what an adventure in learning it is.

Impressed by Morrie's sayings, she formed a new concept of death and aging. As regards death, she noticed,

> Some people afraid of the sight of death, and don't know how to face death and wouldn't like to face death coming. Because we don't know where we go and that is an unknown world.

When we realize death, we don't fear and see everything much differently (OR-Jo-2-4).

Regarding the fear of aging, she was aware that aging was normal. It is not just decay, as Morrie said, it is also growth, because life is a series of cumulative experiences (Mitch, 1997). Joyce concluded, "Every stage of our life has its meaning. We should delight to accept. Aging was valuable" (OR-Jo-2-5). She did not make this statement naively; instead, she understood it thoroughly through both reading Morrie and taking care of her grandparents (O-21). Again, she presented the close relationship between her reading/writing and her life and concerns. This connection promoted her critical consciousness and so empowered her in both thought and deed (Bentley, 1999; Freire, 1993; Freire & Macedo, 1987).

Joyce considered finishing Tuesdays with Morrie as her major accomplishment as a reader (SE-Jo-2-6), because, as she said, "it was the first book that I completely read and it taught me how to love and self-grow" (SE-Jo-2-5). In addition to Tuesdays with Morrie, she read articles and books related to the philosophy of life (Em-Jo-13), such as The Happy Prince, The Little Prince, Education of the Little Tree, Why Am I Afraid to Tell You Who I Am, etc. (Em-Jo-14, O-18, 22, SE-Jo-2). As a result of forming the habit of reading English books and gaining an interest in writing English, she became a reader and a writer (RJ-28). The preface of her portfolio spoke clearly for her growth:

> Because of the need of working, I must contact English everyday. But I don't think that it is learning. It is just my job. I have to read paper and do the routine report. ....
> Before entering this class, I never knew what the real English writing ... was. But since the first class last semester, I had a different feeling. ...
> For me, the most gain is I could write down my impression as we read some articles, even though there is just a sentence. And this semester, I feel my most accomplishment is I have finished reading a book, Tuesdays with Morrie. It also causes my

interesting for reading English. I think I won't fear to read English book further.

During preparing the portfolio, I never have so great achievement. Because not only I am interested in English writing and reading, but also I learn how to live. The course opens a window to guide me to the way of learning English. Thank my dear teacher and my classmates.

(PP-Jo)

5.4.3 Good (32-28)

Anne was the only student rated at this level.

5.4.3.1 Anne's Personal Growth/Empowerment

Anne, a woman without any writing instruction prior to this class, improved her writing performance and built her confidence in writing after a year of learning. She also showed personal growth in several ways.

Anne wrote in her final self-evaluation,

> I think there are three accomplishments this year as a writer, the first is observing the society more soft, the second is thinking more about life, and the last is ever trying to write my ideas on the paper in English (SE-A-1-6).

According to Freire (1970, 1993), conscious beings would have action and reflection upon their world. Anne's observation of society with a tender heart and her thinking more about life indicated her development in the process of humanization.

Moreover, that she valued these achievements of being a writer showed her newly formed concept of a writer. The connection she made between reading/writing and society/life revealed that she connected the word and the world as well as the self and the word (Freire & Macedo, 1987; Wink, 2000). Further evidence was shown in the preface of her portfolio:

> For most government employees, it isn't usual to have an "English reading and writing" lesson, especially a lesson like we had this year. …. In our reading practice, it's not only language training but also life study. … we know the relationship is more important than others. … (PP-A-1 & 2).

Also, her gracious attitude toward people around her showed her tenderness while interacting with others. The gratitude she showed in the preface can be summarized in the following sentence "Thank you all for bringing these good things into my life" (PP-A-3), which illustrates the soft way she observes society.

Her self-perception as a reader and a writer changed in the year of learning. In the beginning of the school year, she never thought of practicing reading and writing English. Her major concern was to improve the listening and speaking of English (Em-A-1). However, after being engaged in the learning of theme cycles, her major accomplishment as a reader was "I learn some good words, good opinions, and spent some more time to read English articles" (SE-A-2-6). Even when she mentioned how to improve her reading, she emphasized "remember more and more vocabulary by reading different kinds of articles, and practice to guess the meanings when I first read a vocabulary" (SE-A-2-8). The emphasis on reading articles of different genres and meaning suggests that she had formed a belief that learning a language should go from whole to part and meaning should be obtained from the context. Learning reading by reading more became her motto and so she had confidence in saying, "If the ability of English is not good, it would be hard to read by yourself, but it can be approved by reading more and more" (SE-A-2-10).

In addition, through frequently reading English articles at home (SE-A-2-2), she noticed that good writing did not necessarily contain complex sentences or big words. Instead, she appreciated writing "using simple sentence or simple words to describe deep feeling or some situations that made readers realize clearly what the author would like to say and made readers think it over and over" (SE-A-2-9). This comment showed her growth in reader awareness. Her reading awareness was not obtained from a series of lectures but from pleasure reading and group discussion. By appreciating well-written English articles and books as well as sharing reading responses interactively with others, she recognized that simple words and sentences used properly can draw tremendous attention of the readers and could have a dramatic impact on them (O-26, RJ-28). Therefore, she applied these techniques to her own writing. When she was asked what her strengths were as a writer and what areas she needed to improve, she answered with confidence "I think my strength is ... I have my own thinking, my own words to say about life and society et al." (SE-A-1-7), and "I think I can ... make my writing easier to read and to be more vivid" (SE-A-1-8). As we can see, Anne not only changed her perception of what a reader is, but also altered her perception of being a writer. The strong connection between writing and the writer as well as between the writer and the reader is further shown by her saying, "... if something moved you, write it down and that always can move others" (SE-A-1-9).

All in all, Anne's personal empowerment was presented in various ways. She was fond of reading and writing and believed that she had the potential to write well (SE-A-1-10). She recognized that reading is a guessing game and words are meaningful only in context. Also, she noticed that writing is person-related and that simple words and expressions can be powerful and touching as long as the writer is first moved.

5.5 Discussion of the Results

The results of this study prove the efficacy of implementing whole-language-based theme cycles in an adult EFL reading-writing class. The results can be explained by assuming that the whole-to-part view of language, the integration of learning and learners, and the value of interaction and collaboration provided students with a sound learning environment, in which they improved their writing, changed their attitudes, and gained empowerment.

From the Whole-to-part View of Language and the View of Meaning Making

Language is learned as a whole. Because "language learning is easy when it's whole, real, and relevant" (Goodman, 1986, p. 26), in this study, the target language was always presented to the students in a complete form. They read complete articles, like essays, short stories, news articles, poems, lyrics, jokes, and so on. The discussion of these reading materials was always in context. Whether they did summary making, paraphrasing, retelling, recreating, or responding, meaning was always the first concern. The writing they did was never sentence patterns practice, transformational grammar practice, or model-based paragraph writing. There were no fill-in-the-blank exercises or multiple-choice lessons. They always wrote real writing pieces, which were generated by the writer, full of the writer's inquiries, and delivered with the writer's unique style. Draft discussion was the only time they focused on the structures and forms of their writing and was usually carried out at the point of their needs.

Writing is a journey of meaning making. Goodman (1986) advocated, "Language learning is learning how to mean" (p. 26), and Weaver et al. (1993) argued further, "The learners construct meaning for themselves by actively transacting (interacting) with other people, with books and other printed matter, ... and materials in the external world" (p. 32). The concept that language learning should take place from whole to part and that writing is a meaning-making process, unshackled the students from the pressure of making errors in language components. Moreover, students were given the freedom to regard making errors as a process of literacy development. This change in their view of language and language learning unchained their writing and allowed them to improve in all aspects: voice, content, organization, and language. These impressive results were not gained from a single writing piece or from a single rater with bias. Instead, they were the results of the scrutiny of two professional raters, rating 80 writing pieces, written by 8 students. Though some research has argued that students instructed with drills or model-based practices would also improve their writing (Chiang, 1999), it did not mention whether it resulted in more writing or a keener interest in writing. On the other hand, our study not only showed the better writing of students in the general sense, but also presented their progress in confidence, interest, and individual development. Besides the improvement of content and organization, the students' writing had more vivid expression, figurative language, and authentic voice. Their improvement was beyond the expectation of rigid rule-controlled correctness and reached for the anticipation of liveliness and heartiness.

Risk taking is encouraged in a supportive community. Along with the emphasis of meaning, teachers "are responsible for creating a supportive community of learners in which everyone (including the teacher) is free to take risks without fear of negative consequences, and in which everyone is supported by others" (Weaver et al., 1993, p. 41). The emphasis on meaning was also revealed in the teacher's comments. While making comments on students' essays and journals, the teacher would first focus on the meaning conveyed in their writing and then suggest alternative approaches for the revision. For example, when the teacher responded to Peggy's journal on the issue of married life, she wrote

> What else I can say! You indeed made brief but profound comments on marriage life. Yes, to respect each other and to solve communication problems are important for both the husband and the wife. However, in daily life, such common understanding usually becomes the hardest principles for any couple to carry out. Maybe that's why we all need to make our efforts to 'cultivate' our personality and interpersonal relationship. Thank you for the insights and sharing! (j-p-2)

Also when she commented on Judy's theme writing on traveling, she wrote

> I can tell you are good at preparing for a wonderful trip. ... I also believe that those who read your piece will definitely consider more carefully about their trip because you ... provide them with ... useful suggestion. Nice sharing. Thanks! ...

As for the colorful "responses," can you guess what they refer to? Generally speaking, the pink ones refer to the problems of sentence structures. For example, … (J-Ju-4).

Learners are respected as unique individuals. "In order to help students engage themselves wholeheartedly in learning, learners must be confident that they will be safe from negative repercussions. That is, the environment for learning must reward risk, not punish it" (Weaver et al., 1993, p. 34). The emphasis on meaning is also related to the value of a student's voice, the voice that makes writing authentic and powerful and changes the student's perception of being a writer. Because the class put value on a student's voice, in this study they did not need to sacrifice their ideas or personality for the sake of sentence structure and form. Therefore, they did not suffer from being simply automatons, who produce correct (but with no individual voice) and "good" pieces; instead, they regarded themselves as thinking beings with ideas, identities, personalities, intellect and emotions. Focusing first on thoughts, students began to view themselves as real writers and thinkers. Knoblauch and Brannon (1984) strongly stated:

> People write because it enables the making of meaning, the discovery of coherence, the communicating of valued ideas, not merely because they enjoy technical accomplishment. When teachers regard the composing process as an elaborate multiplication of skills, they are working from a pseudoconcept. They are not just overlooking the motivations that make writing worthwhile by emphasizing control of a technology; they are treating the thinking and forming processes as though they themselves were technologies, when they are not (p. 91).

From the View of Learner-centered Learning

Learners own their learning. As Goodman (1986) emphasized, "Language development is empowering: the learner "owns" the process, makes the decisions about when to use it, what for and with what results.

Literacy is empowering too, if the learner is in control with what's done with it" (p. 26). The integration of learning and learners has a positive influence on students. In this study, the integration was presented in various ways, such as self-selected themes and topics, writing about their professions, reflection on their lives and experiences, etc.. The themes students chose for reading and writing were always self-initiated. There were no assigned topics or irrelevant materials. Their professional knowledge, concerns, interests, experiences, and the social events happening in their daily lives were always selected and included. For example, Anne wrote about air transportation; Jenny introduced a light-transit system; Joyce examined the natural environment, and Peggy often discussed social events. They all gained confidence through writing about their specialties. Furthermore, with reflection on life's issues, the distance between the learning and the learners was shortened. It can be clearly seen in Judy's experiences in travel, Ken's observations on busy life, Linda's depiction of family life, and Maria's profound thoughts on art and love. Writing and the writer were inseparable in theme cycles learning and so English writing became close and relevant to the students. This integration promoted students' motivation and performance. No wonder students reported that they enjoyed seeing their ideas on paper and that they would like to share their writing with others. As whole language proponents claim, "when lessons begin with students' interests and experiences, students are naturally more motivated to engage in learning" (Freeman & Freeman, 1998, p. 107), and their learning would never be short-term rote memorization (Short, Harste, & Burke, 1996).

Negotiation promotes ownership. "Since choice is an important factor in learning, the curriculum is in many respects negotiated among the teacher and the students" (Weaver et al., 1993, p. 36). Learner-centeredness in this study was also revealed in course design and evaluation. Though there was a tentative syllabus in advance, the detailed schedule was decided by and negotiated among the teacher-researcher and the students. Both the teacher and students could suggest reading materials, lead the discussion, or provide relevant information. As with the use of contracts suggested by Rogers (1983), students involved with course design are well motivated, actively participate in activities and are driven to achieve cognitive objectives. Students feel that they are the masters of their own learning. Ownership and authorship are enhanced.

Self-evaluation is emphasized. "Self-evaluation is an important component of assessment and evaluation. ... Self-evaluation provides a basis for decision-making and goal-setting, as does mutual evaluation of the learning experiences in which the students and teacher have engaged" (Weaver et al., 1993, p. 44). Self-evaluation was emphasized in this study. The forms of self-evaluation were varied and often integrated into presenting and publishing, such as journal sharing, peer/group discussion/editing, portfolios, etc.. Formal self-evaluation was conducted as well, such as filling in questionnaires and final self-evaluation forms. This on-going self-evaluation was employed to dispel any preconceived notions that learning English is test-and-grade-driven and that learning outcomes are controlled by the teacher. Furthermore, the emphasis on this on-going self-evaluation was to strengthen the students' responsibility for learning. To paraphrase Carl Rogers (1983), with high motivation, enhanced ownership, and strengthened responsibility, it is not surprising that students in this study invest their whole being in the learning process, which tends to make their learning deeper, proceeding at a faster rate, and more pervasive in their lives and behaviors.

From the View of Interaction and Collaboration

Sharing and responding are encouraged. Goodman (1986) claimed, "Language development is a holistic personal-social achievement" (p. 26). Weaver et al. (1993) also asserted, "Individual learning is promoted by social collaboration: by opportunities to work with others, to brainstorm, to share, to try out ideas and get feedback, to obtain assistance. That is, learning is facilitated when the classroom is genuinely a community of learners" (p. 35). With the emphasis of interaction and collaboration, this study, therefore, reversed the traditional perception of writing and writing class. Constant sharing and responding raised the awareness of readership and highlighted writing as a process of social interaction. In this study, a variety of sharing and discussion was conducted throughout the school year. From the beginning of the course, students shared and discussed their theme selections. When reading and writing, students shared their reading responses via journals, essays and oral presentations. At the end of the course, they appreciated each others' individual portfolios. This teacher-student interaction as well as student-student interaction made real readers and audiences available in this study. The teacher-researcher was not the only reader of the student writers; instead, the whole class formed a community of readers and writers. In such a community, students learned and grew. Those students who engaged in theme cycles learning will no longer regard writing as an isolated activity. With collaboration instead of competition, students interacted with one another in a symmetrical context, in which they all gave and received something (Sladky, 1994). Like being engaged in a satisfying conversation, they were motivated to keep the interaction going and to produce meaningful written discourse. Collaboration and symmetric interaction drew students closer to one another and so reduced the anxiety that can be caused by competition and comparison. It is not surprising that all the students in this study showed a decrease in their writing apprehension.

Reciprocal dialogue is valued. Freire (1993) highlighted, "Only through communication can human life hold meaning. The teacher's thinking is authenticated only by the authenticity of the students' thinking. The teacher cannot think for her students, nor can she impose her thought on them. Authentic thinking, thinking that is concerned about reality, does not take place in ivory tower isolation, but only in communication" (p. 58). Besides promoting symmetric interaction among peers, the asymmetric interaction between the teacher and the students was dispelled in this study. Rather than playing the role of a lawyer examining a client's document for all possible ambiguities and misinterpretations (Shaughnessy, 1977), the teacher in this study was always a real reader trying to understand what she was reading. There was always dialogue between the teacher and the students. They discussed reading, writing, social events and life issues throughout the school year. In both spoken and written conversation, they shared firm positions, changing concepts, and unsolved confusion. The students were always respected and trusted in these reciprocal dialogues (Gadotti, 1994; Freire, 1970, 1993). Their potential was highly valued. Because of the trust and acceptance, students were willing to be risk takers, challenging their own learning and limitations. Though this humanistic way of learning often draws criticism, the concerns of chaos arising in class or having students pampered with a lack of discipline (Yu, 1990) did not occur in this study. Students took their learning responsibilities seriously and helped one another to grow. The results reflected Freire's (1993) argument on cooperation and dialogue:

> Cooperation can only be achieved through communication. ... Dialogue, as essential communication, must underlie any cooperation. ... Dialogue does not impose, does not manipulate, does not domesticate, does not "sloganize" (p. 149).

This study reconfirmed the need for a new teacher-learner relationship, in which learning proceeds via the dialogical process.

CHAPTER

CONCLUSIONS

AND RECOMMENDATIONS

6.1 Summary of the Study

This study investigates the writing progress of students in a whole language post-bachelor reading-writing class. It also explores whether the students in this class increased their writing confidence and/or decreased their writing anxiety. Finally, it questions whether students changed their perceptions about reading/writing and their understanding of themselves as readers and writers, and whether they experienced personal growth and empowerment. The goal of this study is to raise awareness of the importance of relevant material, person-centered learning, and reciprocal interaction in the learning process.

In all stages of this research, ethnography, case studies, and the teacher-as-researcher methods were used. These stages are course design, data collection, data presentation, and data analysis. The ideas for the course design were based on participant observations and reflective journals in a pilot study, informal interviews, and document analysis. Ethnography describes the teacher-researcher and her teaching philosophy. During data collection, the methods used were observation by the teacher-researcher, informal interviews in both oral and written form, the recording of reflective journals, and the collection of written documents such as essays, journals, and portfolios. At the data presentation stage, case studies are portrayed in detail. Individual changes in writing performance, writing attitudes, and personal growth are also presented.

Data analysis includes: case studies, content analysis of essays, and thick description in ethnography. In addition to qualitative research methods, an SPSS 8.0 package was also used for finding the mean scores of essay writing and questionnaire outcomes to examine interrater reliability, and for investigating the t-test on the overall progress of the class.

The researcher relied heavily on the theories and framework of whole language, Carl Rogers' whole-person learning, and Paulo Freire's education of liberation. The features of these theories framed the design for this study as well as the findings on the changes in the students throughout the year of learning.

The major findings of the study are as follows:

1. All of the students made progress in their writing performance in terms of voice, content, organization and language, after engaging in the learning of theme cycles. Three students improved their writing from Weak to Good, four students from Average to Good and one student from Weak to Average.

2. All of the students made progress in their writing voice. Though their voice was occasionally hindered by unclear language, their authenticity and personality in voice grew stronger throughout the year of learning.

3. All of the students made progress in writing content. At the beginning of the course, they knew neither how to generate ideas nor how to connect their ideas with their writing. What they had in mind was always more than what they were able to write. However, in the process of learning, they became able to generate more ideas for each paper and managed to develop adequate content. They also skillfully connected what they knew with what they intended to convey.

4. All of the students made progress in writing organization. The amount of illogical and non-fluent expression was greatly reduced during the learning process. The confusing and disconnected ideas were mostly replaced by understandable and coherent expression towards the end of the school year. With

constant reading and writing, they were aware of the importance of idea development.

5. All of the students made progress in their use of language. In terms of sentence structure, they not only gained knowledge but used more sophisticated structures in their writing. In terms of grammar, they became aware of s-v agreement, verb tenses, word forms, word order, and the appropriate use of modals and connectors. In terms of vocabulary, they began to take risks in different word choices, illustrated by the use of figurative language, vivid expression, allegory, similes, and synonyms/antonyms. Though their writing was not perfect, their progress in language use was obvious.

6. All of the students increased their writing self-efficacy in various writing tasks as well as in different writing component skills. One student raised her writing confidence from Low to High, four students from Low to Middle, and three students from Middle to High. Their progress in writing confidence helped change their self-perception as readers and writers.

7. All of the students decreased their writing apprehension after a year of theme cycles learning. One student lowered her writing anxiety from High to Middle, six students from Middle to Low, and one student from higher Middle to lower Middle. The decrease in writing apprehension correlated to the increase in writing self-efficacy. It also encouraged students to write, and write more frequently.

8. All of the students demonstrated changes in their perception of reading and writing as well as their understanding about themselves as readers and writers. They became more interested in the reading and writing of English and even formed the habit of doing so.

9. All of the students demonstrated the self-directed learning. They began to consider learning as a life-long process, and not limited to a classroom or a certain time period. They searched for their own reading materials, shared their findings, and presented their reading responses. They learned not only

language and research skills but also reading/writing and sharing/responding. They began to take responsibility for their own learning.

10. All of the students experienced personal growth and empowerment. With profound reflection on their reading and their lives, the students searched for the meaning of life, the value of human beings, human relationships, and the harmony of society. Through constant inquiring and problem-posing, they viewed issues from different perspectives. They became more patient with others and more patient with themselves.

6.2 Implications of the Study

The results of this study prove that it is possible to implement theme cycles learning in an adult EFL reading-writing class. Since the design of the theme cycles learning used in this course was based on the philosophy of whole language, Carl Rogers' whole-person learning, and Paulo Freire's liberation of education, the implications relating to these theories and philosophy are worth consideration.

First, the findings imply that learner-centeredness arouses motivation, enhances ownership and authorship, and reminds students that learning is their responsibility. It is possible to encourage EFL student writers to choose their favorite themes for exploration. They can then develop, individually or collaboratively, their own learning according to their professional knowledge, interests/concerns, and their desire to discover. In order to stimulate learning, rather than assign the same work to all students, the teacher suggests possibilities for individual or collaborative learning experiences (Weaver et al., 1993). Since there are no assigned topics and no dominant viewpoints, students will have "freedom to experiment and risk without fear of negative feedback" (Weaver et al., 1993, p. 208). As Scott (1996) mentioned,

> Motivating students to write can be elusive because the assigned topic is often arbitrary and artificial. However, ... when the teachers play collaborative roles, never dominating nor insisting on their personal views, students will be more likely to engage in the scholarly activity of exchanging ideas regardless of the topic (p. 148-149).

Second, the results suggest that relevant materials may bridge the gap between the writing and the writers. This happens if students choose materials that interest them for their theme project and if in-class reading and discussion is related to either their theme project or is connected to a universal theme, such as humanity or life. Through reading, sharing, writing, and discussion, students are inspired to participate in constant introspection and retrospection. The reading and writing of English is then no longer something apart from themselves, but is integrated into their life and breath. This greatly benefits the generation of ideas. Because the distance between learning and the learner is diminished, students cease to regard writing as a subject or a discipline. They begin to view writing as a way of presenting themselves, their identities and their thinking. Thus, their perception of writing changes, and in the process, they gain the confidence to write.

Third, the study provides evidence that the emphasis of meaning promotes students' writing. Emphasis of meaning encourages students to view writing as a meaning-making process, a journey of discovery, and an opportunity to clarify their thoughts. In order to fully express their thoughts, students are willing to spend more time on idea generation, organization, and development. In striving to be understood by their readers, they tend to spend more time on revision. By doing this, students simultaneously improve the content of their writing along with their writing skills, without pre-packaged or pre-scheduled grammar lessons that so often dominated the writing curriculum. Raimes (1983) supports this argument:

> When FL students are required to write beyond the sentence level from the start, they learn to communicate ideas with a reader, without the pressure of face-to-face communication, to

record experience, to explore a subject, to become familiar with the conventions of written discourse in the target language, and to discover the link between writing and thinking (cited in Scott, 1996, p. 167).

The emphasis on meaning also reinforces the importance of writing as an integral part of learning. Since Goodman (1986) claimed that the whole is always more than the sum of the parts, writing lessons which focus on the entire meaning must, therefore, be preferred over writing lessons which focus on separate components. Moreover, in a study which values meaning, the linear or hierarchical view of teaching writing, which emphasizes that writing should be learned from words, phrases and sentences to paragraphs, will be de-emphasized. In other words, "the traditional paradigm, which included writing in the FL curriculum after students had already attained some mastery of the target language, is no longer valid" (Scott, 1996, p. 167).

Fourth, it appears that constant sharing and responding raises the awareness of readership and highlights writing as a process of social interaction. Through sharing, responding to, and publishing what they have written, students have a real sense of audience. This audience then becomes their stimulus and purpose for writing (Simic, 1993). When they have a sense of audience, they want to see that readers understand their meaning. With this strong desire to be understood, they will, without having to be forced or reminded, continue to work on grammar and spelling (Nelson, 1991). As Sladky (1994) mentioned, "only when he felt he was getting something from the exchange was he willing to contribute something to the process."

Fifth, the outcomes lead us to believe that the reciprocal dialogue between the teacher and the students is the key to facilitating all aspects of learning. The teacher not only serves as a role model, demonstrating what it means to be a literate person and a lifelong learner (Weaver et al., 1993) but also plays the role of co-learner and proposes a dialogical way of learning (Freire, 1993). It is helpful when the teacher welcomes input from the students and listens without judgment. The students are encouraged when the teacher can view the world through their own eyes

(Rogers, 1983; Weaver et al., 1993). Students will benefit if teachers show themselves to be real people with conviction and genuine feelings, and frequently share, with their students, their thoughts, personality, and life stories. That the teacher has faith in humanity and hope in education will elicit the potential of each student and enhance their self-esteem. This teacher/student interaction promotes critical thinking and personal growth and facilitates learning. As Rogers (1983) repeatedly emphasized, none of the methods are effective unless the teacher's genuine desire is to create a climate in which there is freedom to learn.

6.3 Limitations of the Study

A major limitation of this study results from the small size of the group participating in the research. It involved only one class with eight students. Therefore, the research results of the effects of theme cycles learning may not be generalized to all adult EFL learners.

The second limitation of this study results from the lack of gender diversity. Since there is only one male student participating in this research, the tendency of theme selection, the responses to reading, and ways of negotiation may not be the same when equal numbers of both genders are represented.

The examination of only first and final drafts of each essay is the third limitation. The comparison of first and final drafts, in this study, clearly shows the progress of students' writing. However, without investigation of multiple drafts, it is difficult to explain the process of progress in details.

6.4 Recommendations for Future Research

This study proves the efficacy of implementing theme cycles learning in an adult EFL writing class and has shown positive outcomes in the writing performance, writing attitudes, and personal growth of the students. Further research, however, is still warranted.

First, it would be interesting to know how theme cycles learning can influence writing performance. This study presents the changes in students' writing but does not investigate how these changes occur through the process of theme cycles learning. Examination of how these changes occur can shed more light on the subject and further assist those interested in applying theme cycles learning in their writing classes.

Second, it would be helpful to know whether the majority of adult EFL learners would benefit from theme cycles learning. The students in this study were all government employees with academic degrees and professional knowledge. It remains to be seen whether adult EFL learners, other than government employees, would have the same results, and whether adult EFL learners with no academic background would show the same progress.

Third, future research might look at whether college students would also benefit from theme cycles learning. The investigation could focus on both English majors and non-English majors to see if there is any difference. Since most college students have already learned to write English in high school, it would be interesting to find out whether theme cycles learning and portfolio preparation would bring them the same sense of accomplishment experienced by the adult learners. In other words, the research could compare results from learners who have had experience writing English with those who have not.

Fourth, future research could be done with a group having equal numbers of male and female participants to see if the outcome is the same. Since there was only one male but are seven females participating in this study, curiosity is aroused as to whether the results would be different if there had been a higher percentage of males. The question is whether females are more willing than males to write about their per-

sonal lives. If males usually do prefer "report" talk, while females enjoy "rapport" talk, would this distinction be reflected in the effectiveness
of theme cycles learning?

Fifth, since the interaction between teacher and students is a key
factor in this study, the reasons for avoidance of reciprocal dialogue
warrants further scrutiny. Though this study shows that reciprocal dialogue between teacher and students is not only possible but effective, we
need to find out whether it is because of the common concerns shared by
both sides. If there is a considerable gap between the teacher's interests and the students' concerns, would these reciprocal dialogues still be
possible? Another question is whether age difference plays a role. In
this study, the teacher is close to the average age of the students, which
means they shared certain experiences while growing up. If the teacher
and the students belong to different generations, with fewer common
experiences, would this reciprocal dialogue be possible?

Sixth, an investigation on teacher's growth and empowerment
could be done in the future. If teachers are co-learners and constantly
involved in a dialogical way of learning, whether they would change
their perception of English teaching and whether they would also be
empowered are worth further scrutiny.

6.5 Conclusions

The goal of this study is to raise awareness of the importance of
relevant materials and to investigate an alternative way of learning—theme cycles—to assess their influence on the learning outcomes
of adult EFL writers. According to the changes recorded in the students' writing performance, writing confidence and anxiety levels, and
personal growth and empowerment, we have successfully reached our
goal. The significance of this is echoed in the statement made by F.
Smith (1994b) in his *Writing and the writer*,

> Writing is not learned in steps; there is no ladder of separate and incremental skills to be ascended. Writing develops as an individual develops, in many directions, continually, usually inconspicuously, but occasionally in dramatic and unforeseeable spurts. And, like individual human development, writing requires nourishment and encouragement rather than a restrictive regimen (p. 221).

Writing is a process of shaping language, a process of creating ideas, like delivering a baby, full of the power of life, requiring labor but worth celebrating. It should be an enjoyment with great respect. It is a pity that most adult EFL writers experience the difficulty of delivery but seldom experience the joy of a new born life. Overshadowed with frustrating learning experiences, adult EFL writers usually assume that they are failures in the writing of English and that they *cannot* write (F. Smith, 1994b). Fortunately, whole-language-based theme cycle learning renders these assumptions insignificant. In a whole language class, the concept of "failure" does not exist (Weaver et al., 1993) and there is no discrimination towards different rates of learning (Goodman, 1986; Weaver et al., 1990, 1994). Instead, students are respected as capable and unique, and are, therefore, always eager to deliver their "brain baby" with pride. With trust, collaboration, and reciprocal dialogue, both the teacher and the students experience a sense of achievement, the satisfaction of fulfillment, and the thrill of triumph. The teacher's reflections on this year of learning offer the best conclusion for this study:

> Their perseverance, tenderness, profundity and frankness show me that we can really challenge the limitations. To the students, the limitations may be their tight schedules or low proficiency in the reading and writing of English. To me, the limitations are the doubts and uncertainty of trying new things with busy adult learners. With their collaboration and participation, we all experienced the joy of breakthrough. (RJ-30)

REFERENCES

Altwerger, B., & Flores, B. (1994). Theme cycles: Creating communities of learners. *Primary Voices K-6, 2* (1), 2-6.

Andrews-Sullivan, M., & Negrete, E. O. (1994). Our struggles with theme cycle. *Primary Voices K-6, 2* (1), 15-19.

Arthur, B. M. (1991). Working with new ESL students in a junior high school reading class. *Journal of Reading, 34*, 628-631.

Bandura, A. (1986). *Social foundations of thought and action: A social cognitive theory.* Englewood Cliffs, NJ: Prentice Hall.

Barnes, G. A. (1981). *Crisscross: Structured writing in context.* Englewood Cliffs, NJ: Prentice Hall.

Bartolome, L. I. (1994). Beyond the methods Fetish: Toward a humanizing pedagogy. *Harvard Educational Review, 64* (2), 173-194.

Beane, J. A. (1995). Curriculum integration and the disciplines of knowledge. *Phi Delta Kappan, 76*, 616-622.

Bentley, L. (1999). Paulo Freire: A brief biography [On-Line WWW]. Available: http://www.unomaha.edu/~pto/paulo.htm

Bergeron, B. S. (1990). What does the term whole language mean? Constructing a definition from the literature. *Journal of Reading Behavior, 22* (4), 301-329.

Berthoff, A. (1985). [Review of the book *The politics of education: Culture, power, and liberation*]. *Journal of Education, 167* (1), 140-143.

Bialystok, E. (1990). *Communication strategies: A psychological analysis of second-language use.* Cambridge, MA: Basil Blackwell.

Bird, L. (1987). What is whole language? In "Dialogue," D. Jacobs (Ed.), *Teachers networking: The whole language newsletter, 1* (1). New York: Richard C. Owen.

Blanton, L. (1987) Reshaping ESL students' perception of writing. *EFL Journal, 41* (2), 112-118.

Brinton, D., Snow, M., & Wesche, M. (1989). *Content-based second language instruction.* New York: Newbury House.

Brophy, J. (1988). Research on teacher effects: Uses and abuses. *Elementary School Journal, 89*, 20.

Brown, D. (1988). *Understanding research in second language learning: A teacher's guide to statistics and research design.* Cambridge, UK: Cambridge University Press.

Brown, H., & Mathie, V. (1991). *Inside whole language: A classroom view.* Portsmouth, NH: Heinemann.

Cambourne, B. (1988). *The whole story: Natural learning and the acquisition of literacy in the classroom.* Auckland, New Zealand: Scholastic.

Carl Rogers, core conditions and education [On-line]. (2001). *Encyclopedia of Informal Education.* Available http://www.infed.org/thinkers/et-rogers.htm

Castro, E. (1994). Implementing theme cycle: One teacher's way. *Primary Voices K-6, 2* (1), 7-14.

Chang, Y. L. (1988). Pen pal letter activity in written instruction for college students and high school students. *Proceedings of the 5th Conference on English Teaching and Learning in the Republic of China*, pp. 193-209. Taipei: Crane.

Chapman, M., & Anderson, J. (1996). Putting theory into practice: A day in two classrooms. In V. Froese (Ed.), Whole-Language: Practice and Theory (pp.). Boston, MA: Allyn & Bacon.

Chen, H. C. (1988). Computer assisted writing in Taiwan: Methods and perspectives. *Proceedings of the 5th Conference on English Teaching and Learning in the Republic of China* (pp. 173-191). Taipei: Crane.

Chen, Y. M. (1994). The whole language approach to language instruction: Philosophical beliefs, theory, and practice. *Journal of National Chung Cheng University, Sec. I: Humanities, 5* (1), 365-397.

Chen, Y. M. (1996). To revise or not to revise: A comparison of single-drafted writing vs. multi-drafted writing. *Proceedings of the 13th Conference on English Teaching and Learning in the Republic of China*, pp. 63-72. Taipei: Crane.

Chen, Y. M. (1997). An investigation of EFL students' perceptions of revision in English composition. *Proceedings of the 14th Conference on English Teaching and Learning in the Republic of China*, pp. 273-292. Taipei: Crane.

Chen, Y. M. (2001). The whole language approach to teaching reading. *The National Chi Nan University Journal, 5* (1), 161-180.

Cheng, Y. S. (1998). A qualitative inquiry of language anxiety: Interviews with Taiwanese EFL students. *The Proceedings of the 7th International Symposium on English Teaching*, pp. 309-320. Taipei: Crane.

Cheng, Y. S. (1999). A study of second language writing anxiety and individual learner variables. Paper presented at the 8th International Symposium on English Teaching, Taipei, Taiwan (November).

Cheng, Y. S. (2001). Learner's beliefs and second language anxiety. *Concentric: Studies in English Literature and Linguistics, 27* (2), 209-223. Taipei: NTNU.

Chiang, M. C. (1999). *The effects of model-based instruction on Chinese students' English writing.* Unpublished master's thesis, National Taiwan Normal University, Taipei.

Clark, J. (1992). *Whole language literacy for at-risk learners.* Washington, DC: ERIC Clearinghouse.

Cochran-Smith, M., & Lytle, S. L. (1993). *Inside/outside: Teacher research and knowledge.* New York: Teachers College Press.

Connor, U. (1984). A study of cohesion and coherence in English as a second language students' writing. *Papers in Linguistics: International Journal of Communication, 17,* 301-316.

Crawford, A. N. (1993). Literature, integrated language arts, and the language minority child: A focus on meaning. In A. Carrasquillo & C. Hedley (Eds.), *Whole Language and the Bilingual Learner.* Norwood, NJ: Albex.

Cumming, A. (1989). Writing expertise and second language proficiency. *Language learning, 39* (1), 81-135.

Daly, J. A., & Miller, M. D. (1975). The empirical development of an instrument to measure writing apprehension. *Research in the Teaching of English, 9,* 242-249.

De Carlo, J. E. (1995). *Perspectives in whole language.* Boston, MA: Allyn and Bacon.

Denzin, N. K. (1990). Interpretive interactionism. Newbury Park, CA: Sage.

Dewey, J. (1963). *Experience and education.* New York: Macmillan.

Dirkx, J. M. & Prenger, S. M. (1997). *A guide for planning and implementing instruction for adults: A theme-based approach.* San Francisco, CA: Jossey-Bass.

Edelsky, C., Altwerger, B., & Flores, B. (1991). *Whole language: What's the difference?* Portsmouth, NH: Heinemann.

Elbow, P. (1973). *Writing without teachers.* London: Macmillan Education.

Elbow, P. (1998a). *Writing without teachers* (New ed.). New York: Oxford University Press.

Elbow, P. (1998b). *Writing with power: Techniques for mastering the writing Process* (New ed.). New York: Oxford University Press.

Elias, J. L. (1994). *Paulo Freire: Pedagogue of liberation.* Malabar, FL: Krieger.

Engstrom, Y. (1986). The zone of proximal development as the basic category of educational psychology. *LCHC Quarterly, 8,* 23-42.

Faigle, L., Cherry, R., Jolliffe, D., & Skinner, A. (1993). *Assessing writers' knowledge and processes of composing.* Norwood, NJ: Ablex.

Feeley, J., Strickland, D., & Wepner, S. (Eds.). (1991). *Process reading and writing: A literature-based approach.* New York: Teachers College Press.

Flynn, S. (1986). Production vs. comprehension: Definition underlying competencies. *Studies in Second Language Acquisition, 8,* 2, 135-164.

Flynn, S., & O'Neil, W. A. (Eds.). (1988). *Linguistics theory in second language acquisition.* Boston, MA: Kluwer Academic.

Freeman, D. E., & Freeman, Y. S. (1988). Whole language content lessons for ESL students. Paper presented at the Annual Meeting of the Teachers of English to Speakers of Other Languages (22nd, Chicago, March 8-13). (ERIC Document Reproduction Service No. ED 295 468)

Freeman, D. E., & Freeman, Y. S. (1991). Practicing what we preach: Whole language with teachers of bilingual learners. In Y. M. Goodman, W. J. Hood, & K. S. Goodman (Eds.), *Organizing for whole language* (pp. 348-363). Portsmouth, NH: Heinemann.

Freeman, Y. S., & Freeman, D. E. (1989). Evaluation of second-language junior and senior high school students. In K. S. Goodman, Y. M. Goodman, & W. J. Hood (Eds.), *The whole language evaluation book* (pp. 141-150).

Freeman, Y. S., & Freeman, D. E. (1992). *Whole language for second language learners.* Portsmouth, NH: Heinemann.

Freeman, Y. S., & Freeman, D. E. (1998). *ESL/EFL teaching: Principles for success.* Portsmouth, NH: Heinemann.

Freire, P. (1970). *Pedagogy of the oppressed* (M. B. Ramos, Trans.). New York: Continuum.

Freire, P. (1971). *Extension or communication?* Rio de Janeiro: Paz e Terra.

Freire, P. (1985). *The politics of education: Culture, power, and liberation.* South Hadley, MA: Bergin & Garvey.

Freire, P. (1993). *Pedagogy of the oppressed* (New revised 20th-annversary ed.) (M. B. Ramos, Trans.). New York: Continuum.

Freire, P. (1994). *Pedagogy of hope: Reliving pedagogy of the oppressed* (R. R. Barr, Trans.). New York: Continuum.

Freire, P., & Macedo, D. (1987). *Literacy: Reading the word and the world.* South Hadley, MA: Bergin.

Freire, P., Fraser, J. W., Macedo, D., McKinnon, T., & Stokes, W. T. (Eds.). (1997). *Mentoring the mentor: A critical dialogue with Paulo Freire.* New York, NY: Peter Lang.

Friend, H. (1985). The effect of science and mathematics integration on selected seventh grade students' attitudes toward and achievement in science. *School Science and Mathematics, 85*, 453-461.

Froese, V. (1991). *Whole-language: Practice and theory.* Boston, MA: Allyn and Bacon.

Fromkin, V., & Rodman, R. (1988). *An introduction to language* (4th ed.). Fort Worth: Holt, Rinehart, Winston.

Gadotti, M. (1994). *Reading Paulo Freire: His life and work* (J. Milton, Trans.). New York: SUNY Press.

Gadotti, M., & Torres, C. A. (n.d.). Paulo Freire: A Homage [On-line WWW]. Available: http://www.nl.edu/ace/Homage.html

Gaies, S. (1976). Gradation in formal second language instruction as a factor in the development of interlanguage. Paper presented at the meeting of the Midwest Modern Language Association, November 4-7.

Gass, S. M., & Madden, C. G. (Eds.). (1985). *Input in second language acquisition.* Boston, MA: Heinle and Heinle.

Gass, S. M., & Selinker, L. (1992). *Language transfer in language learning.* Philadelphia: J. Benjamin.

Goetz, J. P., & LeCompte, M. D. (1984). *Ethnography and qualitative design in educational research.* Orlando, FL: Academic Press.

Goodman, K. (1967). Reading: A psycholinguistic guessing game. *Journal of the Reading Specialist, May*, 126-135.

Goodman, K. (1969). Analysis of oral reading miscues: Applied psycholinguistics.

Reading Research Quarterly, 5, 9-30.

Goodman, K. (1986). *What's whole in whole language.* Portsmouth, NH: Heinemann.

Goodman, K. (1992). I didn't found whole language. *The Reading Teacher, 46* (3), 188-199.

Goodman, Y. (1989). Roots of the whole-language movement. *The Elementary School Journal, 90* (2), 113-127.

Graman, T. (1988). Education for humanization: Applying Paulo Freire's pedagogy to learning a second language. *Harvard Educational Review, 58,* 4, 433-448.

Graves, D., & Hansen, J. (1983). The Author's Chair. *Language Arts, 60,* 176-183.

Gunkel, J. (1991). Please teach America: Keisuke's journey into a language community. *Language Arts, 68,* 303-310.

Gust, J. (1994). *Enhancing self-esteem: A whole language approach: Esteem-building thematic units.* Carthage, IL: Good Apple.

Gutloff, K. (Ed.). (1996). *Integrated thematic teaching.* West Haven, CT: National Education Association Professional Library.

Hall, N. (1994). Written dialogue with young children: Making writing live. In A. D. Flurkey & R. J. Meyer (Eds.), *Under the Whole Language Umbrella: Many Cultures, Many Voices* (pp. 343-356). Urbana, IL: National Council of Teacher of English (NCTE).

Halliday, M. A. K. (1977). *Explorations in the functions of language.* New York: Elsvier North-Holland.

Hamayan, E. V. (1989). Teaching writing to potentially English proficient students using whole language approaches. Program Information Guide Series, National Clearinghouse for Bilingual Education. Illinois Resource Center. Number 11, Summer 1989. pp. 1-15.

Hamayan, E., & Pfleger, M. (1987). *Developing literacy in English as a second language: Guidelines for teachers of young children from nonliterate backgrounds.* Washington, DC: Center for Applied Linguistics.

Hansen, J. (1992). Literacy portfolios: Helping Students know themselves. *Educational Leadership, 49,* 66-68.

Harste, J. C., Pierce, K. M., & Cairney, T. (Eds.). (1985). *The authoring cycle: A viewing guide.* Portsmouth, NH: Heinemann.

Hatch, E. (1992). *Discourse and language education.* New York: Cambridge University Press.

Heald-Taylor, G. (1989). *The administrator's guide to whole language.* Katonah, Y: Richard C. Owen.

Heaney, T. (1995). Issues in Freirean Pedagogy. *Thresholds in Education* [On-line WWW]. Available: http://nlu.nl.edu/ace/Resources/Documents/FreireIssues.html

Hsu, Y. (1994). *Whole language and ESL children.* Washington, DC: ERIC Clearinghouse on Language and Linguistics.

Huang, Y. K. (1997). Changes in freshman English programs for non-English majors at universities in Taiwan. In J. E. Katchen & Y. N. Leung (Eds.), *Proceedings of the 6th International Symposium on English Teaching* (pp. 332-341). Taipei: Crane.

Huang, Y. K. (1998). Whole language and fluency first applications: Ideas that work. In J. E. Katchen & Y. N. Leung (Eds.), *Proceedings of the 7th International Symposium on English Teaching* (pp. 537-546). Taipei: Crane.

Hydrick, J. (Ed.). (1991). Whole language: Empowerment at the chalk face. *The Proceedings of the 1989 National Council of Teachers of English Day of Whole Language.* New York: Scholastic Inc.

Hymes, D. H. (1972). On communicative competence. In J. B. Pride and J. Holmes (Eds.), *Sociolinguistics.* Harmondsworth, UK: Penguin.

Jacobs, G. (1988). Cooperative goal structure: A way to improve group activities. *EFL Journal, 42* (2), 97-101.

Jacobs, H. L., Zingraf, S. A., Wormuth, D. R., Hartfiel, V. F., & Hughey, J. B. (1981). *Testing ESL composition: A practical approach.* Rowley, MA: Newbury House.

Jama, V. (1992). *Integrating English as a second language instruction with the regular elementary- and middle-school curriculum: Can it work?* Paper presented at the Annual Meeting of the Teachers of English to Speakers of Other Languages (TESOL), Vancouver, B.C., March 3-7.

Janopoulos, M. (1992). Writing across the curriculum and the NNS student. Paper presented at the International TESOL Convention, Vancouver, B.C. (March).

Johns, A. (1986). Coherence and academic writing: Some definitions and suggestions for teaching. *TESOL Quarterly, 20* (2), 247-266.

Johns, A. (1991). Interpreting an English essay competency examination. *Written Communication, 8* (3), 379-401.

Johnson, D. M. (1992). *Approaches to research in second language learning.* New York, NY: Longman.

Kameen, P. (1978). A mechanical, meaningful and communicative framework for ESL sentence combining exercises. *TESOL Quarterly, 12* (4), 395-401.

Kaplan, R. B. (1988). Contrastive rhetoric and second language learning: Notes towards a theory of contrastive rhetoric. In A. Purves (Ed.), *Writing across languages and cultures: Issues in contrastive rhetoric* (pp. 275-304). Newbury Park, CA: Sage.

Kaspar, G., & Blum-Kulka, S. (1993). *Interlanguage pragmatics.* New York: Oxford University Press.

Katchen, J. E. (1987). Coordination in the EFL curriculum: Writing and public speaking. *Proceedings of the 4th Conference on English Teaching and Learning in the Republic of China,* pp. 275-289. Taipei: Crane.

Kirschenbaum, H., & Henderson, V. L. (Eds.). (1989). *Carl Rogers: Dialogues.* Boston, MA: Houghton Mifflin.

Knoblauch, C. H. & Brannon, L. (1984). *Rhetorical traditions and the teaching of writing.* Upper Montclair, NJ: Boynton/Cook.

Krashen, S. D. (1981). *Second language acquisition and second language learning.* Oxford: Pergamon Press.

Krashen, S. D. (1982). *Principles and practice in second language acquisition.* Oxfrod: Pergamon Press.

Krashen, S. D. (1985). *Inquiries and insights: Second language teaching, immersion and bilingual education, literacy.* Hayward, CA: Alemany.

Krashen, S. D. (1999). *Three arguments against whole language & why they are wrong.* Portsmouth, NH: Heinemann.

Kroll, B. (1991). Teaching writing in the ESL context. In M. Celce-Murcia (Ed.), *Teaching English as a Second or Foreign Language* (2nd ed.), (pp. 245-263). New York: Newburry House/Harper Collins.

Lamb, H., & Best, D. L. (1990). Language and literacy: The ESL whole language connection. (ERIC Document Reproduction Service No. ED 324 915)

Lehman, J. R. (1994). Integrating science and mathematics: Perceptions of pre-service and practicing elementary teachers. *School Science and Mathematics, 94,* 58-64.

Leki, I. (1989). Academic writing: Techniques and tasks. New York: St. Martin's Press.

Li, L. T. (1996). Enhancing sensitivity to human needs: EFL learners in Taiwan. Paper presented in TESOL '96 Convention in Chicago, USA; accepted for inclusion in the ERIC database of educational documents. [ED 403 756]

Li, L. T. (1997). Enhancing sensitivity to human needs: Whole language application. *The Proceedings of the 14th Conference on English Teaching and Learning in the Republic of China,* pp. 143-156. Taipei: Crane.

Li, L. T. (1998a). Integrating EFL Learning Using Collaborative Taped Journals. Paper presented in TESOL '98 Convention in Seattle, USA.

Li, L. T. (1998b). Publishing Students' Writing: A Magic Wand for EFL Writing. *The proceedings of the 7th International Symposium on English Teaching,* pp. 649-658.

Li, L. T. (2000a). A Chinese EFL Learner Overcomes the Fear of English Listening and Speaking. *Jieng-E, 11* (4), pp. 35-48.

Li, L. T. (2000b). Beyond Language Skills: A Whole Language Teacher's Monologue. *Jieng-E, 12* (1), pp. 47-58.

Li, L. T. (2001). Theme cycles: Empowering adult EFL writers. Paper presented at the 10th International Symposium on English Teaching, Taipei, Taiwan (November).

Lim, H. L., & Watson, J. W. (1993). Whole language content classes for second-language learners. *The Reading Teacher, 46,* 384-393.

Lincoln, Y. S., & Guba, E. G. (1985). *Naturalistic inquiry.* Newbury Park, CA: Sage.

Liou, H. C. (1991). A whole language class. *Journal of Huang-Pu, 24,* 247-252.

Lipson, M., Valencia, S., Wixson, K., & Peters, C. (1993). Integration and thematic teaching: Integration to improve teaching and learning. *Language Arts, 70,* 252-263.

Loewe, M. A. (1998a). Implementing whole language in a university-level ESL curriculum. In C. Weaver (Ed.), *Lessons to share: On teaching grammar in context* (pp. 260-278). Portsmouth, NH: Heinemann.

Loewe, M. A. (1998b). Meeting the special needs of the English as a second language (ESL) students in public schools. In C. Weaver (Ed.), *Lessons to share: On teaching grammar in context* (pp. 244-259). Portsmouth, NH: Heinemann.

Lou, Y. H. (1998). What it whole language? *English Teaching and Learning. 23* (1), 76-90.

Lu, Y. L. (2002). Teaching ESL literacy through the whole language approach. *Journal of Ging-Chung Business College, 5*, 191-200.

MacGowan-Gilhooly, A. (1991). Fluency first: Reversing the traditional ESL sequence. *Journal of Basic Writing, 10* (1), 73-85.

MacGowan-Gilhooly, A. (1996a). *Achieving clarity in English: A whole-language book* (3rd ed.). Dubuque, IW: Kendall/Hunt.

MacGowan-Gilhooly, A. (1996b). *Achieving fluency in English: A whole-language book* (3rd ed.). Dubuque, IW: Kendall/Hunt.

Manning, G., & Manning, M. (Eds.). (1989). *Whole language: Beliefs and practices, K-8.* Washington, DC: National Education Association.

Manning, M., Manning, G., & Long, R. (1994). *Theme immersion: Inquiry based curriculum in elementary and middle schools.* Portsmouth, NH: Heinemann.

Mansfield, B. (1989). Students' perceptions of an integrated unit: A case study. *Social Studies, 80*, 135-140.

Maslow, A. H. (1954). *Motivation and personality.* New York: Harper & Row.

McCallum, G. P. (1970). *Idiom drills: For students of English as a second language.* New York: Harper & Row.

McKee, M. (1983). Academic writing vs. composition. *TECFORS, 6* (5), 7-11.

McLaren, P. (1999). A pedagogy of possibility: Reflecting upon Paulo Freire's politics of education: In memory of Paulo Freire. *Research News and Comment, 28* (2), 49-56.

Merriam, S. B. (1988). *Case study research in education: A qualitative approach.* San Francisco, CA: Jossey-Bass.

Mills, H., & Clyde, J. (Eds.). (1990). *Portraits of whole language classrooms: Learning for all ages.* Portsmouth, NH: Heinemann.

Mitch, A. (1997). *Tuesdays with Morrie: an old man, a young man, and life's greatest lesson.* New York, NY: Doubleday.

Mitchell, D. (1982). *The process of reading: A cognitive analysis of fluent reading and learning to read.* New York: Wiley.

Moll, L. (1990). *Vygotsky and education: Instructional implications and application of sociohistorical psychology.* New York: Cambridge University Press.

Murray, D. (1982). *Learning by teaching.* Upper Montclair, NJ: Boynton/Cook.

Murray, D. (1985). *A writing teacher teaches writing* (2nd ed.). Boston, MA: Houghton Mifflin.

Murray, G. (Ed.). (1980). *Language awareness and reading.* Newark, DE: International Reading Association.

Nash, T. (1987). The continuing development of an English department writing program. *Proceedings of the 4th Conference on English Teaching and Learning in the Republic of China*, pp. 317-326. Taipei: Crane.

Nash, T., Hsieh, T. L., & Chen, S. I. (1989). An evaluation of computer-aided composition. *Proceedings of the 6th Conference on English Teaching and Learning in the Republic of China*, pp. 313-323. Taipei: Crane.

Nehls, D. (1988). *Interlanguage studies.* Heidelberg, Germany: J. Groos.

Nelson, M. W. (1991). *At the point of need: Teaching basic and ESL writers.* Portsmouth, NH: Heinemann.

Newman, J. M. (Ed.). (1985). *Whole language: Theory in use.* Portsmouth, NH: Heinemann.

Newman, J. M., & Church, S. M. (1990). Myths of whole language. *The Reading Teacher, 44* (1), 20-26.

Nickel, G. (1989). Some controversies in present-day error analysis: "Contrastive" vs. "non-contrastive." *International Review of Applied Linguistics in Language Teaching, 27* (4), 293-305.

Nigohosian, E. (1992). *Meeting the challenge of diversity: Applying whole language theory in the kindergarten with ESL Korean children.* ERIC Clearinghouse.

Nissani, M. (1995). Fruits, salads, and smoothies: A working definition of interdisciplinarity. *Journal of Educational Thought, 29*, 121-128.

Olarewaju, A. O. (1988). Instructional objectives: What effects do they have on students' attitudes towards integrated science. *Journal of Research in Science Teaching, 25*, 283-291.

Pack, A., & Hendrichsen, L. (1981). *Sentence combination: Writing and combining standard English sentences.* Rowley, MA: Newburry House.

Pajares, F., & Johnson, M. J. (1994). Confidence and competence in writing: The role of self-efficacy, outcome expectancy, and apprehension. *Research in the Teaching of English, 28*, 313-331.

Pajares, F., & Johnson, M. J. (1996). Self-efficacy beliefs and the writing performance of entering high school students. *Psychology in the Schools, 33*, 163-175.

Pajares, F., & Valiante, G. (1997). Influence of self-efficacy on elementary students' writing. *The Journal of Educational Research, 90* (6), 353-360.

Patton, M. Q. (1990). *Qualitative evaluation and research methods* (2nd ed.). Newbury Park, CA: Sage.

Peetoom, A. (1986). *Shared reading: Safe risks with whole books.* Richmond Hill, Ontario: Scholastic-TAB.

People you should know: Freire [On-line WWW]. (n.d.). Available: http://www.nl.edu/ace/Resources/Freire.html

Peyton, J. K. (Ed.). (1990). *Students and teachers writing together: Perspectives on journal writing.* Alexandria, VA: TESOL.

Peyton, J. K., & Reed, L. (1990). *Dialogue journal writing with nonnative English speakers: A handbook for teachers.* Alexandria, VA: TESOL.

Peyton, J. K., & Staton, J. (1992). *Dialogue journal writing with nonnative English speakers: An instructional packet for teachers and workshop leaders.* Alexandria, VA: TESOL.

Piaget, J. (1955). *The language and thought of the child.* New York: Meridian.

Popp, M. (1996). *Teaching language and literature in elementary classrooms: A resource book for professional development.* Mahwah, NJ: Lawrence Erlbaum Associates.

Purves, A., & Purves, W. (1986). On the nature and formation of interpretive and rhetorical communities. In T. N. Postlethwaite (Ed.), *International Education Research: Papers in Honor of Torstern Husen* (pp. 45-64). Oxford: Pergamon.

Raimes, A. (1983). *Techniques in teaching writing.* New York: Oxford University Press.

Raimes, A. (1985). What unskilled ESL students do as they write: A classroom study of composing. *TESOL Quarterly, 19* (2), 229-258.

Reid, J. M. (1982). *The process of composition.* Englewood Cliffs, NJ: Prentice Hall.

Reid, J. M. (1993). *Teaching ESL writing.* Englewood Cliffs, NJ: Prentice Hall Regents.

Rice, M. K., & Burns, J. U. (1986). *Thinking/writing.* Englewood Cliffs, NJ: Prentice Hall.

Richards, J., Platt, J., & Platt, H. (1992). *Longman dictionary of language teaching & applied linguistics.* UK: Longman.

Ridley, L. (1990). Whole language in the ESL classroom. In H. Mills & J. A. Clyde (Eds.), *Portraits of whole language classrooms: Learning for all ages* (pp. 213-228). Portsmouth, NH: Heinemann.

Rigg, P. (1985). Petra: Learning to read at 45. *Journal of Education, 167,* 1, 129-139.

Rigg, P. (1991). Whole language in TESOL. *TESOL Quarterly, 25* (3), 521-542.

Rivers, W. (1964). *The psychologist and the foreign language teacher.* Chicago: University of Chicago Press.

Rivers, W. (1968). *Teaching foreign language skills.* Chicago: University Press.

Rogers, C. R. (1961a). *On becoming a person: A therapist's view of psychotherapy.* Boston, MA: Houghton Mifflin.

Rogers, C. R. (1961b). This is me. In C. R. Rogers, *On becoming a person: A therapist's view of psychotherapy* (pp. 3-27). Boston, MA: Houghton Mifflin.

Rogers, C. R. (1980). *A way of being.* Boston, MA: Houghton Mifflin.

Rogers, C. R. (1983). *Freedom to learn for the 80's.* Columbus, OH: Charles E. Merrill.

Rogers, C. R., & Freiberg, H. J. (1994). *Freedom to learn (3rd ed.).* New York: Macmillan.

Rogers, C. R., & Stevens, B. (1967). *Person to person: The problem of being human.* Moab, Utah: Real People Press.

Rolheiser, C., Bower, B., & Stevahn, L. (2000). *The portfolio organizer: Succeeding with portfolios in your classroom.* Alexandria, VG: Association for

Supervision and Curriculum Development.

Rosenblatt, L. (1978). *The reader, the text, the poem: The transactional theory of the literary work.* Carbondale, IL: Southern Illinois University Press.

Samway, K. D. (1992). Writers' workshop and children acquiring English as a non-native language. National Clearinghouse for Bilingual Education. Program Information Guide Series. Number 10, Spring 1992, pp. 1-27.

Santos, T. (1988). Professors' reactions to the academic writing of non-native speaking students. *TESOL Quarterly, 18* (4), 671-688.

Santos, T. (1992). *What do we teach when we teach ESL writing?* Paper presented at the International TESOL Convention, Vancouver, B. C. (March).

Saussure, F. (1966). *Course in general linguistics* (W. Baskin, Trans.). New York, NY: McGraw-Hill.

Schachter, J. (1990). Communicative competence revisited. In B. Harley, P. Allen, J. Cummins, & M. Swain (Eds.), *The development of second language proficiency* (pp. 39-49). London: Cambridge University Press.

Schell, J. W., & Wicklein, R. C. (1993). Integration of mathematics, science, and technology education: A basis for thinking and problem solving. *Journal of Vocational Education Research, 18*, 49-76.

Schenk, M. J. (1988). *Read, write, revise: A guide to academic writing.* New York: St. Martin's Press.

Schmidt, W. H., Roehler, L., Caul, J. L., Buchman, M., Diamond, B., Solomon, D., & Cianciolo, P. (1985). The uses of curriculum integration in language arts instruction: A study of six classrooms. *Journal of Curriculum Studies, 17*, 305-320.

Scott, V. M. (1996). *Rethinking foreign language writing.* Boston, MA: Newbury House.

Selinker, L. (1991). *Rediscovering interlanguage.* London: Longman.

Shanahan, T. (1997). Reading-writing relationships, thematic units, inquiry learning ... In pursuit of effective integrated literacy instruction. *The Reading Teacher, 51* (1), 12-19.

Shaughnessy, M. (1977). *Errors and expectations.* New York: Oxford.

Shell, D., Murphy, C. C., & Bruning, R. H. (1989). Self-efficacy and outcome expectancy mechanisms in reading and writing achievement. *Journal of Educational Psychology, 81* (1), 91-100.

Shen, T. C. (2000). The "whole language versus direct skill instruction" debate: Perspective from L1 literacy classrooms. Paper presented at the 9th International Symposium on English Teaching, November 10-12, Taipei.

Shook, R. (1978). Sentence-combining: A theory and two reviews. *TESL Reporter, 2,* 4-7, 12, 15.

Shor, I. (Ed.). (1987). *Freire for the classroom: A sourcebook for liberatory teaching.* Portsmouth, NH: Heinemann.

Shor, I. (1992). *Empowering education: Critical teaching for social change.* Chicago: University of Chicago Press.

Shor, I., & Freire, P. (1987). *A pedagogy for liberation: Dialogues on transform-*

ing education. South Hadley, MA: Bergin & Garvey.

Short, K., Harste, J., & Burke, C. (1996). *Creating classrooms for authors and inquirers.* Portsmouth, NH: Heinemann.

Simic, M. (1993). *Publishing children's writing.* ERIC Digest. Washington, [ED 363 884]

Sladky, P. (1994). *Why we need to publish student writers.* Nashville, TN. [ED 371 352]

Smith, F. (1983). *Essays into literacy.* Portsmouth, NH: Heinemann.

Smith, F. (1994a). *Understanding reading* (5th ed.). Hillsdale, NJ: Erlbaum.

Smith, F. (1994b). *Writing and the writer* (2nd ed.). Hillsdale, NJ: Lawrence Erlbaum Associates.

Smith, F. (1997). *Reading without nonsense* (3rd ed.). New York: Teachers College Press.

Smith, M. K. (2002). Paulo Freire and informal education [On-line WWW]. Available: http://www.infed.org/thinkers/et-freir.htm

Smoke, T. (1987). *A writer's workbook: An interactive writing text for ESL students.* New York: St. Martin's Press.

Sommers, N. (1980). Revision strategies of student writers and experienced adult writers. *College Composition and Communication, 31,* 378-388.

Spack, R. (1984). Invention strategies and the ESL college composition student. *TESOL Quarterly, 18* (4), 649-670.

Spack, R., & Sadow, C. (1983). Student-teacher working journals in ESL freshman composition. *TESOL Quarterly, 17* (4), 575-594.

Taylor, B. (1981). Content and written form: A two-way street. *TESOL Quarterly, 15* (1), 5-13.

Teng, C. S. (1985). How I use the overhead projector to reach English composition in my classroom. *Proceedings of the 12th Conference on English Teaching and Learning in the Republic of China,* pp. 259-265. Taipei: Crane.

Tseng, Y. H. (1997). Attacking mythology: EFL whole language in a Taiwanese classroom. *The Proceedings of the 14th Conference on English Teaching and Learning in the Republic of China,* pp. 157-168. Taipei: Crane.

Tung, C. A. (1995). The teaching of basic writing: A more effective approach. *Proceedings of the 9th Conference on English Teaching and Learning in the Republic of China,* pp. 363-379. Taipei: Crane.

Uchniat, J. D. (1990). Language and culture: N.T.U. students of English composition and their responses and reactions to a western pedagogy of modern composition theory. *Proceedings of the 7th Conference on English Teaching and Learning in the Republic of China,* pp. 117-132. Taipei: Crane.

Ueland, B. (1987). *If you want to write.* Saint Paul, MN: Graywolf Press.

Vacca, R. T., & Rasinski, T. V. (1992). *Case studies in whole language.* Philadelphia, PA: Harcourt Brace Jovanovich College Publishers.

Valencia, S. (1990). A portfolio approach to classroom reading assessment: The whys, whats, and hows. *The Reading Teacher, 43,* 338-340.

Vygotsky, L. (1978). *Mind in society: The development of higher psychological process.* Cambridge, MA: Harvard University Press.

Vygotsky, L. (1986). *Thought and language* (E. Hanfmann, & G. Vakar, Trans.). Cambridge, MA:MIT Press.

Wasserstein, P. (1995). What middle schoolers say about their schoolwork. *Educational Leadership, 53* (1), 41-43.

Watson, D. J. (1989). Defining and describing whole language. *The Elementary School Journal, 90* (2), 129-141.

Watson-Gegeo, K. A. (1988). Ethnography in ESL: Defining the essentials. *TESOL Quarterly, 22*, 575-592.

Weaver, C. (1988). *Reading process and practice: From socio-psycholinguistics to whole language.* Portsmouth, NH: Heinemann.

Weaver, C. (1990). *Understanding whole language: From principles to practice.* Portsmouth, NH: Heinemann.

Weaver, C. (1994). *Reading process and practice: From socio-psycholinguistics to whole language (2nd ed.).* Portsmouth, NH: Heinemann.

Weaver, C. (1996). *Teaching grammar in context.* Portsmouth, NH: Heinemann.

Weaver, C., Chaston, J., & Peterson, S. (1993). *Theme exploration: A voyage of discovery.* Portsmouth, NH: Heinemann.

White, R. V. (1987). *Writing advanced.* Oxford: Oxford University Press.

Wilson, K. (1993). *Whole language ESL: Reading, writing, and speaking.* Paper presented at the National Conference on Migrant and Seasonal Farmworkers, Denver, CO, May 9-13.

Wink, J. (2000). *Critical pedagogy: Notes from the real world* (2nd ed.). New York, NY: Longman.

Wohl, M. (1985). *Techniques for writing: Composition* (2nd ed.). Rowley, MA: Newburry House.

Yao, C. K. (1997). An overview of writing theory and research: From cognitive to social-cognitive. *The Journal of National Chung-Hsin University (Taichung Campus, Evening Division), 3*, 183-202.

Yu, A. (1990). Discipline and freedom. [On-Line WWW] Available: http://seamonkey.ed.asu.edu/~alex/education/essays/discipline.html

Yu, T. H. (2001). The literature review of "whole language with respect to learning English as a second language." *Journal of Te-Ming College, 18*, 189-201.

Zamel, V. (1980). Re-evaluating sentence-combining practice. *TESOL Quarterly, 14* (1), 81-90.

Zamel, V. (1982). Writing: The process of discovering meaning. *TESOL Quarterly, 16* (2), 195-209.

Zamel, V. (1983). The composing processes of advanced ESL students: Six case studies. *TESOL Quarterly, 17* (2), 165-187.

王備五。(民 73)。基礎英文作文教材教法。*中華民國第一屆英語文教學研討會論文集*，頁 455-465。

江光榮。(民 90)。*人性的迷失與復歸:羅傑斯的人本心理學*。台北市：貓頭鷹出版；城邦文化發行。

沈添鉦。(民 80)。簡介「全語言」的語文教學。*教師之友，第 32 卷第四期*，27-31。

沈添鉦、黃秀文。(民 86)。全語教學在國小實施的個案報告。*八十六學年度教育學術研討會論文集(3)語文教育組，* 頁 881-905.

吳芝儀，李奉儒（譯）。(民 84)。*質的評鑑與研究*。台北縣：桂冠圖書公司。

林春仲。(民 73)。從作文理論探討英文作文教學。*中華民國第一屆英語文教學研討會論文集*，頁 383-394。

官美智。(民 75)。高中英文作文—引導式作文看圖作文教學之研究與設計。*中華民國第三屆英語文教學研討會論文集*，頁 115-124。

高實政。(民 82)。過程寫作教學觀的理論及應用在大學寫作課程的教案設計。*中華民國第十屆英語文教學研討會論文集*，頁 49-64。

陳玉美。(民 87)。國內英文作文教學之回顧與展望。*中華民國第十五屆英語文教學研討會論文集*，頁 331-344。

曾月紅。(民 87)。從兩大學派探討全語文教學理論。*教育研究資料，6* (1)，76-90.

曾月紅。(民 89)。*兒童英語文教學：全語文觀點*。台北市：五南圖書出版公司。

張強仁。(民 73)。中學作文教學與聯考作文之回顧與展望。*中華民國第一屆英語文教學研討會論文集*，頁 395-402。

趙涵華。(民 83)。整體語言教育—理論、研究、特質、及問題。*台北市立師範學院學報，第 25 期*，389-402。

趙涵華。(民 84)。全語文教育的精神。*教育心，第 8 期*，52-53。

劉賢軒。(民 75)。談科技英文寫作教學。*中華民國第三屆英語文教學研討會論文集*，頁 87-99。

劉賢軒。(民 76)。從書面語的言談特性談到我國大學階段的英文寫作教育。*中華民國第四屆英語文教學研討會論文集*，頁 99-110。

Theme Cycles

(designed by Li-Te Li)

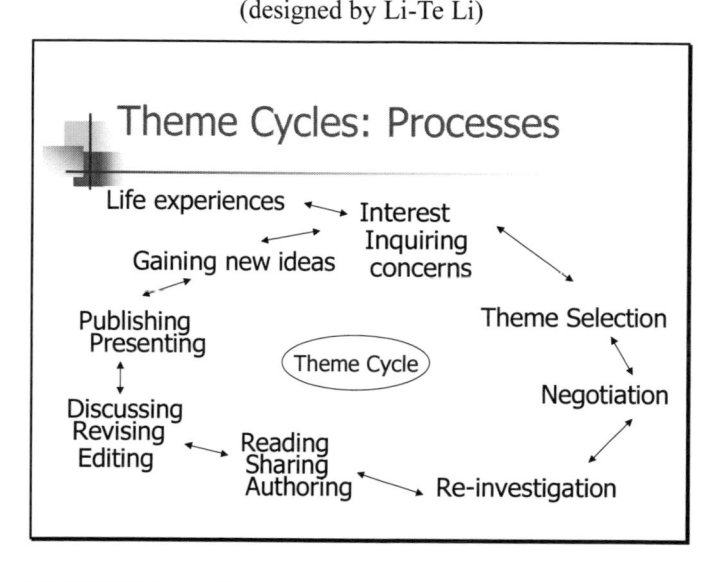

APPENDIX B

Syllabi

(designed by Li-Te Li)

Course: English Reading and Writing (1): Session 20 (Fall 2000)
Monday 6:25 - 9:05 p.m.
Lecturer: Li-Te Li (e-mail: ltli@mail.tku.edu.tw)

Tentative Syllabus

References: 1. Paragraph Development: A Guide for Students of English.
2ed. 1990. (Prentice Hall).
2. Super Dossiers: Modern Issues. 1996. (Phoenix ELT).

Needed Materials: 1. A Folder and disc for keeping essays and journal
writing (or e-mail)
2. Good dictionaries and grammar books

Activities & Assignments:
1. Essay writing: each has to be typed, doubled-spaced, and has
to be revised at least twice (handed hard copy along with disc)
2. Journal writing (e-mail writing): in-class writing or free writing at home, usually based on what you read or experience in
daily life
3. Individual Project: Choose one theme which you are interested in and read at least 5 articles related to the theme and
then write a report and make an oral presentation
4. Group discussion and editing: share your own writing with
other classmates and also give feedback after reading your
classmates' writing
5. Publication: a collection of our own stories

Assessment & Evaluation: based on the attendance, assignments and
participation

Schedule

Date	Reading	Writing	Assignments
09/25 (M)	Orientation	Free writing practice	Questionnaires
10/02 (M)		Overview of writing	
10/09 (M)	Theme reading (1)	Topic sentence/Biography	
10/16 (M)		Supporting TS/Narration	1st draft of 1st essay/Journal (1)
10/23 (M)	Theme reading (2)	Enumeration	2nd draft of 1st essay
10/30 (M)		Draft discussion	
11/06 (M)	Theme reading (3)	Types of Enumeration	3rd draft of 1st essay
11/13 (M)		Description	Journal (2)
11/20 (M)	Theme reading (4)	Description/Punctuation	1st draft of 2nd essay
11/27 (M)		Narration	2nd draft of 2nd essay
12/04 (M)	Theme reading (5)	Draft discussion	
12/11 (M)		Narration	3rd draft of 2nd essay
12/18 (M)	******** Project Report (I) ********		Journal (3)
12/25 (M)	******************** National holiday ******************		
01/01 (M)	******************** National holiday ******************		
01/08 (M)	******* Project Report (II) **** Collection of Our Own Stories ***		

* In-class reading will be different types of articles, such as essays, short stories, news, travel tips, songs, jokes, etc.

Course: English Reading and Writing (1): Session 20 (Spring 2001) Monday 6:25 - 9:05 p.m.
Lecturer: Li-Te Li (e-mail: ltli@mail.tku.edu.tw)

Tentative Syllabus

References: 1. Tuesdays with Morrie.   1997.   (Doubleday).
2. Paragraph Development: A Guide for Students of English.
2 ed.   1990.   (Prentice Hall).

Needed Materials: 1. A folder and disc for keeping essays and journal writing (or using e-mail).
2. Good dictionaries and grammar books

Activities & Assignments:
1. Essay writing: each has to be typed, doubled-spaced, and has to be revised at least twice (handed hard copy along with disc)
2. Journal writing (e-mail writing): one piece per week based on the reading or daily life
3. Outside reading and presentation: read whatever you are in-terested in and make an oral report in the end of the course
4. Group discussion and editing: share your own writing with other classmates and also give feedback after reading your classmates' writing
5. Publication (Portfolio): a collection of our own stories

Assessment & Evaluation: based on the attendance, assignments and participation

Schedule

Date	Reading	Writing	Assignments
02/19 (M)	Orientation		
02/26 (M)	Morrie: pp. 1-25	Cause & Effect	
03/05 (M)	Morrie: pp. 26-47	"	
03/12 (M)	Morrie: pp. 48-68	"	
03/19 (M)	Morrie: pp. 69-79	Draft discussion	1st draft of 1st essay due
03/26 (M)	Morrie: pp. 80-99	Comparison/Contrast	2nd draft of 1st essay due
04/02 (M)	Morrie: pp. 100-122	Draft discussion	
04/09 (M)	Morrie: pp. 123-141	Comparison/Contrast	3rd draft of 1st essay due
04/16 (M)	Morrie: pp. 142-163	"	
04/23 (M)	Morrie: pp. 164-170	Draft discussion	1st draft of 2nd essay due
04/30 (M)	Morrie: pp. 171-180		2nd draft of 2nd essay due
05/07 (M)	Morrie: pp. 181-192	Draft discussion	
05/14 (M)			3rd draft of 2nd essay due
05/21 (M)	***** Project Oral Report (I) ********************		
05/28 (M)	***** Project Oral Report (II) ***** Individual Portfolio Due *****		
06/04 (M)	***** Celebration Party ****** Collection of Our Own Stories ****		

* In-class reading will be different types of articles, such as essays, short stories, news, travel tips, songs, jokes, etc.

---------- Let's enjoy learning English reading and writing ----------

APPENDIX

Analytic Rating Scale

(revised by Li-Te Li)

Categories	Level	Score	Criteria
Voice	Very Good	25 - 21	Very strong, very authentic, full of uniqueness, identity, personality, and resonance
	Good	20 - 16	Adequate strong, adequate authentic, showing adequate uniqueness, identity, personality, and resonance
	Average	15 - 11	Uniqueness and thinking conveyed clearly though not strong or authentic enough
	Weak	10 - 6	Somewhat weak and non-authentic, lacks uniqueness, identity, personality, and resonance
	Very Poor	5 - 1	No individual/personal voice, non-authentic, no uniqueness, identity, personality, or any resonance
Content	Very Good	25 - 21	Ideas presented very clearly, knowledgeable about the topic, fully development
	Good	20 - 16	Most ideas presented clearly, sure knowledge of subject, adequate development
	Average	15 - 11	Major ideas presented clearly, know some of the subject, mostly relevant to topic but lacks details
	Weak	10 - 6	Most ideas presented unclearly, little substance, inadequate development
	Very Poor	5 - 1	Lacks of ideas, non-substantive, not pertinent
Organization	Very Good	25 - 21	Well-organization, very fluent expression, cohesive and coherent
	Good	20 - 16	Adequate organization, mostly fluent, most ideas stated and supported properly
	Average	15 - 11	Main ideas stand out though somewhat loosely organized, limited supported, acceptable fluent
	Weak	10 - 6	Ideas confused and disconnected, lacks logical development, non-fluent
	Very Poor	5 - 1	No organization, does not communicate

Categories	Level	Score	Criteria
Language	Very Good	25 - 21	Effective word/idiom choice and usage, very few global and local errors and mechanics errors
	Good	20 - 16	Minor errors on word/idiom, grammar, and mechanics but *meaning not obscured*
	Average	15 - 11	Several errors on word/idiom, grammar, and mechanics but *meaning seldom obscured*
	Weak	10 - 6	Frequently errors on word/idiom, grammar, and mechanics and *meaning confused or obscured*
	Very Poor	5 - 1	No mastery of English vocabulary, sentence construction rules, and conventions

Portfolio Assessment Form

(revised by Li-Te Li)

Name of Student: _____ Date: _____
Name of Reviewer: _____

Please indicate your evaluation by circling the appropriate number on each of the scales below. Space has been provided for comments about the student's work. Thank you for taking the time to share your valuable feedback.

1. **Quality of Work** (knowledge of content, communication of ideas, ... etc.):

10	9		8	7		6	5		4	3	2	1

   Superior   Good   Average   Limited

   Reasons:

2. **Creativity and Originality** (voice, depth of reflection, ... etc.):

10	9		8	7		6	5		4	3	2	1

   Superior   Good   Average   Limited

   Reasons:

3. **Evidence of Effort** (perseverance, amount of reading and writing, ... etc.):

10	9		8	7		6	5		4	3	2	1

   Superior   Good   Average   Limited

   Reasons:

4. **Evidence of Growth** (depth of reflection and concerns, progress as a reader and writer, … etc.):

    10   9   8   7   6   5   4   3   2   1

       Superior   Good   Average   Limited

    Reasons:

5. **Other comments:**

    _____
    _____
    _____
    _____
    _____
    _____
    _____
    _____
    _____
    _____
    _____
    _____

    TOTAL: _____ / 40

APPENDIX  E

Writing self-efficacy questionnaire

(revised by Li-Te Li)

英文寫作自信問卷調查

Background Information

本資料只供研究用，且絕對保密。　班別: 公教班 _____ 級　學號:

1. Gender: a. male　　b. female
2. Age: _____
3. Native language: _____
4. Major: _____
5. Study abroad: a. yes _____ (weeks/months/years)　　b. no
6. Education:　a. high school　　b. Bachelor　　c. Master　　d. Doctor　　e. above
7. How long have you studied English: _____
8. How long have you studied English writing: _____

Directions: How confident are you that you can successfully communicate, in writing, what you want to say in each of the following *writing tasks* (1-17) and how confident are you that you can perform each of the following *writing skills* (18-25)?　You may select any number from the 7-point scale.　(請務必每題作答，並請每題只圈選一個答案)

	Extremely confident ←→ Extremely not confident
1.　Write a letter to a friend or family member.	7　6　5　4　3　2　1
2.　List instructions for how to play a card game.	7　6　5　4　3　2　1
3.　Fill out an insurance application.	7　6　5　4　3　2　1
4.　Write an instruction manual for operating an office machine.	7　6　5　4　3　2　1
5.　Prepare a resume describing your employment history and skills.	7　6　5　4　3　2　1
6.　Write a one or two sentence answer to a specific test question.	7　6　5　4　3　2　1
7.　Compose a one or two page essay in answer to a test question.	7　6　5　4　3　2　1

8. Write a term paper of 15 to 20 pages.   7 6 5 4 3 2 1
9. Author a scholarly article for publication
   in a professional journal in your field.   7 6 5 4 3 2 1
10. Write a letter to the editor of the daily newspaper.   7 6 5 4 3 2 1
11. Compose an article for a popular magazine such as
    Newsweek.   7 6 5 4 3 2 1
12. Author a short fiction story.   7 6 5 4 3 2 1
13. Author a 400 page novel   7 6 5 4 3 2 1
14. Write useful class notes.   7 6 5 4 3 2 1
15. Author a children's book.   7 6 5 4 3 2 1
16. Prepare lesson plans for an elementary class
    studying the process of writing.   7 6 5 4 3 2 1
17. Write a brief autobiography.   7 6 5 4 3 2 1
18. Correctly spell all words in a one-page passage.   7 6 5 4 3 2 1
19. Correctly punctuate a one-page passage.   7 6 5 4 3 2 1
20. Correctly use parts of speech
    (i.e., nouns, verbs, adjectives, etc.)   7 6 5 4 3 2 1
21. Write a simple sentence with proper punctuation
    and grammatical structure.   7 6 5 4 3 2 1
22. Correctly use plurals, verb tenses, prefixes, and suffixes. 7 6 5 4 3 2 1
23. Write compound and complex sentences with proper
    punctuation and grammatical structure.   7 6 5 4 3 2 1
24. Organize sentences into a paragraph so as to clearly
    express a theme.   7 6 5 4 3 2 1
25. Write a paper with good overall organization
    (e.g., ideas in order, effective transitions, etc.)   7 6 5 4 3 2 1

APPENDIX

Writing apprehension questionnaire

(revised by Li-Te Li)

英文寫作焦慮問卷調查

Directions: Below are a series of statements about writing. There are no right or wrong answers to these statements. Please indicate the degree to which each statement applies to you by circling any number from the 8-point scale. While some of these statements may seem repetitious, take your time and try to be as honest as possible. Thank you for your cooperation in this matter. （請務必每題作答，並請每題只圈選一個答案）

	Strongly agree ⟷ Strongly disagree
1. I avoid writing.	8 7 6 5 4 3 2 1
2. I have no fear of my writing being evaluated.	8 7 6 5 4 3 2 1
3. I look forward to writing down my ideas.	8 7 6 5 4 3 2 1
4. I am afraid of writing essays when I know they will be evaluated.	8 7 6 5 4 3 2 1
5. Taking a composition course is a very frightening experience.	8 7 6 5 4 3 2 1
6. Handing in a composition makes me feel good.	8 7 6 5 4 3 2 1
7. My mind seems to go blank when I start to work on a composition.	8 7 6 5 4 3 2 1
8. Expressing ideas through writing seems to be a waste of time.	8 7 6 5 4 3 2 1
9. I would enjoy submitting my writing to magazines for evaluation and publication.	8 7 6 5 4 3 2 1
10. I like to write my ideas down.	8 7 6 5 4 3 2 1
11. I feel confident in my ability to clearly express my ideas in writing.	8 7 6 5 4 3 2 1
12. I like to have my friends read what I have written.	8 7 6 5 4 3 2 1
13. I'm nervous about writing.	8 7 6 5 4 3 2 1
14. People seem to enjoy what I write.	8 7 6 5 4 3 2 1
15. I enjoy writing.	8 7 6 5 4 3 2 1

16. I never seem to be able to clearly write down my ideas. 8 7 6 5 4 3 2 1
17. Writing is a lot of fun. 8 7 6 5 4 3 2 1
18. I expect to do poorly in composition classes even
    before I enter them. 8 7 6 5 4 3 2 1
19. I like seeing my thoughts on paper. 8 7 6 5 4 3 2 1
20. Discussing my writing with others is an enjoyable
    experience. 8 7 6 5 4 3 2 1
21. I have a terrible time organizing my ideas in a
    composition course. 8 7 6 5 4 3 2 1
22. When I hand in a composition I know I'm going
    to do poorly. 8 7 6 5 4 3 2 1
23. It's easy for me to write good compositions. 8 7 6 5 4 3 2 1
24. I don't think I write as well as most other people. 8 7 6 5 4 3 2 1
25. I don't like my compositions to be evaluated. 8 7 6 5 4 3 2 1
26. I'm no good at writing. 8 7 6 5 4 3 2 1

---------- 謝謝您的作答 ----------

APPENDIX G

Final self-evaluation of writing and reading

(revised by Li-Te Li)

I. Writing

1. How many pieces of writing did you finish this year?
    (1st semester)_____   (2nd semester)   _____
    How often do you write at home?   _____

2. What kinds of writing do you like to write (e-mail letter, journal writing, essay: narration, description, enumeration, definition, cause-effect, comparison and contrast, etc.)?
    _____

3. How do you decide what you'll write about?   Where do your ideas come from?
    _____
    _____

4. What kinds of response help you most as a writer?
    _____
    _____

5. Which pieces of writing are your most effective?   Why?   (What did you do as the author?)
    _____
    _____

6. What were your major accomplishments this year as a writer?
    _____
    _____

7. What are your strengths as a writer?
    _____
    _____

8. What are the areas in which you can improve?
    _____
    _____

9. What rules and conventions have you mastered?
    _____
    _____

10. In general, how do you feel about what you write? (Please write on the other side)

II. Reading

1. How many English books/articles did you finish this year?
   (books) _____ (articles) _____

2. How often do you read at home?
   _____

3. What genres are represented (essay, story, news, poems, autobiography, etc.)?
   _____

4. What are your favorite genres to read? _____

5. Which books/articles do you like most? Why? (What did the authors do?)
   _____
   _____
   _____
   _____
   _____
   _____
   _____

6. What are your major accomplishments this year as a reader?
   _____
   _____
   _____

7. What are your strengths as a reader?
   _____
   _____
   _____

8. What are the areas in which you can improve?
   _____
   _____
   _____

9. What literary techniques do you identify and appreciate in the texts you read?
   _____
   _____
   _____

10. In general, how do you feel about English reading?
    _____
    _____
    _____

APPENDIX

Coding system

(designed by Li-Te Li)

Es-I-#-p   Es: essay
            I: initial
            #: essay draft number (totally 8 essay drafts each person)
            p: paragraph number of each essay draft

Pr-I-#-p   Pr: prompt writing
            I: initial
            #: prompt writing number (totally 2 pieces each person)
            p: paragraph number of each prompt writing

J-I-#-p   J: Journals (including messages on discussion board)
            I: initial
            #: entry number of journal
            p: paragraph number of each journal entry

OR-I-#-p   OR: Oral report
            I: initial
            #: oral report number (totally 2 reports each person)
            p: paragraph number of each oral report (in its written form)

PP-I-p   PP: Portfolio preface
            I: initial
            p: paragraph number of preface

SE-I-#-q   SE: Self-evaluation
            I: initial
            #: number of section (totally 2 sections)
            q: question number of each section

Em-I-#   Em: e-mail correspondences (including self-introduction,
        written Interview, and information in document)
        I: initial
        #: number of e-mail letters

O-#   O: observation (in class, field notes)
        #: session number of observation (totally 30 times)

RJ-#-p   RJ: Reflective journal
        #: entry number of reflective journal (totally 30 entries)
        p: paragraph number of each reflective journal entry

APPENDIX

Cover Letter

Dear all,

Here, I have a sincere request. Owing to the needs of my dissertation, I would like to ask for your permission to let me use your writing in my research study. This study is based on the class we had last year and the purpose is to investigate the adult EFL learners' writing, to see whether self-selected reading or inspiring group discussion will positively influence adult EFL learners' writing and in what way the influences reveal, so that English learning/teaching, or at least reading and writing, would be effectively improved. According to the ethics of research, your names on all the drafts will be deleted and a pseudonym or a subject code number will be used instead.

Besides the improvement of writing, the study would also like to investigate the attitude changes toward English writing. Thus, I would also use the questionnaires you filled out—one for writing confidence and another for writing anxiety—also without your names on it. And since it is always important to have learners' self perception on learning, the study would also consult your self-evaluation filled in the end of the school year. Once again, your names will not be shown on any material and all the materials will be used only for the research purpose, not for any other reason.

Since the dissertation would mainly rely on your production, I really appreciate your contribution and help. If you are willing to give me your permission to use your drafts, would you please sign the attached form for me as soon as possible? Thanks a lot.

By the way, if you have any questions about the study or how I will use your drafts, please do not hesitate to contact me at e-mail: ltli@mail.tku.edu.tw or Tel/Fax: (02) ×××××××××.

Your help means a lot to me! Thank you!!

Li-Te

APPENDIX  J

Informed Consent Form

I agree to allow Ms. Li-Te Li to use my writing drafts, filled questionnaires, and self-evaluation form in her research study as part of the requirements for her doctoral degree in the Graduate Institute of Western Languages & Literature at Tamkang University, Tamsui, Taiwan.

The purpose of this study is to investigate the adult EFL learners' writing and to see whether self-selected reading or inspiring group discussion will positively influence adult EFL learners' writing and in what way the influences reveal, so that English learning/teaching, or at least reading and writing, would be effectively improved. Also, learners' attitude change and the learners' self-perception of learning will be consulted so as to provide additional and dynamic evidences for the study.

I understand the study is based on the class I had with Ms. Li-Te Li from Fall 2000 to Spring 2001 and all my drafts and my answers to the questionnaires and self-evaluation will be kept confidential and identified by a pseudonym or a subject code number. My name will not appear on any of the results.

I understand that this consent may be withdrawn at any time without prejudice, penalty or loss of benefits to which I am otherwise entitled. I have been given the right to ask and have answered any information concerning the study. Questions, if any, have been answered to my satisfaction.

I understand that if I later have any additional questions concerning this research study, I can contact Ms. Li-Te Li through e-mail: ltli@mail.tku.edu.tw or at home (02) ××××××××. Group results will be sent to me upon my request.

I have read and understand this consent form.

_____   _____

(Learner's signature)   (Date)

APPENDIX  K

The Discussion of Ken's Writing Performance

According to the scores of prompt writing, Ken's writing improved from the level of W to the level of G-VG. He showed progress in all aspects, like sentence structures, theme development, and organization.

Prompt Writing—All Aspects

Pre-prompt writing. His pre-prompt writing (Pr-K-1) had no title and was full of errors in sentence structures, language use, and punctuation (Ex. 56, s3, 4, 5, 7). The ideas were not fully developed and were roughly organized. Though all the sentences were grouped into three sections, they did not represent introduction, body, and conclusion. Only his voice in pre-prompt writing reached the level of Average. His position regarding the issue of elementary school English education was clearly conveyed (Ex. 56, s5-8).

Post-prompt writing. However, his post-prompt writing showed his progress in all the aspects (Pr-K-2). Besides adding a proper title

---

Ex. 56 Ken's Pre-prompt Writing

(1) About the new education policy of English , I think it is very great. (2) Because English is the important language. in the world. (3) If our children want to learn lastest technology . and knowledge ; (4) English plays the important role .

(5) But I wish. the teaching methods. that not like our before ones, just focusing on the grammar and. lacking the practice of listening and speaking. (6) Listening, speaking, reading and writing. can't lack one of them.

(7) Language is the tool of communication not the project of examine. (8) I really hope our children have a well English ability in the well-designed English environment and. system.

293

Ex. 57 Ken's Post-prompt Writing

(0) About the English education of the elementary school in Taiwan

(1) In order to enter the international society easily and to promote the competition of Taiwan, the Taiwan's government had decided to achieve the English education in the elementary school. (2) In my opinions, I really appreciate the policy of the government. (3) But at the meanwhile, I hope the government must notice some important points:

(4) First, the English education must be focused on stirring the students' learning interests, not focused on examming. (5) If the English education still focused on testing, I believe, our children would just become the test machines, not the happy learning students.

(6) Second, the English education must help the students communicate with one another in English easily. (7) It means the teachers must have the professional skills to teach our children like the right pronaciatoin and spelling ability.

(8) Third, the elementary schools must provide the good learning environment for the students. (9) For example, the schools can make a rule in that the specific day of a week, the students must try to communicate with each other in English, of course, including of the teacher's teaching.

(10) In my conclusion, to promote the English ability of the elementary school is a very correct policy. (11) It will make our children more international and more confident. (12) By learning English, they can touch more regions' knowledge and have a wider world to explore. (13) Before achieving the beautiful targets, all of it depends on the right methods and attitudes of our government. (14) Isn't it?

(Ex. 57, s0), he also provided an appropriate introduction with a clear thesis statement (s3) and made a suitable conclusion restating his main ideas (s10-14). With enumeration (s4, 6, 8) and examples (s5, 7, 9), his ideas were adequately supported and developed. Though there were still misspelling *pronaciatoin* (s7), wrong word form *examming* (s4), wrong word choice *the* (s9), the familiarity of English conventions shown in this piece indicated his progress in language use. His voice in the post-prompt writing reached the level of VG, strongly showing his identity and personality. The best example was the expression "If the English education still focused on testing, I believe, our children would just become the test machine, not the happy learning students" (Ex. 57, s5).

Essay Writing—Organization and Content

Ken's essays also showed his writing progress, though it was not as obvious as the progress in prompt writing. He showed knowledge about the topics in all essay drafts, and with revision, he presented his ideas logically and fluently.

Knowledgeable about the topic. His 1st essay "DVD and Home Theater" (Es-K-2) demonstrated his knowledge about technology. The content was full of information, like the characteristics of DVD player, the functions of AV amplifier, and the main purposes of speakers. Besides the introduction of these indispensable equipments, he also suggested the way of choosing proper products for setting up a home theater. The way he presented his ideas was logic with acceptable fluency. The introduction contained clear thesis statement "To build home theater, we need some necessary equipments as follows: DVD player, AV amplifier, and speakers" (Ex. 58, s5) so as to help readers predict the main content of the article. Each body paragraph contained proper topic sentence, like "DVD player has two important characteristics" (s6) for the second paragraph, "AV amplifier is in charge of decoding digital signals and multi-mode digital sound field processing" (s12) for the third paragraph, and "Speakers are the equipment that transmits signals and electronic current into sound" (s15) for the fourth paragraph. The conclusion restated the necessity of these three equipments for a home theater (s18-21). Most ideas were supported properly along with this organization.

Ex. 58 Ken's Essay 1-3

(1) DVD is the most popular AV product within the latest two years. (2) Using DVD equipments, you can enjoy the high-quality AV effect. (3) Without going to the theater, you can experience the amazing realism of films. (4) Owning entire DVD equipments at home, it is called as "Home Theater." (5) To build home theater, we need some necessary equipments as follows: DVD player, AV amplifier, and speakers.

(6) DVD player has two important characteristics. (7) First, it determines which region of DVD disks the DVD player can read. (8) Like DVD disks of United State that classified one-region, DVD player of Taiwan that classified three-region can't read them. (9) Second, it determines which format of disks that the DVD player can read. (10) Usually, most players can read DVD, VCD, and CD. (11) Besides these formats of disks, some of players can even read CD-R, MP3, and SVCD.

(12) AV amplifier is in charge of decoding digital signals and mutli-mode digital sound field processing. (13) The digital signals include Dolby Digital and DTS Digital Surround. (14) They all provide complete multi-channel audio, including three front channels (left, center, and right), two surround channels, and one subwoofer channel.

(15) Speakers are the equipment that transmits signals and electronic current into sound. (16) It is the center of AV system. (17) Without it, even owning millions of AV equipments, you can't hear anything.

(18) In order to build home theater, all of three equipments that DVD player, AV amplifier, and speakers can't lack anyone. (19) It doesn't mean that you can get the most excellent effect if you buy the expensive products. (20) In my suggestion, it is the most important to choose proper products according to your actual needs and the specification of your room. (21) Of course, you can't ignore the influence of budget to yourself.

Ideas presented clearly. In his 2nd essay "The Doctor" (Es-K-4), Ken tried to make a definition for the profession—doctor. He firstly gave the official definition on the doctor as "a licensed, professional person who uses medical science to remedy patients" (Ex. 59, s1), and then argued that a doctor "should show the enthusiasm and give hope to the patients except for treatment" (s5). With details (s7-9) and examples (s12-16), he developed the argument adequately, and concluded his argument with his own experience (s17-20) as a re-emphasis. Most ideas were presented clearly in a well-constructed organization. Like his first essay, the introduction contained proper thesis statement (s5) to foretell the main ideas. Two body paragraphs covered the discussion on being enthusiastic (s6-10) and giving hope to the patients (s11-16). The conclusion was the restatement on his main ideas (s17-20). The only awkward expression was the last two sentences of the entire article. After making a strong statement as his conclusion "a good doctor should have excellent medical skills, enthusiasm, and friendliness" (s20), he redundantly added "Hope every doctor you will meet is like above. And, this is my hope, too" (s21-22). However, this unneeded expression did not undermine his ideas presentation and overall fluency.

Originality and uniqueness. His 3rd essay "Saying Sorry for Yourself" (Es-K-6) was a narration. It looked like a reading response to the discussion between Morrie and Mitch described in *Tuesdays with Morrie*, but Ken made the responses closely related to the struggles he experienced in writing. The introduction explained the reason why he chose this topic:

> ... I spent a lot of time thinking how to write the first draft, but I failed! Suddenly, I got an idea! Why not writing something about saying sorry to yourself?" (Es-K-6-1)
> ... Morrie seemed to emphasize on not being self-pity. However, I wanted to talk about the good effects of saying sorry to yourself (Es-K-6-2).

Ex. 59 Ken's Essay 2-3

(1) The doctor is a licensed, professional person who uses medical science to remedy patients. (2) When we fall ill, the doctor will check us and understand what's wrong with us, such as fever, cold, and snivel. (3) According to the information about ours, he will give us several suggestions like what to do and what not to do. (4) After diagnosing, he will also give us proper medicine to take. (5) Besides, I think the doctor should show the enthusiasm and give hope to the patients except for treatment.

(6) In the process of treatment, the doctor can't only concentrate on treating illness by himself. (7) He should ask the patient more questions and talk with the patient about the life. (8) In the process, he can make the patient easy and relaxed. (9) At the same time, he can also let the patient trust him. (10) Showing enthusiasm can make the doctor be close to the patient and understand the reasons of illness more easily.

(11) Giving the patient hope is also an important access to treat. (12) The doctor can't tell the patient, like "You got a serious cold and I fear you would have a long time to treat. (13) And unfortunately, the opportunity of recovery is rare." (14) This is wrong. (15) Even though it is a serious illness, the doctor should give the patient hope and encourage him to live. (16) By giving many successful examples, the doctor can make the patient trust that he will recover in the future and enjoy his life with his family.

(17) The doctors that I had ever met are almost serious. (18) The doctor just wrote something on the pages and told me to go out and wait for medicine after checking you in a while. (19) Soon, the patient next to me came in. (20) For these bad experiences, I consider, a good doctor should have excellent medical skills, enthusiasm, and friendliness. (21) Hope every doctor you will meet is like above. (22) And, this is my hope, too.

Ex. 60 The 3rd, 4th, and 5th paragraphs of Ken's Essay 3-3

(9) First, … , when I spent so much time but had no gain, I could not help but stop thinking and accepted my poor ability. (10) Meanwhile, I said sorry to myself. (11) And when I faced the fact, I didn't condemn myself too much and expected that I should make more efforts to improve my ability in the future. (12) After all, every improvement just needs time.

(13) Second, due to understanding myself, I would not waste more time doing unmeaning struggle and could save the time to focus on other stuff, like my recent examination[1].

(14) Third, I could relax more and not to be so anxious. (15) This would help me stir my brain and gain more ideas about this homework. (16) Now, what you read is the achievement of saying sorry to myself.

This article was not involved with professional knowledge or argument on definition, but it also showed Ken's understanding of this issue. His understanding came from his experiences and he presented his experiences with logical organization and acceptable fluency. He used enumeration to discuss three advantages of saying sorry to oneself respectively in three body paragraphs (Ex. 60, s11, 13, 15), and provided details and examples as supporting evidences (Ex. 60, s12, 13, 16).

In conclusion, he reconfirmed that this article was the best proof of saying sorry to oneself:

At the same time, I also want to say sorry to my teacher, … . In fact, I originally wanted to write an essay about the controversial Japanese comic book, On Taiwan. But it is too hard to finish. Then I gave up. I said sorry to my teacher again and again, until I said sorry to myself. In the end, when I understood the impor-

---

[1] Ken was preparing for the entrance exam for graduate school at that time. The work, study, and the preparation of the exam made his life extremely busy and hectic.

tance of saying sorry to yourself, this draft had been finished (Es-K-6-6).

This was a piece of writing about writing. While presenting the difficulty of writing and illustrating the process of composing, Ken finished this article. The content of this article and the way he described the ideas showed his creativity and uniqueness in the connection of reading, life, and writing.

Logic and coherence. The 4th essay "Sense and Sensibility" (Es-K-7/8) revealed that the content and organization in Ken's writing reached the level of maturity. He compared and contrasted sense with sensibility point by point and argued for the equal value for a pleasant life. With a strong statement "Unlike machines or animals, human beings own sense and sensibility at the same time" (Es-K-8-1, s1) he started the introduction. Then, in the body paragraphs, he firstly discussed the differences in terms of definition and application (Ex. 61, s4-6) and then talked about the similarities that distinguished humans from animals as well as helped develop our life.

After analyzing the differences and similarities, he concluded the article with a firm suggestion:

> To emphasize sense or sensibility strictly is not good for us. To stress sense strictly will ignore human's feelings and values. By the same token, to focus on sensibility seriously will result in being too emotional and helpless for reality. Therefore, to equally press both of them and to hold the golden mean are just good for our life (Es-K-7-4).

Ex. 61 The 2nd Paragraph of Ken's Essay 4-1

> (4) In definition, sense emphasizes data analysis and situation judgment; sensibility focuses on emotional expression and instant reaction. (5) In application, sense can be applied to science, like statistics, chemistry and mathematics; sensibility, on the contrary, can be applied to art, like literature, music and panting. (6) Hence, sense helps us analyze reality and search the best solution, and sensibility gives us mind touch and spiritual stir.

The ideas in this article were clearly presented and were adequately developed. The expression was properly organized with logic and coherence. This progress was parallel to the progress shown in his prompt writing.

Essay Writing—Language

The progress of language use was shown in his revision, usually related to alternative expression. Other changes, like word choice, were obviously presented as well.

Proper expression. In essay 1-1 "DVD and Home Theater" (Es-K-1), for example, he had unclear expression "Just at home, you have probably experienced the amazing realism of films in the theaters, so called 'Home Theater'" (Es-K-1, s3), but in essay 1-3, he changed it into "Without going to the theater, you can experience the amazing realism of films. Owning entire DVD equipments at home, it is called as 'Home Theater'" (Es-K-2, s3-4). By utilizing a sentence led by a preposition phrase *Without going to the theater* (Ex. 58, s3) and participial phrase *Owning entire DVD equipments at home* (Ex. 58, s4), he not only made his expression understandable but also presented his understanding of sophisticated sentence structures. The misuse of the subject *it* in the main clause (Ex. 58, s4) connected to the participial phrase did not make his ability questioned. Also, by changing the unnecessary present perfect sentence *you have probably experience* (Es-K-1, s3) into *you can experience* (Ex. 58, s3), he made the expression a general statement.

Similarly, in essay 1-1, he explained the features of DVD player as "it determines you can see which region DVD disk" (Es-K-1, s6). In essay 1-3, the awkward sentence was changed into "it determines which region of DVD disks the DVD player can read" (Ex. 58, s7) with the reduced form of the relative clause *the DVD player can read*. In conclusion, the suggestion "it is not the meaning to buy the expensive products that you can get the most excellent effect" (Es-K-1, s18) was changed into "It doesn't mean that you can get the most excellent effect if you buy the expensive products" (Es-K-2, s19). The use of *it doesn't mean* and *If-clause* made this expression fluent and acceptable as well as showed his improvement in sentence structures. Also, in the 2nd essay, by deleting the comma and the misused subject *it*, he corrected the dangling phrase "Giving the patient hope, it is also an important access ... " (Es-K-3, s11) into a complete sentence "Giving the patient hope is also an important access ... " (Es-K-4, s11).

The revision on expression could be seen in the 3rd essay as well. In essay 3-3 "Feeling Sorry for Yourself" (Ex. 60), he substituted "I spent a lot of time thinking how to write the first draft" (Es-K-6, s2) for "I really spent so much time thinking how to write the first draft" (Es-K-5, s2) by deleting the over-emphasized expression *really* and *so much*. When he narrowed down his thesis into the advantages of saying sorry to oneself, he wrote "I wanted to discuss it from other views ..." (Es-K-5, s9) in essay 3-1, but revised it into "I wanted to talk about the good effects of saying sorry to yourself" (Es-K-6, s8) in essay 3-3. The revised sentence—*good effects of saying sorry to yourself*—precisely explained the thesis of this article. Besides, while talking about the second advantage of saying sorry for oneself, his ambiguous and ungrammatical statement in essay 3-1 "due to accept my poor ability on this section, ..." (Es-K-5, s14) was changed into a concise and grammatical expression in essay 3-3 "due to understanding myself, ..." (Es-K-6, s13).

In essay 4-3 "Sense and Sensibility" (Es-K-8), there were other examples on utilizing alternative expression. The obvious one was the revision on the topic sentence of the third paragraph. In essay 4-1, he wrote "Even though the extreme effects to us for sense and sensibility, ..." (Es-K-7, s7) and revised it into "Even though sense and sensibility have such extreme opposite effects on us, ..." (Es-K-8, s7) in essay 4-3. By adding the word *opposite*, he clearly linked the previous discussion on differences with the following expression on similarities.

Word choice. Ken's language progress was also revealed in word choice. In essay 2-3 "The Doctor" (Ex. 59), he replaced *treat* (Es-K-3, s1) with *remedy* (Es-K-4, s1), revised *unless* (Es-K-3, s5) into *except for* (Es-K-4, s5), changed *the treating process* (Es-K-3, s6) into *the process of treatment* (Es-K-4, s6), and modified *even* (Es-K-3, s15) with *even though* (Es-K-4, s15). Also, in essay 4-3, he replaced *let* with *make* in the sentence "They make us develop technologies and own self spirit" (Es-K-8, s10).

Essay Writing—Voice

Ken's unique ideas were usually identified with his authentic voice. No matter what the writing was about: technology or personal matters, he presented himself directly and straightforwardly.

One of the examples was the suggestion he provided in essay 1-3:

> It doesn't mean that you can get the most excellent effect if you buy the expensive products. In my suggestion, it is the most important to choose proper products according to your actual needs and the specification of your room. Of course, you can't ignore the influence of budget to yourself (Es-K-2, s19-21).

In the 2nd essay "The Doctor," his authentic voice was obviously revealed and caused strong resonance for the readers. From the beginning of this article, he showed his uniqueness in the statement "I think the doctor should show the enthusiasm and give hope to the patients ..." (Ex. 59, s5). Then, he re-emphasized the need of showing enthusiasm with strong voice "Showing enthusiasm can make the doctor be close to the patient and understand the reasons of illness more easily" (Ex. 59, s10). While restating the need of giving hope to the patients, he strongly addressed

> Even though it is a serious illness, the doctor should give the patient hope and encourage him to live. By giving many successful examples, the doctor can make the patient trust that he will recover in the future and enjoy his life with his family (Es-K-4, s15-16).

The resonating voice was reinforced in his 3rd and 4th essay. In essay 3-3 "Saying Sorry for Yourself," he showed his uniqueness and creativity in a humorous way. He implied more than once "what you read is the achievement of saying sorry to myself" (Es-K-6, s16) to highlight how suffering composing might be and how exhilarating when it was gone through. The delicate integration of what he read and what he wrote proved his uniqueness. The similar authenticity was shown in the 4th essay as well. To depict the differences between sense and sensibility, he firstly stated the different definition and application (Ex. 61) and then summarized the comparison with his opinions "Hence, sense helps us analyze reality and search the best solution, and sensibility gives us mind touch and spiritual stir" (Ex. 61, s6). In conclusion, he underlined the equal value of sense and sensibility with reconfirmation "Therefore, to equally press both of them and to hold the golden mean are just good for our life" (Es-K-8, s14). The firm position and straightforward expression clearly indicated his personality and identity.

The Discussion of Maria's Writing Performance

According to the scores of prompt writing, Maria's writing improved from the level of Average to the level of Good. Her progress was shown in all aspects, like organization, content, language, and voice.

Prompt Writing—All Aspects

Pre-prompt writing. Her pre-prompt writing was about the new garbage policy in Taipei[1] (Ex. 62). It was an article without title and lack of supporting ideas. Though she mentioned the advantages of carrying out this new policy (s6-8, 11), she did not develop the ideas further but only stated the citizens' complaints (s3, 5). The language of

---

Ex. 62 Maria's Pre-prompt Writing

(1) The new garbage policy in Taipei was stat in July this year. (2) What a good news and policy! (3) Though some people don't like that policy and have many complain. (4) They said the government didn't take enough time to education the people how to fallow the rule.

(5) Namater what they complain, that's only a short time. (6) Taiwan is only a small island. (7) There's not enough space for people here. (8) Does it could supply enough space for the garbage they make? (9) If we recognize that, we would support the new garbage policy in Taipei.

(10) More than that, the policy should go through Taiwan. (11) That will make our enviopment more clean.

---

[1] Maria did not attend the first class for writing her pre-prompt writing on English education at elementary school because she was on her trip to Australia. Therefore, the prompt writing she wrote for this program's entrance exam (about new garbage policy) was considered as her pre-prompt writing for this study.

this article was full of errors, like incorrect spelling, wrong word form, and incorrect use of modal. She misspelled *stat* (s1) for *state, fallow* (s4) for *follow, enviopment* (s11) for *environment,* and *namater* (s5) for *no matter.* She misused the verb *complain* (s3) for the noun *complaints* and the noun *education* (4) for the verb *educate.* She also made a question with incorrect formation of a modal as *Does it could supply ...?* (s8). It is fortunate that the meaning of her pre-prompt writing was not obscured because of these errors. Similarly, despite of these errors, her voice along with her thinking was still clearly heard in her pre-prompt writing.

Ex. 63 Maria's Post-prompt Writing

> (1) I think the policy that children learn English from elementary schools is very good. (2) It's a good time for children to learn language. (3) And children could learn English through a more nature way.
>
> (4) I remember I nearly couldn't speak Chinese when I went to elementary school. (5) I admired the classmates who could speak Chinese well. (6) Perhaps I forgot the pain to learn Chinese. (7) But I really believe it's easy for children to learn to speak a new language. (8) Learning to speak language for children is just like to learn standing up, and running. (9) It's easy.
>
> (10) We usually lear English over 13 years after graduated from universities, but we still couldn't speak English well. (11) How shame!! (12) Months ago, I came back to my mother school, and I found there are English name cards on every thing as trees have their own name cards on them. (13) We should learn English from the things around us in every day. (14) Learning English in elementary schools could creat a more good environment and a more native way for children.
>
> (15) We should happy to see children start their learning English from elementary schools. (16) Hope their speaking English ability would improve and would speak more well than us.

Post-prompt writing. Her post-prompt writing was about English education at elementary school. Though the topic was different from that of the pre-prompt writing, both of them were position paper responding to a new policy in Taipei. Her post-prompt writing (Ex. 63) contained four paragraphs: an introductory paragraph, two body paragraphs, and a conclusion. In introduction, she showed her support to this policy (s1-2) and raised the concerns "children could learn English through a more nature way" (s3). In the body paragraphs, she firstly took her experience of learning Mandarin as an example (s4-7) to emphasize how easy and nature for a kid to pick up a language as "learn standing up, and running" (s8). Then, she stated how ineffective the previous English education might be (s10-11) and moved her argument to the conclusion that the new policy might help children build their English ability (s14-16). Besides this acceptable organization, with examples (s4-7) and explanation (s12-13), the ideas were adequately developed. Though there were still errors in language use (s10, 11, 15, 16), the meaning was not confused. Her voice in this article was clear as well, especially in the statement "I really believe it's easy for children to learn to speak a new language" (s7) and in sentence "We usually lear English over 13 years …, but we still couldn't speak English well. How shame!!" (s10-11)

Essay Writing—Organization and Content

Maria improved her organization and content by providing proper details and examples. Also, her later essays showed logical development and expression more often than her earlier essays.

Informative. Her essay 1-1 was entitled "Olympics Games in the World" (Es-M-1, s0) and was renamed as "Olympics Games and Sydney" (Es-M-2, s0) in essay 1-3 owing to the re-consideration of her content. Since the thesis focused mainly on Olympic Games 2000 in Sydney, the revised title properly foretold the main ideas in this article. Both essay 1-1 and essay 1-3 were long articles, containing 5 paragraphs and 8 paragraphs respectively. She provided abundant information in her 1st essay. Besides the Olympic Game in Sydney, she also briefly introduced the origins and spirits of the Olympic Games (Es-M-1-3/4).

In essay 1-3, she even added three entirely new paragraphs to the discussion of Sydney 2000 (Ex. 64). The addition further indicated that she was knowledgeable about the topic and made the readers gain more information about the Olympic Games in Sydney.

However, she did not present the information logically or coherently. Though she tried to well connect the added paragraphs with the original expression by inserting a sentence "The opening ceremony was all about celebrating Australia's diverse culture, and the colorful closing ceremony celebrated Australia's entertainment" (Es-M-2, s26) in the beginning of the subsequent paragraph, the conclusion, the overall organization was somewhat loose. The whole article had no thesis statement or topic sentences to lead the readers to predict what the article would report. Moreover, the focus of her discussion switched back and forth. That is, she started with Sydney 2000, and moved to the history of Olympics, and then moved back to Sydney 2000, without any transitional signals. This caused confusion and non-fluency to certain degree.

Supporting explanation. Her essay 2-1 "Prague—European City of Culture 2000" was another long article, full of information in content

---

Ex. 64 The 5th, 6th, and 7th paragraphs of Maria's Essay 1-3

> 2000 Olympic Games was held in Sydney, Australia. Sydney, Australia's oldest city, claimed for the British by Captain James Cook and settled as a penal colony in the 1780s, is where it all began for modern Australia. Today, the Rocks, the site of Australia's first settlement, house many of Sydney's best hotels, shops and restaurants.
>
> Sydney Harbour and the Opera House was the backdrop for several of the most visually spectacular Olympic events- the triathlons and sailing.
>
> Sydney 2000 was called the "best Game ever," fans from around the globe were treated to inspirational performances, the kind of dramatic surprises only the Olympics can provide, and a glorious glimpse of one of the world's most beautiful cities.

Ex. 65 The Last Paragraph of Maria's Essay 2-1

> The Prague-European City of Culture project is based on three fundamental programmatic elements. These are The Story of the City, The City of Open Gates, and City to Live in, which reflect current trends in the cultural development of Prague.

but lack of supporting ideas in organization. As her essay 1-1, her essay 2-1 also contained five paragraphs, in which rich content and interesting information were provided. She started the article with the introduction of a project named "European Cultural City" in 2000, and then presented Prague, one of the cultural city, with brief description of the city's social and economic transformation and its potentials to be a European metropolis. In conclusion, she mentioned three basic elements that promoted Prague as a popular city, like the Story of the City, the City of Open Gates, and City to Live in. Despite the informative content, in terms of organization, this article did not present all the ideas in a logical way and even did not further explain what these basic elements referred to (Ex. 65). Without clear thesis statement or topic sentences, this article failed to foretell the main ideas at the proper time (Es-M-3-1/2). Without enough supporting details to illustrate the ideas, this article was somewhat incoherent in expression (Es-M-3-3/4).

However, with revision, the organization of essay 2-3 was improved. In essay 2-3, she still had the same introduction and the first body paragraph talking about the social and economic transformation happened in Prague (Es-M-4). After that, she addressed three elements with detailed explanation and proper examples. She added three entirely new paragraphs in essay 2-3 so as to provide further explanation of the Story of the City, the City of Open Gates, and the City to Live in (Ex. 66).

In concluding paragraph, she stated that Prague had potentials to be a European metropolis (Es-M-4-7). Though there were still no thesis statement or topic sentences, with detailed explanation and rearrangement of ideas, the expression in her essay 2-3 was presented logically and fluently.

Ex. 66 The 6th paragraph of Maria's Essay 2-3

> 3. The City to Live In
>
> Prague is a city in which over one tenth of the Czech Re-public's inhabitant live, work and spend their free time. At the end of the 20th century, European cultural life in the modern metropolis is entering a new phase: these cultural expressions are characterized by the use of non-traditional spaces and mod-ern technologies. Another tendency is to take the culture and art out of traditional spaces and to bring them into the stress, squares and other public spaces in order to address the broadest possible and most random public. Contemporary cultural pro-jects try to make efforts to go beyond the limit of art and cul-ture, and access to other field, such as education, environment, information and lifestyles.

Ideas and examples. Unlike the 1st and the 2nd essays that were related to different cultures and cities and were presented without her personal emotion involved, Maria's 3rd and 4th essays were her reading responses to *Tuesdays with Morrie* and written with her strong feelings and profound introspection. In essay 3-1 "Love" (Es-M-5), she dis-cussed various kinds of love, such as love between lovers, love toward human beings, and love to the nature and other creatures in the world. She presented wonderful ideas. Though there were no clear thesis statement (Ex. 67), topic sentences, or complete development (Ex. 68), the lack of these components did not undermine her expression. In-stead, her understanding of love was fluently conveyed.

Ex. 67 The 1st paragraph of Maria's Essay 3-1

> How magic life is! Maybe we could say, "Love creates the human beings." Because of love, because of man and women, the limited life could be passed from the generations to genera-tions.

Ex. 68 The 4th paragraph of Maria's Essay 3-1

> Respect all the lives and things, even though they can't talk nor move. Don't kill the world; don't let her down. Than we can see the loving world we like to live in. And you will smile to the world. So the country where we live, Taiwan, would not as notorious as people know. All kind of the environment, including politic, economic, and nature, would not as bad as now.

In essay 3-3, more details and examples were added to further illustrate her ideas. For the introductory paragraph, she not only rephrased the expression (Ex. 69, s1, 2, 4) but also added clear thesis statement (s7-8).

In order to fully describe the love between lovers, in essay 3-3, she took Puccini's opera, Turandot, as an example (Ex. 70). This added example enriched her explanation of lovers' love.

The revision on the paragraph discussing the love toward the nature and other creatures was tremendous. She firstly moved the sentence "Don't kill the world; don't let her down" (Ex. 71, s32) forward so as to make it as a proper topic sentence, and then rearranged the ideas in a logical way (s35-38).

Ex. 69 The 1st paragraph of Maria's Essay 3-3

> (1) Maybe we could say in this way, "Love creates the human beings." (2) Life starts from the attraction between men and women. (3) Because of love between men and women, the limited life could be passed from generations to generations. (4) How magic life is! (5) There're still thousands of questions we can't understand, but life can just create itself. (6) How simple life herself is! Because of love, people would like to suffer all kinds of pain and are willing to burn themselves to warm the others whom they care. (7) Love could be shown not only between lovers but all kinds of lives. (8) There're many kinds of love—love between lovers, love between human beings, love to the nature and all kinds of lives in the world.

Ex. 70 The 2nd and 3rd paragraphs of Maria's Essay 3-3

> Love between lovers receives high praise most. As you know, there're so much stories to describe it. For example, Puccini's last opera, Turandot, really moves many people.
>
> In ancient China, the vengeful Princess Turandot had decreed that anyone seeking her hand in marriage must answer three riddles or die. Calaf, a foreign prince, was struck by Turandot's beauty and resolved to win her, despite of the plea of his blind father and the begs by the slave girl Liu, who loved Calaf deeply. Calaf answered the three riddles correctly. Turandot begged her father, the emperor, to release her from this stranger, but he refused. Calaf offered to die if Turandot could guess his name by the next morning. That night, Turandot sent her troops throughout Peking to discover Calaf's name. She found Liu and tortured her, but Liu killed herself and his secret died with her. Turandot wouldn't guess his name - by dawn he would be the victor. It was morning. Despite Turandot's pleas, Calaf declared his love, and forced a kiss on her. Turandot melted, and Calaf revealed his name. Turandot summoned her court and declared she had learned the stranger's name - it was "Love."

Ex. 71 The 6th Paragraph of Maria's Essay 3-3

> (32) Don't kill the world; don't let her down. (33) We should extend our love to those not moving or talking. (34) Respect all the lives and things, even though they won't against nor argue with you. (35) When we respect all the nature, the nature will smile to us. (36) Then we can understand how lovely the world is and how magic the life is. (37) If all the people who live in and take advantage from Taiwan could love all the life in this country, Taiwan will not be as notorious as people regard. (38) All kind of the environment in Taiwan, including politics, economy, and nature, would not be as terrible as now.

Ex. 72 The 7th Paragraph of Maria's Essay 3-3

There's an English woman's adventurer, Jane Goodall, in Africa had taught us amazing things about some of the animals who share the earth with us. She grew up reading Tarzan book and spent much time outdoors. At age 23, her curiosity led her to Kenya, Africa, where she watched and studied a group of Chimpanzees. What she observed has forever changed the way people think about animals. Jane's discoveries have taught us a lesson to look at chimps and all others in the animal world in a completely new way and give a greater respect to them. We have begun to realize that animals, like us, can experience emotion, and they know both joy and sadness. She is constantly talking to people about the need to protect animals and preserve their environment.

She also added Jane Goodall as an example to further explicate the love toward the nature (Ex. 72). Jane Goodall, a female English adventurer, has been well-known for the efforts she made on wild animals protection. By referring to Jane's anecdotes, Maria reconfirmed her position on the broad definition of love.

With these added examples, rearrangement of ideas, and detailed explanation, the revised draft, essay 3-3, was not only full of information but also presented with fluency and coherence. This change proved Maria's progress in content and organization.

Idea development. The similar progress was revealed in the revision of the 4th essay. Her essay 4-1 "Morrie Schwartz and the Buddhists" was also her reading responses to *Tuesdays with Morrie*. She started with her observations that there were similarities between the thoughts of Morrie and the philosophy of Buddhism (Es-M-7-1/2). Then, she described how Morrie faced death and learned from it (Es-M-7-3). Finally, she stated "The meaning of life they get and the attitude to face it are similar though the way of their thinking is different" (Es-M-7-4) as the conclusion. As shown in the title, she planned to compare Morrie's saying and the concepts of Buddhism, especially their views on the meaning of life (Ex. 73).

However, the comparison was incomplete, because she did not really mention the concepts of Buddhism and because the different thinking ways she mentioned in conclusion were not further explained (Ex. 74).

Ex. 73 The 1ˢᵗ Paragraph of Maria's Essay 4-1

> "I think, so am I." Thought make one's will strong. After reading the book," Tuesdays with Morrie", I fell what Morrie Schwartz mentioned before death is similar to the Buddhism. They all learn from death and get the meaning of life.

Ex. 74 The 4ᵗʰ Paragraph of Maria's Essay 4-1

> The meaning of life they get and the attitude to face it are similar though the way of their thinking is different. If you want to be at peace with yourself, you must extend your love broadly to all the life surrounded you and devote yourself to the people around you.

Ex. 75 The 6ᵗʰ Paragraph of Maria's Essay 4-4

> Buddhism is appealing to the public for recognizing life is unstable and will die unexpectedly. No matter how strong and mighty we are, or how wealthy we are, we may die at any time. As time flies, our life is approaching to death second by second, day by day. When you die, you have to leave all the things you own and all the people around you. When you're dying, many things will be far away from you but Buddhist doctrine will help you. Thus, they inspire themselves to practice Buddhist rules and collect the essence of life. Recognizing life is unstable and will end unexpectedly is the easiest and powerful initial approach to become a Buddhist for the beginner. Then they could turn their heart to Buddhist doctrine and destroy all the magic of worry. Finally, they could get peace in the future world and get free from the transmigration and become Buddha.

Ex. 76 The 9th Paragraph of Maria's Essay 4-4

Buddhists think we are so lucky to get the body to present life so we should cherish it. We shouldn't be controlled by the harassment, which makes us experience pain. We should understand the purpose of living is not only to get the personal peace and solve the personal problems, but should help those who are suffered from the misery and eager for peace to get far away from the misery and to get to the way to have peace. Don't we get peace and happiness from other people? How dare we just cherish ourselves, but abandon other people! If you only concentrate on yourself and only pursuit your own happiness, the trouble from greed and displeasure will come. Then you will hurt yourself and others. Those who have power but without love will hurt people. In our life, the most important and praiseworthy thing is to develop the heart to be full of kindness and love. That's the root of peace.

In essay 4-4, the comparison was shown obviously. Both content and organization were improved by the utility of adequate details and explanation. The main ideas were fully developed and properly supported. For example, to respond to Morrie's saying on death, she added a paragraph discussing how Buddhism dealt with death (Ex. 75).

Also, when she reacted to Morre's saying about meaningful life, she added another paragraph talking about the meaningful life defined by Buddhism (Ex. 76).

With added examples and further discussion, essay 4-4 successfully connected Morrie's saying with the concepts of Buddhism, and fluently expressed the main ideas. This revision indicated that Maria gained awareness of content and organization.

Essay Writing—Language

In terms of language use, Maria also presented her progress throughout the school year, especially in revision. The most obvious progress was shown in the use of word choice, sentence structures, and correct spelling. In addition, she started utilizing vivid language in her later essays.

Word choice and spelling. While revising the 1st essay "Olympics Games and Sydney," she solved the problems of misspelling and incorrect word choice. For example, the misused *scream* in "people ... watched the Games through TV, big scream" (Es-M-1, s6) was changed to *screen* (Es-M-2, s6), *bought* in "French Baron Pierre de Coubertin bought the Olympic tradition back to life" (Es-M-1, s8) was revised into *brought* (Es-M-2, s8), and *than* in "Than the Olympic flame was lighted in a ceremony ..." (Es-M-1, s24) was replaced by *then* (Es-M-2, s29). The incorrect listing signals, like *First, ... Second, ... Another ...* (Es-M-1, s12-14) was also re-written as *First, ... Second, ... Last, ...* (Es-M-2, s12-14).

In essay 3-1, there was still confusion about word choice and spelling. When she revised the 3rd essay "Love," she gained knowledge about word forms and sentence structures. For example, in essay 3-1, she wrote "All kind of the environment, including politic, economic, and nature, would not as bad as now" (Ex. 68, s16), and in essay 3-3, the words with wrong word forms *politic* and *economic* were changed into *politics* and *economy* in "All kind of the environment in Taiwan, including politics, economy, and nature, would not be as terrible as now" (Es-M-6, s38). In this same sentence, she also revised the incorrect sentence structure *would not as bad as now* into *would not be as terrible as now* by adding the copula *be*. The revision on conclusion was another evidence of her understanding of word forms. In essay 3-1, she wrote "Without good health, we can't live energy, powerful, and colorful" (Es-M-5, s21). Because the words *energy, powerful,* and *colorful* in this sentence carried wrong part of speech, she replaced these words, in essay 3-3, with their adverbs *energetically, powerfully,* and *colorfully* so the sentence became "Without good health, we can't live energetically, powerfully, and colorfully" (Es-M-6, s50).

Sentence structure. The revision of the 4th essay showed her overall progress in language use, like word choice, spelling, sentence structures, etc. For example, the sentence in essay 4-1 "We usually don't know cherish life and ... our immortal body ... will polished by age must decay ..." (Es-M-7-2) was rewritten as "We usually don't know how to cherish our life and ... our mortal body ... will be perished by age and must decay ..." (Es-M-8-2). By adding *how to* between "don't know" and "cherish life" and adding *and* between "will be perished" and "must decay," she solved the problem of run-on sentences. By substituted *mortal* for *immortal* and replaced *polished* by *perished*, she precisely conveyed the meaning. By revising *will polished* into *will be perished*, the correct formation of passive voice was presented.

Vivid language. Besides the changes shown in revision, that she started utilizing vivid language was another proof of her language progress. Using flowers giving pollen to bees as an analogy in the 3rd essay "Love," she vividly depicted the concept of love coming from sharing:

> Love comes from sharing. One could not feel love alone without others. Only when we give the things we get, love could be understood and be showed up. Just as flowers give their love—pollen—to bees, so the nectar could be made, and the seeds could be produced (Es-M-6-4).

Essay Writing—Voice

With vivid language, she strengthened her voice. Her uniqueness and authenticity were interwoven with her getting-mature language. Like in essay 3-3, while talking about the magic of love, she wrote "Because of love, people would like to suffer all kinds of pain and are willing to burn themselves to warm the others whom they care" (Ex. 69, s6). She also mentioned in the same article "Only through love, we could learn how to understand and forgive, and smooth all the uncomfortable part in heart" (Es-M-6, s30). Her profound reflection and understanding of love were extended to the love toward human beings, which was emphasized in essay 4-4 and revealed in this sentence "If you want to be at peace with yourself, you must extend your love broadly to all the life surrounded you and devote yourself to the people around you" (Es-M-8-7).   With resonating expression, Maria presented her concerns and raised awareness of love and meaningful life.   The conclusion of her essay 3-3 showed her voice to its fullest:

> Opening the page of history, we see that wars and wars make the history of human beings. We learn one could rule the world and open a new age in his country, but without love, he can't win the people's hearts. "Love wins. Love always wins."
>
> Without breath, we can't live.
>
> Without good health, we can't live energetically, powerfully, and colorfully.
>
> Without heart, we can't feel love.
>
> Without love, we can't see the beautiful and wonderful part of the life and we won't hear the charming melody in the journey of our life (Es-M-6-8).

APPENDIX

The Discussion of Peggy's Writing Performance

According to the scores of prompt writing, Peggy's writing performance improved from the level of Average to the level of Good. The obvious progress was shown in content, organization, and language.

Prompt Writing—All Aspects

Pre-prompt writing. Talking about elementary English education, her pre-prompt writing brought up two concerns: different policy for schools in city and in countryside as well as the overloaded pressure for elementary school students. She, therefore, concluded that she disagreed with the policy of teaching English in elementary schools and suggested that the government should pay more attention to environment/ecology education instead of foreign language learning (Ex. 77).

Ex. 77 Peggy's Pre-prompt Writing

(1) Although I am not familiar with this topic, I still have two opinions about this policy.

(2) First, Cities and countries don't have the same standard to develpe this course, including equipments , teachers.... (3) In other words , if we teach English in the elementary school , students will enlarge their clearning abilities.

(4) Second, elementary school students start to study Chinese . (5) Right now add new class in this system. (6) Do students learn more or confuse their language abilities.? (7) In this modern world, elementary school students have many pressures on them. (8) Therefore , I disagree add new course in the elementary school.

(9) The most important is that the government should develop natural learning environments, not add foreign language courses.

What she intended to convey in this article was meaningful and reflected the current dilemma our government faced. However, some of her ideas were not clearly presented due to the lack of details and explanation. For example, when she mentioned "Cities and countries don't have the same standard to develpe this course, including equipments, teacher ..." (s2), she did not provide further discussion but incoherently started talking about "if we teach English in the elementary school, students will enlarge their clearning abilities" (s3). Moreover, these two irrelevant sentences were connected by the transitional phrase "In other words" (s3). Though she made a clear thesis statement "I still have two opinions about this policy" (s1) and used enumeration to list her points (s2, 4), she did not make topic sentences clear and not fully develop the main thesis. In terms of language use, there were frequent errors on words and grammar, such as misspelling *develpe* (s2) and *clearning* (s3), fragment *Right now add new class in this system* (s5), and incorrect sentence structure *I disagree add new course* ...(s8). In this article, only her voice reached the level of Good, which revealed her authenticity and uniqueness without reservation. The statement "...students have many pressures on them. Therefore, I disagree add new course in the elementary school" (s7-8) and the suggestion "The most important is that the government should develop natural learning environments, not add foreign language courses" (s9) were the best evidences.

Post-prompt writing. After a year of learning, while composing her post-prompt writing, she not only showed awareness of coherence and detailed explanation but also changed her position on the issue of elementary school English education (Ex. 78).

In this article, her stand was to support the policy of teaching English in elementary schools. In order to further explain her position, she firstly emphasized the need of international communication (s2-4), and then referred her opinions to the research of psychologists and sociologists (s6-7). Furthermore, she argued from the perspective of reducing social stratification and distance (s9-17). Finally, she restated the necessity of starting teaching English in elementary schools (s18). In her post-prompt writing, she showed that she was acknowledgeable

Ex. 78 Peggy's Post-prompt Writing

(1) In the agriculture time, most of the people only can speak their mother tongue language. (2) However, as the industrial era coming, it is very common to exchange international goods. (3) Taiwan is a sea island, undoubledly, it can't be excepted in this world trend since the global time is the only main trend, tool to communicate each other is using the same languages. (4) We all know that English is the most popular languages in the world. (5) So, it is basic to learn English especially in the childhood period. (6) Most psychologists and sociologists approve that people in the childhood period can learn more than in the adulthood. (7) We, adults, have the same experience, aren't we? (8) How can we say that it is not important to learn English in the elementary school?

(9) Besides, if we have some English lessons in the elementary school, the social stratification's distance can be reduced. (10) In Taiwan, some rich families send their children to learn English after classes dismissed. (11) But, poor families don't have enough money to let their children to learn something. (12) So we can see that Taiwan's English standards has apparent distance (13) Poor families always have fewer educational resources. (14) But, rich families' children always have enough and abundant information and resources. (15) It results in rich families' children will have higher achievements in the future than in the poor ones. (16) So if we teach English lessons in the elementary school, it can reduce poor-rich, and high-low social status differences. (17) Everyone has the same opportunities to learn basic English speaking and writing skills.

(18) Cnclusionally, no matter from the international bussiness view, professions' opinion or reducing social stratification's point, it is the basic technology to have speaking and writing English language abilities.

about this issue. Especially when she mentioned the phenomena and influences of social stratification, she discussed it not only from a student writer's point of view but also from a social worker's professional observations. With extended discussion, her ideas were properly supported and adequately developed. Her voice presenting her personality was also heard. The contrast between rich family and poor family was the best proof (Ex. 78, s10-16). As for the language use, there were still errors on spelling, word choice/form, and sentence structures. For example, she misspelled *undoubledly* (s3) for *undoubtedly*, used wrong word form *Cnclusionally* (s18) for *In conclusion*, and constructed incorrect sentence *it can't be excepted in this world trend since the global time is the only main trend, tool to communicate each other is using the same language* (s3). However, the amount of errors was greatly reduced and the existing language problems did not make her meaning obscured.

Essay Writing—Organization and Content

The similar progress in all the aspects was shown in her essay writing as well. For organization and content, the most obvious progress was shown in logical development of ideas, clear topic sentences and supporting details, and vivid expression and description.

Informative and meaningful content. Her 1st essay "American Music" was based on her theme reading. She briefly introduced American Music chronologically (Ex. 79). The content was informative and full of illustration and explanation (s23-27, 36-37). The ideas were properly presented, though there were no topic sentences to foretell the main discussion in each paragraph.

The 2nd essay "The Titanic Riddle—Should a Good Feminist Accept Priority Seating on a Lifeboat?" was also the reaction to her reading. She started with the scene that the captain of Titanic asked women and children got in the lifeboats first (Ex. 80, s1-3), and rephrased the opinions proposed by the magazine article[1]—"If women, especially feminists still insist men should let women go first, it is demeaning women" (s6).

---

[1] The article "The Titanic Riddle" she read was written by Charles Krauthammer and published by *Time Express* on April 13, 1998.

Ex. 79 The 5th and 6th Paragraphs of Peggy's Essay 1-1

(21) In the early 1900's, the blues was born in South. (22) When the civil was over, the blacks worked on the farms and construction sites. (23) However, the life was difficult. (24) Many people lived alone, without their families. (25) On the weekends, the workers were together to drink and picnic. (26) And the travel black singer entertained them. (27) Their songs' contents expressed having no money, no job, no lover, no house. (28) These songs were called blues. ...

(35) During the 1930's, there were many economic problems in America. (36) Many people expressed their troubles in the folk music. (37) Folk music likes the country music, but they are more serious and traditional. (38) In 1960's many people were against the war in Vietnam. (39) Many folk singers wrote many songs to anti the war, like Bob Dylan.

Ex. 80 The 1st and 2nd Paragraphs of Peggy's Essay 2-3

(1) The captain shouts, "The Titanic will be sunken by hitting the iceberg. (2) There are not enough lifeboats, so women and children first!" (3) When the audiences see men trying to sneak on with—or ahead of the ladies, everyone hisses them. (4) This mores—let women first—seem natural without saying. (5) But, the author feels so strange why in the modern times, women still own all of the special rights?

(6) If women, especially feminists still insist men should let women go first, it is demeaning women. (7) It is because that during 1900s, women were only allowed in the private sphere and the social structures limited women to develop their life career. (8) Therefore, they were incapable to dissolve and handle emergencies. (9) One day, if something happened, undoubtedly women could be granted special protections like children, including the fact that they could go first. (10) In contrast, in this day of the most extensive societal restructuring to grant women equality in education, in employment, in government, in athletics, in citizenship, why entitles women to the privileges? (11) I have some opinions to debate with the author.

To argue against the author's saying, Peggy made her points skill-fully and persuasively.   She referred to the diverse roles humans played at different developmental stages (Ex. 81, s12-16) and the reality and the need of humans' interdependency (s17-18).   Then, based on these facts, she claimed "It, 'women go first,' shouldn't be supposed to helpless and pitiable dependence as the children" (s20) but a reflection of the physi-cal differences between male and female in nature.

She also urged that women should not be "the donkey in the lion's skin" (Ex.81, s26); otherwise, there would be "another gender oppres-sion from women to men" (s33).

Ex. 81 The 3rd, 4th, and 5th Paragraphs of Peggy's Essay 2-3

(12) Everyone has his(her) role to play and developmental tasks. (13) First, on the basis of the age, babies learn to walk, eat, bath, etc. ...   (14) The children and youth learn knowledge from the school. (15) The adults organize families and develop careers. (16) The old pass on their experiences to the next generations, and the young generations should respect the old.

(17) Second, from the view of social stratum, farmers, la-bors, fishers, teachers, officers, engineers and other careers con-stitute a mutual dependence social network. (18) No one can live by himself and society must be operated by all of them.

(19) Identically, different genders also have their own functions and tasks such as women have the ability to breed and men have more physical strength. (20) It, "women go first," shouldn't be supposed to helpless and pitiable dependence as the children. (21) In simpler terms, women and men originally have divergent roles to play. (22) It is the same as different ages, and social stratums. (23) Everyone contributes his(her) own ability to the society. (24) The author seems to make a fuss over a trifling matter.

Ex. 82 The Last Paragraph of Peggy's Essay 2-3

> (25) Besides, I caution against one thing. (26) Women should be careful not to be the donkey in the lion's skin. (27) A friend of mine complained to me that when some heavy things were needed to pick up, the female colleagues turned their head on him and say, "It is right you, undoubtedly." (28) However, while there are something good, female always are the first to get and grab. (29) He says, "I really don't like this situation, but I can't say any words. (30) I will be labeled as a chauvinism." (31) This situation needs to be carefully considered. (32) If women have the priority to get good things and throw bad things to men by the reason of gender equality, I think it loses the essence of equality. (33) It will become another gender oppression from women to men.

The ideas in this essay were presented clearly. With fluent expression, her thoughts were properly developed and reflected. The way she constructed the article was also well-organized. The short sentences, like "the author feels so strange why in the modern times, women still own all of the special rights?" (Ex. 80, s5) and "I have some opinions to debate with the author" (Ex. 80, s11), signaled the follow-up discussion and prepared the readers to interact with the argument. The progress in organization helped convey the informative and meaningful content.

Idea development and coherence. In her 3rd essay "What Do I See 'Girl Lashes Out at Dad in Court' Event?" (Es-P-5/6), she again revealed her professional concerns—be sensitive to the society. She wrote her reaction to a social event, in which a teenage girl, Hsiao-tse, sued "her biological father for not supporting her life expenses" (Es-P-5, s1). She first briefly described the background of this event and then raised two inquiries to have further discussion. The inquiries were whether "children born in single-parent families [would] contribute to more negative behaviors than two-parent family" (Es-P-6, s7) and whether "Hsiao-tse's methods [would] influence our society?" (Es-P-6, s8) In terms of content, the ideas in this essay were clearly presented

Ex. 83 The 3rd Paragraphs of Peggy's Essay 3-3

(9) According to foreign and Taiwan domestic researches, single-parent families have more negative effects on their children. (10) These negative effects include the difficulty of adapting oneself to his/her community or school life, lower self-esteem, oppressing emotion and so on. (11) Hsiao-tse's abnormal behavior seems to testify this point. (12) But what is the casual relationship between single-parent families and deviant behaviors? (13) First, Hsiao-tse's mother is an unmarried woman. (14) Traditionally, people can't accept unmarried woman having children. (15) In some degree, her interpersonal relationship may be affected and limited. (16) We can guess that in Taiwan, she will suffer more external critiques. (17) Besides, she is an out-of-work woman. (18) Her social network is smaller than working people. (19) Third, Taiwan's social welfare system doesn't provide enough economic and mental help to unmarried women. (20) Therefore, She can only use radical ways to express her needs including kneeling down in front of her husband's company. (21) It looks as if she made living lonely. (22) No kin, no friends, no neighborhood, no colleagues and no government helps her. (23) Naturally, in this circumstance, Hsiao-tse learns some defense mechanisms from her mother. (24) Furthermore, during 1980—2000A.D, some people express their voices through unusual and even more biased ways. (25) For example, fight and remonstrate. (26) Often, if person uses these ways, his(her) issues will be noticed and solved. (27) As mass media developed, people imitate these behaviors and actions. (28) We can't deny that Hsiao-tse or her mother was influenced by the mass media. (29) In sum, we can find out single-parent families have more weakness than two-parent families. (30) As a result of having more weaknesses, children from single-parent families have more deviance than two-parent families.

and fully developed (Ex. 83).   Details (s13-23) and examples (s24-27) were adequately provided.   It was not only informative but also problem posing, which drew attention to the consequences of single-parent family and the legitimization of Hsiao-tse type of protestation.

In terms of organization, this essay had appropriate introduction with clear thesis statement (Es-P-6, s7-8).   The ideas in the body paragraphs were stated with logic and properly supported.   The revision on the second paragraph of essay 3-3 indicated her understanding of the necessity of coherence.   In essay 3-1, the second paragraph was written in this way:

> From this event, we can discuss some issues. First, why do children who were born in single-parent families contribute to more negative than two-parent family? Second, will Hsiao-tse's methods influence our society? (Es-P-5-2)

However, in essay 3-3, she revised it into:

> After the mass reported the events, we need to take some potential phenomena seriously. First, will children born in single-parent families contribute to more negative behaviors than two-parent family? Second, will Hsiao-tse's methods influence our society? (Es-P-6-2)

By adding the sentence "After the mass reported the events, we need to take some potential phenomena seriously" (Es-P-6, s6-8), she made clear connection between the event and the possible consequences. The only weakness in organization of this essay was the lack of conclusion after investigating those two inquiries.

Vivid language.   In her 4th essay "Web Bookstore vs. Traditional Bookstore" (Es-P-7/8), she made comparison on two different kinds of bookstores.   In the introductory paragraph, she briefly mentioned how web bookstore made things different and proposed that there were many differences between traditional bookstore and web bookstore as the thesis statement (Es-P-8, s10).   Then, she started discussing the differences point by point in body paragraphs (Es-P-8-2/3/4). With clear topic sentences (Es-P-8, s11, 17), the discussion was well foretold and organized. With vivid language and description (Ex. 84, s18-19, 22, 25), the ideas were presented thoroughly and fully developed with details (Ex. 84).

The conclusion was to emphasize the luckiness of the modern readers for the choice they had (Ex. 85).

Ex. 84 The 3rd and 4th Paragraphs of Peggy's Essay 4-3

(17) We can buy books in these two bookstores; however, web bookstore is 7-11—24 hours open. (18) When I am sleepless, I can jump out of my bed and go to the web bookstore immediately. (19) Right now, when I can't fall asleep, my antidote is browsing the web bookstore. (20) As opposed to the web bookstore, traditional bookstore has running hours limited. (21) Customers are restrained to its operating styles. (22) The traditional bookstore is confined to its location and book collection. (23) While I have am emergency to look up some references, I usually don't go to the traditional bookstore; on the other hand, browsing the web bookstore becomes my first step to solve my problems. (24) In other words, I can buy all sorts of books in the web bookstore.

(25) Although the web bookstore has strong searching functions, the traditional bookstore tends to keep friendly and human characteristics. (26) In the traditional bookstore, we can skim through the whole book quickly, then, deciding whether to buy it or not. (27) However, in the web bookstore we only can glance at few introductions briefly. (28) Therefore, we may buy more wrong books in the web bookstore than in the traditional ones.

Ex. 85 The Last Paragraph of Peggy's Essay 4-3

(34) There are many differences between the two. (35) However, it is the most fortunate for the readers because we are capable of choosing and shopping in any kind of bookstores.

Generally speaking, Peggy's 4th essay was another evidence for her progress in content and organization.

Essay Writing—Language

The use of language in her essays was also improved throughout the school year.   She made progress in punctuation, like the use of *'s*, in word choice and word order, and in effective expression.

Punctuation.   In essay 1-1 "American Music," she seemed to have problems utilizing correct form of *'s*.   While mentioning the date, she misused *1900's, 1930's, 1950's, 1960's* (Es-P-1, s21, 31, 42, 38) for *1900s, 1930s, 1950s, 1960s,* and when she referred to the performers of "minstrel show," she misused *Its'* (Es-P-1, s18) for *Its* in the sentence "Its' characters are that whites wear blackface sing and dance and tell funny stories" (Es-P-1, s18).   Also, she seemed confused about the use of definite article *the*.   In essay 1-1, she incorrectly used *the* in "Chicago, was the center of the jazz" (Ex. 79, s30) and in "Music is the part of America" (Es-P-1, s56).   The similar problem of using *the* was also seen in essay 2-1, in which she misused *the* in the transitional phrase "In the contrast" (Es-P-3-2).   With revision and gained knowledge of the proper usage, she tremendously reduced these errors in subsequent essays.

Sentence structure.   Besides, Peggy also gained awareness of sentence structures.   In essay 1-1, she had difficulty on sentence like "Folk music likes the country music" (Es-P-1, s37).   With understanding of the difference between the verb *like* and the adjective *like*, the sentence was revised into "Folk music sounds like the country music" (Es-P-2-6).   Though the revision on this sentence "American started to listen black music" (Es-P-1, s15) was not complete—it only changed *to listen* to *listening* but not replaced *listen black music* with *listen to black music*, the revised one "American started listening black music" still showed her awareness of the sentence structure to certain degree.   Also, in essay 2-1 "The Titanic Riddle—Should a Good Feminist Accept Priority Seating on a Lifeboats?" she used incorrect passive voice and wrong s-v agreement in the sentence "the social structures were limited women to develop her life career" (Es-P-3-2).   In essay 2-3, she revised

329

it with the deletion of *were* and the utility of *their* to make the sentence grammatically correct as "the social structures limited women to develop their life career" (Es-P-3, s7). In the conclusion of the same article, she misused *careful* for *carefully* and *consideration* for *considered* in the sentence "This event needs to be careful consideration" (Es-P-3-6). The revision "This situation needs to be carefully considered" (Es-P-4, s31) indicated her understanding of part of speech. Similarly, when she mentioned the advantages of using web bookstore at home, she, in essay 4-1, wrote "When I am sleeplessness, I can jump out of my bed ..." (Es-P-7-3). With understanding of the part of speech, she, in essay 4-3, properly substituted the adjective *sleepless* (Es-P-8, s18) for the noun *sleeplessness*.

Word choice, word order, and effective expression. Her progress in language was also shown in word choice, word order, and effective expression. In essay 3-3 "What Do I See 'Girl Lashes Out at Dad in Court' Event?" she revised *self-concept* into *self-esteem* (Es-P-6, s10), modified *her father's company's door* into *her father's company* (Es-P-6, s20), and replaced unclear expression *our design* with precise saying *our social structure's design* (Es-P-6, s42). She also rephrased the sentence "These negative effects include adapting difficulty in community and school life ..." (Es-P-5-3) into "These negative effects include the difficulty of adapting oneself to his/her community or school life ..." (Es-P-6, s10). By using *the difficulty of adapting oneself to his/her community*, this meaning of the sentence was effectively conveyed. By changing the word order of *temporarily were coped with* into the order of *were temporarily coped with*, the revised sentence "It seems that her problems were temporarily coped with" (Es-P-6, s34) was well presented. The progress in word choice and effective expression was also revealed in her 4th essay "Web Bookstore vs. Traditional Bookstore." In essay 4-4, she replaced *deleted* in "my trouble has deleted completely" (Es-P-7-1) with *disappeared* to make the meaning of this sentence "my trouble had disappeared completely" (Es-P-8, s6) clear. Also, in essay 4-3, she replaced *questions* with *problems* for sentence "browsing the web bookstore becomes my first step to solve my problems" (Es-P-8, s23). Another example of effective expression was shown in the closing inquiries of essay 3-3 after the discussion of Hsiao-tse's protest:

> ... this event reminds us to examine our social institutions. Why can't people obeying social norms get justice? Does our social structure's design keep up with time? Does it have accessibility, availability, accountability, integration, affordability and quality? If the structure's design falls far behind people's needs, how can we improve and make it better? (Es-P-6-4)

Essay Writing—Voice

Peggy's unique voice and concerns were shown more clearly in her later essays than her earlier essays. She usually presented her voice with vivid language and lively description.

The quoted example (Es-P-6-4), the expression made by Hsiao-tse, not only proved Peggy's use of effective language but also revealed her strong voice. With a series of questions, she presented her concerns intensively in the following paragraphs of the same article. When she inferred how Hsiao-tse's mother was negatively influenced by the unsound social welfare system, her unique voice was strongly presented as well:

> ... Taiwan's social welfare system doesn't provide enough economic and mental help to unmarried women. Therefore, She can only use radical ways to express her needs including kneeling down in front of her husband's company. It looks as if she made living lonely. No kin, no friends, no neighborhood, no colleagues and no government helps her (Es-P-6-3).

Then, when she questioned whether Hsiao-tse's protest would have any side effect on the public, what she expressed showed her personality directly:

> ... If Hsiao-tse's protest becomes normal, I am afraid our society will be deconstructed and disordered. Everyone will deem it to use unusual methods as the only fast and proper ways. And then, people using regular ways to obey social rules will be sacrificed. I can't imagine what the world will be (Es-P-6-4).

In addition to the 3rd essay, her 4th essay "Web Bookstore vs. Traditional Bookstore" demonstrated her authenticity strongly. She started with the article with vivid language and lively description:

> This winter was a little lousy cold and the ground was always full of incredible wet. I, who am the laziest person in the world, like to read. Can you imagine? When the bad winter meets with me, what will it happen? Often, I, as Hamlet, always hesitate--to be or not to be—whether going outside to search books crazily or not. Now, my trouble has disappeared completely. Do you know why? The reason is that the web bookstore was born. I only use one figure to kick my keyboard relaxedly; then, books will come to my home automatically. ... (Es-P-8-1)

This vivid language and lively description carried her unique voice and drew the readers' attention, which, in turn, helped reach the function of resonance. In the following paragraph of the same article, when she mentioned the first difference between web bookstore and traditional bookstore, she also interwove the vivid language with her uniqueness perfectly:

> In the web bookstore, I can easily put my clothes on. Not only can I wrap myself in the heavy blanket in the winter, but also I can be naked in the summer. No one will notice I am a terrible monster or a beautiful lady. On the contrary, when I am in the traditional bookstore, I have to be a person. It means that I have to wear appropriate clothes in the right time. I can't choose what I want to wear (Es-P-8-2).

By making fun of herself and being humorous, she not only effectively conveyed the meaning but also moved her writing into a new territory.

APPENDIX N

The Discussion of Ken's Attitudinal Changes on Writing Self-efficacy

According to the results gained from *Writing Self-efficacy Questionnaire*, Ken's writing confidence was improved from 2.6 to 4.1, which referred to the progress from the level of Low to the level of Middle. The means of each subscale indicated similar changes. The change of the first subscale was from 2.4 to 3.9 and that of the second subscale was from 2.9 to 4.6. These changes proved that Ken increased his writing self-confidence on composing various writing tasks and performing different writing skills.

The distribution of his frequency checks on the questionnaire of writing self-efficacy showed the same improvement in details. Before engaging in theme cycles learning, no check fell in the category of "confidence" (point 5, 6, 7). There was only 1 out of 25 checks for "undecided" (point 4) and the rest of 24 were all for the category of "no confidence" (point 1, 2, 3). Among the 24 checks, there were 15 for point 3 (fairly unsure), 6 for point 2 (strongly unsure), and 3 for point 1 (extremely unsure). However, after the learning of theme cycles, there were 10 out of 25 checks belonging to the category of "confidence" (point 5, 6, 7), 6 for "undecided" (point 4), and only 9 for the category of "no confidence" (point 1, 2, 3). Among the 10 "confidence" checks, 5 were for point 5 (fairly confident) and 5 for point 6 (strongly confident). Among the 9 "no confidence" checks, 7 were for point 3 (fairly unsure), 1 for point 2 (strongly unsure), and 1 for point 1 (extremely unsure).

In terms of writing tasks, the most obvious change was shown in his answer to Item-17 "Write a brief autobiography." Before learning, he showed his lack of strong confidence (point 2), and after learning, he became strongly confident (point 6). The increased confidence in writing an autobiography was revealed in the answer to Item-5 as well. The answers to Item-5 "Prepare a resume describing your employment history and skills" were point 4 (undecided) before learning and point 6 (strongly confident) after learning. This tremendous change was also proved by his gained motivation and intention in writing self-introduction. In the beginning of the class, while writing a self-introduction, he only wrote 6 sentences (Em-K-1) explaining his fondness of English and his wish to go abroad, but during the winter vacation, he wrote a complete autobiography, including his family background, schooling, work, and future plan (J-K-13). Not to mention the content and structure of the complete autobiography, that he gained confidence to present himself in a written form was clearly revealed.

In addition, he also gained confidence in composing different types of articles. The answers to Item-11 "Compose an article for a popular magazine such as Newsweek" first showed his lack of strong confidence (point 2) and then indicated his fair confidence (point 5). His responses to Item-16 "Prepare lesson plans for an elementary class studying the process of writing" were fairly unsure (point 3) before learning and fairly confident (point 5) after learning. The same progress was indicated in the answers to Item-4 "Write an instruction manual for operating an office machine" and Item-1 "Write a letter to a friend or family member": from being fairly unsure (point 3) to being fairly confident (point 5). For "Write a one or two sentence answer to a specific test question" (Item-6), his answers were changed from point 3 (fairly unsure) to point 5 (fairly confident).

Ken's confidence also had tremendous changes on performing different writing skills. Before learning, the answers to the statements regarding writing skills (from Item-18 to Item-25) were all in the category of "no confidence": 7 for point 3 (fairly unsure) and 1 for point 2 (strongly unsure). However, after a year of learning, only 1 answer fell in the category of "no confidence": 1 for point 3 (fairly unsure) and others were all for the category of "confidence," including 3 for point 6 (strongly confident). The most remarkable changes were shown in the answers to Item-18 "Correctly spell all words in a one-page passage," Item-19 "Correctly punctuate a one-page passage," and Item-24 "Organize sentences into a paragraph so as to clearly express a theme."

For these three statements, his responses were all changed from a fair lack of confidence (point 3) to having strong confidence (point 6).

All in all, Ken gained confidence in both communicating in various writing tasks and performing different writing skills.

APPENDIX  O

The Discussion of Peggy's Attitudinal Changes on Writing Self-efficacy

According to the results gained from *Writing Self-efficacy Questionnaire*, Peggy's writing confidence was increased from 3.0 to 3.9, which referred to the progress from the level of Low to the level of Middle. The means of two subscales indicated similar results. The first subscale, regarding the confidence on various writing tasks, had its means changed from 3.1 to 3.9. The second subscale, regarding the confidence on performing different writing skills, had its means increased from 2.9 to 4.0. The distribution of frequency check also showed similar increase and presented the changes in details. Before learning, there were 5 out of 25 checks falling in the category of "confidence" (point 5, 6, 7), which were 2 for point 6 (strongly confident) and 3 for point 5 (fairly confident). Besides, there were 3 out of 25 checks belonging to point 4 (undecided), and 17 for the category of "no confidence" (point 1, 2, 3), including 7 for point 3 (fairly unsure), 5 for point 2 (strongly unsure), and 5 for point 1 (extremely unsure). However, after learning, there were 6 out of 25 checks falling in the category of "confidence" (point 5, 6, 7), which were 1 for point 6 (strongly confident) and 5 for point 5 (fairly confident). Eleven checks were for point 4 (undecided). Most importantly, there were only 8 checks out of 25 belonging to the category of "no confidence" (point 1, 2, 3) after learning, which included 7 for point 3 (fairly unsure) and 1 for point 2 (strongly unsure). No response was for point 1 (extremely unsure).

In the first subscale, the most tremendous change was the responses to Item-13. For the statement "Author a 400 page novel" (Item-13), she responded with point 1 (extremely unsure) before learning and point 5 (fairly confident) after learning. This change indicated that Peggy gained confidence in composing different types of articles. Similar changes were revealed in the answers to Item-9 "Author a scholarly article for publication in a professional journal in your field" and Item-10

"Write a letter to the editor of the daily newspaper": both from point 1 (extremely unsure) to point 3 (fairly unsure). Though the changes occurred within the category of "no confidence," the increase of her writing confidence was still presented.

In addition, Peggy gained confidence in using writing for school learning. For example, the responses to Item-8 "Write a term paper of 15 to 20 pages" were point 1 (extremely unsure) before learning and became point 3 (fairly unsure) after learning. Although the answer still fell in the category of "no confidence," the improvement was clearly presented. If the answers to Item-6 and Item-7 were investigated, the evidences of progress were further provided. For the statement "Write a one or two sentence answer to a specific test question" (Item-6), she answered with point 4 (undecided) before learning and point 5 (fairly confident) after learning. Also, for the statement "Compose a one or two page essay in answer to a test question" (Item-7), she responded with point 4 (undecided) in the beginning of learning and point 5 (fairly confident) in the end of school year.

Also, Peggy gained confidence in functional writing. In answer to the statement "Prepare a resume describing your employment history and skills" (Item-5), she chose point 3 (fairly unsure) before learning and point 6 (strongly confident) after learning. The responses to Item-4 "Write an instruction manual for operating an office machine" also showed the increase from point 3 (fairly unsure) to point 4 (undecided), though the change was not obvious.

In the second subscale, the most obvious changes were shown in the responses to Item-21. To respond to the statement "Write a simple sentence with proper punctuation and grammatical structure" (Item-21), she chose point 3 (fairly unsure) before learning and point 5 (fairly confident) after learning. Others like the answers to Item-20 "Correctly use parts of speech," Item-22 "Correctly use plurals, verb tenses, prefixes, and suffixes," and Item-23 "Write compound and complex sentences with proper punctuation and grammatical structure" were all changed from point 2 (strongly unsure) to point 4 (undecided). As for the statement "Organize sentences into a paragraph so as to clearly express a theme" (Item-24), she answered with point 3 (fairly not confident) in the beginning of learning and with point 4 (undecided) in the end of school year. Concerning the overall organization stated in Item-25 "Write a paper with good overall organization," she first responded with point 1 (extremely unsure) and then with point 3 (fairly unsure). Though none of these responses belonged to the category of "confidence," the increase of her writing confidence could not be denied.

The Discussion of Maria's Attitudinal Changes on Writing Self-efficacy

According to the results gained from *Writing Self-efficacy Questionnaire*, Maria's writing confidence was raised from 4.0 to 5.3, equal to the progress from the level of Middle to the level of High. The means of two subscales indicated the similar results. The mean of the first subscale raised from 3.6 to 5.1 and the mean of the second subscale increased from 4.8 to 5.8. The distribution of frequency check revealed the same outcomes in details. Before learning, only 9 out of 25 checks fell in the category of "confidence" (point 5, 6, 7), and all these 9 checks were for point 5 (fairly confident). There were none for point 6 (strongly confident) or point 7 (extremely confident). However, after learning, 19 out of 25 checks belonged to the category of "confidence," in which 6 were for point 5 (fairly confident) and 13 for point 6 (strongly confident). Moreover, before learning, there were 7 checks for "undecided" (point 4) and 9 checks for the category of "no confidence" (point 1, 2, 3), among which all 9 checks were for point 3 (fairly unsure). However, after learning, there were 6 checks for "undecided" (point 4) and none for the category of "no confidence." In other words, after a year of learning, Maria remarkably raised her writing confidence.

In terms of confidence on various writing tasks, that Maria gained confidence in functional writing was revealed in the answers to Item-2, Item-3, and Item-4. While responding to the statement "Fill out an insurance application" (Item-3), she chose point 3 (fairly unsure) before learning and point 5 (fairly confident) after learning. In answer to the statement "List insurance for how to play a card game" (Item-2), she chose point 3 (fairly unsure) in the beginning of learning and changed it into point 5 (fairly confident) in the end of learning. Similarly, to respond to the statement of Item-4 "Write an instruction manual for operating an office machine," she first showed a fair lack of confidence (point 3) and then presented with fair confidence (point 5).

In addition, Maria's responses indicated her changes in using writing for school learning as well as in composing different types of articles. Regarding the changes in using writing for school learning, she had point 4 (undecided) before learning and point 6 (strongly confident) after learning for the statement "Write useful class notes" (Item-14). Concerning the changes in composing different types of articles, her changes were clearly revealed in her responses. For example, to respond to the statement of Item-15 "Author a children's book," she chose point 4 (undecided) before learning and point 6 (strongly confident) after learning. In answer to the statement "Prepare lesson plans for an elementary class studying the process of writing" (Item-16), she answered with point 4 (undecided) in the beginning of learning and changed it into point 6 (strongly confident) in the end of learning. Also, for the statement "Write a brief autobiography" (Item-17), she firstly responded with point 4 (undecided) and then answered with point 6 (strongly confident).

As for the confidence on performing different writing skills, Maria also presented the increase of confidence, though the changes were not as obvious as the changes shown in the first subscale. For example, before learning, her answer to "Write a paper with good overall organization" (Item-25) was point 4 (undecided) and was point 5 (fairly confident) after learning. The same change happened to Item-18 "Correctly spell all words in a one-page passage," the responses of which were from point 4 (undecided) to point 5 (fairly confident). Others like "Correctly punctuate a one-page passage" (Item-19), "Correctly use parts of speech" (Item-20), "Write a simple sentence with proper punctuation and grammatical structure" (Item-21), "Correctly use plurals, verb tenses, prefixes, and suffixes" (Item-22), "Write compound and complex sentences with proper punctuation and grammatical structure" (Item-23), and "Organize sentences into a paragraph so as to clearly express a theme" (Item-24), her responses were all from point 5 (fairly confident) to point 6 (strongly confident).

APPENDIX

The Discussion of Ken's Attitudinal Changes on Writing Apprehension

According to the results gained from *Writing Apprehension Questionnaire*, Ken's writing anxiety was reduced from 4.5 to 3.0, equal to from the level of Middle to the level of Low. The distribution of frequency check told the decrease of anxiety in details. Before learning, 12 out of 26 checks fell in the category of "anxiety" (point 5, 6, 7, 8), including 1 for point 7 (strongly anxious), 5 for point 6 (very anxious), and 6 for point 5 (fairly anxious), but after learning, there were only 2 out of 26 checks for the category of "anxiety," both of which were for point 5 (fairly anxious). Moreover, before learning, there were 14 checks fitted in the category of "no anxiety" (point 1, 2, 3, 4), including 9 for point 4 (fairly unafraid) and 5 for point 3 (very unafraid), but after learning, 24 responses were for the category of "no anxiety," which were 4 for point 4 (fairly unafraid), 12 for point 3 (very unafraid), and 8 for point 2 (strongly unafraid).

The most tremendous change was the answers to Item-15. To respond to the statement "I enjoy writing" (Item-15), he had point 2 (strongly disagree) as his answer before learning, and after learning, he chose point 7 (strongly agree). That he became enjoying writing was revealed in many aspects. For example, in answer to Item-11 "I feel confident in my ability to clearly express my ideas in writing," he firstly chose point 3 (quite disagree) and then changed the answer into point 7 (strongly agree). The responses to Item-23 "It's easy for me to write good compositions" were changed from "quite disagree" (point 3) to "quite agree" (point 6). As for the statement "I like seeing my thoughts on paper" (Item-19), he chose point 4 (somewhat disagree) first and then had point 7 (strongly agree) as his answer. For the statement of Item-10 "I like to write my ideas down," he also made changes from "quite disagree" (point 3) to "somewhat agree" (point 5). Besides gaining confidence in writing his own ideas, the answers to Item-20 showed remarkable decrease of the anxiety for sharing his writing with others. The answers to Item-20 "Discussing my writing with others is an enjoyable experience" were point 3 (quite disagree) in the beginning and point 7 (strongly agree) after learning. Similar results were also seen in the responses to Item-12 "I like to have my friends read what I have written" and Item-25 "I don't like my compositions to be evaluated." The former had answers from point 3 (quite disagree) to point 5 (somewhat agree), and the latter had point 5 (somewhat agree) as an answer in the beginning and then had point 3 (quite disagree) as an answer.

In addition, his answers to Item-1 and Item-17 depicted the overall picture of the decrease of his writing apprehension. For Item-17, he somewhat agreed (point 5) with the statement "Writing is a lot of fun" before learning and strongly agreed (point 7) after learning. For Item-1, he somewhat agreed (point 5) with the statement "I avoid writing" in the beginning and then strongly disagreed (point 2) in the end of the school year. As mentioned above, Ken's attitudinal changes on writing apprehension were presented clearly.

APPENDIX R

The Discussion of Maria's Attitudinal Changes
on Writing Apprehension

According to the results gained from *Writing Apprehension Questionnaire*, the mean of 26 responses was reduced from 4.4 to 3.1, which means Maria's anxiety level was lowered from the level of Middle to the level of Low. With the investigation of the distribution of frequency check, the decrease of her writing anxiety was clearly presented. Before learning, there were 11 out of 26 checks fell in the category of "anxiety" (point 5, 6, 7, 8), among which 7 were for point 5 (fairly anxious), 3 for point 6 (very anxious), and 1 was for point 7 (strongly anxious). However, after learning, only 3 out of 26 checks belonged to the category of "anxiety," including 1 for point 5 (fairly anxious) and 2 for point 6 (very anxious). Moreover, before learning, there were 15 out of 26 checks belonged to the category of "no anxiety" (point 1, 2, 3, 4), among which 9 were for point 4 (fairly unafraid) and 6 for point 3 (very unafraid). However, after learning, the number of checks falling in the category of "no anxiety" was increased, which was 23 checks. Among these 23 checks, there were 3 for point 4 (fairly unafraid), 11 for point 3 (very unafraid), and 9 for point 2 (strongly unafraid). This change clearly indicated the decrease of Maria's writing anxiety.

That Maria lowered her writing anxiety level was revealed in several aspects. First, she reduced nervousness. Before learning, her response to Item-7 "My mind seems to go blank when I start to work on a composition" was point 5 (somewhat agree), and after learning, she changed the answer to point 3 (quite disagree). The answers to Item-13 "I'm nervous about writing" showed similar change: from point 5 (somewhat agree) to point 3 (quite disagree). Second, she gained confidence in her writing ability, which in turn reduced the anxiety. To respond the statement of Item-11 "I feel confidence in my ability to clearly express my ideas in writing," she chose point 4 (somewhat disagree) in the beginning of learning and point 6 (quite agree) in the end of school year.   Similarly, in answer to Item-23 "It's easy for me to write good compositions," she responded with point 4 (somewhat disagree) before learning and point 6 (quite agree) after learning.   Third, she became interested in seeing her thoughts on paper.   The answers of Item-19 "I like seeing my thoughts on paper" were the case: from point 5 (somewhat agree) to point 7 (strongly agree).   Others like the responses to Item-3 and Item-10 showed greater differences after learning.   For the statement of Item-3 "I look forward to writing down my ideas," she answered with point 3 (quite disagree) before learning and point 6 (quite agree) after learning.   Similarly, for the statement "I like to write my ideas down" (Item-10), her responses were changed from point 4 (somewhat disagree) to point 7 (strongly agree).   Fourth, she started viewing sharing her writing with others as an interesting and a joyful thing.   For example, while being asked whether "discussing my writing with others is an enjoyable experience" (Item-20), she responded with point 5 (somewhat agree) before learning and point 7 (strongly agree) after learning.   Even when she was asked whether "I would enjoy submitting my writing to magazines for evaluation and publication" (Item-9), she answered with point 3 (quite disagree) to point 5 (somewhat agree).

All these changes obviously spoke for the decrease of her writing anxiety and could be concluded by her answers to Item-15 "I enjoy writing": from point 5 (somewhat agree) to point 7 (strongly agree).

The Discussion of Peggy's Attitudinal Changes on Writing Apprehension

According to the results gained from *Writing Apprehension Questionnaire*, the means of Peggy's anxiety decreased from 3.8 to 3.0, equal to the changes from the level of Middle to the level of Low. If the distribution of frequency check was investigated, the decrease of Peggy's writing anxiety would be presented clearly. Before learning, there were 10 out of 26 checks fell in the category of "anxiety" (point 5, 6, 7, 8) and 16 were for the category of "no anxiety" (point 1, 2, 3, 4). However, after learning, 8 out of 26 checks belonged to the category of "anxiety" (point 5, 6, 7, 8) and 18 were for the category of "no anxiety." Most importantly, before learning, only 3 out of 16 were for point 1 (extremely unafraid), and after learning, among these 18 non-anxiety checks, 11 were for point 1 (extremely unafraid).

The most remarkable change in Peggy's writing anxiety was that she became interested in sharing her writing with others. While being asked whether "Discussing my writing with others is an enjoyable experience" (Item-20), she responded with point 3 (quite disagree) before learning and with point 7 (strongly agree) after learning. Even in answer to Item-9 "I would enjoy submitting my writing to magazines for evaluation and publication," she chose point 4 (somewhat disagree) in the beginning of learning and point 8 (extremely agree) in the end of school year.

The second obvious changes were about taking a composition class and her writing process. The responses of Item-18 "I expect to do poorly in composition classes even before I enter them" were firstly point 4 (somewhat disagree) and then point 1 (extremely disagree). While being asked whether "My mind seems to go blank when I start to work on a composition" (Item-7), she answered with point 6 (strongly agree) before learning and with point 3 (quite disagree) after learning.

In addition, Peggy became a writing lover. For example, in answer to Item-10 "I like to write my ideas down," she chose point 6 (quite agree) in the beginning of learning and point 8 (extremely agree) in the end of school year. Also, to respond to the statement "I like seeing my thoughts on paper" (Item-19), her responses were changed from point 6 (quite agree) to point 8 (extremely agree). The extreme agreement clearly proved the decrease of her writing anxiety.

APPENDIX  T

The Discussion of Peggy's Personal Growth/Empowerment

Peggy's personal growth was presented in three different aspects. First, she became self-directed learners. Second, she started placing value on discussion. Third, her thinking was widened and deepened.

Throughout the year of learning, Peggy read 2 English books and at least 20 articles (SE-P-2-1). She often read at home, almost 3 times a week (SE-P-2-2). The genres she covered included story, news, autobiography, essay, and poems (SE-P-2-3). The variety of reading materials and the frequency of real reading indicated that she did not read for homework but for her interest and inquiry. Because of theme cycles learning, she had chance to further explore the issues interested to her. The enjoyment and the difficulty she encountered while conducting the theme project were often revealed in her e-mail letters:

> Recently, I read some articles about American music. Because of difficult cultures, I have to guess many singers, background, ... etc. ... (Em-P-5).

> This week I read another article, so I send this one to share it with you. This topic is about "Chicago Jazz and the Dixieland revival." ... After reading these "music" articles I think if I want to understand it more deeply, I must take more time to study especially Jazz. Jazz is marvelous sphere. I try to know it. ...
> I like this class to let me search some interesting things (Em-P-8).

Although there were still difficulties in reading and understanding, she overcame the obscurities with strong motivation and curiosity (O-10, 13).

Peggy also changed the perception of discussion. In the beginning, she, like most Taiwanese students, was not used to sharing her opinions or her writing with others. The unavoidable embarrassment and shyness scared her away from sharing and discussion (O-7; RJ-10; Em-P-31). However, after engaging in the learning of theme cycles, with plenty of encouragement and interaction, she started considering sharing and discussion as benefits to reading and writing. She not only once mentioned that others' feedback helped her to be a writer (SE-P-1-4) and having ideas exchange with classmates was one of her major accomplishments as a writer (SE-P-1-6). Along with the change of conception, she became an active learner who often shared reading materials and feedback with the class. For example, she shared her nervousness of using English and how she overcame the anxiety (Em-P-4); she actively responded to Lin's essay draft and shared her opinions and suggestion as peer discussion (Em-P-33; O-7); and she informed everyone in class an English learning website she found (Em-P-22). She even helped Ken solve his calculus problems (Em-P-14; O-22) when Ken was preparing for his entrance exam of graduate school. The most remarkable sharing was the time she brought a news article for class reading and discussion:

> I have heard that NEW YORK TIMES reported about "Comfort Women" columns. Hence, I go to the homepage of new york times to search this article. Fortunately, I got it. In this article, there are some new and unfamiliar English words which we often speak in Chinese. Therefore, I will bring it into class next Monday (Em-P-11).

Before bringing this news article to class, she sent an e-mail letter along with the article to the teacher-research. At that day in class, she made enough copies for each classmate (O-19). Her active participation proved that students could also be information givers and indicated that she was not any more a shy woman without voice in class. As Rogers (1983) proposed, students are full of choice to co-develop curriculum or course design with the teacher. Peggy's active participation reflected her automatic learning and sharing.

In addition, her thinking was widened and deepened. Majoring in social work and social welfare, Peggy was cultivated to be sensitive to social events. Throughout the year of learning, engaging in the learning of theme cycles, her sensitivity was enhanced and her critical thinking was reinforced. Most importantly, she started integrating her sensitivity and critical thinking into English reading and writing, and began to value this integration. As she mentioned in final self-evaluation, she considered "writing ... discipline me to think more logically" (SE-P-1-6) as one of her major accomplishments as a writer, and regarded "To think my life deeply and seriously" (SE-P-2-6) as her major accomplishment as a reader. She enjoyed the process of learning, and stated, "I really like what we read. They always make me recall what I learned in the university, especially the sociology course" (Em-P-7). She further explained why her thinking and reflection were enhanced through reading and writing:

> Because when I read this kind of articles, I have strong feeling about my life experiences. It seems that I undergo these social events directly and they can let me reflect my daily life (SE-P-2-5).

The depth of her reflection was clearly revealed in her writing. For example, when she responded to the article "Donkey in the Lion's Skin," she referred to a Sociologist's saying and pointed out the weakness of human beings:

> ... everyone in the stages hopes to gain others' praise and encouragement, so he only presents advantageous parts and hides unfavorable parts. ... He wanted to be an idle, respected, and own powers. However, he made the big mistake. Because he forgot who he was, he did too much beyond himself. Maybe this story drops a hint that owing power will make people forget to be in reality as well as in name. One in mutual interactions will pretend something to gain others' good images, but he can't play roles far away from himself (J-P-3).

353

When she reacted to the issue of education, like dropouts, she strongly disputed the solution proposed by certain schools—using money as an incentive:

> ... education should not be changed as material or goods. It is a learning process. If students don't want to go to school any more, it may represents that the ecology systems get some problems, such as the students have some family reasons to let them not go to -- family violence, poverty, economic etc, and educational systems-- teaching techniques and education ad-ministrational design —-can't attract students to go to school. Therefore, if students are uninterested the courses, we should think the real reasons. Do not use money, lotteries, or material ceremony to solve this complicated problems. Education can't be exchanged in the market (J-P-4).

She continued her strong voice and firm argument in the following discussion:

> ... I am worried about that these will have some stigma on these students. For example, some schools hold some pizza parties for potential dropouts. If students come to parties, it implies that these groups are different, abnormal, potential problem makers. ... It labels bad marks on these students. In other words, it will disturb the students learning attitudes.
> On the whole, the officers, principals, and teachers and even all of us must think what's wrong in this educational system. We can't take it for granted that ... students want some money, ... We should think why the students don't want to go to school any more and stand on the same side to feel their moods and thoughts then try to dissolve this problem directly (J-P-4).

Her concerns about young people were not limited to the dropouts. Instead, while facing the increasing rate of juvenile delinquencies, the inquiries she raised were worth careful considering:

> ... Accessibility of motorcycles and firearms is obviously a key
> issue here. Why these kids would choose these tools to express
> their feelings? What do they think about themselves? Do these
> teenagers get in trouble in their family and school life? Or our
> society is so disorder that the teenagers don't have any model to
> seek their identification! ... (J-P-10-2)

As an adult, she never thought adults should ignore juvenile delinquencies:

> ... they are our responsibilities that how to instruct the kids to
> distinguish what is wrong and right and build some paths to let
> them to speak out their voices and get out love and let it come
> in (J-P-10-2).

Besides youth problems, she also cared the marriage life. She was concerned that "Social events happen day by day. Most events are family abuses. People in the family have risks to hurt and to be hurt" (OR-P-2-2). "What's wrong with ... marriage ...?" was a question she asked (OR-P-2-2). After reading the article "The Unicorn in the Garden" and the book *Tuesdays with Morrie*, she watched the movies "America Beauty" and "The Bridge of Madison County" and also read the references about these two movies (OR-P-2; O-28). She would like to explore the issue and found out the problems in marriage life. Though she was not married yet, her understanding of marriage was presented in her writing. She considered "marriage is [an] art" (OR-P-2-6) and the couple should run their marriage together wholeheartedly (J-P-2-3). "Not only should they listen, talk, share their mood, but also they should ... try to change bad attitude and habits" (J-P-2-3), she emphasized. She believed that "finding problems, then taking actions to change is the only one path to have good marriage" (J-P-2-3).

Peggy extended her concerns to the policy made by our government, like the reaction to a comic book *On Taiwan* by Kobayashi, a

Japanese cartoonist (J-P-9). Besides emphasizing "Taiwan is a democ-racy country" (J-P-9-2) and Taiwan should respect "freedom of speech" (J-P-9), she also urged "It's time for us to think where Taiwan will sail" (J-P-9-3). Her strong statement reflected her thinking, position, and introspection. From Freire's (1993) perspectives, the dialogical way of learning promotes human beings "to reflect on their own 'situationality' to the extent that they are challenged by it to act upon it" (p. 90). In so doing, people are empowered. Peggy's concerns and reflection shown above echoed Freire's argument.

In sum, throughout the year of learning, Peggy became a self-directed reader and writer, formed a habit of sharing and discussion, and enhanced her thinking and reflection. Her growth and her changes were clearly described in the preface of her portfolio:

> I recall that when I was in senior high school, there is no mean-ing for English lessons but texts. Although I learn a lot from my attending schools, I think there should be some diverse and interesting areas I don't know. Fortunately, I entered [this class] to pick my books again. When I started to study, I already know my dream will come true (PP-P-1).
>
> [These] articles attract me to involve my surrounding life events and take some actions such as listening jazz music, accompany-ing my families with more time, and caring my colleagues' feel-ings. Discussing with classmates also makes me ... enlarge my visions and think deeply. ... (PP-P-2)

APPENDIX

The Discussion of Maria's Personal Growth/Empowerment

Maria took risks to try difficult issues, like Olympic Games (Es-M-1), European City of Culture (Es-M-3), the philosophical definition of love (Es-M-5), and the comparison and contrast between Morrie and Buddhists (Es-M-7). The challenge she encountered and the way how she overcame the difficulty showed the power she gained in the process of learning.

In her e-mail letters, she not only once shared the difficulty she faced in reading and writing. For example, while conducting the theme project on European City of Culture, she wrote

> ... This original article ... is difficult for me to understand. I ... try my best to understand her article and reorganize them. Another difficult for me is I just know ... Prague ... from paper and video, but never being there ... (Em-M-6)

Because Prague was a place she looked forward to visiting after she finished taking this course (PP-M-3), she would like to spend time discovering this city, no matter how difficult the article might be. Also, when she composed the last essay "Morrie Schwartz and the Buddhists," she felt into a dilemma and encountered a tremendous difficulty:

> Sometimes I think maybe I should change another easier topic for me to write. I have a feel on this topic and I don't want just threw it away, though I'm not a Buddhist and I still can't totally understand it until now (Em-M-11).

The difficulty did not scare her away. She overcame the difficulty with a great deal of reading. Besides, she spent a lot of time discussing the philosophy of Buddhism with his father, who knew Buddhism very well (O-29). With better understanding of the issue, she finally finished composing this article with detailed comparison and contrast (Es-M-8). The way she explored an issue indicated that she did not work for assignment but for her interest and curiosity. By so doing, she integrated her life into learning, and discovered new knowledge that was meaningful to her (RJ-13, 29, 30). As Rogers (1983) argued, in self-chosen and self-initiated learning atmosphere, the learner tends to invest the whole person in the learning process, and such learning "tends to be deeper, proceeds at a more rapid rate, and is more pervasive in the life and behavior of the student" (p.189). Maria's perseverance reflected her investment of her whole person in theme cycles learning, which, in turns, empowered herself and made her growth.

In addition, that she chose difficult issues to explore sometimes made her feel she was not an effective writer, because she always spent much time on a single piece (SE-M-1). However, her insistence on exploring whatever interested her showed her perseverance in reading and writing. This perseverance, in turns, brought her the sense of achievements:

> I'm glad to see the collection of my essays … Though they were not as good as I hope, that's all I had work hard at this academic year. Though they are not as much as I expect for, that's all I had tried my best to capture the voice from my heart (PP-M-1).

She considered finishing reading *Tuesdays with Morrie* as her major accomplishment as a reader (SE-M-2-6), because she thought "it's hard to read books in English completely and patiently" (SE-M-2-6). Moreover, the intensive sharing and discussion of this book made her feel like a real reader. Though she still needed to polish her skills (SE-M-2-8), she admitted that "my ability in English reading is improving" (SE-M-2-10).

She regarded the essay "Love" (Es-M-6) as the most effective article she wrote(SE-M-1-5). The process of writing "Love" (Es-M-5) revealed her eagerness to convey her ideas:

> Some inspiration came to me when I lay in bed before fall in sleep at deep night. I didn't want to miss the inspiration after hours, so I rose up and write them down. Interestingly, I ... got part of the outline and the main idea about my essays. ... [It] was almost pictured in one amazing deep night. And I like this piece of my writing most (PP-M-4).

Having inspiration before falling asleep was considered as her major accomplishment as a writer. She proudly said, "Maybe somebody think it's funny. But for me, it's amazing. I appreciate the inspiration coming before fall into sleep" (SE-M-1-7).

With the persistence on writing whatever interested her and valued the inspiration as well as her insightful and thoughtful ideas, she changed her view of writing in the end of school year:

> Writing is not only to write down the words and sentences correctly, but to reflect the thought after reading and find the hidden meaning in them (SE-M-2-9).

In general, Maria, a risk taker, successfully challenged her limitations. Even though the class was over, it is believed that her growth and "transformation" would go on as she continually interacted with the word and the world (Freire, 1993; Freire & Macedo, 1987).

APPENDIX  V

The Discussion of Ken's Personal Growth and Empowerment

Ken was a professional firefighter. Though his work always occupied his time and tired him out, he still continually came to class and accomplished all the assignments. Whenever he had no time reading or writing, he felt unsatisfied:

> This week, I have a full schedule so that I can't read and write. In morning, I had to spend 80 minutes going to Taipei. And took all day to learn about computer. ...
> When I got up in the morning today, I felt a little empty and regret in my mind. Even though I usually read the ... article in the rapid train ... I still liked to spend some time reading and writing on the desk. Only this, I consider I have studied some things, but this week, I think I must do more effort to program my schedule and care more at my study. ... (J-K-4)

His hard working was not only revealed in completing this course but also shown in his preparation for the entrance exam of graduate school (RJ-13, 14, 19, 20). However, he was not a workaholic. Instead, he concerns his life and usually had deep reflection on it:

> In this Monday morning, I pass by a park near my office. There are so many people that accompany the music to dance with each other. They look so happy and healthy. But I think myself I have to ride my motorcycle and go to work. I feel a little sad.
> In our short life, we must spend ... much time working and earning money. Since we retire, we begin to learn how to enjoy ... life. But we can't keep our health and energy ... we would lose some important things in our life. For example like different taste, sport, interest, activities, and so on.

> So I think despite work and earning money are very important
> in life, we can't ignore the leisure, interests, and the thoughts ...
> After the hard work, we should ... relax and think how to
> award ourselves. Like listening music and watching the movies
> we like. And keep our passion for life and not all the work.
> (J-K-2)

The struggle for the balance between work and rest was often revealed in his sharing (O-9, 10; J-K-4, 2). Rather than give up either
one of them, he indeed squeezed his time out for certain recreation, like
watching movies. He smartly integrated his movie watching into his
first-semester theme project, and by so doing, he made learning interesting and enjoyable:

> I thought my themes for final project are "Movie" and "Com-
> puter". And in order to see the movies of DVD without Chi-
> nese display, I buy a DVD player last Saturday. As my expect,
> it is so fanstic. Although it is hard to understand all meaning in
> the cinema, I will practice again and again. ... (Em-K-3)

In the second semester, while preparing for the entrance exam of graduate school, his struggle for a balance life and good time management
was getting severe. However, he did not hide his struggle or ignore
this difficulty. Instead, he wrote about the pressure he was facing and
the solution he was searching for (Es-K-5/6). By transferring his stress
into written words, he released himself from the tension and completed
his homework at the same time. It is obvious that he tried to manage
his time wisely by connecting his learning with his life. No wonder
after a year of learning, he could confidently said,

> Through the whole of the school year, I found I have learned
> not only English ability but also time management ... (PP-K-1)
> ... it is very important to learn how to manage my time be-
> tween work, study, and relationship. Fortunately, I thought
> myself having no big trouble on it (PP-K-3).

In addition to searching a balance life, Ken also showed his perseverance in realizing his dream. Although he had to bear heavy and diverse responsibilities, he never lost his vision or gave up his ideals. His insistence in solving calculus problems (O-21; Em-K-11), his acceptance of a graduate school of a National University (O-26; RJ-27), and his determination in improving his English were all the evidences. That he valued dreams and ideals was clearly presented in his reflection:

> ... I think dreams or ideals are very important. Without dreams or ideals, the life can be dim and not brilliant. The life will be a circle day after day until death, because you never want to be or want to do (OR-K-1-12).

Besides his life and his dreams, Ken also concerns the people around him. Greatly impressed by the movie "Patch Adams" (OR-K-1), he reconsidered the relationship with others:

> ... it is also important to keeping touch with people. My meaning is not only to make friends with people, but also to help them if you can do. By helping people with selflessness, you will get more happiness with everybody than with self. ... (OR-K-1-13).

This understanding was not limited to his reading responses but extended to his life and his view on his profession—firefighter:

> You know, I am a fire fighter. In order to rescue people and process the recovery after the typhoon, I had four days not to take off! Rarely sleeping well, I can't concentrate my attention on studying. And needless to say, I can write something. All of my wish is let me take off and sleep well, but it can't come true unless everything recovers! So please bless for all people in disaster regions and me ...... Amen............. (Em-K-7).

Though he revealed his being exhausted, he also showed his concerns toward the people suffered in floods. His work, study, and life were interwoven and so a new Ken emerged. In the end of school year, while making his theme report on *Tuesdays with Morrie*, he shared his discovery—Love should be the center (OR-K-2). As a firefighter, he would rather view himself as a person helping others than view his work as a job merely. He further illustrated,

> Love should be the center. With love, we will really value other people's life and property. Also, with love, it is then possible for us to advance our facilities in fire station (OR-K-2).

After reading *Tuesdays with Morrie*, the short story "Chinese School," and the article "Dropouts," he also had reflection on our culture and education. In terms of education, he strongly declared

> I think education should teach students the right values for life and stir their learning desire and talent. Let they have the pleasure of learning and growing. Education should be not all tests, exams, and marks, but to enjoy knowledge exploring and satisfy ourselves' curiousness (J-K-15).

His emphasis on education was not a naïve reaction. Instead, he spoke from his experiences. Though he has never been a teacher, he has been a student for years. Looking at his schooling, he could not but state:

> Since I began to study in school, the teacher never asked me what I wanted. They just taught me in the routine schedules and held the regular and irregular examinations. In my dim memory, the only experience that my teacher asked me what I wanted is the title of writing …
> … I never thought how we could argue with the teacher in any subject. … (J-K-14)

He further described the "tragedy" he faced after he tried to voice himself out:

> ... in my college time, ..., I just argued the unfair standard of folding bedquilt in public so that I was classified the bad student. Of course, ... I felt into a situation that usually suffered odd punishment without reasons. And after two years, I became a student by labeled and always was accepted several special taking care. From then on, I learned that I had to be quiet in public, and ... not daring to insist my opinion in public when I face a controversial situation (J-K-14).

He has been silenced since then, but after engaging in the learning of theme cycles, he got his voice back (OR-K-1; PP-K). In the year of learning, through reading, writing, and discussion, he exchanged ideas with peers and negotiated meaning with himself and others. From Freire's (1970, 1993) perspectives, Ken had been silenced in banking education and was empowered in this dialogical way of theme cycles learning. He not only learned the skills of negotiation but also recognized he should not follow the crowd:

> ... I like this ... 'See what no one else see. See what everyone else chooses not to see out of fear and conformity. See the world anew each day.' I think ... not to be a yes man. Understand where you go, what you want, and how to do. Insist your ideals out of caring others' view and keep your mind on achieving your goals (OR-K-14).

Trying not to be a person saying "yes" all the times, he, instead, decided to be himself with self-confidence and tenderness (OR-K-2; O-29; RJ-29).

These changes, along with the understanding of strengths and weaknesses in his writing (PP-K-5), proved his personal growth in the year of learning. In the first class, he revealed his expectation:

> I will do my best to learn and hope that I can toward my English ability to a new space that I can't dare to think! (Em-K-1)

Though he never clearly defined the "new space," he confirmed his achievements after a year of learning:

> ... I read many good articles in this year. Unlike before giving it up without finishing, I continued to read them and had a lot of mental contact. It contacted my deep mind and made me discover the other side of myself that I never touched (PP-K-4).

With the learning of theme cycles, he had chance to explore the depth of his mind and to discover a self that unknown even to himself. His growth was obviously and remarkably.

實踐大學數位出版合作系列
語言文學類　AG0065

The Effects of Implementing Theme Cycles on Adult EFL Writers
主題探索式課程對成人英文寫作學習者的影響

作　　者	李利德（Li-Te Li）
統籌策劃	葉立誠
文字編輯	王雯珊
視覺設計	賴怡勳
執行編輯	林世玲　詹靚秋
圖文排版	張慧雯
數位轉譯	徐真玉　沈裕閔
圖書銷售	林怡君
網路服務	徐國晉
法律顧問	毛國樑律師
發 行 人	宋政坤
出版印製	秀威資訊科技股份有限公司
	台北市內湖區瑞光路583巷25號1樓
	電話：(02) 2657-9211
	傳真：(02) 2657-9106
	E-mail：service@showwe.com.tw
經 銷 商	紅螞蟻圖書有限公司
	台北市內湖區舊宗路二段121巷28、32號4樓
	電話：(02) 2795-3656
	傳真：(02) 2795-4100
	http://www.e-redant.com

2006 年 9 月
BOD 一版
定價：440元

讀　者　回　函　卡

感謝您購買本書，為提升服務品質，煩請填寫以下問卷，收到您的寶貴意見後，我們會仔細收藏記錄並回贈紀念品，謝謝！

1. 您購買的書名：_____

2. 您從何得知本書的消息？

  □網路書店　□部落格　□資料庫搜尋　□書訊　□電子報　□書店

  □平面媒體　□ 朋友推薦　□網站推薦　□其他_____

3. 您對本書的評價：(請填代號　1.非常滿意 2.滿意 3.尚可 4.再改進)

  封面設計____　版面編排____　內容____　文/譯筆____　價格____

4. 讀完書後您覺得：

  □很有收獲　□有收獲　□收獲不多　□沒收獲

5. 您會推薦本書給朋友嗎？

  □會　□不會，為什麼？_____

6. 其他寶貴的意見：_____

  _____

  _____

  _____

讀者基本資料

姓名：_____　年齡：_____　性別：□女 □男

聯絡電話：_____　E-mail：_____

地址：_____

學歷：□高中(含)以下　　□高中　　□專科學校　　□大學

　　　□研究所(含)以上 □其他_____

職業：□製造業 □金融業 □資訊業 □軍警 □傳播業 □自由業

　　　□服務業 □公務員 □教職　　□學生 □其他_____

(請沿線對摺寄回,謝謝!)

秀威與 BOD

BOD（Books On Demand）是數位出版的大趨勢，秀威資訊率先運用 POD 數位印刷設備來生產書籍，並提供作者全程數位出版服務，致使書籍產銷零庫存，知識傳承不絕版，目前已開闢以下書系：

一、BOD 學術著作—專業論述的閱讀延伸
二、BOD 個人著作—分享生命的心路歷程
三、BOD 旅遊著作—個人深度旅遊文學創作
四、BOD 大陸學者—大陸專業學者學術出版
五、POD 獨家經銷—數位產製的代發行書籍

BOD 秀威網路書店：www.showwe.com.tw
政府出版品網路書店：www.govbooks.com.tw

永不絕版的故事・自己寫・永不休止的音符・自己唱